GENTLY, TRYING TO KEEP HER SELF-CONTROL, SHE RAN HER FINGERS ALONG THE INTERIOR EDGES OF THE CASKET. . . .

She had hoped to find something her fingers could grip. When she yanked at the material, it tore away. Small upholsterer's tacks landed on the bottom of the casket with strange little *pings*. This did nothing but expose the wood beneath.

The speed of Lutetia's movements picked up as her thin grip on calm slipped away; she tore at the lid with bruised fingers. Frantically, she tried to bite into the lid with her teeth. But once through the satin, her bleeding lips touched a wall of wood. Losing herself completely to panic, she went back to her futile, terrified shrieking, her voice growing raw in her agony and pain. . . .

UNHOLY MOURNING

David Lippincott

A DELL BOOK

Published by
Dell Publishing Co., Inc.
1 Dag Hammarskjold Plaza
New York, New York 10017

Dell ® TM 681510, Dell Publishing Co., Inc.

ISBN: 0-440-19224-2

Printed in the United States of America

First printing—November 1982

AVANT PROPOS

The boy sat on the beach, shifting uncomfortably on the pebbles beneath him. As with all of the Great Lakes, the beach at St. Max had more small stones than sand; grown-ups took it in their stride, but it was painful to an eight-year-old's bottom.

In front of him the waters of Lake Michigan shimmered in the unexpected blush of a mid-September sun; Jorbie luxuriated in the unusual warmth, letting his eyes almost close from the hypnotic effect of the light shimmering on the water. The day was so unusual, St. Etienne Parochial School had brought its children to the beach; there was little chance of another day like this before the howling cold of a northern Michigan winter froze the sky white above them.

Across from Jorbie his twin continued building the sand castle Jorbie had abandoned out of boredom. When both of them had been working on it, the castle had grown quite elaborate, a maze of towers and moats and cleverly balanced arches. For a second, Kenneth stared at his twin, eyes silently asking why Jorbie had given the project up. Slowly Jorbie moved his head back and forth in a single smooth motion. The two of them frequently communicated this way—saying nothing—a strand of psychic waves making words superfluous.

The identical twins were a startling sight in St. Max, as they would have been anywhere, with deep, honeyblond skin, hair the intense jet of night, and black eyes softened by overly long lashes. "The Little Princes," their mother had called them. But that was last year and she had died and there was no one to call them that anymore. Jorbie shuddered.

Farther down the beach more of St. Etienne's children played in a large, boisterous group; another set of boys—fifteen- or sixteen-year-olds—lay flat, sunning on a small raft anchored in the lake. Usually this late in the fall the raft had been hauled ashore for the winter, but for some reason it had so far been overlooked. The raft jauntily bobbed up and down as if it itself had made the arrangements to stay on—specifically so it could enjoy this day.

From his left Jorbie suddenly saw a shadow fall across them and looked up. She had been sitting farther down along the beach with Sister Honorée, helping keep track of the other children. Jorbie couldn't remember her name, but he did know she was one of the lay teachers at St. Etienne—Sister Honorée was the sole remaining nun—and that she played piano in Assembly every morning and tried to train the children's uncertain voices to present a reasonable imitation of a choir. Kenneth continued working on his sand castle; Jorbie looked up and gave the teacher one of his most winning smiles. Smiling, the teacher patted him on the head absently, her eyes studying Kenneth. Jorbie guessed she liked him well enough, but knew she liked Kenneth more. A lot of people did. The sun suddenly seemed too hot.

"My," the teacher said, smiling again. "What a wonderful castle you two have built. Magnificent."

"See this little spire over here?" Kenneth asked suddenly, looking up at the teacher for the first time. "It's made of sand diamonds and—"

Jorbie cut him off. His twin was shy, and whenever he tried to talk to a grown-up, he sounded like a baby. "Down below here," Jorbie said with authority, "are the dungeons. And the windowless cells. And the rack. In the basement, they have a dragon that blows fire, and the moats—see the moats?—are kept full of alligators. Snap, snap."

"Oh, my," the teacher said, putting her hand beside her mouth as if frightened. "Is there a damsel in distress, too?"

Both Jorbie and Kenneth looked at her blankly. Tilting her head to one side, the teacher laughed again. "No, I guess both of you are a little young for that yet. But in a few years . . ."

Jorbie smiled at her to show that he understood what she meant, which of course he didn't. Kenneth continued to stare at her with a vacant expression.

The teacher sighed. "I've got to go back and keep an eye on the other children. You should play with them more, you know."

Automatically, Jorbie and Kenneth drew closer together. They neither needed nor wanted other children; they lived in a private world of their own. Jorbie, particularly, resented intruders into this world. They didn't always listen to him or do what he commanded the way Kenneth did.

Silently they watched the teacher walk slowly down the beach until she got back to where Sister Honorée was sitting. His twin began work again on the castle, but Jorbie was completely bored with it now. And the teacher had stirred something unpleasant inside him. He looked out across the water. "Let's swim out to the raft. Look, there's Doobie deCarre and Hank Tierney and Whale Berringer and Larry Coombs."

Kenneth looked at him for a second, then returned to patting the sand smooth on a new tower. "I want to finish the castle," he argued, already suspecting he was going to lose.

"You're scared."

"No, it's just that—I mean—we've spent a lot of time getting it this far and—"

"Sissy."

"There's one whole wall over here that's too high, and we ought to tear it down and—"

Jorbie jumped to his feet. Deliberately, he strode through the sand castle, his bare toes flinging sand in every direction, flattening almost everything. Stopping, he stared at Kenneth, fixing him with the hard look of the man in charge. "There. That lowers the wall. Now, let's swim to the raft."

"It's a long way," Kenneth complained. "I can't swim like you can, you know that. The current and everything. Those boys are much older than us, anyway. Somebody'll grab me and hold my head under. . . ."

Reaching down, Jorbie pulled his twin to his feet. "Look. I promise. I'll stay right beside you the whole time. I'll stay beside you while we're swimming out, and when we get to the raft, I'll stay right with you there, too. It's a solemn promise, Kenny. Cross my heart and hope to die."

"Point a finger at the sky?" added Kenneth wistfully. The solem ritual was complete, filled with promise of dire events if Jorbie broke it. Still, Kenneth could never be sure of what his twin would really do.

" 'Course I do," said Jorbie breezily. "C'mon. Let's go."

Defeated, Kenneth shrugged. He always lost these battles. He wasn't a good swimmer and the water frightened him. So did the older boys on the raft; they could be so *mean*. But he had no choice. Slowly, he joined Jorbie and shuffled toward the water's edge. As they got there the wind suddenly picked up and the day's first clouds scudded across the sun, their shadows moving quickly across the beach and the water. Shivering a little, Kenneth gritted his teeth and began swimming out toward the raft beside Jorbie.

The Great Lakes, properly speaking, have no tides. But in the area around St. Max, near the narrow Straits of Mackinac, a strong wind from either east or west can force the water between Lake Michigan and Lake Huron to race through the Straits at a furious clip. Then the tide along the beaches rises as quickly and ominously as at St. Michelle.

By the time the two of them had swum halfway to the raft, the first waves were already lapping gently at what was left of the battlements of their castle. A sudden wave from the lake rushed clear across the fortress, leaving only a soft, rounded mass of wet sand behind, as if the lake knew something about the castle-builders no one else was yet aware of.

By the time they got to the raft, Kenneth was complaining bitterly. His side hurt, he said, and the waves kept filling his mouth with water. Shaking his head, Jorbie took Kenneth around to the far side of the raft, away from where the teen-agers were lying, and told him to hang on to a rope that was swagged around the edge of the whole raft. A sudden burst of laughter at something unheard made Jorbie, treading water beside Kenneth, strain his neck to try to see what was going on. Kenneth could sense what was going to happen.

"You promised," he sputtered as more water splashed into his mouth. "You promised you'd stay with me. You promised and—"

But Jorbie was gone. Kenneth could see his legs disappear into the water as he dove beneath the raft to come up on the other side where the older boys were.

When Jorbie broke the surface, he was about three feet from the raft. Without pausing, he swept his arm back and splashed a huge sheet of water over the older boys. They roared in mock fury; he was, after all, only eight. A second sheet of water drenched them. With the sun suddenly hidden behind the racing clouds and the wind rising, the splashed water felt cold and uncomfortable. The teen-agers crowded to the edge of the raft, leaned over, and began splashing back, threatening to jump in and hold Jorbie's head under water if he didn't stop. Jorbie paid no attention; more bellowing from the older boys. It was relatively good-natured, with a lot more laughing than real anger, the teen-agers rushing back and forth on the edge of the raft to splash water at Jorbie from either end.

On the far side of the raft, Kenneth was having increasing trouble keeping his grip on the rope as the small raft heaved up and down from all the activity on the other side. A particularly violent lurch brought the underside clear out of water; when the raft crashed back onto the surface, a powerful sheet of water hit Kenneth square on the face, filling his mouth until he coughed and gasped. He grabbed at the rope, but it seemed to go suddenly limp, as if it weren't attached to anything.

The second he realized he was alone in the water without anything to hang on to, Kenneth panicked. He could feel the current racing through the Straits begin to tug hard at his body, sweeping him farther away from the raft every moment that passed. Kenneth struggled to flail against the tide and get back to the raft, but his inexpert swimming and his feeling of panic and the strength of the current were too much for him. The harder he struggled, the farther the sweep of the waters seemed to carry him away from the raft. He yelled and shrieked for someone to help, but the teen-agers' laughing and yelling buried the sound of his words in the wind. He thrashed in the water; his head kept slipping beneath the surface; each time he tried to scream, his mouth filled with water again.

Farther out, having his own sudden problems with the new power of the current surging through the Straits of Mackinac, swam Quentin Losee, a man of about fifty. He saw what was happening to the eight-year-old and began swimming toward him; the child was ob-

viously in trouble. Losee had once been a strong swimmer, but he was out of condition now, and the current
made his progress toward the boy slow and painful.
The farther the child was swept out in the lake, the
more strongly the tide seized him, dragging the youngster toward the vortex of the Straits.

Losee called to the child to stop fighting the tide and
let himself drift with it, but the youngster was so terrified Losee could see his arms begin flailing more wildly
and his head disappearing under water. Losee swore.
The God damned current, if it would just let go of the
kid for a couple of seconds . . . but the current wasn't
listening to Losee any more than the child was; he saw
the boy disappear under the surface completely.

When he finally reached him, Quentin Losee was exhausted. The boy appeared dead; he was facedown in
the water, the body lifeless. If they'd been on the shore,
Quentin Losee would have tried mouth-to-mouth, but in
the water it was impossible. He started to tuck the body
under one arm in the fireman's carry, but suddenly felt
himself in almost as much trouble as the youngster had
been. Carried by the race of the tide, they had passed
the jutting point of land that separated St. Max from
the Straits; beyond was the long bridge to the Upper
Peninsula. This left them completely unprotected from
the current. The pull on Losee and his deadweight burden was overwhelming, here where the water sped up to
pour into the Straits.

Beyond, Losee could glimpse the wide expanse of
Lake Huron; if he let himself be carried through the
Straits into Huron, he would be far out in the lake's
center, with no certainty whether or not he could fight
the tides back to shore. He looked again at the little
boy. His eyes were closed; there was no sign of life.
Slapping him on the face produced no reaction. Feeling
self-conscious, he whispered a soft little "good-bye" and

released the child's body into the raging current, striking out for shore with his dwindling reservoir of strength. The boy was already dead, Losee kept telling himself.

By now, Kenneth had been missed. People were running up and down the shore calling his name; three men were dragging a dory to the edge of the shore so they could begin searching the water. Quentin Losee appeared first as a dot, jogging slowly down the beach toward them. Feeling inadequate, he explained he'd had to let the boy's body be swept through the Straits; he'd have drowned himself trying to bring it ashore.

Still on the raft, a guilt-ridden Jorbie heard the news and began screaming. "You killed him, you killed him!" he shrieked at the older boys, the senselessness of his charge stunning them. By then, the dory was in the water and already alongside. Jorbie was put in it, sobbing, and the men rowed him back to the beach.

The shocked teacher turned to Sister Honorée. "If you can watch the other children, I'll try and help him," she said. "He's one of my pupils; I know him pretty well." Sister Honorée nodded and began trying to collect the rest of the children, milling around in a combination of excitement and fear. Running down to the water's edge, the teacher lifted the crying Jorbie out of the dory and carried him to a section of the beach where no one else was. With her she had brought a large towel and what some other children said were his clothes. Stripping off his wet bathing suit, she dried him hard, whispering anything comforting she could think of into his ear.

"It was my fault," sobbed Jorbie. "I killed him."

"It wasn't your fault, sweetheart. You mustn't think that. It was very foolish of Kenneth to swim out so far when he didn't know how to swim very well."

There was a pause that she barely noticed, as if an idea had just struck Jorbie. "I tried to stop him," Jorbie said. "I tried everything I could think of to make him not go. I stayed right beside him, but somehow he got away from me. It's my fault."

"Shhh. Don't even say that, darling. Look. I know how terrible you feel. Losing someone as close as Kenneth seems like the end of the world. And at first it doesn't seem to make sense, I know that, too. But remember, darling, Kenneth wouldn't have died unless God wanted him in Heaven with him. He loves children." The crying seemed to have slowed a little, but the moment she stopped talking, it began again. The teacher, even though a devout Catholic, was about to get into an area that felt uncomfortable and uncertain. "Sweetheart, what I'm trying to explain to you now is a very grown-up thing and something very hard to understand. But, you see, when someone dies, it isn't the end of everything. For Kenneth, it's the *beginning* of everything. It's the beginning of a new life, a life even after he's died, a life where there's no fear or suffering or pain.

"So don't think of Kenneth as having left you, darling; think of him as waiting for you in Heaven. Kenneth's alive up there, laughing and playing and being loved just as much as when he was here. . . ."

Jorbie looked at her. It *wasn't* his fault? It wasn't his tricks and things that had killed Kenneth? And Kenneth was waiting in Heaven for him? Maybe he could explain to him he was sorry. . . . Rubbing his eyes with his fist, Jorbie nodded his head slowly. He would remember. Because the teacher had told him what he wanted to believe—that it was no one's fault. Except maybe God's.

* * *

About a month later Jorbie sat on the edge of a rock just off the Straits, in a narrow inlet that opened into their property. In spite of his jealousy he missed Kenneth terribly; they had always felt part of each other. In his loneliness he came to this spot often, talking to the rock as if were Kenneth himself. He loved the sting of the spray in his face and the feeling of the wind through his hair, and although the rock never answered back, Jorbie was sure he sometimes heard Kenneth's voice, very far away, just audible above the wind. To make himself feel less guilty, he'd remember what the teacher had told him, and imagined Kenny living his wonderful new life in Heaven, playing and laughing. Sometimes, if he let his imagination work hard enough, he'd feel the old jealousy return, thinking how much better off Kenneth was. It was just like it had always been; everybody still liked Kenneth better than him. Even God.

With a sigh, Jorbie stood up and walked slowly down the beach. About a hundred yards from the rock a sudden throbbing sound seemed to come from somewhere down near the water, a muffled pulsing like what Dr. L'Eveque had let him hear through his stethoscope one day. Throbbing like the sound of his own heart, the pulsing grew louder. As suddenly as it had begun, it stopped. But down by the water, he saw a flash of color showing between two rocks, a piece of cloth somehow vaguely familiar.

When he walked over to see what it was, Jorbie realized it was Kenneth's bathing suit. Facedown, wedged between the two rocks, was Kenneth's body, until this moment never recovered. His twin had come back to visit him from his new life. It was kind of a funny way to arrive, but maybe, along with everything else in Heaven, God had given Kenneth a sense of humor. A little timidly, he called out Kenneth's name, turning him over on his back.

A wave of shock surged through him. The fish and

crabs and sea scavengers had been busy; Kenneth's body was torn and open with strands of loose flesh hanging from it in long white shreds and floating in the shallows. His body was a whitish-green color, bloaty and swollen out of shape. But it was his eyes that were the worst; they had been eaten out of their sockets.

Jorbie ran screaming from the water toward his home; he ran along the dunes and hammered on the door of his house, pleading for someone to help him. There was no answer.

Jorbie threw himself on the ground, sobbing so hard he gagged from the heaving that racked his body. That was where his father found him when he came home that night. The teacher had lied to him. There was no wonderful, happy life after you died at all. You just rotted and fell apart, like the family cat the year before.

He would never trust anyone again.

PART I

Chapter One

If you walk all the way down to the end of St. Max's main street, you come to a sagging sign showing the way to Deliverance Road. When I was a child I used to take that sign literally, and believed that one day everybody in St. Max would suddenly turn around and like me. Or that at least I'd be allowed to get completely away from St. Max to someplace else. And up until recently, I still believed it.

Most of the people in St. Max, you see, have always hated me. Some people like Mrs. Pardee—damn, but she's a nice woman—say that I've got it all wrong, that most people really do like me, but I just don't give them a chance to show it. I know better. They've hated my guts ever since, ever since—well, ever since I can remember.

For a while I did make it out of St. Max entirely, you know. Deliverance Road. My escape came when I got the chance to go to pre-med at Marquette. What a different world it was! Sure as hell, nobody hated me there. Christ, when my work on bacterial isolation modes cracked the anthrax scare that had been driving this part of Michigan up the wall, the professors said I was at least a prodigy and maybe a genius. I liked that.

But then came the accident and I had to come back to St. Max again. Only now it's worse than ever. The streets look smaller and more beat-up than before, the storefronts more falling-down, and the people meaner. They pretend it's just the business I'm in, but I can feel it's something that goes a lot deeper than that.

The other day I noticed that even the sign Deliverance Road had disappeared. I guess that means I'm stuck in this God damned town forever. Some deliverance.

> *Jorbie Tenniel—to the rock,*
> *5:14 P.M., September 27th*

The gymnasium of St. Etienne Parochial was trying to look festive. It was not succeeding. Looking around her, Angie Psalter found the effort poignant; she and the gym shared a kinship of failure.

At the peak of the ceiling a few dozen balloons clustered forlornly, as if hoping to escape to the open air beyond; strands of bunting hung limply around the mesh-covered windows in a desperate, futile effort to add a touch of gaity. Still, in spite of its dusty, depressing promise, tonight's affair—a money-raiser for the school's athletic program—would be well attended. For St. Etienne served not only the town of St. Max itself but a cluster of towns farther down the Michigan peninsula—Charlevoix, St. Ignace, Groscap, Petoskey, Alpena—small towns much like St. Max, sticking like frozen fingers into the frigid waters of Lake Michigan.

Some of the guests were already arriving, blowing on their hands against the early cold of winter, trying, like the gym, to approach the evening of buffet supper followed by dancing with an enthusiasm they did not yet entirely feel.

Angie Psalter did not want to be here at all. She loathed parties because they made her feel more of an outcast than usual. She had no choice in the matter. As a lay teacher at St. Etienne her presence was required to help dish out the buffet and serve the watery purplish punch. More revelers appeared, slapping their hands against their sides and moving quickly away from the entrance doors, where the wind rushed in and it was cold and drafty. By general agreement it was decided they were having an unusually cold November.

It was *always* cold in St. Max, Angie realized. On this frigid spit of land touching the Straits of Mackinac, at a longitude farther north than either Ottawa or Montreal but untempered by any closeness to the sea, temperatures of minus thirty and forty for weeks at a time were not in the least unusual.

Even during the short two-month summer season, Angie thought sadly, it remained chilly, a feature relished by the waves of rugged sportsfishermen and other lovers of the outdoors who flew in every summer. They came from as far away as Chicago, Detroit, Toledo, and Milwaukee to relax in the peninsula's unspoiled wilderness. These tourists were the core of the area's economy, since the ferrous mines that had once supported the communities had long ago become defunct. "Take away the tourists," a survey for the State of Michigan had recently observed, "and you might as well give St. Max and the counties back to the Chippewa"—a decimated tribe who now huddled in their tepees on the Bay Mills Reservation, not really any more uncomfortable than the white man who had conquered them.

Angie Psalter watched as more people from various towns began arriving, steeling herself against the moment she would start serving food from behind the makeshift buffet counter. All of it had been donated by the ladies of one town or another, who presently clustered around Pyrex chafing dishes kept warm over alcohol burners, stirring their ragouts and stews and chattering with each other. Although known to most of them, Angie was largely ignored. She was used to it.

There was nothing ugly about Angie. In fact, she had really quite good features and an excellent figure, although she did nothing to enhance either. She wore little or no makeup, her hair was pulled straight back, and her clothes were what could only be described as dowdy. It was not that Angie didn't care, because she did. *Desperately.* But over the years, beaten down by the inevitability of rejection and the habit of failure, she no longer tried to fight back.

Slowly the gym—to Angie it felt airless and over-heated—was filling. One by one the men, appearing uncomfortable in suits that inevitably appeared too large or too small, wandered over and sampled the punch, sipping it with a glimmer of hope. As always, they were disappointed. Some of the more prescient had stopped off at bars in Alpena and Charlevoix before coming, loudly excusing themselves by muttering about how cold the weather had suddenly turned.

Across the room Angie saw her father, almost a stranger to her in his tie and jacket. Mr. Psalter needed no excuse to stop off at any bar anywhere any time. At twenty-one Angie had difficulty remembering a single day when he had been fully sober. And when he drank really heavily, sometimes a streak of dark, peculiar passion overcame him; it was the town's awareness of this extraordinarily ugly side to him that had made his daughter—from the time she was a little girl—St. Max's blameless but confirmed outcast, it's untouchable, its pariah. Looking at him, Angie shuddered.

Apparently Henry Psalter had tried to shave for the occasion, but his hand had seemingly shaken so badly his whole face was dotted with tiny pieces of toilet paper, making him appear the victim of some rare disease. She could resent him; she could not hate him, Angie decided almost sadly.

The buffet began. Everyone seemed to be talking at once and laughing with one another. If they even noticed Angie behind her serving dishes, it was not evident; she filled the plates of a faceless army of people who seemed to look more through than *at* her. Then they would withdraw, still talking and laughing, commenting on how well this year's committee had put the meal together. When the last of them had disappeared to tables and chairs at the rear of the gym, Angie put a tiny portion on a plate for herself, viewing the food with the same discomfort as she regarded the party.

Almost completely hidden behind part of a pillar and the edge of an old kitchen screen, Angie swallowed her meal without pleasure or interest, suffused by the same degree of enthusiasm with which a hospital patient faces a solitary Christmas dinner.

A few moments later a sudden noise brought Angie's head up. The Petoskey Five, a combo whose players were ordinarily busy as carpenters, fishermen, clerks, school-bus drivers, or mechanics, took up position on the small stage. Besides a shortage of ability, the Petoskey Five had other singular features: there were—and always had been—six players instead of five, and most of the men came not from Petoskey but from Alpena. Neither of these peculiarities in any way helped to explain their total lack of talent.

With a flourish, the cymbals crashed, the accordion squealed, and an arpeggio shook the piano; the violin sounded open chords to prove it was in tune, while the saxophonist's instrument groaned, and the bass player plucked at his giant strings with simulated abandon. It was time, the Petoskey Five's leader announced, fighting the squeals that had begun pouring from the PA system the moment he turned on the mike, it was time, he finally managed to say, for the dancing to begin and would everyone please help move the tables off the floor? Barely a minute later, his voice could be heard again: ah-one, ah-two, ah-three!

Angie Psalter tried to give the Petoskey Five the benefit of the doubt, but their playing had the same desultory quality as the gym's decor. Yet, as she looked around the room, she had to wonder if perhaps something wasn't wronger with her than with the party. Almost everyone else seemed to be enjoying themselves, laughing and calling to one another, happy for this excuse to cut up a little, the men occasionally slipping out to their cars to supplement the watery purple punch. She would have liked, now that dinner was out of the way, to go home and watch TV or read a book or listen to records or even just stare at the safety of her walls. But she couldn't. Sister Honorée expected her and the other lay teachers to stay until after everyone had left so they could help with the final cleanup.

Startled, Angie spun around as a sudden voice spoke to her cheerfully. "Delicious, Angie, delicious. Even better than last year, I think. I could have done without Gwen Lyttel's salad, but most people probably loved it." Shyly, Angie smiled at Edith Pardee, one of the warmest, kindest, and most thoroughly likable women in the entire area. She always had something pleasant to say to everyone, and seemed to make a special effort to be particularly pleasant to Angie. Once, a long time ago, Angie remembered, Mrs. Pardee had been a lay teacher at St. Etienne herself. Music, she thought. The wonderful smile that seemed a permanent part of her face fixed itself on Angie, simultaneously offering what was both a question and a suggestion. "You shouldn't just be sitting over here all by yourself, Angie. You ought to be out there mixing and dancing with people. They rarely bite, you know."

Angie felt a flush of embarrassment surge through her. Edith Pardee was right, of course. But how could a prominent woman like her be expected to understand what years of always being on the outside of everything did to someone? Edith Pardee was—and, Angie suspected, always had been—popular, attractive, and steeped in the self-confidence of total acceptance. "Oh, Mrs. Pardee, I'm waiting for someone I'm supposed to meet," Angie lied vaguely. "They're late."

From Edith Pardee's expression it was clear she

knew Angie wasn't even near the truth; it was also obvious she would never challenge the lie. "Well," said Mrs. Pardee with a gentle laugh, "I've got to find George and haul him back out onto the floor. Hard on the feet, but I wouldn't want the Petoskey Five to think I was boycotting them." With a pleasant little wave and an encouraging smile, Edith Pardee disappeared into the crowd.

A quarter of an hour later the Petoskey Five announced a ten-minute break. Most of the couples headed for the tables and chairs set up in the back of the gymnasium. Across the dance floor from Angie stood a long line of wooden chairs with their backs pushed tight against the wall. In the center of the long row, empty chairs stretching out from either side of him, sat Jorbie Tenniel. Perhaps it was the void surrounding him, but Angie couldn't remember ever seeing anyone look quite so alone. On impulse—she would never know what prompted her to make so uncharacteristic a move— Angie suddenly crossed the abandoned dance floor and sat down beside him. Blankly, he stared at her, appearing a little hostile, a little surprised, and completely baffled.

"Hi, Jorbie," said Angie cheerfully. "You looked so terribly lonely." She knew that Jorbie, much as herself, rarely went to parties and was here only because someone had to maneuver his father around in his wheelchair.

The word "lonely" had apparently rung some bell deep inside him. "Lonely? Tonight, just *tonight*? I've been lonely all my life." He stopped abruptly, apparently as surprised at what he'd said as she was to hear him say it. After a tight, strained laugh he recovered. "See, Dad's profession didn't exactly make me the most popular kid in town." He stopped again, his eyes clouded with confusion. "At Marquette, everything was so different. So damned different. . . ."

For a moment Angie felt a sudden bond surge between them; Jorbie Tenniel apparently considered himself as much of an outcast as she herself did. But the notion quickly faded; it was pure fantasy, Angie decided. Look at the difference in their situations. How could he possibly feel unwanted? Jorbie was incredibly handsome, with fine, sensitive features, a winning smile, and, in his own way, was almost beautiful. To that, add that he was admired, looked up to, respected. And was spectacularly bright. Brilliant, she supposed. Look at that thing he'd done during the anthrax scare; everyone in St. Max respected him for that.

The only negative thing she'd ever heard about Jorbie was his standoffishness, but what might have been considered stuck-up in others was, in his case, attributed to brilliance. People with the kind of esoteric talent he had, it was generally agreed, always lived in private little worlds of their own.

Angie let her eyes drift over to Jorbie again, studying him, trying to make sense of what he'd said. Well, yes, some people were a little thrown by his family's business, of course. But Jorbie had so many positives to make up for it that for him to apparently feel as she did—like an outcast—was ridiculous.

Angie wanted to say something about his curious attitude but decided against it; she didn't know him well enough to be that personal. To fill the awkward silence, Angie changed the subject. "It was sad about your father. I mean, the accident. It must have put a terrible burden on you."

She watched his face closely. He shrugged, seeming to disappear into his own thoughts. Actually, a kaleidoscope of nightmare events was crowding through his brain. The picture of his father's car skidding on a rain-slicked Michigan 383 to crash head-on into another car. The spinning red lights of the state police and the ambulance streaming unevenly across the puddles on the road. The sudden 1 A.M. call to Marquette's med school finally reaching him. The surgeon at Saginaw Memorial, wearing OR green and a grim expression, telling Jorbie what he'd already guessed. "He'll live, for which he may or may not be thankful. There isn't a damned thing anybody can do to put that spine of his back together. Two crushed vertebrae, anterior, and all the nerves gone with them. Hell, you're a medical student, I don't have to play games with you. Paralyzed from the waist down. For good. Life in bed and, if he's lucky, an occasional wild spin in his wheelchair. I wish there was something I could say that sounded a little more hopeful. . . ."

Two days later, his shocked faculty advisor at med school had listened incredulously as Jorbie told him he'd have to withdraw. "But, my Lord, Mr. Tenniel, with a future like yours! Your plans for research medicine. We all had such big hopes. Why, that work of yours in pulmonary anthrax . . . brilliant . . . it would be a tragedy for you to withdraw at this juncture. . . ."

"I don't have any choice," Jorbie had answered. "Someone has to take care of my father. Hell, they're not even sure yet if he'll be able to use a wheelchair. And someone has to take over his business. Without it, I couldn't afford med school anyway."

The professor was not willing to give up this easily; Tenniel was the most promising student the med school had had in years. "Certainly someone can be found to take care of your father. A male nurse of some kind. And perhaps the school can find someone willing to subsidize a brilliant future like yours. As for your father's business . . ." The professor had paused, aware he didn't have the faintest idea what the business was, but stared at Jorbie waiting for the student to tell him. Wincing, Jorbie did.

"In St. Max. He was the undertaker. Now I guess *I* am."

A pained expression crossed the professor's face. What a waste of a brilliant future. Shaking his head, the professor glanced at his watch again, scurried down the corridor, and disappeared.

For Angie, there was something almost painful in letting Jorbie sit lost in his private silence. She tried talking to him, but at first got no answer. When he finally came out of whatever it was he'd drifted into, his entire mood seemed electrically charged. "Want to dance?" he asked suddenly.

Angie felt herself begin to tremble—part delight, part fear. She wasn't sure she could get away with it. Would Jorbie take a few steps with her and quickly suggest they sit back down? And people in the gym might laugh at the sight of her out on the floor, pretending to be something she was not.

Jorbie seemed to be reading her mind. "Of course," he added. "I'm a little out of practice . . ."

"That still puts you way ahead of me."

Jorbie flashed her a smile of encouragement. What a wonderful smile it was, thought Angie. The mischievous smile of a misbehaving little boy, she decided, a little boy so appealing he didn't even *pretend* to be good. "Okay," Jorbie smiled sheepishly, letting the last barrier crumble. "I've never even tried. Not once in my whole life."

"You're making fun of me."

"I'm not. Cross my heart." Jorbie spoke with a child's solemnity and stared Angie directly in the eye. "Cross my heart and hope to die. It's something I just never got around to learning."

Angie was still having trouble believing him, but he was being so charming about it she found herself half accepting what he said. "Point a finger at the sky?" she added, falling into Jorbie's game of children.

"Point a finger at the sky," he repeated. A small, mystified frown crossed his face as he said it, but quickly disappeared. "C'mon. What they're playing just now is so slow it might be halfway easy."

"I may fall down," Angie warned him. Her own smile was a grateful one, still not really believing him.

Tentatively they stepped out onto the floor, holding each other a little clumsily, two children playing grown-up, and began to dance. They weren't very good, but standards in Mackinac County were mercifully low and they were able to get away with it. Angie felt breathlessly happy. Did Edith Pardee see her? Cathy Springer? Sister Honorée? By now she wished she'd worn something less severe than her shapeless gray wool, but then, she didn't *own* anything much less severe. That would have to be remedied. She wished she'd worn makeup. She wished she'd done something more with her hair. She wished—but Jorbie appeared oblivious, chattering and laughing.

This was the real wonder of it—his pretending to have so much fun with her. There were other, far more attractive girls at the dance, so, to Angie, it *had* to be pretending. Faintly she remembered his lonely words about being shunned all his life, words she might have said herself. Perhaps it was this sense of shared experience—wrong as his was—that drew him to her. Perhaps it was the mutual emotion of their reaction to the town. Perhaps—no, it was all in her head.

"You don't need to apologize for your dancing, you know," Jorbie noted with a smile. "I mean, the way I—"

Angie felt herself blush. "Well, I haven't tripped on anything yet. Maybe it's just that there's a little tiny slice of dancer in any woman—"

"Salami."

"Salome," corrected Angie automatically, before she realized it was a joke and laughed with him. It wasn't a very good joke, but everything either of them said had suddenly become very funny. They talked of everything and of nothing. They looked back, they looked forward. They laughed. They sat together on the long row of empty chairs and talked some more. Suddenly, from Jorbie:

"Next Friday. Veterans' Day. School's closed, isn't it?"

Angie nodded, not sure where he was headed.

"Well, I was thinking. We could take a picnic lunch and drive over the bridge to the Upper Peninsula—you know, up toward Sault Sainte Marie . . ."

Angie's heart leapt. The whole world was changing around her. "I could make lunch. Deviled eggs, sandwiches. And, if you want, beer . . ."

"Heineken. Very cold."

"On ice. And—" She stopped.

Jorbie's face was suddenly ashen, his eyes fixed straight ahead of him. "Jorbie . . ." He didn't seem to hear her.

His mind was a million years away. The thumping of the Petoskey Five's double bass, reverberating through the gym, had picked up a sympathetic vibration from something in the room, amplifying itself. The sound fascinated at the same time that it terrified, simultaneously familiar and foreign. It grew inside his head, drowning out everything, beating so loudly his whole skull throbbed.

"Jorbie . . ." he heard Angie say again, followed by something else. He stared at her in confusion. The frightening, throbbing sound seemed to come from her, suddenly a stranger. The face opposite him kept going in and out of focus, intermittently replaced by somebody else's. Jorbie could hear another voice speaking to him urgently, but could not recognize it; it was a voice familiar yet distant. The face and the voice and the pulsing, throbbing sound all belonged to this someone, someone he had known, but someone he could not be-

gin to place because the muffled throbbing had grown
so intense it overwhelmed rational thought.

As if from a great distance he heard Angie's voice.
"Jorbie, you look terrible . . . are you all right? Is
there anything I—"

As abruptly as he had slipped away, Jorbie returned,
his expression apologetic. "Hey, I'm sorry. I do that
sometimes. Just sort of float away." It was a lie, of
course. Noticing the anxious look Angie still wore, Jorbie forced his most winning smile. "I guess I should
warn people. Otherwise they could take it personally."

A small shiver that Angie couldn't explain ran
through her. Jorbie's "floating away" was frightening to
witness, but she dismissed it quickly because that wonderful smile of his had come back, touching something
deep inside her. Soon she managed to put it out of her
head entirely.

A little later they watched their neighbors perform
during the dance intermission: Mr. Lewitt and his
highly unreliable card tricks. Mrs. deCarre and her
Basque folk songs. The Petoskey Five's accordionist in
his annual rendition of "Lady of Spain." And two little
girls from Alpena who tap-danced until one of them fell
down and burst into tears. Jorbie took the opportunity
to see if his father needed anything; across the room
Angie caught her friend Cathy Springer's eye. Instead
of looking happy for her, Cathy appeared troubled. Angie finally looked away, confused and a little hurt.

Intently she watched Jorbie, dark and slimly erect,
walking across the floor and back to her; a shudder of
pride ran through her. "How is he?" Angie asked of his
father.

"Fine, fine. He did say if he had to hear 'Lady of
Spain' one more time, he's going to crawl into the coffin beside one of our customers and pull the lid shut.
Crowded, sure. But that's the way the cadaver crum-
bles."

As with his smile, Angie decided, Jorbie's sense of humor was also that of a little boy's: designed mostly to shock. She wondered what he'd been like as a child—in fact, Angie wanted to know everything, every last little detail, about him, to absorb him, to inhale him—she sensed there were certain parts of him kept secret. Apparently there were some things you didn't discuss with Jorbie Tenniel.

Not too much later Hardy Remarque, chief of St. Max's one-man police force, came over and told Jorbie his father wanted to leave now. Angie found a lot of things she suddenly wanted to say—she had intended to bring up the picnic again and make it official—but Remarque planted himself beside them, standing alongside Jorbie, like a federal marshal waiting to escort a prisoner to court. Remarque intimidated Angie completely.

"I thought you could use some help getting his chair through this mob," Angie heard him explain to Jorbie as they walked over toward his father. Jorbie nodded.

From the far end of the room Angie watched as the two of them maneuvered the wheelchair across the floor, Hardy Remarque forcing his way through the crowd like a linebacker. When Jorbie reached the door, he seemed to pause for an instant, and Angie wondered if she hadn't seen him smile at her, but couldn't be sure; his hands were too busy handling the wheelchair to return her wave, she supposed. A moment later he was gone.

That night Angie had a terrible time getting to sleep. What Jorbie looked like, what he sounded like, his way of speaking, his voice, the picnic, the dancing, the crazy boyish smile, kept her turning from one side to the other. Usually, not being able to sleep infuriated Angie; tonight it made her tremble with excitement.

Farther up the coast, along the Straits of Mackinac, where the wind never stopped and the waves crashed ceaselessly on the rocks below the mortuary, Jorbie Tenniel also lay sleepless.

But his thoughts were not about Angie. He would do it, damn it, he would. Ever since he'd gotten back to St. Max after being forced to leave Marquette, a dark idea had been growing in his brain. This hateful little town full of hateful little people. Until tonight he had always dismissed the idea as something he would probably just play with, but certainly never get around to carrying out.

Now, for reasons he didn't understand, things were different. The idea had taken on new urgency; it was no longer an idle thought but something he suddenly knew had to be undertaken.

Chapter Two

*It's funny, Angie Psalter and me hitting it off like that.
I can't pretend she's terribly pretty, but maybe that's
because she doesn't work at it. That can happen if a
town like St. Max gives you the business long enough.*

*Now, there's a subject I know all about. Christ, but I
resent this town. I know it's crazy, but I can't get away
from the notion that the people in St. Max are why I
had to give up Marquette. It's as if they reached out,
grabbed me, and hauled me back. Stupid. They weren't
behind the wheel of my old man's car, they didn't make
it rain that night, they didn't make the car skid. Still.*

*Somehow Angie knows exactly how I feel about St.
Max; she sensed it right off. Anyway, it's nice to have a
friend like her, someone you can talk to, someone who
means what they say.*

*I don't know how to bring it up to her, but she sure
as hell could use some makeup—you know, lipstick and
powder and stuff. Without it, she looks sort of washed
out and unhealthy.*

*Unhealthy? Hell, we got healthier-looking people
right downstairs in the freezer.*

> *Jorbie Tenniel—to the rock,
> 10:00 A.M., November 5th*

"Damn it, I saw you with my own eyes. I'm not blind.
You spent most of the party with him, for Christ's
sake."

Angie and her father were sitting in the kitchen while
he pretended to have breakfast. It was the morning
after the dance at St. Etienne's, and he was furious. On

the counter in front of him was all the breakfast he ever
had: orange juice and black coffee. As always, he was
spiking the orange juice with vodka, something she always pretended not to see him do. But from the shape
he was in this morning, Angie knew he'd been downstairs for a long time before she got there and had already had quite a lot of vodka—undiluted with Sunkist.
Her father swore as he knocked over his water glass
and sent it careening off the counter onto the floor.

Angie said nothing, just mopped up the mess the best
she could. Moodily, her father stared at the shattered
pieces. "Damned crazy little water glasses with itsy-
bitsy bases. Always falling over," he muttered angrily.

Angie remained mute. Inside her were a thousand
things she would like to say, but it never proved anything, so she didn't bother.

"Damned crazy," her father began again, infuriated
by the obstinacy of inanimate objects this morning.
"Just like that bastard Jorbie Tenniel. Crazy. The
whole Tenniel family, all of them, bad news. Undertakers, for Christ's sake. Ghouls. Grave robbers. Body
snatchers. And *you*—for the love of God. Dancing
with, *touching* Jorbie Tenniel! How the hell do you
know where his hands have been last?"

Inside, Angie flared. Crossing her father when he
was two-thirds gone like this was pointless; he'd yell at
her, curse her, and by evening forget the whole thing
had happened. Usually she avoided such confrontations
by keeping quiet, saying nothing, and getting away from
him as soon as she could. But today he'd attacked her
in a particularly sensitive area. "You don't know anything about Jorbie," she said, trying to keep her voice
calm. "He's a wonderful person. Bright, funny, understanding. We had a great time at the party. I'm going to
see more of him, lots more. He likes me."

Mr. Psalter's moist, puffy eyes rose in his bloated
face to stare at his daughter. He gave a dry little laugh,

as spiteful sounding as it was intended to be. "I guess, considering what a bust you are in this town, even an undertaker's a pretty good catch for you."

Something in her exploded. Angie rarely lost her temper, but he had pushed the right button. "If my father hadn't been the town drunk all my life, maybe I wouldn't be such a bust." The moment she had said it, Angie regretted her words. She was too kind, too gentle a person to be so cruel to her own father. Or for that matter, to anyone. As she opened her mouth to make some sort of apology, he took one hand and swept everything off the counter. The moist eyes, filled with hurt, stared at her as he stood up, knocking over the chair, and stormed out the kitchen door. Hanging in the air like two great burning clouds, the hurt eyes stared balefully at Angie for a long time after he'd left the kitchen.

Angie glanced at the clock on the side wall and slowly began clearing up the carnage, aware she was already late for her job at St. Etienne. She should have followed her usual course and kept silent. That was the trouble with trying to deal with a drunk: they were allowed to be as mean to you as they wanted, but if you returned any of the meanness you wound up feeling guilty about it. But damm it, her father shouldn't have attacked Jorbie.

"In my opinion, it looks superb, mam'selle. Your coloring, you see. And the size is perfect."

Angie Psalter stared at herself in the mirror. The light woolen skirt, woven in some sort of houndstooth pattern, with the pastel shade sweater-top blouse, looked rich and colorful. They appeared to have been lurking on some secret shelf of Madame Solo's, expressly waiting for Angie to walk through the door and claim them. To her, the effect they created was magical. But the price appeared equally as possessed by spirits.

She winced. Her eyes kept traveling back and forth between the blouse and skirt, the mirror, and the price tag. She finally sighed and took two in different colors.

To Angie, paying such a sum for clothes—and this, she knew, was only a beginning—was so extravagant it verged on the immoral. That she had the money was beside the point; she spent little, and had for years. This was why her account at the Petoskey Savings Bank bulged with money; the black figures marched down the "Deposits" column like a Roman phalanx as seen from a helicopter. Nothing, virtually, was ever spent on herself, and her other living expenses were minimal. She lived rent-free in her father's house, and it was he who paid for the food, the electricity, and the oil. In return, Angie cooked the little he ate and did her best to straighten the house up behind him. Her salary from St. Etienne Parochial was not large, but her cost of living was infinitesimal. With what she had in the bank, she could have bought the entire contents of Madame Solo's and never batted an eye.

She and her only real friend from St. Max, Cathy Springer, were in Sault Sainte Marie, across the Upper Peninsula and just over the border into Canada. Sault Sainte Marie was the largest town for miles—over eighty thousand people living along the complex of locks that separated Michigan and Lake Huron from Superior—and Angie felt the French touch might give her new clothes an added flair, not realizing most of the woolens came from Ontario and were almost as English as treacle.

She moved on to where the salesgirl began showing her more formal items—dresses, scarves, coats, shoes—completely outfitting herself dress by dress, skirt by skirt, blouse by sweater. Before she made each purchase, she would turn to Cathy, searching for approval of the things she was sure of, seeking advice on those that left her balanced between certainty and confusion.

Cathy was helpful, but said a bare minimum; she was not stupid, and the reason behind the outlay was clear enough to her—clear, and a little frightening.

Even to herself, Angie had to admit that she was going overboard. Last night, after all, had only been a fleeting exposure. But she seemed unable to help herself. Jorbie had mentioned something about taking her on a picnic; that, Angie had decided, was at least an indication of interest.

While the small mountain of purchases was being carefully wrapped in pink tissue paper and placed in long, gleaming boxes, Angie turned to face Cathy. Cathy seemed very subdued, her lips compressed, and looked uncomfortable. Angie's conversation with her began on the lower of two levels. "You don't approve, I guess. It sort of shows."

"It's your money, Angie. God knows, you deserve to spend it on anything you want."

"But you don't approve."

"The clothes? Sure. You need them. You've needed them for a long time."

"That isn't what I meant, Cathy, and you know it."

Cathy shrugged and fixed Angie with her eyes. Abruptly the conversation changed levels. "Well, it's just that—"

"You think I'm losing my head over one evening . . ."

"No, not that either. It's just that Jorbie Tenniel, well, I can't exactly put a name to it, but there's something strange about him. Spooky, sort of. I'm afraid I've always felt that way. I can't tell you why."

With a sad little smile Angie looked at her friend; she already could guess, she thought, what Cathy was skirting so delicately, and while she might have expected it from some people, she hadn't from Cathy. "The undertaker thing," Angie noted with disappointment. "Everybody holds it against him a little, I guess, but Jorbie thinks it makes people hate him. Which is ridiculous.

Besides, it isn't his fault that he had to come back and go into it; he was a pre-med student until that awful accident paralyzed his father. How can you hold that against him?"

"It isn't the undertaker thing, Angie. It's *him*—him as a person." Cathy was lying. It *was* the undertaker thing—at least one particular facet of it—that disturbed her. She had never been particularly fond of Jorbie; some people have a long-standing chemical aversion to someone else they can never explain satisfactorily, even to themselves. Jorbie, however, had given a specific trigger to her vague dislike, something she could use to rationalize her feelings.

Cathy had come to Tenniel's that day—was it six months ago?—to drop off some flowers for Miss April Claybourne, a fellow teacher at St. Etienne Parochial. Her death had had some unsettling overtones. For years April Claybourne had lived with her brother, Fred, who worked as a janitor at the town hall. Unlike most brothers and sisters, the pair were so close people sometimes snickered behind their hands.

As if to prove how close they really were, when a heart attack struck April Claybourne, it was only a few minutes before her brother suffered the same fate. With people who have lived together their entire lives, Dr. L'Eveque said, the phenomenon was not an unusual one.

Cathy stood outside Tenniel's, the flowers clutched in one hand, pressing the doorbell with the other. It was answered by Jorbie.

"Come in, Cathy," he said, "come in. Always a sad business, twin deaths like this." Jorbie was being at his most charming, and as she sat chatting with him in the living room, Cathy could feel herself overcoming a lot of her native reservations about him.

"Dying like that. Just minutes apart," Cathy said. "It seems so strange."

Jorbie had nodded. "World is full of strange things." Suddenly he stood up. "Let me show you something, Cathy—something kind of strange—that shows how close April and Fred Claybourne *really* were."

Taking her by the hand, Jorbie led her downstairs. Cathy'd never been to Tenniel's before and wasn't entirely sure where they were going, except that it was through a room filled with large bottles of chemicals and rolling white enamel carts. Something made Cathy begin to hold back.

With a sweep of his hand Jorbie suddenly threw open a heavy door. Stretched out on two adjoining tables were April and Fred. Fred's face still wore the expression of pain and horror that had hit him along with the impossible pain in his heart. April's wore a surprised look, her mouth twisted into what was almost a smile by the sudden wonder of the pain she was experiencing. Apparently Jorbie had made no effort to straighten out their features before rigor mortis set in and the bodies were still pliable. In a sick, macabre joke, however, he had placed Fred Claybourne's left hand halfway up April's nightie; the suggestion of a surprised smile on her face and the look of startled pain on his made the tableau shockingly realistic. "Now that," commented Jorbie, beginning to laugh as a look of horror crossed Cathy's face, "*that* is what I call close."

For a second Cathy stood there in stunned silence. Her earlier feelings about Jorbie returned, converted now from dislike to loathing. Her stomach turned, her head felt light. "You sick bastard," Cathy hissed. She wanted to scream, to slap his face, to throw up. Instead, Cathy ran, out ot the room, out of the house.

Right now Cathy wished she could explain it to Angie, to tell him what Jorbie had done, and how sick it proved he was. But she couldn't. She never would be able to; to her, it was a scene of private horror, one she could never tell anyone. Her reaction to it was too personal. Waffling, she looked at Angie.

"I wish I could explain what it is about Jorbie that bothers me, Angie. I don't know what it is," she lied. "It's just there. Something funny, something a little sick. And it worries me: you could get hurt." Cathy shuddered, studying Angie's face anxiously.

Not sure of what Angie's reaction would be, Cathy kept waiting for a reply, braced, because she expected it to be an angry one. There was no reaction at all. Talking about Jorbie—even with Cathy in such a negative mood—had excited Angie to the point she was no longer even able to hear what her friend was saying. She had spotted a scarf—it was a pretty silly thing, brightly colored and with some sort of motif that suggested an extremely awkward couple dancing—and Angie had to have it. The dancing couple, stylized as they were, would amuse Jorbie, reminding him of the St. Etienne's dance.

Studying her, Cathy gave up. Angie was gone. Nothing she or anyone else could say was going to change her mind. Yes, she told Angie helplessly, it was certainly a pretty scarf.

The water hitting the rocks on either side of him flew into his face, stinging, but somehow familiar and reassuring. In front of him, whipped by the same wind—it always tore across this little inlet off the Straits of Mackinac below the mortuary—was his private rock, the water ebbing and surging around it.

Jorbie Tenniel had been coming here since he was a child. He let the ceaseless wind pummel him, as it did his rock; his hair flew wildly in it, his clothes were pressed tightly against his body by the endless blast of cold air that tore across the chill Straits. It did not bother him. This place was a special place to him; the howling of the wind was a special music to his ears; the stinging spray was a special feeling upon his face.

Standing here, whipped by the elements, Jorbie would talk to the rock as if it were a person, sometimes chiding it, sometimes imploring it, pleading with it, yelling in fury at it. The event that began this strange ritual—Kenneth's death—was so traumatic it had long ago been erased from his mind. Jorbie did not remember that it was to this rock he had come in his loneliness, talking to it as though it *were* Kenneth, and hearing, somewhere beyond the pounding of the waves and the screaming of the wind, Kenneth's voice answering him.

Today, Jorbie's conversation with the rock was a strange one, so strange he was even troubled himself. "Rock," he cried over the moaning wind, "I don't know what's happening. Those dark thoughts I've had for so long. They're growing darker. Something inside is pushing me to carry them out. I don't know what started them again, or why they feel so urgent. I think it's something that happened the last day or so, but I can't really be sure. That party at St. Etienne—did you know I even *danced*?—for the first time in my life I actually danced. And all of a sudden I knew there's something I have to do—I'm still not sure why, but I think it began at the party."

For a moment there was silence as Jorbie listened to the roar and hiss of the water. Defiantly, he stared at the rock. His voice changed, suddenly strident and furious. "Rock, damn it, tell me, for Christ's sake! Tell me what or leave me alone."

Staring at the silent rock for a moment longer, a frightened Jorbie Tenniel abruptly spun on his heel and, slipping and sliding on the wet stones, ran up the steep hill to the safety of the mortuary and the body of Blaine Escarre, too long out of the freezer and becoming a little high.

* * *

"I don't know why you'd want that kind of stuff—we sure as hell don't get much call for it—but, yeah, we carry it, mister." Muttering, the man in the chemical supply center disappeared, returning a little later with a pile of miniature retorts and flasks, which, after he had shown them to his customer, he carefully wrapped and put gently into a box. This was happening about the same moment that Angie's purchases, equally carefully wrapped, were being tenderly placed into the gleaming white boxes for her.

Jorbie Tenniel had spent most of the afternoon here in Saginaw, picking up his supplies. Some of them were for the business—Saginaw was a bustling town of almost a hundred thousand people, and you could get just about anything there.

Some of his purchases were for the experiments he was conducting. It had been almost four months since Jorbie had been at Marquette, but his interest in research medicine remained strong.

To keep the work viable, he had set up a small lab off the mortuary's main work area; he was still at work on the experiments he had been involved with when his future was so cruelly changed by a speeding car and a rain-slicked pavement. At Marquette the work had been part of research into new kinds of anesthesia; when Jorbie left, he had brought—stolen—a large supply of the various drugs he'd been using in his experiments.

For hours, in his makeshift laboratory, he would stand in front of the cages that lined the wall, each filled with the inevitable lab hamsters. Whistling softly, Jorbie would study them as the tiny mammals would stand or sit or pace restlessly from one end of their prison to the other, giving their sharp little squeals every time something frightened them. They had plenty to be frightened of. Jorbie had injected each of them with a different drug or a different dosage, noting in his meticulous hand on his clipboard, which thrived, which reacted as expected, or which simply fell over dead.

There was one drug in particular that especially fascinated Jorbie. It was the one drug of Jorbie's that was in short supply—*bonaro,* an exotic, little-known member of the curare family. For reasons Jorbie could not understand, the drug completely enraptured him; he found himself virtually hypnotized by it. It's sole functional property—and Jorbie at the moment could think of no particular use for it—was its capacity to reduce any of his hamsters to a virtual state of suspended animation for hours at a time. Day after day he extrapolated the dosage of *bonaro* into the amount it would take for the drug to produce the same effect upon other species. More and more he found the *bonaro* absorbing him; pointless as the drug appeared to be, he felt increasingly unable to tear himself away from his experiments with it. Crazy, he told himself. Some sort of vestigial hangover from his days of glory at Marquette, he decided.

Walking down the street in Saginaw, doing various formulations in his head with *bonaro* and the hamsters, he suddenly saw the man and ducked into a doorway. Jorbie had difficulty imagining what he was doing here, but the man was Dr. Vincent deLac, one of the more unpleasant members of Marquette's faculty.

Jorbie despised him; so did all the other students. The man was sarcastic, pompous, unpleasant, and thoroughly mean—sometimes almost savage in his contempt of the young men he taught. Unlike Jorbie, the other students only disliked him as a person, while repecting him for his brillance as a doctor.

Jorbie didn't respect deLac in any area. The roots of his loathing were personal. When the breakthough had happened, deLac blithely wrote a paper about Jorbie's experiments in immunology that had cracked the pulmonary anthrax outbreak two years earlier. In it, deLac took all the credit for himself, carefully avoiding any mention of even Jorbie's name. It was unpardonable.

Jorbie was aware this kind of thing happened frequently in the fiercely competitive little world of medicine, but deLac had compounded his sorry treatment of Jorbie by being totally condescending to him, raising his eyebrow in a way that implied it was bad form for a medical student to touch on such a presumptuous subject. That slithering, stealing, slimy creep deLac, Jorbie thought. And then . . . and then . . . a strange idea suddenly slipped into Jorbie's brain, as evil as deLac himself. Jorbie struggled with himself. The idea was so awful he wasn't sure of what it was entirely, or who it was meant for, or what to do with it. Shaken, he walked slowly around the streets of Saginaw, the idea only half completed, unaimed, and certain only in its enormity.

That was the trouble with great ideas, he told himself; frequently no one, not even their creator, was sure what to do with them.

All right, so she wasn't Bo Derek. But not bad, not bad at all. Angie stood in front of the long mirror in her bedroom and studied herself. She looked completely different, she decided. It was amazing what a little makeup could do for you. Oh, she'd used it before, of course, lots of times, but never as part of a total package. The beauty shop had cut, trimmed, and set her hair, which seemed somehow to change the entire shape of her face. They had taught her how to use the right lipstick to set off her coloring; they had even tried to introduce her to the wonders of eye-liner, but there Angie had drawn the line.

Maybe later. Angie stood now, looking at herself— her new self—dressed in the bright plaid skirt and the pastel cashmere cardigan. To Angie the total effect was awesome. She picked up and held one of the dresses in front of her; the material felt slippery, fragile and sensual between her fingers. But the dresses, like the eyeliner, would have to wait until later. Her first exposure to Jorbie would be in one of the sweaters and skirts, on his picnic next Friday.

It was stupid, Angie told herself, to let the mere thought of this day affect her so; she was trembling all over. Sitting down on her bed suddenly, Angie hugged herself. My God, life was wonderful.

In this lab, Jorbie Tenniel was not hugging himself. But, like Angie, he had just realized the wonders of life were limitless. Before him stood the cage with one of the hamsters, its eyes open, lying on its side, apparently dead. Only it wasn't: 2 1/2 cc of *bonaro* had kept it in suspended animation for six hours, and as Jorbie watched, the animal began flexing its muscles, slowly coming back to life as it regained the use of its muscles. If the dosage were multiplied by ten and factored out by weight, a large dog could be kept in such a state for six days, an average-size human for three.

Jorbie felt a shiver run through him. It had no possible use with humans. Or did it?

Chapter Three

*I've never understood what makes guys like deLac tick.
The man's bright—really bright, you can tell that—but
he's such a damned prick. Mean. Sadistic. That's not
just my opinion, understand; lots of the other guys at
Marquette reached the same conclusion. See, he gets
some kind of kick out of putting people down, of beating on them. And not just people he doesn't like—
anyone.*

*I suppose that's why he had to go into teaching instead
of private practice. What a bedside manner he'd have
had! Can you see him telling a patient what was wrong
with him? "Jesus," he'd say, shaking that oversize head
of his, "Jesus, are you sick. If you ask me, you'll be
damned lucky to make it through the night. Oh well.
Easy come, easy go. . . ."*

*What old deLac needs is a king-size shot of bonaro.
Improve his disposition no end. Then he ought to be
put in a—hell, there's that idea again. It keeps creeping
up on me like that all the time.*

*And Christ, what a thought. I ought to go soak my
head in a bucket of formaldehyde for even toying with
it again.*

Maybe, in the last analysis, I'm just as mean as deLac.

> *Jorbie Tenniel—to the rock,
> 11:15 P.M., November 6th*

"Watch him," Jorbie commanded, "and come wake me
if he moves a whisker." They were in the lab off the
mortuary preparation room, he and Pasteur, standing in

front of a cage with a hamster lying still as death on the cage's floor.

Pasteur looked confused, repeating the words aloud. "Wake you if it moves a whisker." Pasteur turned suddenly. "They can really move their *whiskers,* Mr. Jorbie?"

"Oh, shit," Jorbie groaned. "Just wake me if he moves, Pasteur." Pasteur was his assistant at the mortuary; he was willing, he was devoted to Jorbie, but he wasn't very bright, and therefore a pain in the ass.

There was something essentially sad about Pasteur. He was not quite as dim-witted as he appeared, although the fact was frequently difficult to accept. In part, Pasteur's aspect of stupidity came from his giant, oaflike size, his shambling gait, and a speech pattern that verged on that of a child's. He shuffled rather than walked, his face suffused with a huge smile, trying to win favor in a world that had little time for anyone that strayed from the norm in the most minimal degree.

In essence, this attitude of the world's toward him lay behind Pasteur's total, almost mindless, devotion to Jorbie. Quite simply, Pasteur worshiped him. Mr. Jorbie was—and always had been—kind to him; no one else had. Mr. Jorbie talked with him; no one else in St. Max did. Mr. Jorbie had given him a job; no one else would. And most wonderous of all, Mr. Jorbie had even gifted him with his own secret name—Pasteur.

It never occurred to Pasteur that almost everything Jorbie appeared to do for him, he actually did for himself. Or that there was an essential cruelty behind all of Jorbie's apparent kindness. Yes, Jorbie talked to him, but in reality he was talking to himself; Jorbie merely used Pasteur as a sounding board for his ideas and for his rage against the world of St. Max. Yes, Jorbie had given him a job—with Pasteur doing all the heavy, loathsome work, work requiring no brains, work of a kind that very few other men in St. Max would have even considered.

Cruelest of all was the name he'd given him. To name this giant, slow-brained creature Pasteur was as cruel as labeling a paraplegic Bruce Jenner. Yet Pasteur loved his name. To him, it was proof of the private relationship between him and Mr. Jorbie, a secret relationship unshared by anyone else in the world. He wore the name proudly, lulling himself to sleep at night with the magic sound of it. In a thin and dangerous world, Pasteur was happy.

The bell rang sharply, making Pasteur's head snap upright. The ringing, shrill and incessant, came every half hour, triggered by a small automatic timer. Directly following the ringing of the bell, a low-level electric shock would be sent coursing through the dead-appearing hamster. Each time, Pasteur could see the animal's body quiver from the electricity, but the tiny creature exhibited no movement of its own, so Pasteur knew it was not yet time to follow his orders and go wake Mr. Jorbie.

Earlier, Pasteur had watched as Mr. Jorbie injected a shot of *bonaro* into the animal's rump. "Aw, the poor li'l fella," Pasteur had groaned, squeezing his eyes shut so he wouldn't have to see the hamster struggle from the pain of the injection. "The needle's so big and *he's* so small." When he had looked at Mr. Jorbie, hoping to see some sort of sympathy written across his face, all Pasteur could see was a look of contempt. And knew the scornful look was not only intended for the hamster, but for him as well. To avoid further confrontation, Pasteur had busied himself at the far end of the lab.

A small shout had suddenly come from Mr. Jorbie, and Pasteur hurried to the other end. "Thirteen minutes. Look. Thirteen minutes is all it took," Jorbie had said excitedly, checking the stopwatch hanging beside the cage. Pasteur peered inside blankly. On the floor lay the hamster, motionless, its eyes open and staring at him with reproach, looking very dead. This time, Pasteur hadn't said anything; he didn't want that scornful look turned in his direction again.

Settling back in his hard chair, Pasteur concentrated on keeping himself awake. Doing this was not easy, sitting here all alone in the dead stillness of the lab, with only the ticking of the wall clock to keep you company. It was unsettling to remember that in the freezer, just outside the lab door in the preparation room, bodies lay in a frozen stillness even more final than this room's.

With time, Pasteur had adjusted himself to working in the Tenniel Funeral Home fairly well; he had grown accustomed to the strange sights, sounds, and bitter smells of the preparation room, to the feeling of cold flesh against your hands, to the piercing stare of sightless eyes that glared at you as accusingly as the hamster's. Hardest to get used to, Pasteur thought, was the cavalier treatment the bodies were subject to. His God, Mr. Jorbie, was, he supposed, no different from any other undertaker—with him, he'd once visited the undertakers in Saginaw, the lone time in his life he'd been so far away from St. Max, and saw the same curious behavior—but Pasteur still felt the bodies should have been treated more respectfully than they were. They had, after all, once been alive, with families and hopes and dreams of their own. When he'd mentioned this to Mr. Jorbie, all he'd gotten was one of the usual scornful stares. Pasteur let the subject drop, something never to be raised again.

Four more times the automatic bell rang and the electric shock was administered; four more times its automatic nervous system made the hamster twitch, but without exhibiting any movement made of its own will.

At three thirty-seven Pasteur's half-closed eyes saw the animal slowly begin movement, first a forepaw, then a blink of the eyes, then a heavy, awkward movement of its whole body. Fascinated, Pasteur continued to stare. From the hamster finally came a high-pitched squeal as it rose on all fours. He raced upstairs to get Mr. Jorbie.

Racing into the lab, Jorbie almost knocked Pasteur down going through the door. Alongside the cage, Jorbie glanced at the hamster to see that it was once again fully mobile, then pressed a button that made the bell ring manually without need of the timer. A high-pitched squeal came from the hamster and it leapt high in the air, even though the electric shock it had been receiving while under the effects of the *bonaro* was not administered.

Jorbie was beside himself. "I knew it, I knew it!" he said gleefully, pummeling Pasteur on the arm and shoulder. "The old Pavlov thing, of course, but my part proved out too. God damn."

Pasteur stared at him blankly, pleased to have been included in Mr. Jorbie's excitement but totally baffled as to what it was all about. Jorbie took the opportunity to sound off, talking, as usual, more to himself than Pasteur. "See, that was what *bonaro* was originally used for. Centuries ago, by the Amazonian pygmy people. They used to tip their blow-darts with it; when they hit an animal, they depended on its unique paralyzing properties to keep their catch alive and fresh until they wanted to eat it. Like a spider. They do the same thing with bugs they trap in their webs."

Numbly, Pasteur nodded. He didn't dare ask questions: Mr. Jorbie might realize he hadn't understood a word of what he said. "See," Jorbie continued, "to all appearances that hamster appeared medically dead—flat brain wave, no pulse, no heartbeat, nothing. I don't think even the most sophisticated equipment would detect any sign of life. Only that hamster was alive, Pasteur, *alive*. Look at him now. *Bonaro*'s victims, if you get me, are in a state of suspended animation."

Pasteur nodded again, although he was biting his lower lip as he desperately tried to understand. Jorbie saw the biting and was well aware that he was far beyond Pasteur's limited capacity to understand, but kept right on talking. It excited him to hear his own words as he explained that in the state of suspended animation brought on by the *bonaro,* the hamster had been unable to move, make a sound, or react, yet was fully aware of everything. That it could see and hear and be conscious of all that went on around it. "It's a medical research breakthrough, Pasteur, a tremendous discovery." He glared at Pasteur, annoyed by his apparent lack of any reaction whatsoever.

Pasteur knew that some comment or compliment had to be produced. "That's swell, Mr. Jorbie. Congratulations." To Pasteur a great discovery in medicine meant only one thing, and he had to find out where this discovery fitted into his limited picture of science. "Will it make people feel better *fast,* Mr. Jorbie?"

"Oh, shit. Look, Pasteur. Remember what I said. That hamster, to anyone who didn't know better, would have been pronounced dead. It wasn't. What's more, the damned animal was completely aware of what was was happening to it. *That's* the breakthrough, you jerk."

"I was just trying, Mr. Jorbie, just trying to understand better. . . ."

A small smile slipped across Jorbie's face. Through the open door he could see the edge of a coffin, waiting for Simon Lavendou's laying-out in the morning. "You only have to understand one thing, Pasteur. Listen. What you can do to a hamster, you can do to a person. Got it?" The smile flickered across his face again. The pieces were beginning to come together.

Moving quickly, Jorbie telephoned a number he had written on a small slip of paper, dialing the number in Marquette city with infinite patience. "It's ready, mis-

ter, it's ready," the voice on the other end assured him.
"You will be pleased, mister." Jorbie mumbled something and told the man—his heavy accent always made
dealing with him difficult, and Jorbie was never entirely
sure of how much of what he said was entirely understood—he would drive up this morning. "Please," the
man said, "no later. Everyone else in town all closed up
today. Armistice Day, Veterans' Day. Whatever." The
man said, "Okay, mister," a few times more and hung
up.

If Jorbie left around eight, it would mean he
wouldn't get much sleep, but what the hell. He was too
excited for sleep anyway. Instead, he busied himself
with preparing Mr. Lavendou. Then he went upstairs to
chat with his father, Caleb Tenniel. He had to go away
for most of the day, but Mr. Lavendou was all set, Jorbie told the old man, settled uncomfortably in his bed
watching *Good Morning America* on the small color TV
set that stood just beyond his wheelchair.

"Pasteur will take care of the people and everything.
I wouldn't usually go on a laying-out day, but I don't
have much choice. Pasteur can do it, Dad. He'll make
you lunch, too."

Caleb fixed his son with a questioning eye. He didn't
like Pasteur; he loathed having him anywhere near him.
The food was one thing, he supposed, but letting Pasteur handle people from St. Max—Mr. Lavendou's relatives and friends—was something else. To avoid a
fight on the matter, Caleb Tenniel turned his eyes back
to the TV. Reproachfully, he watched Jorbie walk out
of the room. When his son stopped back in to wave
good-bye, Caleb pretended to be so deeply absorbed in
an early-morning soaper that he didn't notice him. How
else could a crippled father criticize the son who kept
him alive?

*   *   *

Standing outside the house, wiping off the windshield to get ready for his trip—it was a good two hundred miles or so in each direction—Jorbie was startled to see another car drive slowly into the driveway. Angie got out, waving cheerfully. She seemed all dressed up, somehow looking better than he'd ever seen her—had she done something different to her hair, or what?—and carrying a picnic basket over her arm.

"Hi, Jorbie. I see you're getting ready. Even this late in the year, the windshield certainly picks up a lot of bugs. I don't know where they come from, and by the time I get around to asking them, they're all squished."

Jorbie forced a small laugh, but his face remained a total blank. Inside herself Angie felt a sudden stabbing, a deep inner pain as if someone were probing her insides with an ice pick. Was it possible—no, it couldn't be—could he have forgotten about Veterans' Day? The picnic and everything? It was her own fault, damn it. She should have called and reminded him. Firmed up the date somehow. It was a woman's responsibility to check things like that out, wasn't it?

The whole thing came back to Jorbie in a rush. Friday. Veterans' Day. Shit. "I tried to call you at your house," he lied, "but you must have just left. God, I feel awful about this . . ." In a strange way, Jorbie did. It wasn't just that Angie was looking damned attractive—with whatever she'd done to herself—somehow it went deeper than that. He didn't want to blow it, but he was afraid he already had. "See," he added, "there's some undertaking stuff I've got to drive down and pick up in Saginaw—right now, today—or Tenniel's will be in real trouble. My fault. I should never have let us run so low. But Christ, I'm sorry. That's what I was calling about. To tell you we'll have to put the picnic off for a few days. I don't know how to tell you how sorry I am. God damn."

Awkwardly, Angie stood in front of him, trying to reassure him that it really didn't matter. Didn't matter? What a lie that was! Unconsciously she kept fingering her new wool skirt, which now seemed the symbol of a shattered dream. Jorbie's story wasn't overly convincing. Of course, she told herself, it *could* have happened that way. In the painful silence that had sprung up between them, Angie struggled to believe that Jorbie was telling the truth. He had to be. The pain inside her— the ice pick still probed—was searing, but she was finally able to believe what he was saying because he was saying what she *wanted* to believe.

"Look," said Jorbie suddenly, "I'll call you tomorrow. We can make plans. If not the picnic, something else."

Still apologizing, Jorbie glanced at his watch and said it was time he got going. He'd told the man who dealt in undertaking supplies he'd be in Saginaw by noon, and the man was staying open on Veterans' Day just to help him out. Angie allowed herself to believe him.

She kept on believing him even when she saw Jorbie's car reach the intersection and turn, not south toward Saginaw but up the highway toward the northwest.

Chapter Four

Man, when I blow one, I really do it good. Forgetting the picnic with Angie was about as stupid as you can get. Particularly since she's someone I want to get close to.

You know, I can't really explain it, but all of a sudden I got this feeling Angie is someone I've known well for years and years. Crazy, when you consider about the most I'd ever exchanged with her before that night of the dance was a casual nod or maybe a distant wave. Crazy? Almost spooky.

> *Jorbie Tenniel—to the rock,*
> *10:30 P.M., November 11th*

She was hiding. In her own home she was hiding like a thief. The one thing in the world Angie couldn't face after today's fiasco with the picnic was the thought of seeing anyone. Particularly her father. They'd had one of their terrible arguments this morning, just before she left to meet Jorbie. For the picnic that never materialized.

When he'd found out who she was meeting, her father lit into her again, yelling at her about "that ghoul grave robber of yours—even *you* should be able to do better than that"—the heavy stench of his vodka breath floating across the kitchen counter like a sweet-sick cloud of marsh gas.

Downstairs, Angie could hear him rummaging around, crashing into things, riding his morning wave of drunkenness like an expert surfer. Worst of all, in an odd sort

of way her father had been right. He'd told her she'd
have a lousy time with "that little bastard Tenniel,"
and she had—or worse, she'd had no time at all with
Jorbie. Leaning against her window, staring out at the
almost empty streets of St. Max, Angie wondered if
Jorbie had any idea of how terribly important the picnic
had been to her, or of how she had been looking forward to it, or, now, of how empty she felt that the
whole thing had crumbled to dust. For an instant she
imagined Jorbie and herself the way she had pictured
them about this time: racing along the road to Sault
Sainte Marie, chattering, laughing, once again talking
about everything and nothing. Damn. She believed what
he'd told her about Saginaw and the supplies. She believed him, she believed, she believed him. Angie said
the phrase over and over in her head as if repetition
could guarantee validity.

Briefly, Angie thought about calling Cathy Springer
and suggesting *they* have the picnic—the food was still
sitting in the hamper—and maybe go to a movie in
Traverse City or something, but almost as quickly as
she fielded the idea, she abandoned it. Cathy knew that
the picnic had orginally been scheduled with Jorbie,
and while she wouldn't come out and say, "I told you
so," her earlier warnings about Jorbie would stand between them like a great stone.

As she turned around Angie's eyes fell upon the
hamper, packed with everything she did particularly
well, and something reached inside and squeezed until
her face was contorted with pain. It was stupid, she told
herself, to let all that good food sit on her bed until it
spoiled; she'd put it in the fridge and she and her father
could eat it over the next couple of days. She waited
until she heard him stumble his way up the stairs into
his room—he usually took a nap around this time,
sleeping the morning's intake off so he could begin all

over again before lunch—and slipped noiselessly down to the kitchen.

Quietly opening the door of the refrigerator, Angie began carefully transferring her movable feast from the hamper to the shelves, slipping off the Saran Wrap and aluminum foil so the strange array of foods would not raise any suspicions in her father's mind. Then she would go into town and keep herself busy somehow— maybe at the library.

"Stood up?" sneered her father's sudden voice from behind her. Apparently he'd come down for a beer to space out the vodka and caught her in the act of moving food out of the hamper and into the refrigerator. Her attempt to hide had failed; the house was too small. "Stood up?" her father repeated. "Even by *that* bum?"

Angie turned and glared at him. Damn it, she wouldn't let him have the satisfaction. She turned back and pretended she was taking the food *out* of the fridge and putting it into the hamper. She wondered if she shouldn't say something to bolster her deception, but decided against it. Even bombed, her father had a shrewd ability to see through her. She turned and glared at him again, slamming the lid on the hamper shut with finality. Wordlessly she walked out of the house and climbed into her car.

As she drove off she could see him standing in one of the windows, swaying slightly, studying her with a quizzical expression. Wondering whether to believe her, she supposed. Just as she had wondered this morning when she saw Jorbie's car turn toward the northwest instead of south toward Saginaw.

"Somewhere between a prodigy and a genius," they had said about Jorbie at Marquette. They were words that had burned themselves into Jorbie's brain; his brilliance in research medicine, even as a pre-med student, had been acknowledged by almost all of the faculty at Marquette. His work on isolation modes that had ended the pulmonary anthrax crisis had only confirmed what everyone already agreed with. At night, lying in his bed, listening to the strange sounds of the university—sounds so different from the mournful roar of the waves in St. Max boiling against the rocks below the mortuary—the words "prodigy" and "genius" had kept returning to him. He could remember the feeling of warmth that would settle over him, a delicious sensation that he was, at last, free.

Because of his acknowledged brilliance in research, Jorbie had been given free run of all of Marquette's labs. And when the accident had forced him back to St. Max, he hadn't surrendered the keys. No one had asked him for them; Jorbie didn't volunteer them. Because it was Veterans' Day (the damned picnic, the crazy, damned forgotten picnic), the med school was pretty well shut down. Getting into the lab with the right key was easy; no one saw him go in, no one would see him leave. With a twinge brought on by recollections of an earlier, better day, Jorbie looked around the lab where he had spent so much time. This was the lab—A33-Res—where he had been working on new concepts in anesthesia when he had to quit school. It was also the lab where he had first developed his thesis about the way *bonaro* worked. His eyes moved slowly around the room and settled on the wall safe where the more exotic drugs were kept. Using another key, he opened this and took out a full flask of *bonaro*—no one, he noticed, was following up on his experiments; this was the same half-liter flask that had been flown in from South America the week before he left—and poured the colorless fluid into an empty flask he found on a lab counter. The flask labeled *"Bonaro"* was filled with distilled water and returned to the safe; his own, he labeled "distilled water" and slipped into his attaché case. Carefully he replaced the other flask in the safe and softly closed the door. No one would know it had been touched.

As he started out of the lab something else caught his eye. Farther along the same wall, set firmly into the plaster, was the door to another safe. This was the refrigerated safe, one where biological material requiring refrigeration was stored. Jorbie knew for instance, that the cultures of several different almost plague-like diseases on which the lab was working were kept inside. More out of curiosity at first than anything else, Jorbie used his key to unlock this special safe, wondering if the lab would still have retained the strain of pulmonary anthrax he had used in his breakthrough two years ago, or whether it would have been destroyed.

It was still there, with his name around the neck of the flasks. Even more carefully than he had handled the *bonaro,* Jorbie withdrew a small flask of the deadly anthrax culture, placed it in a plastic bag surrounded by dry ice inside another plastic bag, and gingerly added this to the contents of his attaché case. He had no particular use for it in mind, but it could be an effective weapon if the occasion arose.

One last time Jorbie looked around the lab. It was like an old friend to him, comfortable, undemanding, smiling warmly upon him, as it always had. Jorbie felt a catch at his heart, realizing this would probably be the last time he would ever see it; the place had been good to him.

Straightening his shoulders, he walked firmly from the room.

Although the wind blowing across the hill above the Straits of Mackinac was cold, she had found a natural sun-trap—one sheltered from the biting wind. It was behind some evergreens, pointing in a direction that allowed her to enjoy both the sun and the view of the lake without becoming overly cold.

Angie had spent most of the day here. Alone. In front of her was the checkerboard tablecloth she had brought along for her picnic with Jorbie; to one side was the hamper with the food she had fixed. She still wore her new sweater and cardigan combination, unwilling to change her clothes to suit the change of occasion. The presence of Jorbie was all around her. It was as if she were holding a picnic for the ghosts of some happier time. The blame for the failure, she was fully convinced, was her own. He *had* gone to Saginaw for supplies, she was equally convinced, just as he said. If his turn at the intersection seemed to be in the wrong direction, it was because she hadn't entirely understood what he'd said. She reproached herself for her lack of faith in Jorbie.

Jorbie was a good man, a fine man, a put-upon man, suffering the results of an accident he had nothing to do with. He wasn't even near St. Max when it happened, yet it had changed his whole life. For a moment Angie wondered unhappily if she would ever have gotten to know Jorbie if the accident to his father *hadn't* happened; immediately a wave of guilt swept across her. Speculating on what had crippled one man and completely shattered the career of another was a narrow, selfish way of looking at things. Jorbie deserved better than that.

This brought her to the one area about Jorbie that still mystified Angie. In St. Max she had never heard any of the derisive comments that he described about either himself or his family. In fact, she had rarely heard anything but complimentary things.

There were exceptions to this, of course. A handful of people in St. Max *did* shun Jorbie because of his undertaking business. But they were small in number—the superstitious, the unbalanced, the irrationally prejudiced. Her own father was something else. For reasons Angie did not understand—and never would—her father had always loathed the entire Tenniel family.

And it was this same father who had made her the outcast that Jorbie seemed to feel *he* was. She would have to get Jorbie over his senseless feeling of rejection; her own new clothes and growing confidence were a start on overcoming her own.

But it would all take time, Angie knew, time and a great deal of understanding. A lot of Jorbie's trying to understand what the town really felt about him, a lot of her own trying to understand herself.

Her father . . . her father . . . Almost angrily, Angie began eating the first of the picnic sandwiches.

They were already stale.

The business section of the town of Marquette has little to recommend it. It looks like any typical college town, a little larger than some, a little more threadbare than others. On its southeast side, toward Harvey, Marquette becomes quite seedy, a collection of small shops having visible difficulty surviving, rundown restaurants, the meager homes of unskilled laborers, and the impoverished. Carefully, Jorbie guided his car through the narrow, uneven streets until he came to an alleyway. He stopped and parked, two wheels of his car half on the sidewalk, outside a dingy storefront.

As he went inside a bell on a spring over the door tinkled noisily. Some beaded curtains rattled, then parted to admit Sezi, the man Jorbie had called from St. Max.

Sezi was an Arab or Armenian or something—Jorbie suspected Armenian. The sight of the man still disturbed Jorbie, even on this, his second exposure. Sezi's eyes were constantly in motion and appeared slightly crossed, so that they seemed able to look in more than one direction at once. Only on the rare occasions that he wore his jeweler's loop was Jorbie actually sure of which way Sezi's eyes were aimed.

"Ah, Mr. Smith," said Sezi in his curious nasal voice that seemed, like an adolescent boy's, about to crack each time he moved from one word to the next. He sighed slightly, a faint, mocking smile crossing his face. "Such an unusual name, 'Smith'; yet I have many customers with that name." Sezi cocked his head knowingly at Jorbie. "Strange, is it not?"

Jorbie nodded, beginning to find the man absolutely unbearable.

"It must have something to do with my line of work," Sezi added, the smile still pasted on his face, like a bad makeup job on a corpse.

Jorbie finally returned the smile; it was obviously part of the ritual of dealing with a man whose principle occupation was the buying and resetting of stolen jewelry. Jorbie tried to hide his impatience but doubted if he got away with it. "You said it was ready," Jorbie prompted him.

"Of course it is ready. Sezi give promise, Sezi keep promise." Carefully, Sezi dusted the counter with a cloth in itself several times dustier than the countertop. Reaching down, he withdrew a small box from a shelf below, and opened it to reveal an overly ornate ring— the band was simple enough, but there was some sort of heavy crest on its top that immediately reminded Jorbie of the prizes you get in cereal boxes as a child. Because of this, to him the ring immediately became his "Captain Marvel" ring.

"Best surgical steel," Sezi announced proudly, holding the ring aloft. He tapped the heavy, solid body of the ring. "In here is the reservoir for your—ah—fluid. On a touch, Mr. Smith, watch what happens." He pressed a small button on the ring's side, and a small, infinitely thin needle sprang upward and fixed itself in position, protruding from the heavy, ornate crest of the ring. "As you requested, hollow; I got it from a surgical supply house. When you are—ah—through, you push down here, and the needle retracts back into the ring."

Jorbie picked the ring up and tried it several times, refusing Sezi's offer to use his jeweler's loop. It was, unquestionably, beautifully crafted, a new type of hypodermic syringe for which Jorbie had great plans. He could give someone an injection without their realizing they had even had one; they might feel a slight stinging sensation, but little more.

"Sezi has done well, no?"

"Very well indeed," agreed Jorbie.

"The price we agreed on—that is, I did not expect the surgical steel to be so expensive, you see."

"But you did agree, Mr. Sezi that—"

"Yes, you have old Sezi at a disadvantage there. However, an extra hundred would cover it adequately."

"Seventy-five," Jorbie answered automatically.

Sezi sighed and gave in. "You are a hard man, Mr. Smith," he noted, and then did some quick figuring on a pad. "That will be exactly five hundred and seventy-five, then." For the first time Sezi laughed. "I do not believe we need worry about a sales tax."

Sezi's laugh had blown a wave of foul-smelling breath in Jorbie's face, one that reeked of rotten lamb fat and was at once sweet and bitter. He counted out the bills carefully.

Sezi was unable to keep his pride in his work under control. "It is, if I may say, one of my better efforts. Do not you agree?"

Impatiently, Jorbie began counting out the money—in small bills as Sezi had requested—all over again.

"I am, of course, filled with curiosity about it, but I know better than to ask," Sezi said, the ceaseless smile pasted back on his face. "I cannot help wondering, though . . ."

"It is, as I told you, Mr. Sezi, magnificent workmanship. I cannot thank you enough."

When Jorbie handed his wad of bills across the counter, his hand appeared to slip and the bills were scattered across the floor behind it.

Both he and Sezi swore, and Jorbie came behind the counter to help the old man retrieve his money. As the old man bent over, trying to fish some stray money out from along the edge of the counter, Jorbie slipped behind him and in one quick movement withdrew a scalpel from his pocket and neatly slit Sezi's carotid artery.

Blood spurted from Sezi's neck as he crumpled to the floor, followed a moment later by a rush of blood from his mouth. His widened, startled eyes stared at Jorbie in disbelief; for once, Jorbie could see where they were looking—directly at him. A faint, bubbling sound came from the man, and then his breathing stopped. Sezi was dead.

Jorbie picked up all of the money except for a few bills, which he left lying on the bloody floor to suggest an attempted robbery, a struggle, and, finally, murder. This was not the kind of death or a manner of killing Jorbie felt comfortable with, but he could not allow Sezi the opportunity to boast around town of his skill at making exotic syringes. Jorbie shuddered. When they had been haggling over the price, Sezi had called him a "hard man." Jorbie only hoped he was hard enough to follow through with what the plan slowly forming in his mind called for.

Chapter Five

When I was about ten, somebody—I don't remember who—gave me a little kitten. I called him Kevin and really fell in love with him, I guess. At first, Kevin was all cuddly and warm and loving, but as he grew older Kevin began getting sort of standoffish and cold. Damn, but that hurt; I thought I must have done something wrong and that was why Kevin had stopped loving me.

It hurt so much that one day I stuffed Kevin into a sack and held it down beside my private rock until the tide came in. From inside the sack I could hear Kevin mewing and crying and then screeching in panic as the water got to him. It made me unhappy for weeks, what I'd done, and still wondering why Kevin had stopped loving me.

Of course, I know now that that's what happens to any kitten: it starts off warm and friendly, and then becomes distant and mysterious as it turns into a cat.

But I still wonder if the same thing doesn't happen with people who get to know me really well. They love me at first, but then when they know what I'm really like, they turn distant and cold. Will that happen with Angie, too? Will she go cold on me?

Hell, it would be hard to stuff her into a sack.

Jorbie Tenniel—to the rock,
8:00 A.M., November 13th

The Monday after the abandoned picnic Angie was still hurting. Thoughts kept moving in on her, dark clouds

that left her wrestling with an agony of self-reproach.
Maybe the new hair and the new clothes didn't make as
much difference as she thought; maybe—my God, it
was possible—Jorbie hadn't even noticed them. She began blaming herself for being foolish enough to think
mere clothes would make any real difference in how
she affected Jorbie. Maybe not calling to check with
him about the picnic the night before—crazy thought—
had hurt *Jorbie's* feelings and made him think *she*
didn't want to go. The idea was completely upside
down, of course, but she could already see that some of
Jorbie's reactions were not always what you expected.
Maybe it was something she'd said at the dance.
Maybe . . .

The sound of the children laughing and running in
St. Etienne's halls brought Angie back to reality. She
struggled to keep up a brave front, doing her best to
appear her usual cheerful best.

Her performance, much as Angie fought to bring it
off convincingly, didn't fool Cathy Springer for a moment. One look, and she grabbed Angie by the arm as
she walked down the hall. "The picnic was a bust?"
Cathy asked anxiously.

For a moment Angie stared at her. She suddenly
found herself unable to speak. The most she could do
was shake her head, turning it away from Cathy.
"There *wasn't* any picnic?" Cathy pressed, suddenly
understanding. Angie swallowed hard, fighting a losing
battle to keep herself under control. But now, besides
being unable to speak, she found herself incapable of
even shaking her head. Watching Angie's eyes grow
blurred behind a welling of tears, Cathy Springer abruptly pushed her into the faculty ladies' room, shoved
her into one of the chairs, and handed her some Klee-
nex she had ripped out of its box.

Angie fell apart. She hadn't allowed herself even to
waver since the aborted picnic, fighting herself, hanging

onto herself, forcing herself to play the stoic. It was like trying to fight the force of gravity, hanging onto a ledge by your fingernails. The accumulated misery of the last several days came bursting out of her all at once, the unhappiness, the self-reproach, the agony of having soared so high and then fallen so far.

"Jor-bie," she sobbed. "At the very last minute. Something about supplies." For a moment she was once again unable to speak. "Only he didn't turn his car to go south, he headed north." Cathy, holding on to Angie as you might an injured, bewildered child, didn't even question what Angie meant by these strange statements but just kept holding on to her, stroking her hair and trying to comfort her.

"Oh, Cathy. It's all my fault. I didn't check with him like I should have and I wonder if his feelings didn't get hurt and he thought I didn't want to go. It's all my fault. I think I probably said something wrong and—"

Cathy, a down-to-earth woman, decided it was time to bring Angie back to reality. "Balls," she said. "Balls it was your fault. And it's a man's role to check with the girl, not the other way around. And if you'd said something wrong, he wouldn't have waited until the last moment to pull out on you. Grow up, Angie. It wasn't anything you did. What happened, is, is, well, just Jorbie, one hundred percent pure Jorbie Tenniel."

Angie looked at her, blinking. She knew the struggle Cathy must be having not to mention she'd tried to convince her someone like Jorbie could only end up hurting her. Cathy'd said it all, and gotten nowhere.

"These kind of things happen when you're deeply involved with someone—happen all the time," continued Cathy. "Two bits you'll hear from him in a couple of days and he'll be all apologies and explanations. Men are like that." As she spoke Cathy found she was hating herself for her own hypocrisy. Men might be like that, but Jorbie Tenniel wasn't like other men. A grim look

settled across her face, conflicting with the brave, encouraging things she was saying to Angie. The best
thing that could have happened, she knew, would be if
Jorbie had hurt Angie so deeply she'd finally see the
truth about what a bastard he actually was.

And if she was a real friend of Angie's, Cathy told
herself, that was precisely what she'd say to Angie.
Only she couldn't. Angie was too vulnerable, too fragile, too inexperienced, and Cathy let the lie grow in
front of her, even helping it along with reassuring
bromides.

A small smile finally showed through the twisted
rubber mask of Angie's face. Cathy was being, as always, wonderful—comforting, reassuring, and, most
important of all, encouraging. "Maybe you're right,
Cathy," Angie said suddenly. "It was some sort of a
mistake, that's what it was. A mistake. . . ."

Cathy stayed silent. She had taken care of Angie's
unhappiness for the moment, but how long could this
hollow kind of deception last with someone like Jorbie
in the picture? He would hurt Angie, again and again,
and again. She remained mute because while letting
Angie deceive herself was necessary for the moment,
she was damned if she'd top her lie with further words.

For Angie, the session with Cathy had been a cathar-
tic. On one hand, Cathy's reassurance had buoyed her
enormously, yet Angie was not stupid: some of Cathy's
unspoken reservations about Jorbie stayed with her. By
afternoon-coffee time Angie was back completely in
control of herself again, something that a few short
hours ago would have seemed impossible.

In the cafeteria she looked around and could find no
one to sit with. Just as well. She didn't feel much like
talking to anyone—even Cathy—just now. Outside the
long glass window she could see the wind sending flecks
of white racing across the Straits, a dark blue dotted
with a starry meshwork of silver. She had to be practi-

cal, she repeated to herself; it was entirely possible Jorbie *wouldn't* call her. That was something she just had to face.

But as she looked toward the door all of the old dreams and hopes and plummeting fears suddenly came riding back, all mixed up with the disappointments and painful fears he'd inflicted on her before.

There, silhouetted in the doorframe, stood Jorbie Tenniel. Carefully he looked around the cafeteria, searching until his eyes found her, and then strode briskly over to her table. In his hand he held a box of some sort. He smiled his shyest little-boy smile at her and asked if he could sit down. Angie almost choked on her sandwich and nodded.

"Jesus, Angie. I really feel like a jerk about Friday and the picnic. See, I let us run almost out of formaldehyde, something an undertaker just can't have happen. Damn, it was stupid of me. What I thought was a full fifty-gallon drum turned out to be an empty fifty-gallon drum. I didn't have any choice; I had to go to Saginaw or we'd be out of business. But hell, that's no excuse. I was just plain dumb. Honest, I'll try to make it up to you somehow." Shyly, he offered the box to her. "For beginners, there's this. . . ."

He smiled again as she took the box. "It's kind of a joke," he added quickly, warning her.

As she began struggling with the wrapping, Jorbie's eyes darted around the room, absorbing everything. "Is this the only time of day—besides luncheon, I mean—this place is used? The whole school's changed so since I was here."

Angie stopped struggling with the box's string for a moment. "No, after school, any minute now, it becomes sort of a snack bar and soda fountain. A lot of the children, you see, can't afford the prices in town, so we run this for them at cost. It keeps them out of trouble."

This was about what Jorbie thought; the means to the end were becoming easier by the moment. He looked at Angie, still pulling hard on the string, too tightly knotted perhaps, and getting nowhere. "Here," he said. "Never underestimate the value of a Boy Scout knife." Skillfully he severed the tough string around the box with one lightning movement of his hand. He hoped Angie hadn't had a chance to study his "Boy Scout" knife too carefully; it was the scalpel with which he'd dispatched Sezi yesterday, still imprudently carried in his jacket pocket.

The box was finally open. Inside was a small spray of spring flowers. "They're sort of used," Jorbie said with a sly smile, "but it seemed a shame to let them go to waste."

The macabre twist to the gift broke Angie up completely, as he had suspected it would. Her reaction, she knew, was out of proportion, but it was the escape valve for the relief she felt, a realization that all of her worst fears were foolish. The old closeness between them, a private communication beamed on their secret wavelength, was suddenly alive and soaring.

As the first of the children using the cafeteria as a soda fountain began filtering in, Angie kept her eyes glued to Jorbie.

"Say," Jorbie suggested suddenly. "Thursday. Why don't we have an early dinner and maybe drive down to Traverse City for the movie?" Jorbie studied Angie's face for some reaction; she sat as if stunned. She was not used to a world in which things reversed themselves so precipitously. Offhandedly, Jorbie pressed his suggestion. "You don't even have to go home first. We can meet right here. I'll sit and have a Coke or something while you're getting ready. How about it?"

"Well . . . I suppose . . . I don't know . . . you could wait in the faculty lounge, if you'd like that better. . . ."

"No, this is fine. It brings back my childhood."

Thinking, Angie found his choice curious but convenient. With him down here she wouldn't have to let the other faculty members—notoriously gossipy—in on her secret. And it would give her time to change her clothes completely, if she should decide to do that. She didn't know yet. "That would be great, Jorbie," Angie said, smiling happily. "I don't know what the movie is, but there's always something in Alpena if the one at Traverse is a dog."

"The movie doesn't really matter anyway," Jorbie noted, staring her straight in the eye and making her heart pound. She hadn't noticed how carefully Jorbie had studied the increasing ebb and flow of children around the long bar of the soda fountain, pushing, shoving, laughing, fighting for their sodas and milkshakes and candy.

She hadn't noticed because she was too excited and relieved to have Jorbie back with her, being charming, as with the invitation, being funny, as with the flowers, and making her feel wanted, as no one she could remember ever had.

On their way out Angie spotted Cathy Springer sitting along one wall and waved to her happily, glad to have Cathy see that everything was all right with Jorbie again. Without her glasses—she wore them as little as possible when Jorbie was around—it appeared to Angie as if Cathy had waved back just as enthusiastically.

If her eyes had been better, Angie would have seen that Cathy's thin smile had an ominous prescience to it, as if the smile could look into Mackinac County's future and see the awful things that lay in store for both St. Max and Angie Psalter.

Chapter Six

It's funny, but the last few days my mind can't seem to keep away from that very simple magnetism experiment the teacher shows the kids in his science class every year.

You know the one: He holds up two identical magnets and shows how, in one position, the two magnets attract and can make a pile of iron filings line up in neat rows between their poles.

Then he flips over one of the magnets—nothing else is changed—and you see how the magnets are repelling each other, and how the iron filings are shooting out to either side to get out of the way of the force lines.

In a way, my whole life's been like that experiment. Things that attract one minute, repel the next. It goes for the people of St. Max; Christ, it even goes for Angie.

I suppose, if I really thought it through, I'd discover that most of all, it goes for myself.

> *Jorbie Tenniel—to the rock,*
> *11:15 P.M., November 14th*

Because it was a Thursday, St. Etienne was unusually filled for late afternoon. The reason was simple. Thursday afternoons were when almost all of the school's extracurricular meetings were held. The Dramatics Club was rehearsing something in one room; in another, the Debating Society was gearing itself up to throw words at some other school. The orchestra was trying to hit the right notes in the auditorium, but Mr. Otella, the music teacher, knew it was a losing battle. Science

Club, Chess, Dungeons and Dragons, backgammon, woodworking, and photography clubs were all in session. The halls of St. Etienne fairly vibrated with activity.

Going down the hall, carrying a small bag with her dress-up clothes inside, Angie sneaked a peak through the glass doors of the cafeteria–soda fountain. She could see Jorbie sitting at a table in the back, his eyes traveling aimlessly around the room. From his expression Angie decided he was in one of his dark moods. Well, she would change that.

In the women's faculty lounge Angie quickly changed into some of her new clothes, wondering if he'd notice them, and, if he did, whether he'd comment on them. Carefully she combed out her hair; she'd gotten up at the crack of dawn to get it done at the beauty shop. The owner had objected violently at opening so early but had given in to Angie's pleadings.

Studying herself in the mirror of the lounge, she had to admit the effect was pretty damned impressive. Jorbie *had* to like it. Angie's own certainty surprised her. It dawned on her that her realization that Jorbie liked her, that he found her attractive, that he was pursuing her, had made her a different person—a sudden, new self-confidence infusing everything she thought and did.

Jorbie's greeting when she swept into the cafeteria and sat down at his table was less confidence-inspiring. He half stood up, nodded to her, attempted a smile, and sat down again. Rather than a mood, Angie realized, his was a depression. He sat in his chair, his eyes continually darting around the room, studying the shoving and pushing mass of children at the soda fountain's bar, and saying very little.

Angie tried. "Cat got your tongue?" she asked lightly.

"I had a cat once," Jorbie announced in a deep, soft voice. "It drowned."

Angie smiled at him, shaking her head sadly. "The awful little tragedies that happen to us when we're kids. They still hurt years later. It doesn't seem fair, somehow. Usually they weren't any of our doing."

"This was. I drowned it."

Thrown, Angie let her mouth slack open in surprise for a second. It was an odd remark about an even odder event. She wanted to go further into it, to ask Jorbie to explain what he meant, but his face had taken on an even moodier and more depressed aspect than before, and she let it drop. Jorbie must have sensed her reaction and took it up.

"I'm sorry to be on such a downer. See, out in the hall earlier," Jorbie lied, "I ran into Blaine Evers. He's a teacher in Charlevoix I used to know, over visiting someone or other. Evers also took some courses at Marquette, so I knew him there, too." Jorbie hit the tabletop; it was made of Formica and his hand produced a loud slapping noise that made Angie jump. "But damn it, I guess he knows what I'm back in St. Max doing now; the bastard just about ignored me." The lie was a pastiche of half-truths; the meeting had been a week ago, the visiting teacher had been Professor deLac from Marquette. "It's the same old damned prejudices again," added Jorbie, looking miserable, his eyes still carefully studying the crush at the soda fountain.

"Jorbie," Angie said softly. "You know, I know you imagine an awful lot of things people feel about you. Like the way you think everybody in St. Max hates you. Crazy. Listen, I've never heard a single person say one thing about you. Except they wished you didn't keep to yourself so much . . . that's the worst I ever heard. Honest."

"Manners. Hypocritical politeness. You just don't know."

Angie found herself suddenly angry. "Don't know!
Look, Jorbie Tenniel, I've been St. Max's number-one
outcast for as long as I can remember. I know why; for
a long time I didn't, but old Dr. L'Eveque finally broke
down and told me. I can understand the reason now,
but it was a long time ago, and I surely wasn't responsible for what happened. . . ."

The pictures raced across Angie's mind again. After
L'Eveque had told her, a lot of things had come back.
Her father, as usual, drunk. Her eighth birthday party.
Her father was trying, she supposed; with the help of
old lady Speirs he'd at least made the effort to give An-
gie something that approached a normal birthday.

Angie could remember him promising her when he
woke her up that birthday morning, "And as a special
little added present, Angie, I promise I won't get—well,
you know—what you call 'funny.' Not for a whole year,
baby. Not a drop. I mean it; it's an honest-to-God
grown-up promise." And Angie could remember hugging him and crying in his arms because she thought
maybe he really did mean it this time. He wouldn't
drink for a whole year. She was the luckiest little girl in
the world.

But the promise had only lasted—unbelievably—
until early that afternoon. Angie struggling to believe
what she knew was happening *wasn't* happening,
stretching every fiber to convince herself that it was her
imagination, that she was wrong, that she *had* to be
mistaken. His promise was so important to her she tried
to close her eyes to its utter meaninglessness, tried to
pretend she hadn't really known all along the promise
would not be kept. Neither the promise nor the breaking of it were entirely new to her, only the intensity and
timing.

Her father trying to hide it from her. Not drinking
openly, as he usually did. But even at eight, Angie

knew the signs too well. The slur in his speech. Forgetting what he'd just said. The endless repetition of the same words. Being too outgoing with the little girls who were her guests, pretending an interest in them Angie knew he didn't really have.

And the sudden awareness that he *did* have an interest in at least one of them that she could neither understand nor grasp. From beyond the barbecue, where all her friends had grouped themselves, across the grass to the small shed to where the tools were kept, came a sudden screaming. It was a terrified scream, one simultaneously crying for help and voicing pain. Angie had looked around. Her father was not with the group any longer. She had torn across the lawn and into the shed. Fi LeBoque was on the ground, held there by her father, who—what was he doing, what was he doing?—who was trying to tear Fi's clothes off her. She could see Fi's panties already yanked off and lying in a small puddle of white cotton on the dirt floor of the shed. Her father's fly was open and she could see this strange pale white thing sticking straight out from his body, quivering, an ugly purple head swelling at its tip.

Fi's screams grew louder; Angie could remember running across the shed and beginning to pound his face and head as hard as she could with her hands, screaming at him in a senseless fury of words. Partly because of what he was doing to Fi, partly because he had broken his solemn promise, made just that morning, to her. She wasn't the luckiest little girl in the world at all. She was pursued by devils, and now a brand-new demon had entered the picture and was breathing his hot, foul breath of misery into her life, too.

As she told all of this to Jorbie—strange, she had never talked of this to anyone else before, although only strangers to St. Max hadn't at least heard the story—the emotions of that day seemed to come back right along with the telling. Dr. L'Eveque had said that, at the time, there was talk of putting her father away, but that the LeBoques—Fi's mother in particular— didn't want to expose their daughter to more trauma and had refused to press charges.

As she unwound this terrible day in her life for Jorbie, she suddenly wondered if not pressing charges had been the right thing to do. The mayor of St. Max and the tiny town council had talked among themselves about what to do with her, she told Jorbie, but couldn't come up with a truly satisfactory answer. There was no one in St. Max who was related to her, so she would have to be put in a county or state home. No one liked that idea. And if Mr. Psalter had objected, the whole thing would have been forced into the circuit court in Saginaw. The town's elders finally made the easiest of the several decisions open to them: granted, living with a drunken father who occasionally molested little girls was a terrible thing to inflict on a child, but then, in all these years, he had apparently never tried anything funny with Angie. Perhaps it was a one-time performance, something brought on by alcohol. She had no relatives in St. Max to send her to, and orphanages were well known for their own corrupting influence. Very well. They would leave the poor, wretched child where she was.

The mothers of St. Max may well have accepted the council's decision intellectually, Angie told Jorbie, but never emotionally. To protect their own daughters, they gave them strict orders to stay away from her home. In fact, they told their children it would be just as well if they stayed away from Angie completely. They were sorry for her, but God knows what the poor child had seen and experienced.

Angie became St. Max's outcast, their personal pa-

riah, at the age of eight. And long after most of the town
had forgotten what the reason behind their spurning of
her was, the habit stayed on. Angie, as harmless a person as ever drew a breath, remained St. Max's outcast,
looked at strangely, sometimes almost feared, with few
people any longer knowing what the reason was or what
had happened, or even when it had happened.

"Now that, Jorbie," Angie said, forcing a small laugh
about a subject she found in no way amusing, "is preju-
dice. *That's* a town not liking you. For something I had
nothing to do with, something that happened so long
ago I didn't even know what it was or that there was a
word for it."

Slowly, Jorbie turned his head toward her. His eyes
had a vacant, faraway look that made Angie wonder if
he'd heard a word of what she'd told him. The head
turned back and Jorbie's eyes went back to where they
had been, riveted emptily on the soda fountain. That
teacher from Charlevoix, Angie told herself, still bothering him, still sending him into this dark depression.

Something at the soda fountain suddenly seemed to
bring Jorbie to life. Glancing at his watch, he said he
thought it was probably about time they got set to leave
for dinner; he wanted to take her to a place he knew in
Alpena, and it would take awhile to get there. "I'm
starving," he added, bending over as if in pain. Happy
to have him back in this world, Angie walked quickly
to the ladies' room, somewhat surprised when he announced he would stay where he was until she got back.

When she came back down the hall, she was even
more surprised to find him standing in the hall outside
the cafeteria—soda fountain. Where he had been depressed before, he was now all life. He was animated,
talkative, excited, smiling. He'd even bought her a Baby
Ruth at the candy counter, something, he pointed out,
he hadn't had since a child. "I recognized them at the
soda fountain even from our table," he'd explained.

Angie, remembering her own fear about acne, had never had one and didn't plan to begin now. But she welcomed the candy bar as if in lieu of diamonds, happy to have him so alive and himself again. Together they walked toward his car and climbed in for the drive to Alpena.

Getting himself a Baby Ruth had been the least of Jorbie Tenniel's considerations. *He* was there; Jorbie could see him now. The boy had walked in and stepped up to the candy counter in just the last few moments. Jorbie studied the boy, standing almost directly in front of him. Flan Tierney, Hank Tierney's little boy. It was going to work. Beautifully. Above the din in the room Jorbie could hear Flan yelling for a malt at the top of his lungs, half leaning across the soda fountain to make sure he was noticed.

He was noticed, all right. Quickly, Jorbie got to his feet and walked over to the fountain. To get the waitress's attention, Jorbie had to lean hard against Flan, holding his money in one hand and waving it gently. He asked for two Baby Ruths, and the waitress, a little annoyed that a grown-up should be acting as impatient as the children, had fished below the counter and found them.

Casually, as if still trying to get something from the waitress, Jorbie pressed one side of the Captain Marvel ring against Flan's stretched-out left buttock. There was an almost inaudible little *ping* as the spring inside the Captain Marvel ring flicked the surgical steel needle into Flan's soft bottom and then retracted instantly.

The eight-year-old showed no reaction, although he did fan the air behind him, as if annoyed by a persistent insect.

Calmly, Jorbie picked up the two candy bars and walked, with no apparent haste, out into the hall to wait for Angie's return. His face was a mask. He felt ex-

cited, yet, at the same time, a little scared and awed by
what he was setting in motion.

The onslaught against certain persons of St. Max,
people selected for reasons Jorbie himself could not understand, had begun.

Chapter Seven

When I was ten or eleven, someone made me a dare about Sister Honorée. Funny, I've never been able to resist that kind of challenge. And the other kids in my class at St. Etienne's knew it. They used to push me into some pretty dreadful situations, just by daring me to do something, frequently something really dangerous or crazy.

Anyway, this time they'd bet me I couldn't stop Sister Honorée's pacing back and forth, up and down the room, while she talked to us. She was due in our classroom to look at our artwork and model-building, and we all knew she'd be pacing like crazy. She always did. Well, I stopped her, all right.

While another kid kept her in one place talking about a shelf full of pottery work he'd done, I pretended to be hammering the last touches into my model on the floor. As she talked on and on about the kid's pottery, I nailed her long black habit to the floor with the hammer I was using on the model, then ambled back to my seat.

Christ, when she tried to move and start her pacing, poor old Sister Honorée found she couldn't go anywhere. She was nailed as tight to the floor as our desks. It was a little scary, but I loved every minute of it.

Scary, I said. A lot of things scare me. Some that are obvious, some not so easy to get a handle on. My feelings for Angie scare me, for instance. Why should that be? It's a perfectly normal set of emotions.

Even scarier—and harder to explain—is the fear that I'll wake up some morning and the Voice will be *telling me it's Angie's turn. Nobody knows it yet, but it's one hell of a way to go.*

> *Jorbie Tenniel—to the rock,*
> *10:30 A.M., November 18th*

The Mackinac Bar and Grill was not much, really, but it was the best the area had to offer. Actually, their steak and broiled chicken weren't too bad, but everything else was a disaster. For a while they'd tried serving lobster, but since it had to be shipped from the East Coast, very few of the lobsters reached the Michigan peninsula alive. Lobster was abandoned.

Jorbie's mood had swung completely around. When Angie had first met him today, in the cafeteria–soda fountain, he'd been in one of the darkest moods Angie had ever seen him in. He'd improved quite a bit by the time he met Angie in the hall with his damned Baby Ruth bars (awful things, shuddered Angie to herself, remembering an adolescence spent anxiously peering into mirrors, waiting for the first dreaded zit to appear).

Now, sitting in the unpretentious glare of the Mackinac Bar and Grill—not much more than a high-priced roadhouse, Angie knew, but the best you could come by around here—Jorbie's mood had turned itself completely inside out. All traces of the dark, brooding introspection had been replaced by a soaring spirit that came very close to a manic state. Angie was baffled. Jorbie seemed to make himself an impossibly difficult man to understand—or predict.

But the change in Jorbie was tonic to Angie; she felt infinitely better and more relaxed. With her habit of always blaming herself for anything that went wrong— a trait that Angie frequently recognized as not only demeaning but self-flagellatory—she had spent the first part of their evening together struggling to avoid anything that might upset Jorbie and send him careening back into his mood. No longer. Jorbie was riding high again, and Angie could tell herself it had been his chance encounter in the hall with the teacher from Charlevoix, not anything she'd said, that had set him off. A weight was suddenly lifted from her shoulders.

When she had been telling Jorbie about her father and the incident that made her a permanent pariah in St. Max, she had suspected Jorbie heard little of what she said. To her surprise, he appeared to have absorbed every word.

"One thing I don't understand about your father," Jorbie said suddenly. "Not just the drinking thing, although I've got to say it's something I would think is pretty easy to cure. I mean, it's not like some disease the victim can't do anything about. I'm sure it's not as easy as it sounds, but all a drunk has to do is stop drinking, and he stops being a drunk. And I can't believe your father—or anyone else, for that matter— *enjoys* being what he is."

Angie studied the tabletop sadly. "No one enjoys it less. Alcoholics hate being alcoholics; they loathe themselves for it. But the stopping that sounds so easy is still where most of them fall down. They seem to play a little game, trying to beat the system, I suppose. They'll only drink beer. They'll only drink wine. They'll only drink when there's something special going on. But when they try this, eventually the system beats *them*. It's like a casino where the house always knows the odds will win for it in the end. They discover, yes, sure, they can get along for a while, for instance, only drinking a little wine or a little beer. But then they tell themselves, 'Boy, have I got *that* problem licked!' and pretty soon the little beer or little wine becomes one whale of a lot of hard booze, and they're right back where they

started. Drunk. Hating it. Hating themselves. The house
has beat 'em again."

"You've tried—"

"Everything. Father Duval tried. Dr. L'Eveque tried.
The local extension chapter of AA tried. They all failed.
Or, rather, my father did."

Angie was continually surprised by Jorbie. He was
serious in discussing what was a serious—and painful—
subject with her, yet the bright shadow of his new, up-
beat mood was woven into every word of the way he
said things. Angie loved him for it; he was trying, it was
obvious he was trying, to understand one of the major
problems in her life, even as he was bursting inside with
playful high spirits. Simultaneously, Angie couldn't help
but being touched by the amount of time he was devot-
ing to talking solely about *her*—something unusual in
her life.

He sat quietly, absorbing what she had said. Angie
saw his chest rise and fall as he gave a sympathetic sigh.
Then: "Something else I don't understand." Jorbie was
hunting for just the right phrases, choosing his words
carefully, like a man stepping delicately through a
minefield. Angie did not know why, but she had the
feeling that just now he had reached the heart of what
his whole conversation was about.

"I don't understand how you could put something
that must have been as traumatic as your father and Fi
LeBoque out of your mind so easily. I understand
blocking out stuff from the past, of course, but I would
have thought something like that would have stayed
with you. Hell, I've got little blocks, I'm sure, but I
don't think I've ever erased anything really important
from my mind. I'm pretty clear on—at least, I think I
am—everything terrible that ever happened to me."
Jorbie was unaware that quite a number of people
would have disagreed violently with that brave statement of his.

Angie merely shrugged, she didn't really have a logical answer. "Well, you have to remember. I was a little girl, only eight years old, and while I saw what my father was doing, it didn't mean anything much to me. I didn't understand what it was all about. All I knew was that it was bad somehow, and that it made my friends' families keep their kids away from me, and that hurt, so I erased it.

"One of the times Dr. L'Eveque was trying to get my father to quit, he mentioned it to me. It was the first time I even remembered it at *all*. He outlined it for me. And then there was a man from AA—he was trying to get Dad to join up, but he wouldn't, of course—he filled in some more details for me. His daughter had been at my birthday party, you see. And then, suddenly, the whole thing came back. Details. Sentences. Words. Fi LeBoque's screams. It was awful, Jorbie. Like living it all over again."

There were a lot more things Angie didn't even go into with him; just talking about it hurt too much. The funny looks from her friends at school. Being shunned. Whispers about her father and prison. Out-of-earshot remarks about orphanages and other ideas terrifying to a child. Her father crying, pleading with her to forgive him. The town growing more and more remote from her. Then a blank. A total blank that hadn't begun to be filled in until Dr. L'Eveque and the man from AA had finally brought the subject back up to her.

Quickly, Jorbie changed the subject. He could tell it was upsetting Angie badly, but for some reason it was upsetting him, too. He still couldn't understand how she could have blocked the incident from her mind so completely for so many years; he couldn't tell whether it was that unanswered question that upset him, or whether it was seeing Angie look so shattered by even talking about it.

He came on strong, and wildly enthusiastic. "Hey,

you know, Angie. I loused up the picnic and I guess it's getting too late in the year for that anyway. But, hell, we could go to Sault Sainte Marie and do the town. They've got restaurants that make this place look like what it is—a quick pit-stop for passionate strangers on their way to the Alpena Motel. They probably change the sheets there about as often as they change the menu here: once a year."

Angie giggled. "I'm sure you'd know, Jorbie."

Jorbie laughed but ignored the tweak, his effusive good spirits carrying them both higher as he spoke faster and more excitedly. "Or there's Saginaw. Almost a hundred thousand people there, which always surprises me. But we could see just about any movie that's out, or, hell, even go bowling. Ever been bowling? If you remember to take your finger out, it's a lot of fun."

Angie opened her mouth to answer, exhausted by the breakneck speed of all that Jorbie was saying, wonderful things, exciting things, things filled with the promise of a whole new kind of existence for her. But before she could even get a word out, Jorbie was back on his joyful, headlong dissertation.

"Saginaw's not too far, really. On a Friday afternoon, we could load up the body-wagon—"

"*Body*-wagon?" Angie stared at him in confusion.

"It's a black station wagon with the back seats taken out. We use it to take—well, bodies—from their homes to Tenniel's. People don't like a hearse parked in front of their house, you see. Anyway, we use the floor of the wagon for one body, and then there's a sort of rack we can put another on in case it's a two-holer." He saw Angie's new confusion and explained before she could ask, using a deceptive little laugh to take the unpleasant overtones out of what he was saying. "A two-holer is when we get two bodies from the same place at the same time. Like from a car accident"—Jorbie shud-

dered remembering his father's—"or when two people
go at the same time in a fire or something." Studying
Angie's face, Jorbie could tell his effort to avoid the
unpleasant overtones hadn't been successful. "Look,"
he said, suddenly taking Angie's hand, "if the body-
wagon bothers you, we can always use my car. But the
wagon's newer and rides better on a long trip like Saginaw." Seeing her smile, Jorbie laughed. "I promise
there won't be anyone in the back."

Angie hooted. That incredible smile of Jorbie's was
infectious. And the thrust of what he was saying left her
almost speechless with happiness, even if it did have its
macabre overtones. She could feel herself literally glowing with pleasure. Jorbie was already talking of them as
a fully established, self-contained unit. A pair, a couple.
Two of them against a hostile world. To Angie, it was a
completely new experience. What a glorious word "we"
is!

The arrival of their meal finally slowed down Jorbie's talkathon. To Angie, the Mackinac Bar and
Grill's food seemed absolutely delicious tonight. Succu-
lent. Tempting. Superb. She knew it was her soaring
happiness about Jorbie that made everything seem wonderful.

Inside, she was bursting with pride just to be seen
with him, aware that people glanced at Jorbie as they
passed; his exceptional dark eyes and his black hair,
slightly tousled, made him appear a dark, sensuous god
from some other planet.

Angie looked up, startled, as a voice suddenly came
from beside their table, its checkered tablecloth now lit-
tered with an array of used dishes waiting to be cleared
so they could move on to dessert. "Mr. Tenniel?" asked
the bartender, his voice tentative, his face solemn.
"There's a telephone call for you, Mr. Tenniel. I
wouldn't bother you in the middle of your meal, but
they said it was urgent."

Jorbie looked perplexed. "It's okay, it's okay," he muttered, and then, turning to Angie, talked, as much to himself as to her. "I don't understand how anyone knew where to reach me. I didn't tell anybody, I don't think." The incredible smile wreathed his face again. "It's the Alpena demon, I suppose. He heard what I said about his favorite motel." Jorbie shook himself and stood up. "Excuse me, Angie. I've got to take it, I guess. I'll be right back."

Signaling the waitress that she could clear the table, Angie watched Jorbie's slim, erect carriage crossing the room to where the bartender was holding out the phone receiver to him. God, she had to be the luckiest woman alive. His face when he returned was long and he seemed depressed again. He appeared tired and certainly not the buoyant man he had been when he'd left the table.

"God, I'm sorry, Angie, but we have to go. I don't know how they found me here, but I've got to go." He spread his hands hopelessly.

Jorbie's pose of surprise about the phone call was a fraud. He had expected the call to come, and it had. Pasteur was instructed to wait in the Tenniel Funeral Home for it, and then to call him immediately. To make sure, Jorbie had given him the restaurant's number, not entirely sure he could count on Pasteur to find it in the phone book. From her vantage point Angie couldn't see that Jorbie, after a brief conversation with Pasteur, had then made a call of his own.

"Not your father?" asked Angie. "Business?"

"Business. There's been a death. A terrible one. Little Flan Tierney. Christ, I saw him just this afternoon at St. Etienne—in the hall. Well, no, maybe it was the cafeteria, I don't remember."

Angie felt something stabbing at her. An eight-year-old. One she knew. Dead. Just like that. "Oh, Jorbie, how terrible. How did it happen? It can't have been some illness; he was fine this morning. An accident?"

"I don't know yet. Father Duval did mention something Dr. L'Eveque had said about 'hidden childhood accidents,' but that's all I have so far. I'll find out more when I go there."

For an instant Angie was startled. "*Go* there?"

"Right. After I drop you off. People are funny about having a body in the house. They don't really want to see them go—it makes everything so final—but they don't want them in their house either. It's really odd."

They made the trip back to St. Max in virtual silence. Jorbie's mind seemed to be elsewhere, and Angie was still suffering from the shock of sudden, unexpected events. Flan Tierney had been a pupil of hers, off and on, for years. He was a nice child, polite for an eight-year-old, reasonably bright, and inevitably full of laughter. For the moment, Angie's good feeling about the evening had vanished, replaced by an out-of-proportion grief she couldn't entirely explain. Leaning against her front door after being dropped off, she watched Jorbie's taillights recede into the night, two twin dots of somber red that seemed as unsure of what was overtaking St. Max as Angie was herself.

The Tierney house was not hard to spot. Every light in it was on, as if their incandescent blaze could somehow scare away harm. Inside, Jorbie was met by Father Duval, the parish priest from Our Lady of Sorrow Church in St. Max. By now the Father and Jorbie were used to each other. Just as Jorbie was the area's lone undertaker, Father Duval was its sole priest. In a way, the two of them were in business together, bustling proprietors of a thriving cottage industry. Deaths and funerals. Twenty-four-hour service. Satisfaction guaranteed or your money back.

"What happened?" Jorbie asked as they walked solemnly across the hall into the living room. Almost hidden in the far corner, Jorbie could see Flan's father,
Hank Tierney, slumped in a chair, plunged deep into
conversation with Dr. L'Eveque. The father's head was
lowered, his back sagged over, his two arms hanging
between his legs with his hands twisting each other between his ankles. The picture he presented was one of
such misery Jorbie almost felt sorry for him, but then,
this was the man for whom Flan had been the surro-
gate. Flan's death, Jorbie knew, would be more painful
to Hank Tierney than his own.

"What happened to Flan?" repeated Jorbie, realizing
the priest was debating whether to join L'Eveque and
Tierney or whether he should stay with him.

Father Duval turned to him, his head shaking sadly.
"No one seems quite sure, Jorbie. They're running the
usual tests down in Traverse City—you know, urine,
stool, blood—but L'Eveque doesn't believe they'll find
anything much. He's quite sure it was what he calls a
'hidden childhood accident.' He played football, you
know. L'Eveque said his body was quite badly bruised
in several different places. He's positive it was an un-
revealed concussion, probably received during practice
yesterday. Wasn't treated because no one knew it had
happened. Child died. Happens all the time, L'Eveque
says. Sad."

Nodding, Jorbie agreed. "Where is the boy?" he
asked the priest.

"Upstairs. He was getting ready for bed when he just
fell over. His mother heard a thud and went in."

Jorbie looked up as he saw Hank Tierney suddenly
rise out of his chair; L'Eveque also turned, but remained seated. Framed in the doorway into the living
room stood Flan's mother, her red-rimmed eyes sweeping the roomful of relatives, close friends, and those
whose professions required their attendance. They

landed on Jorbie, filled with the mixture of fear, loathing, and reproach he saw so often in the eyes of the newly bereaved. It was as if they somehow held the undertaker responsible for the death, instead of realizing he was only there to tidy things up.

Slowly, one finger raised and pointed at him. "*You*. Already?" For a moment she stood where she was, her finger still pointing. Then she began to fall apart, the words tumbling from her in a torrent of misery. Quickly, Hank Tierney moved to her side. She stared defiantly at Jorbie. "Well, you can't have him. He's only eight and you can't have him." Hank tried to comfort her, to silence her, but her voice was raised now to the thin edge of hysteria. "You can't take him from me," she screamed. "Not now, not ever! My God, Flan—he's never been away from me for a single night in his life . . ."

Father Duval had joined Hank Tierney at the mother's side and was trying to comfort her too, holding her arm and gently lowering it so that she no longer pointed at Jorbie. Even across the room, Jorbie could hear L'Eveque whisper to Hank that he'd given her a shot; she was losing control, he said, from the strain of too much happening to her too suddenly. Between her husband, the priest, and the doctor they were finally able to head her out of the room.

A few minutes later Jorbie was taken upstairs by Flan's father. Flan had been moved off the floor and laid on the bed, dressed only in his pajama tops, loosely covered with a blanket. Apologetically, Jorbie had to raise a point that usually unnerved the strongest survivor. "I'll need some clothes for him. For the viewing. His suit, his white shirt, his best shoes, and—oh, yes—his favorite necktie."

Hank Tierney surprised him. "Of course. Those things are all in here," Hank said, opening his son's closet door and taking out the items, one by one. From

Flan's bureau he pulled his single white shirt, and then stopped to look at Jorbie. He appeared almost embarrassed. "I don't suppose there's much point to a handkerchief, but what about undershorts?"

It was a question almost always asked, one way or another, and particularly painful for ancient husbands who had survived elderly wives. "Of course." Hank dipped into the bureau again and handed Jorbie a neatly folded pair of Jockeys.

That was the way they would remain, too—neatly folded. Putting shorts on a body was a study in overkill. At the end of every year, near Christmas, Jorbie, following his father's example of many years, would contribute a mountain of sometimes barely used clothing to the Salvation Army. It would be donated in some town far enough away that there was no possibility of an embarrassing recognition scene. Saginaw was the usual choice.

Fifteen minutes later Pasteur arrived with the body-wagon. Flan was loaded onto the rolling stretcher and covered with a green plastic body-cover, and began his last journey.

For the final few moments at the Tierney's, Jorbie's composure had been an exercise in self-control. From what he had learned talking to L'Eveque, Flan's death had come only eleven minutes from the time called for on Jorbie's schedule.

Even as a child, Jorbie Tenniel had always prided himself on his punctuality.

Chapter Eight

I can see, I guess, why people aren't too fond of under-takers. Although I'm only in the business because I had no other choice, some days even I hate myself for what I do.

People resent this as a trade; well, I can understand that. See, their canary falls over one morning, and they just dump the thing out along with their crushed ciga-rette packs and the stale rolls. A person dies, and they have to go through all sorts of stuff—with doctors, with me, and with priests.

I just wish they wouldn't be so damned mean to me about it; after all, somebody has to do the job. Angie claims they don't hold it against me, but I wonder. I still think St. Max despises me, and that she's just trying to make me feel better. She can't.

Maybe people have the right idea the way they han-dle their canaries. And maybe people should get the same treatment—stuffed in a garbage can and left on the street to be picked up with the rest of the trash.

Then, with no work for me to do here, I could go back to med school. I sure as hell don't know how I'd pay for it. As it is, working full tilt, barely enough peo-ple in this area die to afford a new car every now and then.

> Jorbie Tenniel—to the rock,
> 1:00 A.M., November 19th

"You're a hurry-up job, did you know that? Rush, rush, rush—that's all people think of nowadays." There was no answer; none was expected. Flan Tierney lay on the slab, naked, his eyes staring blankly at the ceiling. The little boy looked much too small for the slab and very much too young to die, but neither of these things appeared to bother Jorbie. He was fussing with small pieces of Scotch tape, making sure Flan's eyes would remain open. Earlier, Dr. L'Eveque, the old-fashioned GP who was all St. Max could support, had closed Flan's eyes and placed half-dollars on them to allow rigor mortis to overtake Flan with his eyes shut. Jorbie had opened them again and was taping them that way.

"You have very excitable parents, Flan, that's why there's all this rushing around. Last night—well, you were upstairs, so you wouldn't know about it, I guess—last night your poor mother looked as if she was going to blow her cork. Screaming at me, Flan. Hysterical."

He set down a pail of sudsy water near the slab and began washing Flan's body from head to toe, flipping him one way or the other to get at the more out-of-the-way spots. "Of course, Flan, I can understand why they're so anxious to get you on view by noon tomorrow. It's a Saturday, and nobody has to be at work or go to school. You should get quite a turnout at the viewing that way. So I promised your mother and father I'd have you ready. See, I'm just a pushover, Flan. A real softie."

In the back of the room Pasteur leaned against a counter and watched. He'd never known Mr. Jorbie to talk to a dead customer before. It didn't make sense. There was also something about the earnestness with which Mr. Jorbie spoke to this dead little boy that bothered and frightened Pasteur.

Briefly he debated taking the subject up with him, but decided against it. He'd just get yelled at.

"You'd have enjoyed watching old Dr. L'Eveque stumble around trying to figure out what happened to you, Flan. It was funny. Have *you* figured it out yet?" Jorbie patted Flan on his bottom—he had been washing between his buttocks—and flipped Flan back right side up. "Someday St. Max—the whole area, in fact—could stand a decent doctor. Somebody up on the new medicine. Of course, it's a help just now that there's no one around here except old Dr. L'Eveque—I think he'd probably have trouble diagnosing athlete's foot. And for the moment, L'Eveque's about all we ever *will* get—a little blind, a little deaf, fumbling along as best he can. See, Flan, bright young doctors go where the money is. And that certainly isn't St. Max. Or Charlevoix. Or St. Ignace. Or Alpena. Or Groscap. If you decide you're going to be a doctor when you grow up, Flan, go pick yourself a big city with—" Jorbie halted in midsentence, laughing at his own foolishness. "But then, of course, you're not *going* to grow up, are you, Flan? Stupid thing for me to say ... ."

Pasteur could contain himself no longer. He rarely commented on what he didn't understand—that would have kept him talking almost constantly—but the strange behavior he was witnessing was too much to ignore. "I never heard you talk to a dead 'un afore, Mr. Jorbie. Poor little tyke can't hear you nohow."

Jorbie stepped back and treated Pasteur to a faint, condescending smile. "Remember the hamster, Pasteur, remember the hamster."

Pasteur shook his head and thought of some work that he could say had to be done outside. What Mr. Jorbie had just said made as little sense to Pasteur as talking to the dead. Only it was infinitely more disturbing.

Jorbie stood back and studied Flan, tilting his head like an artist trying to appraise a new painting. Dressed in a dark blue suit and a neatly pressed white shirt (but wearing no Jockey shorts), Flan Tierney looked better than he had hoped. Children were always troublesome. Take Flan's tie, for instance. He leaned forward and patted it down in a final finishing touch. When he'd asked Hank Tierney for his son's favorite, Jorbie hadn't expected it to be a *bow* tie. Inevitably a bow tie was a pain in the ass. It was hard enough to tie a regular tie backward, but a bow tie defied taming. With Flan he tried something new: he hoisted him between his arms, face forward, his back to himself, and held him up to a mirror, supporting Flan with his forearms while reaching around from behind the boy to do the bow. It worked. Superbly. He picked Flan up, talking to him gently again, and slipped him into the small-sized white coffin that had been delivered this morning. "All comfy, Flan? Good. Now, I'm afraid I've got to close your eyes. Seeing you with them open would really rock your poor mother."

The eyes, so recently taped open, were now taped shut again. Gently, he closed the lower half of the casket, leaving the top open, in display position. His feet hurt, so Jorbie hopped up and sat on the same counter Pasteur had used earlier, taking long, deep drags on his cigarette and giving Flan's coffin a quick, appraising study.

But as he sat there, admiring his handiwork, a sudden unknown fear gripped him. From the body came a muffled throbbing, a flat, toneless pulsing—the kind Jorbie used to hear through his stethoscope while examining patients at Marquette's teaching hospital. At first Jorbie was convinced the sound must be coming from his imagination—product of the last two days' strain—but it was too loud and too insistent to fit such an explanation. The pulsing grew in volume, adding resonance and tone as it grew, twisting and bending itself in the air like a moving projection on the screen of some flexible, plastic pattern.

Within a few moments the sound had become so loud Jorbie covered both his ears with the palms of his hands, his face contorted, his mouth opening and closing as he gasped for air. But the sound had grown deafening and refused to be shut out. It penetrated Jorbie's hands, seared itself into the drums of his ears, and drilled painfully past them toward his brain. He had long ago gotten to his feet. Jorbie, his hands still over his ears, began running up and down the preparation room, yelling senselessly at the sound as if countering it with enough noise might somehow bring it to a halt. Suddenly, as mysteriously as it began, the throbbing stopped.

Rushing in from outside, Pasteur appeared, his face a mask of worry. "Are you all right, Mr. Jorbie? I heard—"

"I'm fine, I'm fine," Jorbie snapped at him, angry that Pasteur should have been witness. "Just practicing some old vocal exercises I used to do at school." He glanced at Pasteur; his story was not being accepted. "I said, damn it, I'm fine."

Jorbie was a long way from fine. The incident left him feeling weak; he could still feel himself trembling. The throbbing reminded him of some event lost in the misty reaches of the past, but Jorbie found himself unable to remember where or under what circumstances the event had happened. Perhaps it never had. Once again, Pasteur tried.

"Mr. Jorbie, you *sure* you're okay? That yelling—"

"Was a vocal exercise. Now look. I don't have all day to stand around looking after your damned nerves. Take the Tierney boy's body up to the viewing room. And be careful, hear"—the crackling snappishness in Jorbie's voice both hurt and worried Pasteur—"be careful you keep the box level. I spent a lot of time getting that kid just right."

To avoid the expression of reproach in Pasteur's eyes, Jorbie turned away from him, busying himself with tidying up the area around the slab. "I'll be there in just a minute to set the room up," Jorbie called over his shoulder. As he heard Pasteur's shuffle begin to recede, Jorbie turned and watched. The man, following Jorbie's orders, somehow looked ridiculous trying to be delicate with the small coffin. His giant hands seemed out of scale carrying the casket by the tiny polished handles on either end. Handling the casket as gently as if it were full of hand-blown crystal, Pasteur moved out of the preparation room and began to climb the stairs. Slowly, the *thump-thump* of his feet on the stairway was replaced by empty silence.

A sudden recollection of the throbbing, the swell of the muffled pulsing, and his own screaming swept over Jorbie. He shook his head, struggling to find some viable explanation. Maybe, somewhere along the line, he'd breathed in too much formaldehyde. He'd heard of undertakers—unlike his peers, Jorbie refused to think of himself as a "mortician"—getting pretty damned high on formaldehyde fumes before.

Sometimes, as well as unpleasant, this business was damned crazy.

Someone coughed, and the sound bounced off the vaulted stone ceiling, ricocheted off a stone arch, and disappeared into the hollow sibilance of muted whispering and the deafening echo of a dropped hymnal. The town was in attendance on Flan (for Flannigan G.) Tierney.

There is something infinitely sad about the funeral of a child.

Lost in the vastness of Our Lady of Misery's apse, Flan Tierney's tiny coffin appeared toy-like, something Flan himself might well be hiding in, waiting to pop out suddenly and make everyone laugh; the pallbearers appeared ill at ease and awkward; the altar, mammoth. The hushed voices of the adults and other children sounded all wrong, as if someone had switched off the sound in the middle of *The Muppet Show*.

Even by the devoutly Catholic standards of St. Max, the turnout at Our Lady of Misery was vast. There were not sufficient pews for this large a gathering, so many of the mourners had to remain standing throughout the service, clustered against the rear wall of the church, just beyond the baptismal font. As a single unit, the entire student body of St. Etienne Parochial came down the aisle to take the rows of pews reserved for them, looking strange in their blue suits and best dresses on a Saturday. At their head walked a grim-faced Sister Honorée; bringing up the rear were Angie Psalter and Cathy Springer. Other teachers were scattered in among the children to insure an orderly arrival and departure, and to make certain the Sister's interdict against talking was obeyed.

In actuality the huge attendance was not really so surprising. Hank Tierney, Flan's father, was a popular man in St. Max, both in business and as a person. Flan had been well liked, not only by his peers but by most of the town's grown-ups. His mother helped Hank Tierney with his business, as well as being very active in church affairs and the Ladies' Auxiliary of the Rotarians.

From the docks of St. Max, Hank Tierney captained one of the last large commercial fishing fleets in the area; at various times he had had as many as two-dozen small fishing boats operating from his loading and freezing dock at the same time. All of his men were at the church as well, looking as strange in their suits and ties as the boys from St. Etienne.

Standing to one side of the altar, Father Duval waited until the congregation quieted, then nodded to the organist. The small choir—all of the boy sopranos and some of the altos were from St. Etienne—broke into Handel's Processional. Duval could not keep his eyes from moving across the jammed rows of worship-

ers. Attendance was, in general, good at Misery—Father
Duval made sure of that—but he could wish it were
always as crowded as it was today. Immediately the
priest reproached himself for the thought; a child had
had to die to deliver this throng to his doorstep.

The Processional wound to its end. Father Duval
faced the mourners and began: "I am the resurrection,
and the life: whosoever believeth in me . . ." At the
close of the prayer Duval added the Special Ending for
the Burial of a Child: "He shall feed his flock like a
shepherd; he shall gather the lambs with his arm, and
carry them in his bosom . . ."

Angie found herself on the edge of tears. All through
the service she had had difficulty controlling herself,
but managed it because she knew it would only upset
the children further to see her lose her own composure.
This self-control was not easy to impose; she could not
look at Flan's coffin without wanting to cry. At the
opposite end of the pew, she could see that Cathy
Springer was having the same struggle with herself.

Twice, Angie had seen Jorbie. He stood to one side
of the altar rail, hidden, most of the time, by a large
pillar, apparently waiting for Father Duval to intone the
handful of words that marked the end of a Service for
the Dead. Jorbie looked solemn, but Angie was disturbed that she could find no indication of real emotion
in his expression. It occurred to her that to Jorbie funerals were just a part of a business, but somehow, she
felt, this was different; this was *Flan Tierney's* funeral.

The only time he appeared genuinely affected was
during the solo performed by a schoolmate of Flan's,
Peter Berringer. Peter was a boy soprano with such pu-
rity of tone any school or church would have been
proud to have him in its choir. Because of this he was
given broad license in his repertoire and had chosen,
instead of something liturgical, to sing part of "Tender
Shepherd" from *Peter Pan*. No one objected. It was a

highly appropriate choice—in the play the Darling children sang it as they said their evening prayers—and the song, after all, had been chosen by one of Flan's friends. A fitting tribute.

When Peter's small, clear voice reached the last line of the song, "One in the nursery, fast asleep . . . fast asleep . . ." Angie saw Jorbie suddenly turn his head away so that no one could see his face; it was as if the song reminded him of something he hadn't heard for many, many years. Angie was mystified, but felt herself ache for him.

A little later Father Duval, members of the family, and close friends followed the hearse out to the cemetery for the burial. Carpas Point Cemetery stood high over the Straits of Mackinac. The ground sloped sharply upward, covered with row after row of headstones in memory of St. Max's past. By the time the procession reached it, the sky had turned dark with heavy, ballooning clouds. The wind, not noticeable earlier in St. Max proper, blew hard across the treeless cemetery ground, making a low moaning sound as it whipped around the edges of the headstones.

On one side, almost at the top of the hill, were gathered the graves of earlier Tierneys; a freshly dug hole—the earth that had been removed was mounded and covered by a green tarp beside the grave—stood waiting to receive the body of young Flan. In the best of weather it was a desperate-looking place to put a child, but in weather like today's, burial here seemed an act of cruelty. A few drops of rain hurled themselves angrily at the mourners; the wind howled; the headstones moaned. The handful of people who had come with Mr. and Mrs. Tierney shivered and pulled their coats more tightly around themselves, partly because the wind was suddenly so frigid, partly because of a sense of forlorn bleakness the grave cast across them, partly because—well, for reasons they could not entirely explain.

Father Duval, his collar turned up to ward off a chill, held the prayer book in his trembling fingers and recited a final prayer for Flan's soul, and then asked the people gathered around the grave to join him in the Lord's Prayer. Their words were swallowed by the wind and disappeared into the frigid void of the lake.

As they neared the end of the prayer Mrs. Tierney's voice suddenly rose above the rest in a heartrending scream. "You can't take him, God. You can't let them put him in that awful hole." She began trying to throw herself into the grave on top of the casket, but Jorbie, Hank Tierney, and Father Duval grabbed her and held her back. They began dragging her away as Duval, making the sign of the cross, nodded to Jorbie that they could start to fill in the grave.

Over her shoulder Mrs. Tierney was still screaming, now to her son, "Oh, Flan, Flan . . . I loved you so . . . but, my God, Flan . . . you can't hear me anymore . . . you can't hear me!"

The lady was wrong, dead wrong.

Chapter Nine

I know Angie was shook up that I didn't show much reaction at Flan Tierney's funeral. It was written all over her face. Well, outside of my being the reason Flan needed a funeral—enough to make anyone sit on their emotions a bit—she probably doesn't realize that, after a while, in my racket, one funeral gets to be pretty much like another.

Unless something unusual happens. For a minute there, when old lady Tierney was trying to throw herself on top of Flan's casket—two months ago, a lady in Groscap did throw herself on top of her husband's coffin, broke an arm, and there was a hell of a mess— but outside of that incident with his mother, Flan's was a pretty run-of-the-mill job.

Angie doesn't appreciate, I guess, that Tenniel's doesn't serve just St. Max, but St. Ignace, Charlevoix, Groscap, Traverse City, and Alpena as well. That's a lot of funerals. I guess about two a week—and more than that if there's been a big accident, or something like that. What's good for Tenniel's isn't good for Mackinac County—or, anyway, too pleasant for it.

One thing I'll have to do is let Angie inside the undertaking racket a little. Show her how it works and stuff.

Flan's funeral seemed pretty much a run-of-the-mill thing. I wonder what Angie would think if she knew how really unusual it was. Only two people know for sure. I'm one. Flan Tierney is the other. I hope he ap-

*preciates the high honor I'm sharing with him. Probably
not. On the whole, kids are an ungrateful bunch.*

> *Jorbie Tenniel—to the rock,
> 7:00 P.M., November 18th*

The telephone jangling through the uncarpeted halls of
the house made her jump; she almost dropped the book
she was holding. Long ago Angie had taken up the car-
pets in the upper floor of the house; her father had
spilled so much beer and vodka on them over the years
the whole place had begun to stink, a sweet-sour-stale
smell that hit you in the face the moment you walked
in. For a while she'd considered some kind of washable
rugs but gave up on that, too; she was damned if she'd
start washing booze-sodden rugs for him. Downstairs,
in the living room and old-fashioned front parlor, she
did finally resort to washable shags. Most of the time
her father rarely went into those rooms; his world con-
sisted of the kitchen and his room. He had a small television set there and watched game shows until they
came out of his ears. Usually, even with the set blaring
its loudest, he was in a drugged sleep. Like a house-
bound child, Angie could recite the openings and clos-
ings of *Match Game, The Cross Wits, The Price Is
Right, Truth or Consequences, The Dating Game,* and
Camouflage by heart.

By the time the phone had gotten halfway through its
third ring, Angie had already flown down the stairs and
grabbed the phone in the kitchen. The one thing that
seemed to wake her father, who had an alcoholic's
perversity, was the sound of the phone, and if the call
was for her—it usually was; very few people bothered
to reach her father anymore—he could give the caller a
start by swearing at them for no reason at all, or drop-

ping the phone, or screaming at them that nobody was home. She didn't want that to happen today; she had a feeling the call would be Jorbie.

It was. "Hi," his voice said cheerfully. Angie jumped higher than she had when she almost dropped the book. What had told her that it would be Jorbie? Maybe there was more to psychic precognition than she'd thought. "I was wondering," he continued a little hesitantly. "Tomorrow is Sunday, and I thought you might like to go to church with me and then, if you want, we could go on to lunch somewhere."

The invitation surprised Angie a little. The lunch part was in keeping, but Jorbie taking her to *church*? Well, his business probably pretty much required him to show up regularly. Jorbie wasn't particularly devout, that much she knew, but then, neither was she. It was one of the many attitudes they shared. And she found no real hypocrisy in his not being devout and going to church, any more than in her own semi-agnostic belief and teaching at St. Etienne.

"That sounds like fun," Angie answered finally. *Fun?* she asked herself. What a strange word to use for going to Sunday church! But, she told herself, it was more the events surrounding church with Jorbie that she had had in mind. The sheer pleasure of being with him all the way through luncheon. That they would be on display in front of all of St. Max as a unit. She couldn't pretend that that facet of the invitation didn't excite her. She, Angie Psalter, the town's personal pariah, in the company of someone who certainly had to be one of its handsomest, brightest young men—even if Jorbie himself wouldn't believe that was the way the town felt about him. "I mean, Jorbie, that wasn't much of an answer. Yes, of course, I'd love to."

A laugh came from the phone. "For a moment there I wasn't sure. You sounded kind of hesitant."

"It's my harelip."

Jorbie was all solemnity. "Strange, I never noticed it."

"It comes and goes, Jorbie. Hare today, gone tomorrow."

Jorbie roared at Angie's awful pun, a roar that grew when he discovered Angie was unable to stop giggling wildly. Every time Jorbie would start to say something, Angie would laugh again; her new high spirits were in possession of her. They were like children, laughing out of control over what really seemed, in the last analysis, to be something that would make absolutely no sense to anyone else. Finally, Angie was able to bring herself under control long enough to agree on the time Jorbie would pick her up tomorrow.

After she'd hung up, Angie stood in the kitchen, staring at the familiar appliances, pans and hanging plants as if she'd just seen them for the first time. With Jorbie every day seemed to bring something new. And just when she'd decided he'd finally tired of her and was trying to slip away, he'd suddenly turn up with a new and startling suggestion that proved he wasn't trying to get rid of her at all—like today's telephone call. Numbly, Angie shook her head. The world was her toy; she could never remember being so happy.

Cathy Springer didn't seem to share Angie's happiness at all. Twice during Father Duval's Sunday service, Angie caught Cathy staring at her and Jorbie. The first time the stare was merely a disappointed one, the look of a mother who had given a child her best advice and then watched as the child went right ahead and did what it wanted anyway. The second was accompanied by an almost imperceptible, sad little shake of Cathy's head, a stare that announced she had precognition too and could see certain disaster creeping up behind her friend.

Angie turned away, as did Cathy. Let her stare, Angie told herself, let her stare. That was not disaster creeping up on her; it was ecstasy.

Outside, in the crowd standing and talking at the bottom of the church steps, Angie was surprised to find Jorbie moving from group to group, talking with everybody and at least *appearing* to enjoy doing it. This outgoing role seemed very much out of character for him.

Considering the length and dullness of Father Duval's sermon, Angie felt surprisingly lively. It was the kind of sermon that usually left Angie on the edge of sleep, but the presence of Jorbie beside her excited Angie, and for the first time, possibly, she had absorbed every one of Father Duval's words.

Suddenly through the crowd Jorbie arrived at her side, Edith Pardee in tow. They had never discussed her, but Edith Pardee was a special favorite, apparently, of both of theirs. Like Angie, Mrs. Pardee had once been a lay teacher at St. Etienne; like herself Angie knew, she had struggled to drag a reasonable sound out of the school's choir. Like Angie, it was obvious that Edith Pardee was extremely fond of Jorbie.

"Why, of course I know Angie, Jorbie. For years and years. I had a long talk with her a week or so ago, at the dance at St. Etienne, I guess it was." Mrs. Pardee turned her always cheerful eyes toward Angie. "Good heavens, Angie. You look wonderful. I don't know whether it's the hair or the clothes or what. . . ."

"Maybe it's me," laughed Jorbie. "I bring out her natural beauty."

"If that's what's doing it, Jorbie Tenniel, you ought to bottle yourself and sell it to Revlon or someone like that. You'd make millions. And I'd be first in line to buy some, although it's really a little too late for me, I'm afraid."

Jorbie laughed. "The last thing you need, Mrs. Pardee, is help from anyone."

"Oh, c'mon, Jorbie, you're such an impossible charmer. An old lady can't believe a word you say." Edith Pardee might say she couldn't believe much of what Jorbie said, but it was obvious she'd like to. Once again she turned toward Angie, yet somehow managed to do it in such a way that her remark to Angie included Jorbie as well. "It's so wonderful, you know, to see two of my favorite young people in St. Max hitting it off the way you two are. Just wonderful."

Angie could feel herself blushing, yet could feel a glow of pleasure surge through her. The world was beginning to learn what Angie already knew: that she and Jorbie were, well, what *were* they?

Abruptly someone called to Mrs. Pardee, who waved back and turned to go. Before she left, though, she managed to squeeze Angie's hands between hers and whisper, "So wonderful, Angie . . ." She kissed Angie lightly on the cheek, then Jorbie, then was gone.

Jorbie seized Angie by the hand to be with him while he continued moving from one group to another. It was interesting for Angie to see him so unusually gregarious, the product, she supposed, of a business need to be pleasant to *everyone.*

Angie was enjoying every minute of it. Jorbie was clearly showing her off, parading their closeness in front of everyone. Together they chatted with Mr. and Mrs. Berringer, Police Chief Hardy Remarque, Mrs. deCarre, Dr. L'Eveque, and Lutetia Losee. "Oh, poor Quentin's still in bed, poor thing," Mrs. Losee said to Jorbie almost apologetically, as if her husband's absence from Mass had to be explained, "Dr. L'Eveque says it may be quite some time." Mrs. Losee talked for a few minutes with Jorbie but didn't make much effort with Angie. Angie tried to be philosophical about it; there was something grotesque in Jorbie's conviction that the town hated him, when they clearly didn't. Set against her own awareness that the person that St. Max really disliked was herself, a fact that she had lived with for so many years, it no longer bothered her at all.

Senseless as it was, though, she could feel Jorbie's conviction that the town disliked him in everything he said to her. There was a defensiveness that shone through, poisoning what he said and how he acted. Angie saw Jorbie narrow his eyes, then shrug; he took her by the arm and suggested it was time they left for lunch.

During the meal Angie tried to explore his feelings. "You know," she said, "you really ought to get over this idea that the town dislikes you. It's crazy, Jorbie. They adore you. But you keep acting like they were making fun of you or throwing stones at your head or something—"

She stopped, stunned by the sudden ugly expression on Jorbie's face. "If you're embarrassed to be seen with me," he snapped, "nobody's forcing you." For the rest of the meal Jorbie said practically nothing. Angie tried humor, tried sympathy, tried apology, but nothing she did seemed to reach him. Where a few minutes ago he had been lively and funny and apparently enjoying himself, he now was sour and withdrawn, his emotions drawn up inside him like the wheels of a jet.

Angie wanted to kick herself. She'd done it again. Her and her damned stupid comments, sticking her nose into things she didn't understand. The luncheon, which had held such promise, had gone wrong— perhaps fatally so. A fear gripped her. A few minutes later she tried again. There was a good movie playing in Charlevoix. Maybe he'd like to go see it with her. For once, she'd take *him* for a meal. Jorbie shrugged.

As he dropped her at her door he looked at his watch and his dark mood suddenly shifted again. "You know,

the idea of that movie sounds great, but I won't let you
buy the dinner. One of these days you can cook for me
at Tenniel's—I realize your house is out. Why don't we
set it for Friday?" When she said yes, Jorbie leaned
across the front seat of the car and kissed her on the
forehead, the way one might a child. "See you" was his
only comment as he pulled the door closed and drove
off.

Walking up the path, Angie sighed with relief.
Everything was all right again. How or why it had gone
wrong lost its importance with this realization. It had
been a wonderful day—except for the lunch she'd
loused up by saying the wrong thing, whatever that was.
She felt the warmth of her happiness flowing through
her, giving her the strength to ignore her father, who
was trying to subject her to a bitter cross-examination
as she walked toward the stairs. Angie felt tremendous.

But Jorbie's sudden swings in mood were certainly
unnerving.

"Oh, what a day, Quentin. For a Sunday, I'd never
have believed it. One thing after another; I think next
week I'll stay in bed and let *you* go."

Lutetia Losee was sitting in a chair in her husband's
room, knitting, while he lay in his bed, trying to appear
cheerful. He had cancer; he knew it. Lutetia knew it.
But they both maintained the fiction that neither knew
what was wrong with Quentin, a tactic that avoided either of them ever having to acknowledge the painful,
inevitable death that would eventually overtake him.
Except on days when the pain became unbearable, the
deceit allowed both of them to remain relatively cheerful in the face of the inevitable.

"I'll be out of this damned bed one of these days. In
the meantime, I don't recommend it to anyone." Quentin paused, a little taken back by the brashness of his
own lie. Particularly since it was a lie Lutetia wasn't

even supposed to believe. "Fill me in on your Sunday, Tish. Sundays are usually so damned quiet in St. Max."

"Not this one," said Lutetia Losee, trying to count the stitches on her needle to see where she had gone wrong. "Mass—a long one today, and one of Father Duval's less inspired sermons, I'd say. I had a quick lunch with the Berringers. Almost as dull as Duval's sermon; they didn't even offer me a drink, but they never do. I wouldn't have gone, but their house is close to the church and they were pretty insistent. After lunch there was a finance meeting with Father Duval and the rest of the Auxiliary Board. Unusual, but we have a lot of things coming up that are going to need funding. Then I had to stop off and see the young Tierneys; they want a plaque done up for little Flan, which means they'll have to make a sizable contribution. I wasn't really sure they could afford one of the size we'll have to get. It didn't seem to bother them at all. And then home to you, Quentin." Lutetia paused for a moment, struggling with herself. "I know it doesn't seem like much when I line it all up like that, but it's left me exhausted."

Quentin Losee nodded, understanding precisely what his wife meant. After fifty-two years of marriage, such understanding came easily.

Quentin laughed. "I hope you weren't hideous to Father Duval, Tish. The way I feel this afternoon, I may need him any day."

As Lutetia Losee talked a strange expression came over her face. She felt suddenly dizzy, and as if someone were dropping a dark veil in front of her eyes. She held one hand out toward Quentin, her mouth opening in surprise as she slowly spun around and crumpled to the floor. Quentin Losee struggled out of bed, trying to get to his wife quickly. Kneeling, he looked into her open, staring eyes and knew that Lutetia had beaten him in his race toward eternity. Maybe it was better that way, he thought. She wouldn't have to see him suffer, she wouldn't have to spend agonizing hours watching him wither into a screaming shell.

At her house, Angie's phone rang about five thirty. Once again she got to it before her father could. It was Cathy. "Had you heard about Mrs. Losee, Angie? I knew if you hadn't, you'd want to know."

"Heard *what* about her?"

"She died, just about an hour ago. Dr. L'Eveque says it was a heart attack. She's had heart trouble for years, apparently."

"Oh, my God. What about poor old Mr. Losee?"

"Taking it very philosophically, I understand. But it's getting a little crazy here, Angie. Last week Flan, today Mrs. Losee."

Angie couldn't explain it, but a sudden shiver ran through her.

As if someone had just walked across her grave.

Chapter Ten

I don't know why Lutetia Losee was chosen to get the Captain Marvel treatment any more than I know why Flan Tierney was. I was ordered to, you see. No explanation, just the order. So I gave her the bonaro shot when we met outside the church, one hand shaking hers, the other clasping her shoulder warmly and giving her the injection.

That explains how; it doesn't tell why. It's a mystery to me why I'd pick someone who, over the years, had been as nice to me as Mrs. Losee. Always kind, always warm, always doing little things for me.

It's that Voice. A Voice that seizes control of my head, telling me who I have to kill next. It seems to work from some kind of crazy list of names I haven't even seen.

Things can be going along quietly enough, and then, all of a sudden out of nowhere, the Voice begins whispering in my brain, giving me my marching orders on who to go after. I have absolutely no control over it.

I hope one day it doesn't whisper Angie's name to me; I really like the girl, but I know I can't fight that Voice. The world really ought to be warned: that Voice makes me just as dangerous to people I like as to people I hate. Maybe more.

*Jorbie Tenniel—to the rock,
8:15 A.M., November 19th*

Old Dr. L'Eveque's waiting room was not a very comfortable place. By way of furniture, all it had was a few hard wooden chairs and one falling-down sofa. A lot of doctors have magazines that are a month or two out of date; L'Eveque's waiting room had dog-eared copies of *Collier's* and the *Saturday Evening Post* lying around.

For the better part of half an hour, Hardy Remarque had been left sitting in the waiting room, squirming uncomfortably on one of the hard-bottomed wooden chairs, while one patient after another disappeared into L'Eveque's office. Hardy Remarque was not surprised; he knew precisely what the doctor's opinion of the law was.

Tall, slim, gray-haired, Hardy Remarque looked too elegant to be the police chief of a town as small as St. Max. The illusion was further heightened by his custom of wearing a uniform only during the tourist season; the rest of the time he was given to sports jackets of a tweedy sort, making him look more like a British detective than the chief of a one-man police force in the outer reaches of the Michigan peninsula.

L'Eveque's waiting room was almost empty now—it was getting on toward lunchtime—and Remarque lowered the copy of *Look* he had been using as a shield against curious stares and studied the cracks in L'Eveque's walls.

He was troubled. They didn't really get much crime in St. Max; an occasional tourist who got bombed and drove his car into a store window, or the usual petty vandalism brought on by teen-age boredom. Once every year or so there'd be a robbery, usually a break-in of one of the more opulent tourist's homes, and the theft of a few color television sets or stereos. No one knew who committed the breaking and entering; no one ever would.

The worst overall crime Remarque could remember was a Bible salesman who damned near took in the whole town. A real con man, a slick rip-off artist. Remarque could feel his blood pressure rise even thinking of the man. With his glib line of patter he'd sold genuine leather Bibles—to be imprinted with the buyer's name—to about half of St. Max's residents, promising them the Bibles would be delivered as soon as the purchaser's name could be embossed in gold on the outside.

The man took their money—cash or money order only; he'd explained his supplier didn't like checks—and drove off waving cheerfully to some of the customers he'd gotten to know best during his short two-day stay. The Bibles, of course, never arrived. The money was well gone. Hardy Remarque felt very personally about the event; he had been conned along with the rest, waiting three weeks for his own hand-embossed Bible before he began to become suspicious.

Now he had a feeling the town was being conned again. Only on a much higher level. Well, he, Hardy Remarque, was not going to let it happen this time. The door to L'Eveque's office opened and his white head stuck out, beckoning Remarque into his office with a curt little wave that wasn't very friendly. If L'Eveque had ever had a nurse-receptionist, she had left long before Hardy Remarque could remember; the doctor's bills were sent out in the same haphazard fashion he suspected the eighty-plus-year-old doctor practiced his medicine.

Seating him in the chair beside his desk—like the ones in the waiting room, hard and ungiving—L'Eveque stared at him. "What can I do for you?" he growled. "You said you weren't here as a patient."

"That's right."

"What?" boomed L'Eveque. His hearing had grown so bad, Remarque discovered, he had to repeat everything at least twice.

"I'm here on official business, Dr. L'Eveque. Police business."

A ground swell of muttering arose from behind the doctor's desk. His dislike for the law and its guardians was made evident. Remarque had intended to work around to his questions obliquely, but L'Eveque's deafness along with his antagonism quickly forced a more direct route. "Don't you consider," bellowed Remarque, "in a town as small as St. Max it may be kind of peculiar that two people should die within only a few days of each other? Die just a little mysteriously? I do, Doctor."

Eveque shrugged and looked away. "These things happen. Everyone's got to go sometime. Sometime they pick days close to each other. Don't strike me peculiar, Hardy."

Remarque was dogged. "What I was wondering was if we could still do an autopsy on Lutetia Losee."

Remarque watched closely as L'Eveque's head snapped upright, his oddly colorless eyes boring into Remarque. His reaction made the policeman all the more certain his hunch might be right. This was a man who definitely didn't want even to think about autopsies.

Finally, from L'Eveque, an answer. "Too late," he snapped. "Too damned late. She's over at Tenniel's. By now, Hardy, Tenniel's has drained the blood out of her and pumped her full of formaldehyde. That's all embalming is, you know."

Listening, Remarque tried to detect any sign of relief in L'Eveque's voice; all he noticed was the growing hostility. "Anyway," L'Eveque added, growling in his annoyance, "I did my own informal autopsies on both of them. Lutetia, and before her, Flan Tierney. Not the fancy, Saginaw hospital, kind, understand, the fifty-years-of-experience-as-a-doctor variety. The boy—you probably heard it around town, Hardy—hidden concussion, most likely from playing that damned football. Get more broken bones from football in here than anything else. Lutetia? Poor old Lutetia had been playing tag with a massive coronary for years. She knew it.

Tried to get her interested in a pacemaker, but she wouldn't listen. Everybody thought it was Quentin who was sick; Lutetia was the sick one. Had been for years. Lutetia knew that. But wouldn't listen to anything about herself. So now Lutetia's dead and Quentin's still alive. Half alive, anyway. Just to double-check, though, I really went over Lutetia after the coronary. Classic symptoms. Sent blood samples to Saginaw for testing. Nothing. I don't know what you're so worked up over, Hardy. People die. Just like dogs, cats, and flowers. It's part of being alive."

Ignoring L'Eveque's mind-bending rationale, Hardy Remarque got to his real point for coming. The con job. Just like that damned Bible salesman. "Let me spell it out for you, Dr. L'Eveque. Two years ago, when those two cases of pulmonary anthrax showed up and knocked off a couple of summer people, the authorities in this town tried to cover the cases up. Said it was summer flu. Tried to con people. Terrified that it might kill off their damned tourist business. Christ, Doctor, I know how important the tourists are to St. Max; without them we'd all be on relief. You were part of *that* cover-up then. My question—I want a simple, honest answer, Doctor—is whether the same cover-up stunt is being tried again. Are *you* helping them hide a new outbreak of anthrax, this time among the townspeople instead of the tourists?"

L'Eveque, touched on a sore point, fled to the refuge of his deafness. Suddenly, it seemed, he couldn't hear at all. Hardy Remarque couldn't get anything more out of him. "Come on, Dr. L'Eveque," insisted Remarque. "I'm not planning to prosecute anyone. I just have to know; it's my *job* to know."

Abruptly, L'Eveque rose to his feet behind his desk. In an automatic movement Remarque found himself on his feet too. Over the top of the des' L'Eveque glared at him. Hardy Remarque could see the old man's hands, his whole body, trembling in anger. Suddenly he felt sad for him. "I'm sorry, Doctor. I was just . . ."

"Showing off. Being nosy. Getting into areas you don't know a damned thing about." L'Eveque took several deep breaths, trying to get control of himself. It didn't work. "Get the hell out of my office. And don't come back unless you're sick. Real sick. I got people to take care of. People—most of them one hell of a lot sicker than any damned menopausal police chief—to worry about."

When Remarque didn't move, L'Eveque turned and stalked out of the back door of his office and into his home. The door slammed shut, as closed as his mind.

In town, Angie ran across the same sense of uneasiness that was troubling Hardy Remarque. On the street she ran into crazy old Mrs. Lavin, trying to gather a crowd to listen to her Bible theories. When anything happened in St. Max, you could always count on finding Mrs. Lavin somewhere in town trying to show people how accurate her Bible Interpretation and Prediction Charts had been about the event.

She had grabbed Angie by the arm as they passed on the street, taking Angie's nod and smile as encouragement. Her thin fingers were like claws sinking into the flesh of Angie's arm. Trying to be patient, Angie stopped for a minute. "It's all in there," Mrs. Lavin wheezed. "Every bit of it. See? Deuteronomy in Rising Aspect with Habakkuk, opposed by the Second Chapter of Malachi. The Chart foretold everything. You can see for yourself."

To be pleasant, Angie peered at the charts Mrs. Lavin was jabbing with a forefinger of her right hand, muttering darkly about what her charts foretold. It always baffled Angie that her charts seemed to be a sort of zodiac horoscope, with the planets replaced by biblical names, dates, and numbers. Yet what baffled Angie more was that frequently, when Mrs. Lavin predicted something as being about to happen, it happened.

"And the Charts show we are in grave danger. All of us—the whole town. St. Max has become ungodly; some have abandoned prayer. And this cluster of chapter and verse numbers show that God plans to punish St. Max mightily for it. Soon, it says, we will hear Him speaking through the voices of the dead, warning us. We are all doomed."

In spite of the sheer ridiculousness of it all, a cloud had passed across the sun as Mrs. Lavin talked, and Angie felt a shiver run through her. Nonsense, of course, but still . . . Mrs. Lavin appeared to have forgotten Angie was there. Mrs. Tumbril had stopped to watch how Angie would handle this familiar situation and now found herself in the same fix, Mrs. Lavin's fingers gripping her arm in a clawlike vice. Angie fled.

At the drugstore, Mrs. Lavin's son, Nate—he owned it—listened as Angie told him what his mother had said. Nate shrugged, smiling faintly. "Well, Mom's story makes as much sense as some of the explanations I've heard. Except for the voices of the dead. I've got some pretty sophisticated pharmacopoeia stuff here, but the most powerful drugs I can whip up won't make the dead speak. Even for God." Nate laughed nasally, proud of how smart what he said made him sound. Hell, he'd been to pharmacist's college, hadn't he? He had a state license, didn't he? Angie knew Nate's reply would be flashed on all of Nate's customers for the rest of the day.

Telephoning Jorbie—she didn't want the movie Friday to go the way of the picnic—Angie found him harried. "Alpena's having a wave of flu," he groaned. "And older people have a real tough time trying to fight it off. Low white-counts. I wrote a paper on that at Marquette. Anyway, they cave in and that means extra funerals on top of the regular load."

It always threw Angie to hear him talk about embalmings and funerals like a garage mechanic complaining about how many transmissions, muffler adjustments, and spark-plug changes were lined up ahead of him. She supposed it was all in getting used to it.

"Look. I'll have to beg off the movie Friday. I'm getting too far behind."

"I understand, Jorbie." Angie wasn't sure she really *did* understand, but knew she was supposed to act as if she did. Jorbie's cancellation, although understandable, still hurt.

"I've got an idea, though," Jorbie said brightly. "You could come over here, to the mortuary, and I could cook you dinner—upstairs in the house," he added with a laugh, "and show you around. I'm no great cook, but I'm all right with simple things like steak. Dad swears by me."

Angie was torn by emotions pulling in opposite directions. Jorbie's invitation had an intimate ring to it; she'd probably meet his father, too—another step in the framework of intimacy; a dinner cooked by Jorbie, even more intimate. There was, in fact, the promise of closeness in everything Jorbie had suggested.

But she could not entirely escape her own prejudices: being shown around a *mortuary*? An identical shiver to the one Mrs. Lavin had produced passed through Angie. For the second time in one day.

In the end, of course, there was no real battle to the decision she made. "I could do the cooking, Jorbie. Really. I'm good. Very good. Is there anything I should bring with me?"

"Nothing. Oh, maybe a little red wine to go with the steak. But the cooking—well, it's my home and my job. No arguments."

Angie sighed with pleasure. Tuesday evening. Set. A small dark cloud raced across her mind. No matter how you sliced it, an invitation to a funeral home for dinner set a strange stage for a date. But it was something, she knew, she would have to get used to. In the middle of her thought, she paused. Something, Angie corrected, she *hoped* she would have to get used to.

Friday night, dressed in another of her cardigan and skirt combinations—this one a pale daffodil-yellow sweater and dark plaid skirt with a lot of yellow in the tartan—Angie drove down the rocky driveway to Tenniel's. She had seen it before, of course. Over the years, visiting the viewing of St. Max's dead, laid out in solemn wakes on the mortuary's second floor. As a child on a dare. And most recently on the day of the aborted picnic.

The building was an old, gray-shingled Federal. From the center of its roof, where you might ordinarily expect a chimney, rose a severe square cupola. To accommodate the cupola, the chimneys had been built at either end of the house, an unusual arrangement for the architecture of upper Michigan. The side of the first story of the building, as well as both ends, had been faced with red brick; the main entrance had been redone in white-pedimented Georgian, as had the corniced windows. The cheerful, tidy design this produced was, Angie had long ago decided, an effort to make the funeral home less menacing to families and visitors. Beside the door, in chaste script, was a small polished brass sign: JOSIAH TENNIEL & SONS—FUNERAL DIRECTORS. Jorbie's grandfather, Angie speculated. Or perhaps his great-grandfather. She must remember to ask him.

As she stood there the moaning of the wind surprised Angie. She supposed it was always windy here, perched on a promontory above the Straits of Mackinac. The mournful sound washed the place in loneliness; the same constant wind blowing off the deserted sand dunes below had twisted and bent the trees around the house into tortured shapes, their branches, bare now, moving in the wind as if summoning help. Here was where Jorbie had been born and grown up. If he sometimes seemed a little withdrawn, lonely, or possibly a bit paranoid, you only had to see where he'd spent his childhood.

Flicking off her lights, Angie picked up her package and rang the doorbell, trying to dismiss the uncomfortable feeling the place always gave her. Almost immediately the door swung slowly open. There was the shape of a person, wearing what appeared to be a cape of some sort, standing inside, but there was no light in the hall, so it was impossible to know who it was. From somewhere came a deep, sepulchral voice. "Good evening. Come in. Living to the right, deceased to the left." Angie gasped.

The lights all came on at once, and Angie heard Jorbie's infectious laugh. He was standing in the hall, grinning. "I'm sorry, Angie. I couldn't help it. The only way you keep your sanity in a racket like mine is gallows humor. Please, come in. No more games, no more tricks. I promise." He held out his hand and helped her into the now brightly lit front hall. Really quite cheerful, she told herself.

"Oh," Angie said, suddenly remembering. "The wine. I'm not up on my wines, but the man at Sam's in Charlevoix said it was supposed to be quite good. Imported French. Imported, probably, all the way from Sault Sainte Marie."

"Great. It looks great. What's the line?" Jorbie searched the air, trying to remember something, then: "Oh, yes: 'It's a modest little wine, but I thought it might amuse you with its presumption. . . .'" Tossing the bottle in his hands, Jorbie turned to Angie with a shy smile. "Hell, I don't know wines. If it has a red color and twelve percent alcohol, it's wine. If it has a red color, twelve percent alcohol, and is French, it's *good* wine. Some taste better than others, I guess, but this one looks very superior to me. Thank you."

After hanging up her coat, Jorbie took her on a tour of the place. The downstairs living room where people waited before going to the upstairs viewing room. The furnishings were close to Victorian, but the walls were a bright, pale yellow and the room managed not to be too somber. Still there was a detached feeling to what was essentially a small living room; the prints on the wall were bland and dark, and the place was dominated by heavy bronze statuary that glowered from the corners.

"Not very cheerful," Jorbie said, reading Angie's thoughts. "And even depressing, when you consider what its principal use is. But if you think *it's* bad, take a look at the viewing room." Jorbie noticed some hesitation in Angie and was quick to assure her. "No one's laid out for viewing, if that's what's worrying you."

Feeling the depression rising inside her, Angie followed him silently into the viewing room. There was thick carpet on the floor, and some tables lined the walls. Empty vases stood on each table. A somber sofa and a couple of chairs facing the center of the room were the only sittable furniture. The walls were pictureless, painted a speckled brown color. In the room's center was a low dais, and on top of this a cloth-covered platform perhaps two feet wide and six feet long. "It's where the coffin goes," Jorbie explained. "We didn't make an effort to cheer this room up; I think people want this room to reflect their own sadness, not fight it." Jorbie stood in the center of the room, leaning on the platform with one hand. "Besides," he added with a soft giggle, "leaving it alone was cheaper."

Angie found herself growing increasingly uncomfortable. Jorbie's light banter in these rooms that had played host to so much grief in their time only heightened the shabby, depressing atmosphere they kept prisoner within them. "My office," Jorbie said as they went back through the waiting room, "is through that door. Nothing unusual about it. Standard desk, standard chair. Only unusual feature is a large wall calendar. Some guys have naked girls on their calendars, promotion gifts from *Penthouse* or *Playboy*. Mine's different. It has little squares for the undertaker to fill in. See? Right here, you write in your customer's date of death, and the date you interred him. The picture—well—the picture's from Forest Lawn's 'Famous Cemeteries' series. Neat."

Angie didn't know whether Jorbie was kidding again or whether he was merely relating an honest—if bizarre—fact about his business. "Sounds cheery," she said, an answer that could be taken either way.

Jorbie led her down a flight of steep stairs that led to the semibasement workrooms, underground on the front side of the house, aboveground in the rear where the land ran downhill. Out its windows you could see the Straits of Mackinac and the shore of Lake Michigan.

The workroom area was a nightmare to Angie. It looked like a chemistry lab, except that instead of worktables the room was dominated by two huge marble slabs. On one lay the body of Lutetia Losee, naked but partially covered by a sheet, her eyes staring at one corner of the ceiling. The sight made Angie's stomach churn, and she gave a little gagging noise. Quickly, Jorbie pulled the sheet up so that Lutetia was completely covered. "I'm sorry," said Jorbie. "I forgot you knew her. It always gives people a turn the first time."

Pulling Angie behind him, Jorbie explained the various machinery that stood against the walls of the room, leaving out the gorier details. "And over here," continued Jorbie, "is our freezer. It's a regular walk-in job, except, outside of myself, most of the people who go inside roll in, not walk."

It mystified Angie that Jorbie could be so insensitive to her feelings, that he could keep rolling forward with his tour in the face of her obvious squeamishness. Or maybe he *wasn't* that insensitive; maybe he knew exactly what he was doing; maybe he derived some perverse sort of satisfaction in exposing her to the horrors of this place. Impossible. He was too nice a man. Still, he was either guilty of colossal callousness, or some form of psychological sadism, in the way he dragged her on through this macabre tour.

With a flourish, he threw open the freezer door. "Meet Herr Dietrich Schwarz, late of Alpena. Before that, Bremerhaven, I believe." As a joke, Jorbie had frozen the German immigrant's right arm into a Nazi salute to match his Hitlerian moustache. "Since no one quite seemed to know when old Dietrich arrived in this country," added Jorbie, "I improvised a little on history."

Angie spun on him. "That's awful, Jorbie. Brutal. He was a human being."

Jorbie appeared immediately contrite. "I'm sorry. You know, I'm so used to this, I sometimes forget other people aren't. Please forgive me." He closed the freezer door, remembering he would have to come back later and get the two steaks for dinner out of the freezer. Angie was in no mood to discover their evening meal lay on a shelf over Dietrich Schwarz's outstretched right arm.

Angie muttered something about its "being all right," but not meaning it too much. She did her best to quash a rebellious stomach and laugh. "I suppose what's in that walk-in is described on your financial statement as 'frozen assets.' Poor Mr. Schwarz."

Angie's effort to get into the spirit of Jorbie's humor was not entirely a success. There was a sudden strange impression that kept forcing itself to the top of her mind. Standing there, surrounded by bottles and bodies, wiping his hands on his plain white smock, Jorbie suddenly reminded her of the evil scientist she'd seen in some movie somewhere. Charming, brilliant, but consummately evil—and capable of anything. All he needed was a misshapen dwarf as his assistant.

The idea was ridiculous, of course. Jorbie was still the same Jorbie she'd come to know and—well, was it *love*? Yes, it was. Come to know and love. With effort, she shook the faineant notion from her head and forced herself to listen to what Jorbie had just begun to explore.

"Say," Jorbie proposed suddenly. "We could get your bottle of wine and have a little cocktail party right now."

"Upstairs; oh, Jorbie, could we please go back upstairs?"

"Okay. We'll take the wine up and have a drink with my father. He's been dying to meet you again, says it's been years." Angie felt her heart leap; they were so much of a unit Jorbie had been discussing her with his father. She turned as Jorbie spoke again. "You go on ahead; I have something to do first. I'll meet you in the waiting room with the corkscrew and the glasses."

Glad to escape, Angie fled up the stairs.

Downstairs, the moment she was gone, Jorbie folded back the sheet so that Lutetia Losee's head was once again uncovered. Whispering, he leaned down to her. "Sorry, Lutetia. It must be awful to hear, but not be able to see, what's going on. And I want you to see—to see *everything*. Keep the faith, baby."

Affectionately, he patted Mrs. Losee on the stomach and walked toward the stairs, pausing only to pull three steaks out of the walk-in freezer on the way.

Chapter Eleven

I'll never forget my twelfth birthday party. It was the first and last I ever had. Dad knew, I guess, that other kids' families wouldn't be too enthusiastic about their children coming to a birthday party in a mortuary, so he'd arranged for it to be held down on the beach, quite a distance up the inlet. I remember the invitations made a real point of that.

Well, all the boys in my class came, about ten of them. All of my friends—and a few of my enemies. Dad made me invite them, too; see, he was always very big on not letting anyone feel left out.

Right off, of course, the guys who didn't like me started in being mean, like always. And the other kids picked it up—twelve-year-olds are the most tightly knit bunch of sadists on earth.

Man, did I ever get even! I'd seen the body-wagon drive out just after lunch, so I knew no one was home. And I took the entire damned gang of them back to the mortuary and showed them the whole setup, the works. There were two stiffs in the freezer—one of them a girl of about twenty—and I showed those kids what a big man I was by poking my fingers everywhere.

There was a lot of dirty giggling, but most of the kids were turning a little green, scared but not willing to let on they were.

Then, when nobody was looking, I slipped out and slammed the freezer door shut on them. Jesus, you never heard such screaming. When I opened the door again—they can't have been in there more than a couple of minutes—those kids barreled out of the house like the devil was trying to crawl up their ass. Some, I think, ran all the way home.

Christ, was there ever hell to pay. People telephoning all night and the next day. Dad was furious. I don't even know why I did it.

It's sort of like what I pulled with Angie and Herr Schwarz. When I fixed him up with that Nazi salute, I already knew Angie was coming. I was showing off, I suppose, how tough I could be. Just like I did at my birthday party. It was stupid then, and it's stupid now.

Who am I trying to get even with anyway?

> *Jorbie Tenniel—to the rock,*
> *11:15 P.M., November*

Caleb Tenniel, even chained to his bed and with little to keep him company except his television set and Jorbie's hurried visits, was a totally captivating man. Without straining, it was easy for Angie to see where Jorbie's boyish charm came from. Caleb, of course, had no hint of boyishness about him but was the possessor of a puckish, elfin sense of humor that took Angie by surprise and won her to him immediately.

They sat there in Caleb's room, a motorized wheelchair at the bottom of the bed. In this he was able to get to the window and back, or down the hall if he wanted a change of scenery. This room was his prison, his rack, his dungeon, but there was no hint of bitterness about Caleb; the accident had happened and that was all there was to it.

Caleb was studying the label on the bottle of wine Angie had brought, while sipping from his glass. "1970. Good year, if I remember my wines." He smiled warmly, first at Jorbie, then Angie. "With some of the stuff Jorbie brings me, I count myself lucky if it's a good week."

Jorbie laughed. "I never pretended to know wines. If you'd just tell me what to get, Dad."

Caleb was riffling through a pile of pamphlets on the long bookshelf that ran beside his bed. It was filled with reference books, paperbacks, magazines, novels, and an unabridged *Webster's* in three volumes, all of it heaped on top of itself, a jumbled, disorderly stack of reading matter. At right angles to the bed and running along that wall was another, even taller, bookcase, an identical messy jumble of books and pamphlets heaped there in no apparent order. Still, Caleb Tenniel seemed to know exactly where he could lay his hands on anything he was looking for. "There," he said triumphantly, his thick mane of pure white hair flying in front of his face as he spoke, "all the information anyone could want. 'Great, Good, and Fair Years in French Red Wines,'" he read. Solemnly he handed the thin pamphlet to Jorbie. "From now on, ignorance is no excuse." He studied the air for a moment, then stared at his son. "Stay away from Château Lafite Rothschild, though, Jorbie. I think it goes for seventy bucks a bottle these days."

"I can help a little, Jorbie. Believe it or not, knowing how to get a fair wine at a reasonable price was something they taught in home ec."

"Christ," Jorbie groaned, "I'm being ganged up on."

Caleb Tenniel, his pale blue eyes piercing the strands of white hair that hung down over his forehead, laughed and smiled at Angie with warmth. "You see, Angie, you have vastly improved my life just by becoming a part of it. I understand you've improved Jorbie's no end too, by becoming part of *his*. I'm all in favor of improvement. I'd like to start with improved tires that don't lose their traction on wet roads. . . ."

It was to be the only reference Caleb Tenniel made to the accident that night; it was one of the handful of such remarks Angie would ever hear Caleb make. And he made his comment with such good grace, with so large a twinkle in his voice, there was nothing self-pitying in it.

To Angie, who had expected the cocktail hour with Caleb Tenniel to be a painful affair—a bitter, bedridden old man complaining about his lot, his pain, the unfairness of life—Caleb Tenniel represented the answer to a lot of the questions she'd always had about Jorbie. Jorbie, after all, had been raised by his father; the mother had died when he was only seven. It seemed to spell a disastrous future for a child—and yet, Jorbie had emerged as what Angie considered one of the most wonderful people alive. She had wondered where his sense of humor came from; now she knew. She had pondered on the source of his gentleness; now she knew. She had tried to divine the source of his brilliance —as a person and as a student at Marquette—now she knew. Caleb was behind them all. Angie could not help wondering what kind of person she herself—as motherless as Jorbie, and like him, raised by her father—would have been if she'd had a Caleb Tenniel as a father instead of a drunken, pathetic old man with an occasional penchant for little girls.

But there were some things, she realized, that Caleb Tenniel did not explain about Jorbie. The moodiness. The temper that flared. The occasional insensitivity, such as tonight, showing her that poor German, then, even worse, Lutetia Losee. And beyond these superficial facets, something about Jorbie that was a total imponderable, a collection of peculiar actions and pronouncements that sometimes frightened Angie.

She realized Caleb was talking to her again. "You know, Angie, we've been on a nodding basis for years. I can remember you as a little girl, shy, hiding from people; I used to see you pretty often on the street, and then, all of a sudden, you seemed to disappear."

Angie shuddered. "My father . . . well, he—"

Caleb held up his hand, shaking his head, pained that he'd blundered into an unpleasant subject for Angie. "I know all about your father, Angie. I'd just forgotten he *was* your father, that's all, and it's a pretty stupid thing to have to admit. I'm sorry."

"Nothing to be sorry about, Mr. Tenniel. His problems aren't exactly a family secret. For one thing, there's no family."

"Oh, my, Angie, how you have changed," Mr. Tenniel observed, again brushing some of the white hair out of his eyes and studying her more closely. "You certainly aren't shy or hiding from people anymore, which I personally am thankful for. And you look so different! You're really very beautiful now, and you've lost that dour expression you used to have." He turned toward his son. "You've found yourself a knockout, Jorbie. Congratulations. In wines, your taste may be lousy, but in women, superlative."

Angie found herself blushing. She supposed what was impressing Caleb Tenniel was the different Angie he saw now—she knew they'd passed each other on the street just the day before his accident. New clothes, new hair, new makeup, and bobbing on a sea of self-confidence. All of which had been produced by Jorbie, his son. But she couldn't tell him that. To change the subject, she singled out the book that lay shut on one side of his bed and pointed at it. "What kind of books do you usually read, Mr. Tenniel?"

"Oh, this one's Henry Kissinger. Thank God I didn't get the hard-cover; just holding it up could give a man a hernia. But in general I read just about anything. Fiction, biography. Particularly anything with a little humor in it. Most authors today, I think, take themselves too damned seriously. In many ways, life is a big joke. It was something I decided when I was dealing with dead people all day long. A lifetime of it. There they were, you see. After years of slaving, and struggling, and scrimping, where *were* they really? On a slab at Tenniel's, nothing more, nothing less. The things that were so important yesterday, weren't important anymore;

the things they felt yesterday, they didn't feel anymore. It's all over."

"You're not sure of that; neither am I."

Jorbie's comment seemed to trouble Caleb. "You don't really think they can *feel* things, do you, Jorbie?"

"I don't know. It's possible. For a while, anyway."

"Well, then, let's hope they're on the slab and not in the crematorium. That would be awful." Caleb turned toward Angie suddenly. She didn't know whether it was an effort to include her in the conversation or because he was genuinely curious. "Did Jorbie show you the crematorium, Angie? It's about two hundred yards from the main house. I had it built some years ago, but I can't say it was ever very successful."

Jorbie laughed. "Good Catholics don't believe in cremation, as you probably know, Angie. Nothing left to rise up on Judgment Day. But we do get an occasional request for it, and we also do cremations for one or the other of the undertakers in Saginaw. Big town or not, they don't have one down there."

"Listen to us, Jorbie!" Caleb Tenniel said, shaking his head. "You have a beautiful girl over for dinner and we sit here chatting about bodies, funerals, and cremations. Great hosts. Forgive us, Angie; it's a bad habit we have."

"Of course." Angie was relieved. To have *two* of them talking about undertaking was almost more than she could bear. Caleb was certainly far more gentle than Jorbie on the subject—she found it difficult to imagine Caleb freezing Mr. Schwarz's arm into a Nazi salute—but their single-minded concentration on death was upsetting. In fact, the whole conversation stirred some vague disquiet inside her, a ponderous, uneasy sense of something unnatural, something sinister, perhaps even something evil. It was time to change the subject again. "Have you read much Waugh, Mr. Ten-

niel? He can be terribly funny." She suddenly hoped
neither of them had ever read *The Loved One*, Waugh's
book about an undertaker and his girl friends. "I have a
friend at the library, and she can dig up out-of-print
books, some of them quite fantastic. I'd be happy to
bring you some."

Caleb beamed. "Great, Angie. I'd appreciate that."

In his chair, Jorbie suddenly seemed restless. "We'd
better go fall on that steak, Angie. I'll bring you some
up, Dad. Along with a little more wine."

"I'll fall out of bed if you're not careful."

On an impulse, as she left, Angie leaned over and
kissed Caleb on the forehead. He blushed, but treated
her to a wide smile, the light of it making the white hair
above his pale blue eyes seem to glow.

The steaks were great—Jorbie had a way of doing
them that left them tender, rare but crisp on the outside, and with what was almost a crust around the edges
that was positively delicious—but Angie could not escape a feeling that their dinner had somber, uncomfortable vibrations running through it. Jorbie continued to
seem restless, as if there were something on his mind.
His mood was more stable than usual, but on the depressed end of the scale. The feeling was infectious.
Angie became depressed herself, struggling to put her
finger on what was wrong, and beyond that, *why* it was
wrong. The effort was not successful.

At only a quarter past eleven Jorbie grew so restless
that Angie yawned once or twice, making something of
an ostentation of her weariness, and told Jorbie she
really ought to be going home. There were a lot of
things, she said, she had to do; tomorrow was a Saturday and would give her a chance to get them out of the
way.

For a second Jorbie stared at her, just a trace of sus-

picion crossing his face. It almost appeared that he had
guessed the real reason for her early departure, and was
about to ask her, "*What* things?" Instead he shrugged.
From the hall closet he retrieved her coat without comment. Then, in one of those mood changes that Angie
was only slowly growing used to, he suddenly found
some hidden reservoir of energy-charged cheerfulness.

"Hey, let's go out through the back door. You ought
to see what the whole inlet looks like at night. You
know, with the lights of the bridge across the Straits all
turned on, it's quite a sight."

Angie's usual pattern of believing that the dinner
must have been a failure because of something she'd
done or said wrong, fled before his enthusiasm. Turning
on the lights ahead of him, Jorbie once again took her
down into the work area. It was stupid of her to forget
that that was where the back door was; she hated the
place and wasn't sure she would have agreed if she'd
realized it.

"The door's right there—between the two large windows," Jorbie said. His voice sounded as if it were behind her, something Angie couldn't understand; the
moment before, he'd been right alongside her. The explanation came to her suddenly, all at once, and took
her breath away. Jorbie seized her and spun her
around, folding Angie into a long, passionate embrace.
His mouth first brushed hers and, a moment later, by
its pressure, opened hers. His tongue shot inside and
searched and caressed hers, drawing on it, as if Jorbie
were trying to pull the very soul out of her and transfer
it to himself. Angie found herself moaning and, for the
first time, realized that Jorbie was moaning too. She
could feel her heart pounding as his hands moved
across her body, kneading, squeezing, caressing hers.
Through his shirt Angie could feel the pounding of Jorbie's own heart. A tumescent swelling inside Jorbie's
trousers ground itself against her body, making her

breath come in short, uneven gasps. Angie could barely contain the happiness exploding inside her; for the first time in her life she felt truly wanted and needed and loved.

But, in the dim light, one of Mrs. Losee's eyes suddenly locked with Angie's (how had her face gotten uncovered again?)—an eye that stared at Angie in silent reproach. For no reason Angie could think of, the portrait of the evil scientist came back to haunt her.

She gave a strangled little sigh and tore herself loose. Fleeing out the door from what should have been the happiest moment of her life, Angie felt a sudden trembling course through her whole body.

And it was not a trembling that came from Jorbie's kiss.

Chapter Twelve

Sometimes I think the world is pretty much made up of things you can't count on. You can't count on people, I've always known that. You can't count on the weather, you can't count on your family and you can't count on what's going to happen to you tomorrow. Animals? You can't count on any of them except sometimes dogs. That's probably why I've always trusted cats more; I know I can always count on them not to be counted on.

Angie is always making digs about my moods, how she can't ever count on how I'm going to react to things. Well, damn it, she's a little tough to count on herself.

Take last night. All warmth and love, and then WHAM! she suddenly hauls ass out of here like she'd been bitten. It wasn't just because I was playing around with her—well, I don't think it was, anyway. No, it was something else. Something I hadn't counted on, something I still don't understand today.

I like Angie—really like her, you know, but something about her makes me uncomfortable. Maybe it's because I like her too much; maybe it's because I know it's only a matter of time before my damned Voice tells me to add her to the list.

Hell, it's one thing in the world I can count on.

> *Jorbie Tiennel—to the rock,*
> *12:15 A.M.—November 23rd*

Mrs. Henry Tierney was the first to hear it. She'd been half dozing in her chair for an instant and wasn't sure if she was asleep or awake. The gnawing pain of

Flan's death still left her exhausted most of the time. Eight-year-old Flan had been what gave her life meaning; his death left her without purpose, one weary day following another without apparent significance. She still performed her household functions, but automatically, slowly retreating into a hollow existence.

Across the room her husband Hank was either waching a Monday night pro game with the volume turned very low or was asleep himself. These were hard days for the Tierneys: Flan had been their only child.

But Mrs. Tierney's head snapped up, her eyes wide and searching, the moment she heard the voice, the way a mother comes awake instantly at the first soft sound of her baby crying.

From outside or from upstairs—anyway, from *somewhere*—she could hear Flan's voice. Her mouth sagged as she listened, wanting to wake Hank but afraid to miss one word of what Flan was saying. He was calling her, over and over. Silently, her mouth opened and formed the shape of his name, her hands turning white-knuckled where they held the arms of the chair in a savage grip. Confused, dazed, she shook her head hard, trying to make sense of it. Flan sounded like he'd been crying, but every word was distinct, his sentences interrupted, particularly when she first heard him, by the little gasping silences that she knew meant he was trying to stifle a sob. Softly, in almost a whisper, she called for Hank. Her only answer was a muttering snore. She wanted to scream for him, to yell for him to listen, but didn't dare break into Flan's distinct words.

It *was* Flan's voice. She knew the little expressions, the inflections, the cadence, too well for it to be anyone else's. Still hanging on to the arms of the chair, she sat there paralyzed. Around her, the room began spinning. She wondered if she'd gone crazy or was in the middle of some sort of crazy dream or if maybe this thing was really happening.

Flan's message was a short one, but left Mrs. Tierney
gasping. "Mom," Flan's voice said firmly, in a big show
of bravery, "Mom, you shouldn't feel sad. I mean you
shouldn't, y'know? Well, sure, I can't say I don't cry
sometimes, even now, but that's only because I miss
you so much, Mom. *You*—well, you shouldn't be
crying, you ought to be happy about what's happened
to me. Honest."

"Flan, Flan darling, can you hear me?" hissed Mrs.
Tierney, her eyes searching the living room ceiling and
staring wide-eyed into the darkness of the hallway beyond. There was no answer. Flan's voice had stopped
the moment before, leaving Mrs. Tierney in silence.
Slowly, without even realizing she was doing it, Mrs.
Tierney rose halfway out of her chair, repeating,
"Flan—" not sure whether she really expected him to
answer or not. Flan began again.

"See, Mom, I got a whole new life now. A wonderful
kind of life. Nobody is ever scared, nobody ever feels
bad, nobody ever hurts. I'm not even scared of the dark
anymore, Mom. It's what they"—Flan was stumbling
over these particular words, trying to make them come
out right—"it's what I guess they call life after death.
And it's neat, Mom, real neat. Well, it's *called* life after
death"—Flan grew confused again; these words came
hard to him—"but it's not the kind we used to hear
about in Bible class or in church. Just a sort of living on
forever after you die. You'll find out about it someday,
Mom—you and Dad and everybody . . ."

Leaning back a little, Mrs. Tierney had to steady
herself on the arm of her chair. It was impossible, all of
it. Yet, that voice. Flan's voice. No question. And Flan
was dead. Very dead. The words from his funeral came
back to her, Father Duval intoning them from the altar.
"I am the resurrection, and the life: whosoever believeth in me . . . shall live forever . . ."

From the nameless nowhere that contained Flan's voice, Flan began again. "You got to tell people about what I said, Mom . . . tell Aunt Grace, I always liked her. And Bompa. And Peter Berringer and Rene deCarre . . . they got to know to. . . ."

Flan continued on with a list, a list that was long, but intimate. He rattled off a litany of favorite people, friends and relatives, a list really known only to his mother, and possibly his father.

It was too much for Mrs. Tierney. She had survived the shock of Flan's sudden death, not falling apart until those awful moments at the cemetery when she realized he was about to be lowered into that lonely, hellish grave. Slowly, she had been recovering; she would never get over the loss of Flan, but the numbness was gradually leaving her as the days passed. Now Flan was back, his voice as piping and cheerful as ever, talking to her.

The dam broke. Spinning, her hands pressed against either side of her head, she gave a piercing shriek and collapsed into her chair, sobbing. Hank Tierney woke all in one piece, like a small animal, and looked around him, trying to understand what had woken him. He saw his wife, crying, a desperate look on her face, one hand pointing into nowhere. Then he heard the voice. It was Flan. Telling his mother to be sure all the people he mentioned heard about him and his new, wonderful life. And not to be afraid of dying. And, please, be sure his dog, Perky, got fed regularly—he knew they sometimes forgot about Perky, but he was one of the family too, wasn't he?

Hank Tierney blinked as he heard what Flan was saying. He got to his feet, determined to find where Flan was, where the voice was coming from, but hesitated. The voice had stopped. Then it started again. "Well, I gotta go now, Mom. Don't cry for me, please don't cry. I'm happy." There was a little smothered sob.

"Good-bye, Mom, Good-bye . . ." The voice faded
into a nothingness.

Hank Tierney sank into his chair. The voice was un-
mistakable, the details unchallengeable, the message
from Flan about his new life both baffling and profound at the same time.

By outsiders, St. Max was considered one of the
most devout towns on the Upper Michigan Penninsula.
And in this devout town among devout towns, the Tierneys were among the *most* devout.

They sat in their living room, silent, transfixed, staring at each other. It couldn't be, but it was.

Wordlessly, as if on some signal, they fell to their
knees.

A little after ten Angie Psalter retreated upstairs to
bed. Her father was already in his room. Through the
door she could hear his television set and knew he had
passed out: the program was no game show, but a discussion of the political situation in the Far East, something her father would never tune in to of his own free
will. Softly she opened his door and slipped in, switching off the set. He lay, fully dressed, on top of the covers. His head was thrown far back and his mouth was
open. In some ways he looked like the victim of an accident or a war, except that casualties don't snore. The
smell of stale vodka that filled the room sickened Angie, bringing with it a flow of painful memories stretching from her childhood to the present. Shaking her
head, Angie fled.

On the way back to her room, tiptoeing down the
long, carpetless hall, a sound brought Angie to an abrupt halt. From somewhere in the house that she could
not place, she could hear Flan Tierney's voice calling
her by name. "Miss Psalter . . . Miss Psalter . . ." it
said, having the same trouble with the silent P in her

name Flan always did. Angie sank against the wall, her
eyes wide, her mind reeling with confusion. As the
voice went on—with the exception of some asides specifically directed to Angie—it said pretty much the
same things that Flan had said to his mother. The confusion in Angie's mind grew. Flan had been a pupil of
hers, someone she saw virtually every day, and she knew
him well. There was no question about it. Like the
Tierneys, she was absolutely certain the voice was
Flan's.

Angie's reaction, however, was quite different. She
believed in God, she believed in the teachings of Christ,
but she had never been able to accept the literal Catholic interpretation of life after death. Something, perhaps, but not the happy, painless afterlife that Father
Duval—and now Flan—described.

And she was certain that, however the process of
eternity worked, the dead didn't return to speak words
of encouragement to the living. Still, something deep inside her began to question and wonder. . . .

She spent a sleepless night, haunted by the sound of
Flan's voice and the battle to find a solution for what it
meant.

At eleven fifteen Father Duval's phone rang. Sleepily
he raised himself on one elbow and groped for the
phone, wondering if someone else had just died. It was
an odd question to have asked himself, Father Duval
decided as he picked up the receiver.

"I'm sorry to call at such an hour, Father, but something's happened," said Hank Tierney.

"Yes, my son? Tell me. Being told things is why I am
here."

There was a strained silence from the phone and the
sound of a throat being cleared nervously. "I don't
know how to put this, Father. It's Dot . . ."

"Yes?" repeated Father Duval. My God, was Dorothy dead now too? Immediately, Duval reproached himself. Why should anyone's first thought be that someone else was dead in St. Max? He was not acting like a priest; he was acting like a detective in a TV show. "Yes," he said again.

"Well, Father, you know Dot's been under a terrible strain. You can imagine, I'm sure. But I don't honestly think this was the product of nerves or anything. In fact, I'm *sure* it wasn't."

Father Duval was becoming impatient; a terrible suspicion was beginning to haunt him. "What *is* it, Hank?"

"Dot heard something. Something—well, incredible. I heard part of it myself, and I can vouch for it too. It was impossible, yet there it was, happening. A miracle is the only word I can use to describe it."

"I see." Duval's voice was without emotion; he could guess what had happened, and he saw nothing but trouble growing out of it. "Tell me about it, Hank. Please, tell me, my son."

"Flan came back—anyway, his voice did—he spoke to us . . ."

Haltingly, Hank Tierney told Father Duval of the miracle, what Flan had said, what specifically he had mentioned about life after death, and of exactly how much he himself had heard and how much Dorothy alone had been party to.

"Look, my son, I must ask you—no, as your priest, I must direct you—to tell no one of this event. Not a living, breathing soul. Not until you've seen me and we can discuss it. Tomorrow, in the church. I will make special provisions to meet with you. Meanwhile, please, my son, not a word to anyone. I realize this will be difficult for both you and Dorothy, Hank, but it is necessary in the matter of—ah—miracles to be very careful. Very careful indeed. Do I have a promise from you, Hank?"

Muttering agreement, he made an appointment for the following morning. Several more times Father Duval emphasized the need for being extremely careful in such a matter.

Father Duval had good reason to know just how careful. Perhaps an hour earlier he had heard Flan's voice himself—coming from somewhere inside the rectory, he thought. At least, he was pretty sure it was Flan's voice. That was something he would discuss with them in depth in the morning. If it *was* Flan's voice, it was indeed a miracle. He decided against mentioning his own experience; it would only add to the Tierneys confusion.

Duval sighed. Why would Our Lord pick St. Max for a miracle of such awesome implications? The voice in itself indicated—"proved" was perhaps a more suitable word—the sort of life after death described by the prophets, by the Apostles, and frequently referred to by Christ himself.

When he had first heard Flan's voice, Father Duval had been so overcome he had called his bishop's administrative monsignor in Detroit. The man had been worse than skeptical; he had been rude. "Father Duval," he had said, "it's possible we have allowed you to stay in that frozen hellhole of yours too long. Your 'miracle'—sleep on it. You'll find that things look quite different in the morning. The whole thing will be something you'll laugh at later on. In the meantime, maybe you should come down to Detroit for a few days' R and R." He had laughed gently, a very superior-Jesuit sort of laugh, putting one of the local clergy in his place.

Now the Tierneys had heard the voice too. What would the monsignor make of that? Father Duval wasn't prepared to find out until he had a lot more facts lined up. More witnesses. Other examples, if any.

Father Duval struggled with himself. It was all so

clear to him. He did not understand that, like the Tierneys, he was ready to believe what he had heard—Flan's voice—because he *wanted* to believe it. With an angry grunt he threw back the covers; sleep had become impossible.

Downstairs, he walked into his library and began doing what he knew he should have done before he made his call to Detroit. That snot-nosed Jesuit. Moving slowly along the shelves, he pulled out one volume after the other until he had a pile beside his chair perhaps two and a half feet thick. Reference works. Dissertations of early philosophers. Trenchant monographs from later theologians. Metaphysicists. A thin book from Duke University.

Dressed in his wrapper, puffing his pipe and sipping an unusual glass of sherry, Father Duval went through one book after the other, looking for examples of other, similar instances where the dead had reappeared to the living—if only as a voice. He was surprised to discover there was a wealth of them. Mostly, however, they were not of recent vintage. Miracles, it seemed, were not very popular among Catholic theologians of the modern day. But taken as a whole, the the other recorded instances of voices from beyond the grave built a highly impressive case.

He made careful notes on a yellow legal pad, cross-referenced to title, page, and paragraph numbers, so that he could find any of them again relatively easily. Finally, as the first light of morning began edging the long night, Father Duval, feeling his research vindicated, fell asleep sitting in his chair, his face wreathed in a benign smile.

The voice on the phone sounded strong, yet very far away, edged with an echoing sound that baffled her. "Angie," Jorbie said, "I'm sorry you got upset last night. Sometimes I forget other people aren't as accustomed to seeing bodies lying around as I am. It was thoughtless."

As almost always happened to Angie in anything connected with Jorbie, she had already forgiven him before he called. The unpleasantness had disappeared, leaving her with only the memory of the passionate embrace. My God, she loved him, she told herself. Struggling, she managed to keep some of the excitement out of her voice. "Oh, I understand, Jorbie. It was probably stupid of me to react so violently. I'll try and do better next time."

"That's what I called about," Jorbie said, laughing. "Why don't we make the next time tonight? I know it's awful soon, but I really enjoy cooking, honest. Maybe lamb chops this time. And you have my word: we'll steer clear of the work area completely. There's nothing I have to go in there for."

The Angie who had tried to keep the excitement out of her voice a few seconds earlier vanished before the thought of seeing Jorbie once again this soon. And the way he had said "next time"—was he referring to the evening in general or was he suggesting they pick up where they had left off in their embrace? As she told him she would love to she found her hands trembling uncontrollably. She had lost the struggle.

"Oh, for Christ's sake, Angie. When people die, they die. And that's all there is to it. Flan's voice is a crock, somebody's crazy idea of a cruel joke." Jorbie walked over to the fireplace and kicked the log in front with his foot, sending a blazing burst of sparks up the chimney. The log, which had been smokily sending up sporadic licks of flame, sizzled a moment, then burst into a heartening, crackling blaze. They were sitting in the living room, the dishes from their dinner heaped on a tray in front of them. Earlier, Angie had gone upstairs with Jorbie while they had their ritual cocktail with Caleb.

The older man appeared delighted to see her, a little stunned when Angie produced Waugh's *Vile Bodies,* a novel from quite early in his career.

Caleb turned the book over several times in wonderment. "My God, Angie, you only even mentioned Waugh's books last night. I'm going to be spoiled by such attention." His pale blue eyes fastened on her; apparently he was terribly touched by her thoughtfulness. "I'll start this tonight. I'm not up on my Waugh at all. . . ."

A little later, when Jorbie reappeared with Caleb's dinner tray, the same pale blue eyes fastened on the two giant double lamb chops almost greedily. Once again Caleb turned to her. "Jorbie's a wonderful cook, you know. But I have to say our fare had improved remarkably since you started coming around, Angie. A man—particularly a bedridden one—could get fat eating this well."

Jorbie laughed. "I don't think the menu's changed much, Dad. It's just that Angie's face adds a touch of excitement to mealtime. A little zest. Like parsley on swordfish."

Angie felt herself blushing. As she knew was expected of her, she disclaimed any responsibility, making light of both their compliments, yet at the same time savoring every single word of them. Inside her, something trembled. What an incredible pair Jorbie and his father, Caleb, were. Her eyes found Jorbie's—the aftershocks of last night's passionate encounter surged through her again, growing more explosive the more she thought about them—and they went downstairs.

During dinner, Angie kept a light banter running; Jorbie seemed in a lighthearted mood, and she knew how to play to it. Midway through one of her sentences everthing suddenly went wrong. It was when she mentioned having heard Flan's voice. She should have sensed the depth of his reaction and knew she should have sensed it, and *had* sensed it, but blundered ahead blindly in spite of it. "It just isn't that easy to put out of my mind, Jorbie. It was Flan's voice. I taught him; I know. He even had the same trouble with the silent *P* in my name he always had. *Ps* instead of *S*. It was a crazy little private joke we had. . . . Can you explain that any other way?"

"I don't have to explain anything. I'm being perfectly rational, but damn it, you're acting like you don't have both oars in the water." There was an ugly belligerence in his tone, and Jorbie sank deep into one of his dark moods, staring morosely at the log he had kicked, slumping onto the couch with his hands in his pockets like a sulky little boy.

"I'm sorry, Jorbie," Angie said finally. "I didn't realize you felt so deeply about things like that."

Jorbie slowly turned and stared at her, his eyes boring into her. "Shit. You're just like everybody else. I can't trust you." As she listened his voice seemed to rise in pitch, to sound younger. There was almost a childlike quality in it now.

In amazement Angie looked at him, but Jorbie appeared to have retreated completely into his sulk.

Twice more a bewildered and hurt Angie tried to apologize for doing something she wasn't even sure she had done. Silence.

There would be no passionate embraces tonight; Jorbie no longer even responded to direct questions. Crestfallen, she got her coat and left: he had not even made the effort to go to the door with her. Driving home, Angie tortured herself, wondering why it was that things she said so often set him off. Plunged him into his moods. How could she be so stupid as to say something wrong almost every time she saw him?

A more prudent question might have been how she could be so stupid as to continue seeing him at all.

Chapter Thirteen

Finks. Every now and then I get to thinking how all of my life I've been plagued by finks. People who rat on you. That was why Sezi had to be given the new slit in his carotid; I couldn't trust him not to fink.

But it goes back a lot farther than Sezi. Even when I was just a little kid, I can remember how other kids used to tattle on me. To grown-ups. And someone—I can't place the person in my mind—was always telling Dad how mean I was and the awful things I'd been up to. Those stories strike me as one of the things I remember most vividly about my childhood, yet, at the same time, it's all fuzzy and I plain don't know who was behind the tattling or why.

Well, no more. From now on, most of the people of St. Max are only going to believe what I tell them to, and say what I tell them to say. Others, frankly, won't be in a position to say anything.

I don't suppose it'll make the town very happy, but maybe I shou.d remind them that silence is golden.

And you know how expensive gold is these days.

Jorbie Tenniel—to the rock,
11:20 P.M., November 24

She could hear the doorbell ringing somewhere far inside the house. Nothing much happened, and she rang again. Finally, a thumping effect inside told her the bell had been heard.

"Hi," Jorbie said cheerfully, throwing open the door and pulling her inside. "It's cold out there tonight."

Nothing was ever mentioned about his sulk of the

other evening, and to all appearances he had forgotten it. Angie couldn't forget. She just tried to keep it away from the front of her mind. Jorbie had called the morning after the incident, and suggested that she again come over for dinner. Her visits to the mortuary were becoming a daily habit, one that she looked forward to desperately.

There was certainly no hint of sulkiness to him tonight; Jorbie was in one of his "up" moods, flying high, full of life, laughing at almost everything Angie said.

"Look," he said to her, still standing in the hall. "There's a couple of things I have to get out of the way downstairs. I know you can't stand the preparation room, so why don't you go upstairs and talk to Dad. He thinks you're the nuts." For a second, Jorbie turned serious. "For that matter, so do I. But that's another story. Dad's opinion doesn't have the lechery behind it mine does. But with someone as sexy as you, only a man paralyzed from the waist down *could* be immune."

The thrill of expectation that ran through Angie was so strong she ignored his callous comment. She could feel even her toes tremble as the waves of excitement coursed through her whole body. Lightly, she started up the stairs.

Jorbie laughed, waving to her as she continued upstairs to Caleb's floor and he headed downstairs to the workrooms.

Downstairs, no one was laughing. Lutetia Losee was spending what she suspected were her last few moments on Tenniel's slab, a suspicion that grew from something Jorbie had said just before the front doorbell rang and he disappeared upstairs to answer it.

What was happening to her was terrifying. How could any of this be happening anyway? She was dead, Mrs. Losee told herself. By now she'd heard enough people say it so that she'd come to believe it herself.

Heart attack, doddering old Dr. L'Eveque had said. Well, he'd been warning her for years. Wanted her to get fitted with a pacemaker, but she'd refused. Looking where she was now, maybe it hadn't been so smart to refuse after all. Grimly she wondered if the pacemaker would have made any difference.

Dead. They all agreed on that. L'Eveque, all of them. Or *was* she? If so, how was it that she could see and hear and think? A hallucination just *before* death, perhaps. No, if she were still alive, she'd have been at home or in a hospital, not here at Tenniel's. Besides, she could remember hearing L'Eveque telling poor, sick Quentin that she was dead. God, she hoped someone was taking care of Quentin; he was so careless about himself.

Dead. The word kept coming back to haunt Mrs. Losee. And along with it all of the curious, horrifying ramifications of not being able to accept she was dead because she felt so alive. It didn't make sense. But maybe the inexplicable was explained by something only the dead knew: that your brain lived on for a couple of days after you died. You could see and hear and think, but were unable to move or speak or react. Or maybe this was what they meant by life after death. If it was, it certainly wasn't the way she'd imagined it.

Dead. Or maybe she wasn't dead at all; maybe they'd just made a simple mistake. The whole thing was a nightmare. Lutetia Losee desperately wanted to scream, but as hard as she tried, she could produce no sound. A nightmare, hideous, horrifying, dread-filled.

From across the room, she heard Jorbie Tenniel coming back. Given the circumstances, a thought returned to upset her again. It embarrassed her terribly to be seen naked by Jorbie. He was just a child; she was old and fat and puckered, and she hated having him see her this way. Jorbie appeared in the narrow alley of vision above her and gave her a noisy pat on her stomach.

From under his arm he pulled out her best blue, and heaved and grunted pulling it up on her. No underclothes, damn it, just the dress. After he'd lowered her back onto the slab, he stood beside her a moment, panting. He was talking to her again. "You've put on a lot of weight, Mrs. Losee. Bad for the health, you know. But I suppose just now that's academic."

Lutetia Losee strained, trying to move something, anything, somewhere. Nothing responded. It was as if someone had pulled the main switch on her entire nervous system.

"Nice-looking dress," Jorbie said, straightening it out. "The bereaved always like quiet blues—think it makes death seem restful."

Lying on the slab, fully dressed now except for her underclothes, Mrs. Losee stared up at him. She was concentrating everything she had on making some signal with her eyes, something that would let Jorbie know maybe she was still alive. The thought appeared to have reached him; abruptly he reached down and closed her lids with his fingers, fastening them shut with something she assumed was spirit gum. If she *were* still alive, that's how she'd be buried—alive.

A rolling squeak announced that her coffin was being moved over directly beside the slab; she'd seen it waiting there earlier, on a kind of hospital wagon. She sensed that she was being transferred from the slab into the coffin, and heard Jorbie close the bottom half gently, could tell he was adjusting the pillow beneath her head and smoothing her dress, readying her, she supposed, for the session in the viewing room. From just above her she could hear his voice coming closer as he leaned down and almost whispered into her ear. "I'm sorry it had to be you, Mrs. Losee. But my Voice commanded me, you see. You weren't ever mean to me. Not the way some of the people in this damned town were. And still are. It was your husband, Quentin, I want to punish, not you." Lutetia Losee heard Jorbie sigh philosophically. "Sometimes, you see, you have to do to one person what you really want to do to someone else. It's the only way you have."

Jorbie stood back and surveyed Mrs. Losee, who, he decided, looked quite good in her box. Simultaneously, he was considering his last statement to her; so much of his life seemed to have been devoted to doing things to one person, when the person he was really trying to get even with was someone else. A lot of the time he wasn't even sure who. A profound statement, therefore, one he'd have to give more thought to.

He turned away and called loudly for Pasteur. It would take both of them to get Mrs. Losee up the narrow stairs to the viewing room; the wake began tomorrow morning.

Then—there was no warning—it happened again. From the coffin the familiar muffled pulsing began beating on his eardrums. As he stared at the coffin the sound grew. Quickly it became deafening. Spinning, Jorbie covered his ears, but, as before, the sound went right through his hands. He yelled at the sound, screaming at it to stop, to leave him alone, to go away, but it kept on growing louder until his whole body throbbed with its pulsing. His eyes swept the room, as if a door or window might provide him with some way to escape from the sound, although he could already guess that the sound would follow him wherever he went. Screaming, he tried to back farther away, running directly into Pasteur. Pasteur had not needed to be called loudly; he had been standing the whole time, just out of sight, around the corner of the little stairway that led to the outside. Carefully, he had remained very quiet, listening in bafflement to Mr. Jorbie talk to the dead 'uns again. The matter troubled him.

"I'm right here, Mr. Jorbie. I been here some time

now. I heerd you talking to Miz. Losee 'n I don't rightly un'erstan' what's going on, Mr. Jorbie."

"You bastard, you stupid bastard," Jorbie screamed, taking out his nerve-shattered rage on his giant assistant. "You've been sneaking around again. Spying on me. You're always spying, just like the rest of them. Waiting to tattle, you cocksucking prick."

"Mr. Jorbie," pleaded Pasteur, his voice whining. "You know that ain't so. I don't tell nobody nothing what you does, you know that." To Pasteur it was an appeal born of agony. Mr. Jorbie sometimes yelled at him, sure, but he'd never yelled at him like this— screaming, it was, really—and Pasteur was confused and hurt. He'd never told anyone about what his god, Mr. Jorbie, did or said. Even if he'd wanted to, no one would have listened to him anyway. "Please, Mr. Jorbie. Believe me, Mr. Jorbie."

Turning away with a disgusted look, Jorbie waved his hand at Pasteur in a gesture of contempt. Yelling at Pasteur seemed to have helped him; the pulsing sound had disappeared.

"Okay," Jorbie said finally, "help me get the old bag upstairs. She weighs a ton."

Happy to be allowed back into the club, Pasteur took the bottom—the heavier—end of the coffin and cheerfully helped carry it up the difficult stairs.

"Move your chair closer to the bed, would you, Angie? I don't want to have to shout this."

Angie was still upstairs with Jorbie's father, Caleb Tenniel. The old man was being as warm and delightful as always, but had suddenly turned serious. When she was close enough for him, he leaned toward her confidentially. Angie didn't know what to expect.

"Look, Angie, I just wanted to tell you how incredibly lucky I think Jorbie is to have a girl like you. He's been a loner, you know, a loner for so many years I was afraid he was never going to open himself up to anyone." Caleb shoved some of the mass of white hair off his face and sipped on his evening drink. "And what an anyone he found! It's awkward to say things like this right to someone's face, but I just want to be sure you know how really superb I think you are, Angie. I don't mean just the thoughtful little things like the books, although I appreciate them more than you'll ever know. I mean, for Jorbie to find a girl who's as wonderfully bright as you are and as attractive at the same time, Jesus, it's like a dream come true for me. You can do him a world of good, Angie; Jorbie's still all locked up inside himself and you seem to bring him out of that."

Angie was blushing so hard she was having a tough time trying to shape her reply into words. She had never been in a position to say such things before. "Well, Mr. Tenniel—I, that is, well, I have to tell you that what I feel for Jorbie—what I mean is—damn! how do I put this without sounding like a schoolgirl?— well, the closeness with Jorbie, it's just the most wonderful thing that's ever happened to me. It's made me happier than anything in my whole life . . . I don't know, I guess what I'm trying to say is . . ." Angie foundered, unable to continue.

Caleb Tenniel smiled and squeezed Angie's hand warmly. "The word you're looking for, I think, Angie, is 'love.' Never be embarrassed for feeling love, Angie."

"You're right, Mr. Tenniel. Love." There, she had said it, Angie told herself. She had finally voiced to someone what she had known herself for some time. The skies had not collapsed. The sun had not exploded, the world had not stopped turning. It was a safe word to use, it was an exciting word to use. After all of these years. And it had taken old Caleb Tenniel to guide her to it. She was suddenly overwhelmed by helpless gratitude to him. "And it goes further than just Jorbie, Mr.

Tenniel. What I mean is—well, suddenly you're like a father to me. My own father, you know—"

Caleb stopped her. "We touched on that the other night, Angie. It's something you just have to put out of you mind. It's one of those tragic things you have to accept in a family—any family. It's sad, it's destructive—but you have to accept it and rise above it. Your poor father is a grown man; the terrible thing he's done to himself, to his life, to you his child, is *his* responsibility, not yours. Live your own life; don't let a child's guilt convince you it's your job to pander to him forever. Alcoholics are forever doing that to the people closest to them. Trading on guilt to get their own way. Please don't make *that* mistake, Angie; you have too much to offer other people."

Angie wondered if what Caleb said was right. Slowly, as if a giant stone were being lifted from her back, she realized it was; her father had played on her pity, on her feeling that, as a daughter, she owed him something, and on her guilt to get her to accept him as he was, making no effort to change himself or get over his problem. Caleb somehow understood this; he seemed to understand everything.

The area of her father, though, remained a sensitive one, and she changed the subject back to Jorbie. She and Mr. Tenniel talked about him for some time—Jorbie was taking forever downstairs—to both of them he was apparently their favorite subject.

Caleb was frank, filling in a thousand little details about his son. But in one area Angie was mystified. "What was he like as a child, Mr. Tenniel? Bright, of course, but—"

"You know," Caleb said, cutting her off and changing the subject, "he was really doing splendidly at Marquette. A genius, some of his professors called him. . . ." Caleb continued in this vein for a while; Angie tried again.

"I don't mean to nose into the past, Mr. Tenniel, but I *do* want to know everything there is to know about Jorbie. It's a subject I can't seem to get enough of. Now, when he was a child . . ."

This time Caleb Tenniel's evasion left no room for doubt. "Incidentally, Angie, I did want to talk about Waugh's *Scoop* with you. It was his first novel, I gather . . ."

The evasion, the refusal to discuss Jorbie's childhood, was uncharacteristic of Caleb. Usually he was so frank and understanding. But this was a subject he would neither explain to her nor be party to discussing. So both of them, fully aware of how blatant an avolation it was, discussed Waugh. *Scoop, Put Out More Flags, Vile Bodies, Officers and Gentlemen*—all the Waugh Angie had so far been able to get from her friend in the library.

And it was Waugh they were still discussing when Jorbie suddenly appeared with his father's dinner. "There's a bonus glass of wine on the tray, Dad. Médoc, '69. Your book recommended it, and, oddly, the store had some. May it amuse *you* with its presumption." Jorbie laughed. So did Caleb. So did Angie. At what, no one was entirely sure.

Later, when she tried to reconstruct it, Angie was never able to put back together precisely how it had happened. They had come into the living room and were sitting alongside each other on the long couch in front of the fireplace. In front of them were two tray-tables with the dinner Jorbie had cooked. Steak again; Jorbie's repertoire was limited. On the coffee table stood the bottle of Médoc.

They were both, Angie seemed to remember, finishing a glass of the red before they attacked the steak, talking about something quite neutral. Angie was determined to stay away from anything that would send Jorbie into one of his dark moods.

Somehow, she didn't know exactly how, the conversation had come to a dead halt. Turning a little, she looked at Jorbie. He was already staring at her. Abruptly, with not a word said, he threw himself the length of the couch and fell upon her, his mouth once again exploring hers, his hands exploring her breasts, between her thighs, her whole body.

His explorations produced waves of shudders in Angie; a little to her own surprise she found she was exploring Jorbie's body as hungrily as he was hers, her hands moving, almost as if driven by some instinct, to the bulge in his trousers, sliding along the thin khaki material and moving it back and forth.

Wordlessly, Jorbie seized her hand and took her upstairs to his room, tiptoeing down the hall so as not to let his father hear. Inside, he locked the door softly, turning around to face Angie with both arms outstretched, a benign smile lighting his face. It began as an instant replay of the couch, only without clothes. Jorbie's hands were everywhere, filling Angie with more thundering waves of ecstasy; she found, once again, that her hands echoed his, running them over the smooth skin of his face and his neck and his shoulders, driven always downward by some primitive animal force. She found a pulsing, bulging vein along his neck; she discovered it was matched by the same kind of vein on his prick. Her mouth brushed the vein on his neck; her mouth swallowed the one on his prick. Her own aggressiveness startled Angie a little; she had imagined herself in the more passive, surrendering role of Victorian novels. The hell with Victorian novels; she was freeing herself from her virginal notions of passion with a man she considered the most sensual, the most loving, the most wonderful in the world.

Once again she found herself startled when Jorbie suddenly gave a breathless little shout and threw himself on top of her. She had always thought this initial entrance would hurt. Perhaps it did. But Angie was so lost in purely physical delight she felt only what she wanted to feel—Jorbie inside her, rising and falling, groaning, panting, moving ever faster. She kept repeating, "I love you, I love you, Jorbie, my God, I love you." Jorbie was so lost in the moment himself he only responded with grunted animal sounds.

The pace quickened; Angie found herself almost losing consciousness as she shook from the pressure of Jorbie inside her, touching some part of her she was unaware she even possessed; her whole body began to shake more wildly, out of control; she could feel Jorbie's legs thrashing against the mattress in an accelerating tattoo. Then, suddenly, he thrust so deeply inside her, her whole being quivered. Angie screamed. Jorbie gave a tight little cry, one that quickly became a sigh. It was over.

Side by side, their hands holding each other's on top of the covers, Jorbie and Angie lay in his great double bed, silent, spent. Nothing was said; nothing needed to be. To Angie, their moments together, so recent her body was still trembling from it, was the final proof. Jorbie must love her as much as she loved him. She had proof, absolute and positive; no man could perform like that unless he, like Angie, was deeply in love. He hadn't said anything, of course; Jorbie was not the kind to, Angie told herself. And perhaps, in spite of all the bravado and expertise, he was just as shy and innocent about sex as she was. Forcing him to say anything— Angie was convinced it would take little more than a direct question—would only make him nervous.

Half sitting up, Jorbie lit himself a cigarette. In the small talk that followed, he let Angie do most of the speaking; he seemed someplace far away, studying the cloud of smoke that rose from his Chesterfield as if it were the only thing on earth.

"Jorbie," Angie said suddenly. "You know, there are so many things I want to know about you that I don't. I know you're a very private person; I understand that. But darling, I want to be part of everything you are or have been, to inhale your past and make it part of my own." Leaning over, Angie borrowed Jorbie's cigarette and took a puff on it. The gesture was almost a physical representation of what she was saying. She loathed cigarette smoke, and promptly disintegrated into a fit of coughing, something that made Jorbie smile.

"But you know," continued Angie, once she had her breath back, "It's the damnedest thing. Your father's told me quite a lot about you, of course, but every time I asked him something about you as a child, he changed the subject. Jorbie, will you tell—?"

Jorbie's reaction was spectacular. He shot out of the bed as if burned. He began pacing back and forth across his room, his hands clenching and unclenching. He appeared to become suddenly aware that he was naked, and angrily yanked the comforter off the bed and wrapped it around himself.

"Jorbie," Angie began again.

He spun on her. "Shut up, you bitch. You're a fucking whore, that's what you are. A cocksucking busybody. Nothing about me is any of your business, for Christ's sake, unless I decide it is. Shit. You're just like the rest of them—spying on me. A mother-fucking spy. Jesus, even that idiot Pasteur is spying on me now."

"I'm not prying, Jorbie. Really I'm not. It's like I told you, I love you so much, anything about you is something I want to know. Jorbie—" Angie was half crying, pleading with him, trying to calm him down. She got nowhere.

"Bitch," he said again and angrily climbed back into

his clothes, turning his naked back toward her as he dressed, as if she were unfit to see anything more of him than that. Without looking at her, he stormed out of the room, slamming the door behind him noisily in spite of his father down the hall, racing for sanctuary in the one place in the building where he knew she would not follow: the downstairs workrooms.

For a while Angie lay where she was, touching the sheets as if some part of Jorbie had stayed behind. It was impossible to figure out, this behavior of his. Usually, Angie had been quick to assume the blame was mostly her own, and that she was stupid for having said this or that. But tonight she had said very little. A few words about his childhood, words she had expected him to take as indication of how much she felt a part of him. There was something wrong, something preying on Jorbie. This man she loved so desperately—and one who, in spite of the explosion at the end, she was now sure loved her—needed some sort of help. *Her* help to understand himself better. To uncover whatever it was inside that made him react so wildly out of proportion.

Swinging her legs over the edge of the bed, Angie was suddenly embarrassed by the thought of her own nakedness in a man's room. Quickly she dressed, appalled at how far and in how many directions Jorbie had managed to throw each piece of her clothing as he had torn them off her.

Standing in front of his mirror, trying to get her hair back into some sort of order, Angie made what was probably the most dangerous decision of her life. She was not going to let things slide along as they were. She promised herself that, somehow, she would discover whatever it was from his past that was torturing this man she loved so deeply.

Chapter Fourteen

I spent a lot of time this morning trying to figure what made Angie leave in such a hurry last night. Hell, I don't understand it at all, but then I was never much at understanding women anyway. What makes it more complicated in this case is that I don't remember too much of what went on just before she left. That's happening to me more and more these days. I only remember what happens, what I say and do, before and after these blank spots.

Last thing I remember she was trying to find out what I was like when I was a kid. Then comes a big blank, and she storms off into the night. Crazy. I must have said or done something mean, but, damn it, Angie was being awful nosy.

What the hell business is it of hers what I was like when I was a kid? I don't understand why the question should bother me the way it does; I was just about like any only child, a little sulky, sure, but making up for it with straight-on charm. That and those damned long, dark eyelashes of mine. I was born knowing how to bat them at just the right moment to get what I wanted.

Angie keeps insisting she's in love with me. Crap. She's in love with the long eyelashes and my even longer dick. I know women and I can smell those things.

Not that I ever had one before—well, I don't count that pathetic old-bag whore in Saginaw that time—but I'm pretty sure I hid that damned well from Angie. She was too busy orgasming all over my sheets to notice anyway.

So why does Angie keep asking me questions about my childhood, damn it? Nosy as hell. Women always are. They'd sure be better off if they'd just act like men,

*something George Bernard Shaw was always saying in
his plays.*

*Except for now and then when it would be damned
awkward.*

> *Jorbie Tenniel—to the rock,
> 11:00 P.M., November 25th*

"But Cathy, I told you not to tell anybody. It's all over
school: even Sister Honorée's heard about it." Cathy
Springer shrugged her shoulders uncomfortably. The
story about Angie hearing Flan's voice was circulating
like a disease.

Angie stood uncomfortably in Sister Honorée's office, trying not to let it show as she shifted her weight
nervously from one foot to the other. She was not there
by choice. A student had come to her classroom half an
hour earlier and told her Sister Honorée wanted to see
her as soon as the period was over.

Sister Honorée had been sitting behind her desk.
Slowly she got up and walked to the window, looking
down at the Straits below St. Etienne for a few minutes.
She turned back toward Angie, gesturing helplessly.
"Well, if that is what you heard, child, that, I suppose,
is what you heard. Until I get some guidance from Father Duval, though, I suggest you minimize the story,
play it down. It is too late to tell you not to say anything to anyone; I gather it is all over school, and, possibly, all over town already."

"I'll try to play it down, Sister, as you put it, but the
story is so unusual, it's not easy."

"I understand, child. That will be all. And thank
you."

"Thank you."

Out in the hall Angie sagged against the wall in relief. She didn't know why any interview with Sister

Honorée always left her exhausted, but she knew she was not alone in this reaction. The Sister did not mean to appear as stern as she did, but somehow always managed to come off as if she were God's personal representative in St. Max.

That, thought Angie, was what St. Max could use just now: a personal representative of God.

Sister Honorée was entirely correct in one prediction: It would only take a few hours before the story was all over town. So correct, in fact, she found it necessary to call Father Duval almost minutes after Angie had left.

The priest was appalled. "Quash the story as much as you can," pleaded Duval, in what was virtually an echo of what Sister Honorée had said to Angie a little earlier.

"That is what I told the lay teacher involved," responded the Sister. "But I'm afraid it is too late to do much good."

"Try." Father Duval muttered to himself and hung up. After the unsatisfactory call to the monseignor, he had toyed with the idea of going around the Jesuit, directly to the bishop himself. He was stopped by fear of what the bishop's reaction would be; God alone knew, it might be similar to the monseignor's. Now, though, Father Duval felt he had no choice and placed the call. After listening stonily, the bishop was obviously thrown; his voice retreated into short, gasping little sentences. "It could be—ah—overwork, Father. I'm aware of how hard some of you parish priests throw yourselves into your assignments."

No, Father Duval pointed out, it could not be explained away by overwork. The boy's family had heard the same voice; so had a lay teacher from St. Etienne.

"We must—ah—discourage them all from any public statements. Discourage them, Father, until we can get a grip on the—ah—situation ourselves. You can appreciate, Father, that we must move very cautiously. Discourage them."

Wearily, Father Duval pointed out that that was only part of the problem. The voice. After all, he had heard Flan Tierney's voice himself, hadn't he?

The bishop became angry. "No, of course I don't mean to say that you didn't—ah—hear the voice. Of course not. It's just that—for the time being, Father, please follow my directives and—ah—discourage the Tierneys. Until we know more." The Bishop wanted to find a better solution, but couldn't; with the edge still firmly in his voice, he gave his order and hung up. For some time Father Duval stared at the receiver in his hand, not relishing his meeting with the Tierneys at all. Hopelessly, he couldn't help wondering if, somewhere along the line, the Bishop might not have been a Jesuit.

Before Hank Tierney and his wife, Dot, had even left for their session with Father Duval, they had already discovered the story was abroad in St. Max. Extensively. In detail. As soon as Dot Tierney learned that someone else—Angie Psalter, of all people—had heard Flan's voice and was talking about it, she saw no reason to keep her promise to Father Duval. Quickly her story joined Angie's report. By the time they got to Our Lady of Misery the whole town was well aware of both versions.

At the church the Tierneys insisted on having their meeting with Father Duval in the confessional. "I had planned to talk to you in my office," argued the priest. "It seems far more fitting. There are rules governing the use of the confessional, you see, and I—"

"We have committed the sin of not believing enough," broke in Dorothy Tierney. "We think perhaps this miracle—Flan's voice—was our Lord's way of showing us our error. That in itself is a miracle too,

Father. But since it grew out of our not believing enough, that is something we must confess to. That's why the confessional seems to us a very fitting place to have our talk, Father." Reluctantly, Duval gave in and led them to the confessional.

By the end of the meeting no one had confessed to anything, and Father Duval felt in following the bishop's orders against his own conscience, it was perhaps he himself who had sinned. "You see, Hank and Dorothy, you have had an unusual experience. But the strain you were under . . ."

Both of the Tierneys, hidden from the priest by the elaborate grillwork, stared at each other, stunned. What Father Duval was saying was so entirely different from what he had said the night before. "That is a vicious charge, Father," argued Dorothy, growing more upset the longer she thought about it. "I heard the voice. *Flan's* voice. What it means is possibly open to question; that I heard it, is not."

"Damn it," joined in Hank Tierney. "I heard it too, Father. I heard it at the same time saying the same things."

"Yes, my children, I realize you *think* you heard poor little Flan's voice, but——" Duval was perspiring behind his grill. Following the bishop's order was becoming increasingly difficult.

"There is no 'but' in this case, Father," snorted a steaming Dorothy Tierney. "And Angie Psalter—she was one of Flan's teachers—heard it too. Are we supposed to believe *she* only thought she heard Flan?"

Father Duval shifted uncomfortably on his hard bench, pursing his lips, searching for something that would allow him to follow both the bishop's orders and the demands of his own conscience. His nose was itching and he desperately wanted to pick it, but restrained himself; in God's house, if your nose itched, it itched. "I can't speak for Angie Psalter; I haven't had a chance

to talk with her yet. However, I can speak for the
Church in saying that, until there is more evidence, it
would be wrong for us to leap to conclusions. This al-
leged miracle will have to meet certain requirements before—"

What was almost a roar came from an infuriated
Hank Tierney. He had never expected the kind of cynical reaction they were getting from Father Duval. "Jesus Christ," he yelled through the grill. "We came here
to confess, to beg forgiveness. You're making us sound
like a pair of criminals. No wonder the Catholic Church
has lost so many parishioners." Grabbing Dorothy by
the hand, he seized the curtain outside the priest's side
of the confessional, threw the heap of dull green cloth
in Duval's face, and stormed out of the church.

Father Duval crossed himself and leaned his head
wearily against the grill. The Tierneys were now capable of saying or doing anything. He raised his head and
prayed for guidance, almost crying in frustration.

"It was all in charts, dear, all in charts. I tried to get
people to listen, but they wouldn't." Her long, skeletal
finger searched for something on her biblical charts and
predictions, but appeared unable to find what she
wanted.

Angie stood in front of her, feeling uncomfortable in
a living room that smelled faintly of lizard skin. Crazy
old Mrs. Lavin always disturbed her a little, but Angie
had a reason for being here. Mrs. Lavin finally found
what she was looking for on the chart. "See, dear, here
it is, just as I told you earlier this week. Flan Tierney's
voice. You heard it yourself, so now you know how accurate my predictions are. Biblically right. Let me take
the fact that you heard the voice, and add that in. You
see, dear, I believe that Flan Tierney's message was a
warning from God, not a promise. Now, then . . ."

The old lady, her lip trembling so hard that the tiny hairs above her mouth appeared to be waving for help, grew sulky when it became obvious that Angie wasn't really all that interested in either her theories or her charts. To Angie, Mrs. Lavin was a walking history of St. Max; stored away in her was all the information anyone could ask about St. Max's citizens, past and present.

"I was wondering, Mrs. Lavin, what you could tell me about Jorbie Tenniel. Or the Tenniel family. *Anything*." Mrs. Lavin gave a petulant sniff and gazed out of her window into the darkened street, determined not to say anything more than she had to. Young people, she told herself. Young people today were so rude. "Tenniel, Tenniel. There was Adelaide Tenniel. She was Caleb's wife, Jorbie's mother. Died. Died young." Ignoring Angie now, Mrs. Lavin returned to her charts, cross-referencing with two different editions of the King James Bible.

"That's a beginning, Mrs. Lavin. She died of . . .?"

With visible annoyance Mrs. Lavin again raised her head from the charts. "I always thought it was malnutrition. Didn't eat enough to keep a hummingbird going, dear. Her figure, she always said. Pretty woman, she was." As if annoyed by having said so much, Mrs. Lavin returned to her work with great concentration.

"Well, all right. What can you tell me about Jorbie Tenniel?"

The head rose again. In spite of her efforts to remain sulking, Mrs. Lavin was unable not to answer any challenge to her memory, legendary in St. Max. "Jorbie Tenniel. Pretty child, but never healthy. Just like his mother." Mrs. Lavin warmed to her subject, even allowing a trace of a fond smile to cross her face. "Jorbie's twin was the same, too. Poor child died. Can't even remember his name."

"His *twin*?" Angie stood planted in front of Mrs. Lavin, thunderstruck. Mrs. Lavin felt better; her prodigious memory has provided her with the thing she enjoyed most in life: a shocked expression.

"*Identical* twin. You couldn't tell those two apart with a microscope. Loved to play games on people, dear, switching their identities, you know. Fooled everyone, every time." Mrs. Lavin was tiring; she didn't try to conceal the yawn from Angie, returning her eyes to her charts.

"Mrs. Lavin, I'd appreciate it terribly if you'd try and remember more about Jorbie Tenniel's twin. It's very—" A sudden gentle snore told her the old lady had passed quietly from the yawn into deep sleep, one long, thin finger still on the chart, set to prove some point or other to Angie. Tiptoeing—although Angie doubted if such an effort was necessary—she checked her watch and walked quickly to her car outside. She was going to be late for her date at Tenniel's mortuary.

Tonight, Angie didn't have to wait long for someone to answer the doorbell. Almost the instant she pressed in the button, the door opened, as if Jorbie had been waiting inside for her. "Hi, hi, hi," he shouted, folding her into his arms as he swept her into the house and began kissing her. He stopped only long enough to look deeply into her eyes and whisper, "I was afraid you were going to be late. So I stood inside the door, counting each second, trying to make the time go faster—like I used to when I was a kid. It never helped much then; it still doesn't."

Angie had never seen Jorbie in such high spirits. He was bubbling with laughter and fun and that lusty, sexual undercurrent that she had never known anyone except him to communicate. "Come on, Angie. Dad's been asking. I've got some more Médoc for him, and for us"—he leaned toward her conspiratorily—"a little champagne." Grabbing her, he virtually dragged her up the stairs to Caleb's room.

The reason behind Jorbie's sudden burst of ebullience remained a mystery to Angie. But a delicious mystery. And one that was all the more noticeable because it represented such a reversal of where Jorbie had left things the night before. The events of last night were something Jorbie seemed to have forgotten completely; Angie chose not to remind him. He seemed almost a different person. As soon as they left Caleb, they decided against dinner, bringing only the champagne upstairs to Jorbie's bedroom.

Twice, as they made love again—more beautifully, Angie decided, even than before—she thought Jorbie was on the verge of saying he loved her. But at the last moment he would change the words to "Christ, I love—your body," or "Jesus, do I love—the way you do that thing with your mouth. It's incredible." It didn't bother her; Angie was wise enough to realize it would be a long time before Jorbie could break himself away from years of being what Caleb described as a "loner," years before he could bring himself to say what he felt.

Earlier, she had told herself her love for him could not possibly grow any stronger. Tonight, it soared. Out into space along with Angie's expectations and dreams. Wisely, she never mentioned what she had learned from old Mrs. Lavin. That would have to be gone into sometime, but not tonight. No, not tonight. Tonight was too perfect to risk spoiling with one of Jorbie's moods.

It was one of the few prudent decisions Angie made about him during the entire time she knew him.

Chapter Fifteen

*I don't know what it is about Angie Psalter that makes
me like her so much. Put the physical stuff aside for a
moment; she's wild in the sack, and that would make
any guy a little nuts over her, I guess.*

*But way beyond that, there's something about Angie
that's terribly familiar and comfortable, something like
I'd been very close to her all my life, which I haven't,
of course. Along with this feeling, though—a warm
wonderful feeling—there's another side to feeling close
to Angie that isn't either warm or wonderful. It's fear. I
can't explain it worth a damn, but every time I realize
how close I'm getting to her, I feel scared. Wobbly, sort
of, as if it was something dangerous. Threatening.
Crazy. I love her, yet the fact scares the hell out of me.*

*None of this means my suspicion that in the end An-
gie will have to go has changed. One day, out of nowhere, my Voice will whisper her name in my ear, and
that'll be that.*

*I hope for old time's sake I'll be able to spare her the
kind of end that Mrs. Losee is being treated to. It's
pretty hideous. Hideous? Just ask Lutetia Losee.*

*Jorbie Tenniel—to the rock,
9:00 A.M., November 26th*

Funeral services were to be held for Lutetia Losee at
eleven that morning. Lutetia had heard this point discussed enough to be sure of that much. She was hopelessly uncertain about anything else. She found it almost
impossible to believe or accept what had been happen-

ing to her for the last few days. Every morning Jorbie Tenniel and that idiot helper of his would take her casket out of the freezer and carry her up to the viewing room; every night, after everyone had left, they'd carry her back downstairs. Once she was in the freezer, Jorbie Tenniel would send his helper off on some assignment and carefully wrap her in an electric blanket, whispering words of encouragement to her. Then he'd shut and lock the freezer, apparently to keep the helper from seeing the blanket. None of that made sense, but then, things had ceased to make sense to Lutetia Losee ever since she keeled over in Quentin's bedroom.

The viewing room was a nightmare for Lutetia. A poignant one, but a nightmare nonetheless. With her eyes closed she could see nothing of her visitors, while, with the coffin top open, the visitors could see everything of her. How her dress looked, everything. She wondered if they could guess she wasn't wearing underclothes. Probably not. The coffin didn't open down that far. Endlessly, all day long, she could hear their voices—her friends, her enemies, all of the people she knew.

Mostly, what she heard them say was kind, a little sad perhaps, but in general, sincere and genuine. When you're dead, it seemed, even people who weren't overly fond of you when you were alive found something good to say about you. Occasionally—and the people it happened with surprised her—a touch of real meanness would creep into someone's words—only, of course, when Quentin had been wheeled out of the room and no one else was around.

"Looks very natural," Florence Dupres had said.

"If you mean frozen and stiff, yes," answered Kate Liverright.

"You shouldn't say things like that, Kate."

"Terrible dress, too. Ugly. But that's fitting enough."

A small gasp had risen from Florence Dupres. "You shouldn't speak ill of the dead, Kate. It's not Christian. And Tish was a good friend of yours, too."

"The only good friend Tish Losee ever had was Tish Losee," sniffed Kate Liverright. There was a small argument between them, which ended when Kate hissed that Quentin was being wheeled into the room again.

Everyone else quickly left. It was those moments alone with Quentin that affected Lutetia Losee the most, affected her and tortured her for her own frailty in leaving him alone while cancer nibbled determinedly at his flesh. Quentin's way of speaking to her was eviscerating to Lutetia—he would talk to her as if she were still alive—and God help her, maybe she was. Haltingly, stumbling, trying so hard to be brave, Quentin kept returning to the days when they were younger, when they'd met, how they'd fallen in love, their hopes, and dreams, shaken by Quentin's sickness, and now, destroyed by her death. Every now and then she could hear him, facing an agonized and lonely terminal year, crying. It was an agony for Lutetia not to be able to do what she had always done their whole married life: comfort him.

Promptly at ten thirty the last handful of remaining visitors were shooed out and Lutetia could feel her casket being carried out of Tenniel's and put in the hearse. Lying down headfirst is an unusual way to travel, and she became obsessed with the idea that she might become carsick. It was an absurd idea, of course. Hadn't everyone said she was dead? Didn't her being in a coffin and driven to a cemetery in the back of a hearse prove it? The thought that she might somehow still be alive came back to terrify her.

At church, even with the lid closed, she could hear the entire service. Father Duval, reciting the words of the service in his usual flat voice. The choir, singing rather well today, Lutetia thought. The congregation singing the hymns Quentin must have picked; mostly, they were her favorites. Even in her present circumstances she wished he hadn't chosen "Rock of Ages." Father Duval, reading a short eulogy praising her years of work for the church, delivered as drearily and tonelessly as ever. The choir again. More prayers. The ringing of the little bell as the Mass drew to its close. The shuffling of feet as the coffin was taken out of the church and loaded back into the Tenniel's hearse for the trip to the cemetery. Minute by minute the terror inside Lutetia Losee grew; the whole thing was, she kept telling herself, a long-winded nightmare. She would wake in her bed, with Quentin beside her.

At the cemetery Lutetia felt herself lifted from the hearse and carried unevenly toward the grave. The casket was placed on the wide green webbing she'd so often seen used at other people's funerals; the ends were wrapped around some sort of chromium rods that lowered the casket slowly into the grave when the moment came. On the webbing, the coffin seemed to tremble and sway in what sounded like a raging wind, blowing mercilessly across the lonely slopes of Carpas Point Cemetery. The wind always seemed to blow in this forlorn spot, adding to the mournfulness of funerals with its moaning sigh. Lutetia hoped Annette—her sister—had talked Quentin out of coming out here; he was too sick to be out in weather like this.

Over the wind Lutetia could hear Father Duval intoning the final prayers for the dead. The Lord's Prayer was said, but the wind swallowed the words of the frigid group around the grave, so Lutetia said it to herself. "Most merciful Father," she heard Duval say, and knew the service was almost over, "who has pleased to take unto Thyself the soul of this, Thy servant . . ." the prayer was finished quickly. The people standing around the grave must be feeling the cold horribly. There was a sudden silence. It was over.

A moment or two later Lutetia could feel the coffin slowly descending into the grave. She heard little clumps of frozen earth strike the top of the wooden box as the onlookers paid their final, personal respects. Lutetia was desperate to scream and shriek and yell at them that she was still alive and for God's sake to get her out of there, but no sound would come from her. In the distance she heard the starting of many engines and knew it was the sound of people leaving Carpas Point for their homes. This was quickly followed by harsh thunder as shovelfuls of dirt were thrown on the lid of her coffin and the grave filled. Lutetia Losee knew it was all over. But was it over, or was it just beginning?

It was some hours later that Lutetia suddenly discovered her sense of feel was returning. She had no way of knowing that it was exactly two and a half hours later, that this was precisely the moment Jorbie's carefully programmed dose of *bonaro* was scheduled to wear off.

Slowly, one after the other, she found she could move her fingers; her eyelids were able to open partially, although there was nothing for her eyes to see. The fingers and eyes were soon followed by her arms, her legs, her head, and finally everything else.

Suddenly, Lutetia realized her voice had returned; the first sound it made was a strangled crying. Her eyes were fully open now, but stared out into a total blackness. The irreversible, terminal dark. The grave.

The awesome terror of what was happening to her finally bludgeoned Lutetia full force. It had been no freakish twist of her mind. No nightmare. No mysterious projection into the future as she lay in a hospital, comatose, waiting for the Angel of Death to arrive and take her. They had buried her alive. The stupid bastards had actually buried her *alive*.

It took a second or two for Lutetia to comprehend what this meant, the horror building up inside of her.

She began screaming and shrieking, her voice tearing at the air inside the coffin, fully aware that no one could hear her, but having to shriek anyway. She pounded on the lid of the casket hysterically, knowing all the while there was no one to hear. Turning herself a little on her side, she kicked at the casket's top, smashing her legs into it until she could feel bruises rising under her skin.

For a moment Lutetia Losee lay still, trying to assess her situation calmly. She realized she was ravenously hungry, but there wasn't much she could do about that. There had to be some way out of here, she thought, but she was damned if she could think how it could be done. If she could somehow move the lid of the coffin a little to one side, perhaps she could dig her way out with her hands. Did they screw on a coffin lid before they buried someone? She had no idea.

Gently at first, trying to keep her self-control so she could attack the problem rationally, she ran her fingers along the edges of the casket, where the satin-covered sides of the coffin met the gathered material of the lid. Lutetia hoped to find something her fingers could grip, but she was unable to discover anything. When she yanked at the material, she could pull it off, the small upholsterer's nails that fastened it landing on the bottom of the casket with strange little *pings*. This, she realized, did nothing but expose the wood beneath. The speed of Lutetia's movements was picking up again as her thin grip on calm slipped away; she tore at the lid with her hands until she could feel the blood running down her fingers. Frantically, Lutetia even tried to bite a grip into the coffin lid with her teeth, but once through the satin, her lips touched a wall of wood. Her lips bled from where the rough unfinished surface bruised them. Losing herself completely to panic again, Lutetia went back to her futile, terrified shrieking, her voice growing raw in her agony.

Suddenly, as if it were right beside her ear, a calm, whispered voice spoke. "Good evening, Mrs. Losee. I hope you're comfortable. At least, as comfortable as anyone in your circumstances *can* be. I have a little proposition to make to you. . . ."

PART II

Chapter Sixteen

When I was still at Marquette—Christ, I miss that place; they treated me like I really amounted to something—I was into genetic engineering. You know, what the layman calls "gene-splicing."

I studied how you can take the randomization out of heredity and order a gene to be just what you want it to be, giving it instructions through its DNA code on what to do, where to do it, and when. Sometimes I feel just like one of those engineered genes—ordered to do things for reasons I don't understand.

My Voice tells me what to do; I do it. Nothing random there. I don't understand why it picks one person to get Captain Marvel's kiss and leaves another alone, but, sure as hell, I don't have anything to say about it. Neither does a gene. And it can't tell its DNA code to go to hell and decide to do something else. Now that I'm used to it, I kind of like it that way.

There's just one thing that still bothers me. I wish the Voice would lay off kids. I know a kid on my slab isn't any different from an adult on my slab, but adults don't bug me as much. Okay, I agree—that doesn't sound like me at all.

Maybe it's because a big part of me never grew up. Maybe there's a lot of kid still in me, trying to relive whatever I was as a child.

Or maybe I'm a sort of Peter Pan. There's a hoot. Peter Pan with a trick ring, a freezer full of stiffs that aren't really so stiff, and cadavers tearing at the insides of their coffins.

I don't suppose I'm exactly what Barrie had in mind.

> *Jorbie Tenniel—to the rock,*
> *11:35 A.M., November 28th*

"First it was Jorbie Tenniel. Now you're hearing voices," Cathy Springer groaned. "Maybe what you need is a damned good rest somewhere."

"You wouldn't find it so funny, Cathy, if you'd been the one to hear Flan's voice."

Cathy tilted her head to one side, studying Angie, pressing her to test how really serious she was about hearing Flan Tierney's voice.

"It *was* Flan's voice, Cathy, and that's all there is to it."

The firmness in Angie's voice told Cathy it was not a subject to be pushed any further. The two of them were sitting in St. Etienne's cafeteria, having their afternoon coffee. This daily ritual had fallen off recently; there was so much going on, they hadn't had a good talk in days. Dropping one sensitive subject, Cathy managed to walk straight into another. "Okay, okay. That's something you're sure of, and it's not up to me to try and change your mind. But it still leaves you with your biggest problem: Jorbie Tenniel."

Cathy was surprised when Angie laughed. Angie was a little startled herself. But by now she was so sure that Jorbie returned her love she didn't have to be tenuous any more. No more tiptoeing. People who didn't see it themselves, Angie told herself, were to be pitied, not gotten mad at. It was the sudden blossoming of total self-confidence, something Angie, until now, had never experienced in her whole life.

"Cathy, I just wish I could explain it all to you. Jor-

bie's no problem. He's the most wonderful thing that
ever happened to me. He's changed how I feel about
everything. My God, when I'm in his arms, it's, well,
it's like being in a whole other world." She looked at
Cathy for a second. "I don't want you to take this
wrong—how you feel about Jorbie is no secret—but I
just hope some day you experience something as intimate, something as breathtaking, as I do every time I—
let me put this gently—every time I 'see' him."

A pained expression had crossed Cathy's face. "Angie, I hope—"

"There's nothing to use a word like 'hope' about. It's
a fact. I love Jorbie, he loves me. And I don't give a
damn what you or anyone else thinks about it. I don't
know why you're so dead set against Jorbie, but if that's
the way you feel, that's the way you feel. For myself, I
don't want to even hear your reasons. I know everything there is to know about Jorbie (*a lie, a lie, how
could I tell such a lie?*) and he knows everything there
is to know about me. It's like I've been close to him all
my life. Nothing held back, nothing hidden, nothing
mysterious. Only a wonderful openness between us. I'm
sorry, Cath, if you've never experienced what I have
now . . . love. Deep, deep love . . ."

As she spoke Angie could not help listening to herself. She was a little shocked at what she heard. Her
tone with Cathy, her oldest and closest friend, was su-
percilious, fringed with a condescending pity. Worse,
Angie was aware she was being far short of honest.
That she was editing out a great deal when she talked
of how she and Jorbie had no secrets. To Cathy, she
had never mentioned the mysterious identical twin—
any more than Jorbie had to her. To Cathy, she had
never mentioned the dark moods and the wild swings of
disposition that came and went without apparent reason, or how Jorbie's reactions could sometimes border
on violence.

When Angie asked herself why she left these facets unspoken, she realized it was because she wanted everything to sound perfect for Cathy. To herself— secrets, moods, violence, and all—it *was* very nearly perfect, but she was idealizing the relationship so that Cathy could better understand why it was she felt so deeply.

When she was through talking, Angie became aware there was one thing she hadn't been able to edit out; Cathy's expression told Agnie the fact was already as clear to her friend as if it had been blazoned across the sky in ten-foot letters. "Are you sleeping with him?" Cathy asked bluntly.

"It's none of your business, Cathy. But, yes, I am."

"Oh, Jesus."

Angie shrugged. She suddenly found that far from being embarrassed, she was almost proud. To have someone as handsome and bright and wonderful as Jorbie Tenniel bedding you was a fact that any girl— particularly one as emotionally starved as Angie— wanted to shout from the narrow-minded housetops of St. Max. "How could all you smug people," she would bellow at them, "ever have allowed me, little Angie Psalter, to steal someone as fabulous as Jorbie right out from under your noses? How could you let someone like me be the girl Jorbie sleeps with, the girl he becomes involved with, the girl he'll probably spend his life with? God damn, but you're stupid! Stupid, all of you!"

Cathy's face had grown longer and more troubled. "Angie, we've been friends since the beginning of time. But I realize that still doesn't make what you do with Jorbie any of my business. . . ."

"That's right, none of your business."

"And I promised myself I wouldn't try to interfere. That's a fast way to lose a friend. But, look, Angie. I've told you before I thought this thing with Jorbie was—

well—dangerous. There's something really screwed up with that guy, I don't know what, but it's there. And shacking up with him only raises the stakes. Damn it, Angie, the closer you get to Jorbie, the more danger you're in. . . ."

It's a pity Cathy didn't pursue this line of thought more aggressively. If she had, maybe Angie would finally have recognized the growing jeopardy Jorbie was putting her in. But, face to face with Angie, so pathetically eager, Cathy could feel her resolve melt away, making only one final effort to sway Angie before giving up for good. "Can't you see what I mean, Angie?" she asked, her eyes locking with Angie's. "Can't you get out while you're still all in one piece?"

Something inside Angie suddenly robbed her of her composure. Along with the composure went reason. "Damn it, Cathy," Angie said, spilling coffee all over the table as she stood up abruptly. "I think you're jealous, that's what I think. Jealous because you can't stand the idea of your friend, poor little Angie, leaping into bed with anyone as attractive as Jorbie. And that anyone like Jorbie would ask her to. Jealousy is a terrible thing to discover in someone I've known as long as I've known you. You don't have anybody, so I'm not supposed to either. Some friend! I thought you were above that."

Cathy was so stunned by Angie's irrational attack and the harsh tone in which she delivered it, that she could only stare at her friend, unable to speak. She struggled to find something to say, but Angie had turned on her heel and walked out of the cafeteria before she could get a word out.

Angie never even turned around. Somehow the fight had left her oddly euphoric. It had not changed Cathy's mind; it had not changed her own. And Cathy was an old and valued friend, someone who had stood by her over the years. She knew she should have felt saddened by the argument, but she didn't.

Perhaps, she told herself, it was because for the first time in her life, she had a Jorbie to defend.

The ties were uneven, the ballast scattered, and the tracks loose and badly rusted. Yet the spur that ran from Charlevoix down the coast to Grand Rapids was still in operation. At one time, before the giant trucks had stolen most of the freight business, the spur had been heavily traveled. In those times the line could boast almost a dozen trains a day. Business had steadily dwindled, and now it was an unusual day when more than two trains made the run.

Jorbie tripped over one of the ties and swore; Pasteur, walking beside him, grabbed Jorbie's arm to steady him. For his effort he received an icy stare from Mr. Jorbie and a chilly reminder. "For Christ's sake, Pasteur, I'm not a hundred and two—yet."

Pasteur giggled. He wasn't sure that was what was expected of him or whether he was to take Mr. Jorbie seriously; his days were filled with the agony of trying to please Mr. Jorbie, not always successfully. On this occasion he received no reaction at all and decided that his giggle had been what was expected.

A few paces farther on, Jorbie turned around, planted himself in the center of the decayed roadbed, and faced Pasteur. "I think you're trying to irritate me on purpose, Pasteur. Giggling instead of keeping your mind on what you have to do this afternoon." Pasteur watched as Jorbie started forward again, stunned and hurt by the sudden attack, but not wanting to get Mr. Jorbie any angrier by arguing with him about its unfairness. Jorbie stopped again, just as Pasteur had started walking forward, and once more faced him. "I know you don't like what you're going to have to do. I don't really like it myself. But it has to be done, and that's all there is to it."

The statement was entirely accurate. Jorbie didn't look forward to what lay ahead, and he knew that Pasteur dreaded it. He also knew that, in the end, Pasteur would grudgingly do anything that he commanded. To soften the resistance, Jorbie began talking to Pasteur, something he knew Pasteur loved, even if Jorbie was actually talking largely to himself, and though Pasteur would understand little of what he said.

The subject he found himself talking to Pasteur about surprised Jorbie. He had not intended a conversation with anyone on this topic; it just sort of slipped out.

"You know," Jorbie heard himself say, "there's this weird, crazy feeling I get every time I see Angie Psalter. Well, not *every time,* but most of the time. See, it's a feeling like I'd known her before somewhere. And was very close to her. Really *close.* And when I get this feeling, I keep thinking like she was in some terrible kind of danger. And I tried to save her, only instead of saving her, I made the whole thing worse. It was me, see, that put her in danger in the first place. I swear to God, Angie really *does* remind me of someone, and so does the spot I put her in, but I'm damned if I can remember who or what; it's all just very familiar. Damn, but it's weird, you know?"

No, Pasteur didn't know. He didn't understand one word of what Mr. Jorbie was saying, but was enormously pleased that Mr. Jorbie was confiding in him. It never occurred to him that since Mr. Jorbie was really only talking to himself, he didn't expect him to understand, or that Jorbie would never for one moment have gone into the subject if he thought Pasteur *did* understand.

Warmed by Mr. Jorbie's palliative of talking to him

as he would to a card-carrying member of St. Max, Pasteur shuffled happily along beside him, once even doing a little skip that made him lose his balance and caused Jorbie to laugh. Pasteur grinned shyly; even though the joke was at his own expense, that he had made Mr. Jorbie laugh left Pasteur beside himself with delight. The warmth he felt for Mr. Jorbie overcame any remaining reluctance to undertake what lay ahead.

"Right here," said Pasteur. "It's the best place. He should be here in about ten minutes." Officiously, Pasteur rechecked his wristwatch, a cheap Timex Jorbie had given him last year.

"You sure, Pasteur?"

"Yes sir, Mr. Jorbie. I checked him yesterday and the day afore. He always gets here about this time." Proudly, he checked the watch again; it was the most wonderful present anyone had ever given him.

Ahead of them on the tracks was the old railroad trestle, far above Lake Waloon, spanning the narrow inlet the small river made on its way to the lake. The undergrowth on either side of the tracks was dense; it was a perfect place to lay in wait for someone. Even Jorbie was impressed. "You picked a good spot, Pasteur: the undergrowth on this side, and ahead, the trestle. Very good."

Pasteur tingled all over with pleasure at the unusual compliment from Jorbie. Perhaps he was rising in Mr. Jorbie's esteem. "Yessir," he mumbled, too happy to say more.

"I'll go down the tracks about twenty yards or so and hide in that junk growing on the left side of the tracks. You go across the trestle and wait, out of sight, on the other side. When you hear me talking, you'll know it's time to come out of hiding."

Pasteur lumbered over the old trestle, shaking loose dirt and rust and chips of wood as he went; the trestle, like the rest of the roadbed, was in such a state of decay the trains forced to use it rarely did anything much over five miles an hour.

On his side of the trestle, Jorbie picked the likeliest-looking gap in the undergrowth beside the tracks and stepped off the roadbed; briars and loose branches tore at his clothes; a small swarm of gnats appeared from nowhere and began buzzing around his face. Every third breath had to be followed by a wave of his hand or a slap. But the spot was well chosen, perhaps twenty feet short of the trestle. A perfect spot for an ambush. Grudgingly, Jorbie again had to agree with Pasteur's choice of location. Glumly, he pushed on into the undergrowth to wait.

So much of his life seemed spent waiting like this, waiting for someone to come, waiting to do what had to be done, waiting for some vague, indefinable thing to happen. An image of angry, familiar water flashed across his mind, taking him by surprise, making him stiffen. Along with the water, a familiar face he couldn't identify. The face, the water . . . the face, the water . . . the face, the water . . .

In his ears a sudden, terrible pulsing, a muffled throb that made his whole being tremble, seizing him, shaking him, savaging him, forcing him to the brink of crying out in pain. Jorbie swayed back and forth as he struggled against the sound. Covering his ears did no good; the pulsing grew louder inside his brain, exploding against his eardrums.

Suddenly he heard himself scream, unable to control himself any longer; in some distant corner of awareness he realized that Pasteur would eventually hear his screaming and come running. Jorbie threw himself on the ground and buried his face in the loose dirt to stifle his cries. In panic, he dug his fingernails into the palms of his hands—pushed them so deep he could feel blood oozing where the skin was punctured. The pain in his hands overcame the pain in his ears; slowly, the throbbing subsided. Brushing the dirt off his face, he raised himself off the ground a little and blinked at the sounds and smells of the early twilight.

That was the trouble with waiting like this; it gave you too much time to imagine things.

Peter Berringer was feeling good. Several people—including Miss Psalter—had complimented him today on his singing in the rehearsal for *The Messiah;* he had received many congratulations for his work on "Tender Shepherd" at Flan Tierney's funeral. This morning he'd gotten a B on the math quiz, and he usually only had a C or worse to bring home to his father. His old man, Whale Berringer, was a tough man on math marks, but then he was in insurance, where they used that kind of crap a lot.

Maybe he was a little too pleased with himself, Peter decided a moment later when he tripped over one of the rotted ties and almost fell.

Up ahead, he could just make out the old trestle across the inlet to Lake Waloon. He shifted his backpack. It was the one part of the shortcut Peter didn't like. He wasn't supposed to take it at all, but his house was on the last leg of the school bus's circuit, and taking the shortcut meant he didn't have to waste time taking the stupid old bus at all.

It was a forbidden route, of course. His mother had pointed out it was a deserted, lonely walk all the way and if he tripped and hurt himself, no one could hear him. Then, she added, there was the matter of the trestle: rotten, ready to go any minute, very far above ground and thoroughly unsafe. Grown-ups were always saying things like that; it was a conspiracy. He had nodded and promised. Who *wouldn't* accept the promise of someone like himself, with the smile of a cherub and the voice of an angel?

And kept right on taking the shortcut. Every day. Sometimes one of the other kids who lived near his house would join him on his shortcut, but they had all been forbidden to use it too, and rarely flew in the face of the rule. They'd get caught, sure. Probably, Peter decided, because they had neither the cherub's smile nor the angel's voice.

The trestle was dead ahead of him. To face the unpleasant—crossing it—Peter began whistling a tune that was a strange blend of "Tender Shepherd," Handel's *Messiah,* and "Bad Girl, Bad Girl."

The boy felt his heart leap when the man suddenly stepped out of the heavy undergrowth alongside the right side of the track. "Hi, Peter," said the man pleasantly enough, smiling and giving Peter a small, friendly wave of his hand.

"Uh—hi." It was Mr. Tenniel. Peter knew him by sight. Everybody in St. Max knew him by sight; he was the town's undertaker. Peter's first reaction was a desperate desire to run back along the tracks as fast as he could go; there was something terribly frightening about an undertaker popping out of the bushes at you like that.

Mr. Tenniel held up some rocks he had in his hands; Pasteur had learned in town that the boy's hobby was rock-collecting. "Hope I didn't startle you, Peter. I've been following some lignite formations through the underbrush. They're all over this part of the country. Quite remarkable."

Peter's inclination was still to run like hell—he wasn't sure why—but his eyes were drawn to the specimens the man held in his hands. Maybe Mr. Tenniel would let him have one for himself. Still, Peter remained uneasy. The man had moved all the way out onto the middle of the tracks, which made his original temptation to run back the way he came impossible.

His eyes glued to the handful of rocks, Peter uncertainly moved closer to see what Mr. Tenniel was talking about.

"See, Peter," the man began, "this one's metamorphic, this one's sedimentary. You often find them grouped . . ."

The man had placed a hand on Peter's shoulder as he talked. The boy's interest in the igneous, sedimentary, and metamorphic vanished before some vague dread he could not put a name to. Peter Berringer bolted. He could not run the way he had come; Mr. Tenniel blocked that path. With a little yelp of fright, Peter realized there was only one route remaining open to him: *up* the tracks in the direction of the trestle. Dimly he was aware someone now stood at the other end of the trestle as well. He ran toward it anyway.

"Head him off at the end of the trestle," Jorbie yelled at Pasteur. "Quick! He's coming over now."

The boy stopped halfway across, thoroughly terrified but unsure of which direction to run. At one end of the trestle, behind him, was Jorbie; at the other, what appeared a giant. Twice, Peter made a start in the other direction; twice, he stopped, aware he was trapped between the men.

"What's wrong, Peter?" asked Jorbie solicitously. "Just stay calm; no one's going to hurt you." Slowly, Peter saw that the two men were closing in on him from opposite directions. Turning on the ties suspending the track over the ravine, Peter ran a few steps toward Jorbie, who kept up a reassuring flow of words. As Jorbie drew closer Peter turned and ran a few steps toward Pasteur, who seemed farther away. Peter's foot tripped on one of the half-rotten ties, making his whole body teeter from one side to the other.

"Grab him, Pasteur," yelled Jorbie. "Grab him or he'll go over the edge."

Just as Peter Berringer lost his balance and looked as if he might plunge over the side of the trestle, Pasteur took one giant step forward and folded the boy into a great bear-hug.

Peter began screaming, struggling and wrestling in Pasteur's arms so frantically, Pasteur had a hard time keeping his own balance. Jorbie trotted across the rotted bridge ties and joined him; together they were able to carry the terrified boy off the trestle and down the steep sides of the ravine to the stream running beneath the trestle. Winded, Pasteur sat on Peter Berringer's chest to hold him in place, a weight so heavy it took what was left of the boy's breath away.

For a moment they rested, then: "Pull down his pants, Pasteur. Pull 'em down and turn him over." Hearing Jorbie's order, the breathless Peter Berringer suddenly began his frantic struggles again; he'd *heard* about men like that. "Nothing to get upset about, Peter," said Jorbie with a reassuring little laugh. "Just a little pinprick."

The *ping* of Captain Marvel was never even heard by Peter; he found his pants being replaced and the belt buckled. Held flat on the ground, he lay staring up at Jorbie, baffled and terrified, unsure of what was coming next but sure *something* was.

His instincts were correct. Jorbie was well aware that he couldn't afford another accidental death unless it really looked like an accident. "I'll hold him," he told Pasteur, "you do it where I told you. Right there, then up here. Press backward. It'll take both of us for the shoulder thing."

Pasteur grimaced and grabbed hold of the places Jorbie had showed him, pressing backward until there was a sickening crunch followed by a snap. Peter screamed in agony as the bones broke, one after the other. He had passed out by the time Pasteur and Jorbie seized his left shoulder and twisted it until Jorbie could hear the muscles inside rip and bones separate.

Pasteur felt sick. As so often with things Jorbie told him to do, he knew even as he did them that they were wrong. But he worshiped at Jorbie's altar, and what his god commanded was a mission he was required to perform.

Slowly, Peter began to regain consciousness. His struggles were no longer very effective; one fractured leg, one arm broken in two places, and a separated shoulder hurt so much he could barely move, much less fight. "Rip his clothes, Pasteur; scratch his face—this briarbush should do it about right—and put a lot of dirt on him." The helpless Peter watched in confusion as Pasteur ripped his clothes and scratched his face and began taking dirt and rubbing it into his face and hands and anyplace else where skin was visible. Dimly he watched as Jorbie Tenniel yanked one still-tied sneaker off his left foot and threw it some distance from where he lay. The shock was wearing off, and Peter began crying loudly; there was something so final in the way his sneaker was thrown away, as if it were nothing he would ever have need of again. The crying seemed to irritate Jorbie. "Damn it, Angie, shut up," he yelled at Peter. Pasteur looked up, confused, and Jorbie began to laugh at himself. The slip was funny.

Quickly he began rubbing more dirt into Peter's face, afraid the boy's tears might be streaking Peter's dirt makeup job. Again he laughed, this time a little hollowly. Calling the mess of dirt, earth, and grime on Peter's face a makeup job was as crazy as calling Peter Angie. Finally, Jorbie stood up.

Looking at Peter, he knew he made a very convincing accident victim. The touch of the still-laced-up single sneaker would dramatize the force of the impact; the fractures and breaks were about what a boy would receive falling from the trestle into the ravine. The per-

fect finishing touch struck him. Slipping Peter's backpack off him, he scrambled up the ravine and back onto
the trestle. The backpack was left there, its top flap
open, revealing his thermos and some bunched-up wax
paper Peter's luncheon sandwiches had come wrapped
in. Simple, sad scenario: Boy stops halfway across trestle to finish one of his sandwiches or have leftover
Hi-C. Boy fascinated by something he sees below, or tries
balancing on trestle tracks. Boy loses balance and
plunges over side. Backpack remains where he put it
down. Tragic. Deplorable. The mournful hazards of
youth. One more candidate for Tenniel's.

One eye still appraising the job done on Peter, Jorbie
turned to Pasteur. "The *bonaro* will take in about another hour. Until then, you stay here and make sure he
doesn't try to crawl away. Then come back to the mortuary." Jorbie leaned down toward the moaning Peter.
"Sorry we had to hurt you, Peter. But that's the way
it goes. You have a pretty voice; too bad no one will
ever hear it again. Singing, anyway."

Chapter Seventeen

My old man used to have a sister—Prudence Tenniel, I think her name was. There's not a whole lot I remember about old Aunt Prudence, except that she was so superstitious it drove everyone crazy. Raw knuckles from knocking on wood. Could spot ladders to walk around half a mile away. Finally fell over dead one day when a black cat sauntered in front of her.

Looking back, I don't know if this proves her superstitions were right all along, or whether it just means you can worry yourself into an early grave worrying about them. Aunt Prudence was the only person who really knew, and she wasn't saying much at the time.

I never had a damned thing against poor Peter. Or his father, Whale Berringer, either. Yet here I am, doing what the Voice says, and about to bury Peter alive.

More and more the Voice seems to be telling me what to do, and that worries me a little—like it, instead of me, was in charge of my life. Hell, before I know it, the Voice will be ordering me to bury Angie alive. I don't think I'd like that.

I don't want to get superstitious like poor old Prudence Tenniel, but I have a terrible suspicion that's just what's going to happen.

> *Jorbie Tenniel—to the rock,*
> *8:00 A.M., November 29th*

Peter Berringer's body was not discovered until 5:12 A.M. the following morning. There were lights going all night at the Berringer's when he didn't get home from school the afternoon before, and Hardy Remarque's car parked out in front, and a lot of cars with friends of the Berringer's coming and going all night.

Ordinarily, Hardy Remarque might have suspected the boy had run away, but Peter was a model child, always obedient, and simply not the kind of boy who'd get involved with something like that. He did a lot of telephoning of Peter's friends' families during the first rush of fear, but no one seemed to remember anything except that they'd seen him leave school and head for home.

Hardy Remarque still probably wouldn't have called in the Michigan State Police, but he was a man with what he'd once described as "a very acute sense of foreboding." At the moment, all of his antennae were quivering. Or perhaps, like Jorbie Tenniel's Aunt Prudence, he was merely superstitious. Weighing far more heavily on his mind than either was that he had to leave and make the 150-mile drive to Grand Rapids early in the morning. Due there, for Christ's sake, to make a court appearance. He couldn't beg off, yet he didn't feel he could leave without someone's being put in charge.

Reluctantly, at 3:15 A.M., Hardy Remarque called in the state troopers. Almost immediately they descended on the Berringer house, their flashing red-and-white strobe lights adding to the confusion outside the house. After a brief conversation with their sergeant, Remarque left to grab a half hour of sleep before his scheduled departure time, 4:00 A.M.

The state police covered much of the same ground with the Berringers that Hardy Remarque had, but considerably more brutally. Peter's friends, already wakened once, were wakened again—and this time with considerably more results. One towheaded boy, intimidated by the police uniforms and the incredible lateness of the hour, finally admitted he thought Peter had probably taken the shortcut home, walking the old railroad tracks. The poor scared boy admitted he hadn't mentioned it to Hardy Remarque because he didn't want to get Peter in trouble with his family. Peter, he added, did it almost every day.

Two state troopers with heavy flashlights began tracking their way along the same route. Peter's backpack was quickly discovered still sitting in the center of the trestle.

"Down here, down here," called up one of the troopers. "I found him. Shit, what a mess. Right off the trestle. The poor kid."

The radio brought a small armada of state police cars, a police sergeant, Dr. L'Eveque, and a makeshift ambulance, lighting up the bleak wilderness around Lake Waloon as brightly as the Berringer's house had been earlier. The sergeant's report summed up the official police view succinctly:

REPORT OF THE DEATH

29 Nov

Body discovered 4:15 A.M., near track marker 212.

DECEASED: child, white male, approx eleven years of age.

MANNER OF DEATH: Victim, Peter Berringer, fell from RR trestle over inlet to Lake Waloon on way home from school. Backpack discovered on trestle; deceased and one sneaker found in ravine below. Deceased's clothes and skin torn and dirtied by impact; evidence of broken bones, contusions, and other body damage consistent with height of fall (see Medical Report filed by ME, Dr. Harvey L'Eveque, attached).

CONCLUSION: Peter Berringer lost balance while
playing on RR trestle and fell to death. No reason
to suspect foul play.   —

/s/Robert M. Granger,
SERGEANT, #033124,
Michigan State Police,
Area Twelve.

Dr. L'Eveque's report said pretty much the same
thing, except it was packed with medical jargon. "Suffered separate breaks of the fibula and the ulna of the
right forearm, compound multiple fracture of the right
upper leg, and complete separation of the left shoulder." L'Eveque added that Peter's head bore indications of further severe trauma, but less than you might
expect involving a fall from so great a height. Otherwise, he knew the boy to have been in good health at
the time of his death; he, Dr. L'Eveque, had given him
his annual physical only a few weeks earlier. The sover-
ign State of Michigan had spoken; by 9:00 A.M. the
body was already at Tenniel's. There the body awaited
for Jorbie's personal Voice to speak. Everyone appeared saddened, but satisfied; only crazy old Mrs.
Lavin demurred. Peter Berringer's death, she complained, could not be found anywhere on her predictive
Bible charts. No one—not even Mrs. Lavin herself—
appeared anxious to press the point.

"Hi, Mae; Hardy. Sorry I couldn't call earlier.
Damned courthouse has ten thousand lawyers and
maybe two phone booths."
Mae Evers was the lady with a tie-line to Hardy
Remarque's office; when Hardy Remarque wasn't in
his office to pick up the phone himself, Mae Evers did,
taking messages, relaying them, and, in an emergency,
tracking the police chief down wherever he was. And

by listening in to his calls even when he *was* there, she probably knew more of what was going on in St. Max than anyone else—including Mrs. Lavin.

"They found Peter Berringer, Hardy. Under the old railroad trestle. Dead. Fall tore him up pretty bad, I hear from them what saw him."

"Damn. Kids always take that crazy shortcut. Been doing it for years. It's a menace." Hardy Remarque's voice made this pronouncement as if the matter were all settled. Inside, doubt still gnawed. He wanted to believe it was a simple accident—he *had* to believe it was a simple accident—but something kept tugging at his self-proclaimed sense of foreboding, a dull twinge, like a toothache that hasn't happened yet.

"Kids," said Mae, as if the word must explain everything.

"Look, Mae, I should be there. Not that there's much I can do, but I should be there." (The tooth was aching openly now, throbbing in full fierceness, burrowing into Hardy Remarque's consciousness and demanding to be acknowledged.) "See, Mae," continued Hardy, still trying to ignore the ache, "See, court's running way behind schedule. I haven't even been inside a courtroom yet. Grand Rapids is like any other big town—all screwed up. Anyway, I won't get back until at least late tonight, and maybe not even then. Damn, I should be there. There's something all wrong going on in town."

"Don't worry, Hardy," soothed Mae, more than delighted to continue as principal conduit between St. Max and its police chief. "Nothing you could do here anyway. We'll keep the place calm until you can get back."

Hardy grunted and, a moment later, hung up. The damned ache his foreboding represented would not go away. Not yet, anyway. Or maybe he was just being silly.

Neither he nor Mae Evers, tie-line and all, were aware that the foundation for more trouble had already been laid the previous evening.

The first thing Father Duval had heard was a weeping voice. It belonged to a man, but the voice was crying so hard, intermittently racked by sobs, that Father Duval's repeated "Yes? What is it? *Yes*?" produced nothing. Finally, with apparent great effort, the man's voice on the other end of Duval's line had brought itself under some semblance of control.

"It was Lutetia, Father. I heard her. It sounds crazy, but I heard her. Somewhere in the house. . . ."

Inwardly, Duval sighed. "I see." The bishop's orders flashed through his mind and stopped him from saying what he wanted to say. "Well, Quentin, sometimes under the kind of strain you've been suffering . . ."

Quentin Losee suddenly appeared totally in control of himself. In control, and not to be put off by vague allusions that there could be some mistake. "Damn it, Father, it was Lutetia's voice, and that's all there is to it." For a moment, silence. Quentin Losee was apparently considering some additional point, one that he wasn't overly anxious to go into with Father Duval. "She even called me by her pet name, Father. 'Quint.' See, we saw *Jaws* together a couple of years back, and she claimed I looked just like Quint in the movie." Another pause. "I don't think anyone in the world except Lutetia and I knew about that name."

"I see," repeated Duval. It was an inadequate response to what the man on the other end of the phone was trying to tell him, and the man knew it. Father Duval knew it. Everybody knew it except that damned monsignor and his bishop in Detroit. After he'd done his best to comfort the bewildered and upset Quentin Losee, Duval lay back in his bed and considered calling the bishop again. No, not yet. The recollection of the bishop's reaction to his last call was still too fresh in his mind.

Father Duval had thumped his pillows and drunk a little water and done his almighty best to get back to sleep, but still lay there half an hour later, tossing from one side to the other, endlessly pursuing sleep that would not come.

Suddenly the Father sat bolt upright in bed. There was no getting around it. Lutetia Losee was speaking to *him* now, speaking to him just as Flan Tierney had, from somewhere inside the rectory. He could no longer argue with Quentin. It was unquestionably Lutetia's voice; he knew it well from the many church committees she served on. At least twice a week Lutetia Losee's voice drummed in his ears from down at the far end of the table in the rectory's meeting room.

"Father Duval . . . Father Duval . . ." the voice kept repeating. "I mentioned to you at the lay meeting earlier this week that something seemed to be holding you back from expressing what you really believed about poor little Flan Tierney's voice—as if someone had forbidden you to speak your mind."

Lutetia then repeated pretty much what Flan Tierney had said about life after death. Toward the end her voice seemed to change and she added a new and sinister note, far different from anything Flan had said. "If you believe in the voices, Father, speak your mind. Speak loudly and clearly. You must obey in this, Father, or you will be punished, as some already have been."

Lutetia's voice sank even lower into what was a whispered threat. "There are others in this town to be disposed of, too," she continued in a hoarse, sibilant moan. "There is another woman—a young woman, but an important woman . . . a molder of children's minds . . . sad, but necessary . . . for just because I carry to *you* the message of life after death does not necessarily mean that those who disobey will enjoy the afterlife they imagine. For them, it will be an existence so awesomely terrible it defies description. For them, it will be life not in Heaven but one buried deep in the ground, lying there screaming, pounding the sides of their coffins for someone to help them. No one will hear them; no one will help them.

"Speak out, Father. Obey . . . obey . . ." Lutetia Losee's voice faded into a sinister silence.

Duval found he was shaking all over. There *had* been a discussion about Flan Tierney's voice at the last lay church meeting, one that he had ached to join. But the bishop's instructions had silenced him. Lutetia Losee's voice, with her knowledge of that meeting and her plea—no, her *order*—to "speak his mind" was too compelling to write off.

The priest struggled with the ominous warning in Lutetia's message to him. Obey or be punished. For what? To be punished like the others had been. And who was the young, important woman who was threatened . . . "a molder of children's minds . . . sad, but necessary." No one could describe Sister Honorée as young, but that's who it otherwise sounded like. Who then? Who? To lie beneath the ground, screaming, pounding on her coffin for help that would never come. A shudder ran through him. There were too many questions here he could not answer; he needed the help of the diocese.

Duval had one hand already on the phone to call his bishop—in spite of everything, he would call his damned superior-sounding vicar to tell him what was happening and ask for help—when the phone rang beneath his hand.

The sudden sound sent a wave of electricity through Duval. He picked up the phone halfway through its first ring and almost barked into the receiver. It was Lutetia's sister, Annette, in Alpena.

"Father," she had said, "I know you're going to think I'm losing my marbles, but I just heard—"

"Lutetia's voice."

Stunned silence. . . .

Stunned silence. Duval realized he had flown directly in the face of the bishop's orders, and struggled to regain his composure. "What does it mean, Father? What does it all mean?" Annette had asked anxiously. "And now Lutetia says there's going to be another woman punished—buried alive is more what it sounds like. A shaper of children's minds—anyway, something like that, Lutetia said. Who is that supposed to be, Father? Sister Honorée? My God, it could be any mother in St. Max. Horrible, just horrible. Who—do *you* know who she's talking about, Father? What—"

Following the bishop's orders again, back now in control of himself, Father Duval clucked along noncommitally as Annette described a one-way conversation that Duval was already too familiar with. He took a middle position, one neither strongly for nor strongly against believing in the voices. Amy had argued. Duval had countered. Furious, she finally hung up on him in an angry explosion of derision.

Wearily, Father Duval threw his legs over the edge of the bed. The identity of the poor woman Lutetia had mentioned—the molder of children's minds—bothered him, too. There was no point trying to get back to sleep; too much was going through his mind. Wide awake, Father Duval once again had slipped downstairs to his library, searching his books for more instances of the dead speaking to the living. There were many. Lutetia's voice, like Flan's before it, appeared a genuine miracle. The Miracle of the Voices. He was still in his library when the housekeeper came in the next morn-

ing. For an instant she studied his tired eyes and un-
shaven face before she fled to a distant corner of the
rectory. Something was going on in this house—all over
St. Max, in fact—that she neither understood nor particularly wanted to understand. The devil could speak
with many voices. Why not the dead's?

While more and more people heard the Miracle of
the Voices, they remained blind to the danger it
threatened them all with. For both Flan Tierney and
Lutetia Losee shared something in common: They were
intimately related to someone who had been on the
beach the day Jorbie's twin drowned.

And even if the townspeople *had* noticed the coinci-
dence, they probably would have written it off to sheer
happenstance. The town of St. Max was too intrigued by
the Miracle of the Voices to pay attention to such grim
details.

Even though Angie had heard Lutetia Losee's voice
and its threat, the last thing in the world that would
have occurred to her was that *she* was the woman mentioned in Lutetia's warning. This, even though Angie
herself had been on the beach that September afternoon, playing with her kindergarten class from St.
Etienne. But she had been too young to remember.

Even later, when the succession of deaths had mushroomed—still hewing to the same pattern—no one in
St. Max saw the connection. Someone was clearly determined to kill everyone who had been on the beach
that day or, if impossible to kill them, kill their closest
relative. The town was so absorbed by the Miracle that
they remained oblivious to the danger to which they
were all exposed.

It was to be a tragic oversight.

* * *

By the time Hardy Remarque dragged himself back from Grand Rapids, he found he'd returned to a town plunged in the middle of a religious debate. Walking around town, he could find little else on people's tongues other than the voices. This phenomenon disturbed him. For himself, he was a closet agnostic. In a deeply religious town like St. Max it was wiser to keep one's reservations to oneself. And he always had. But he didn't at all believe the dead were coming back to reassure the living—not for a moment he didn't.

In retrospect it seemed strange that a trained policeman like Remarque didn't see how neatly the excitement, the controversy about the voices, kept people—even himself—from thinking very much about the danger that might lie behind them. The one facet of the voices that kept bothering him was the new threat of others still to be punished. His policeman's instinct warned him that the words were there for a reason; they meant something, but neither he nor anyone else seemed able even to guess what.

Walking around the town he heard person after person discussing the voices. Arguments for and against their authenticity (mostly for). Fear generated by the voices' threat to leave them below the earth, screaming for help, should they disobey and require punishment. And who in hell was the woman Lutetia Losee mentioned? A woman, apparently, already marked for punishment of the worst kind.

He could see people's views subtly shifting; the cynics were in hiding, the devout in ecstasy, but both felt an uneasy terror. "The hell with it," Remarque said suddenly, standing on a street corner. Several passersby turned to stare at him; from behind came a rollicking laugh.

"Heavens, Hardy," said Edith Pardee, shaking her head at him in a lilting reproach. "I didn't realize you even knew such strong words. I'm shocked. Only a few yards from Our Lady of Misery, too."

Hardy had to laugh. Like everyone else in St. Max he loved this woman, always so calm, always so cheerful, always so level-headed. For a moment he considered telling her the truth of what was bothering him, but discarded the idea quickly. Instead, he lied. "Thinking ahead is all, Edith. The damned winter. Break-ins. Angry tourists coming back next summer and finding their lodges rifled. No money for a security patrol this winter either." He sighed heavily to underscore how much the situation troubled him.

"It'll work out, Hardy. Somehow. Just hold good thoughts and don't swear on street corners." With another laugh, Edith Pardee walked on. Hardy Remarque didn't. He was right outside of St. Max's lone bar—ill lit, dirty, but gloriously untroubled by matters of the soul.

Sitting on the unevenly padded barstool, Hardy Remarque stared at his own reflection in a mirror smudged with a million thumbprints. In it, for just the briefest second, he thought he saw the reflection of a woman's face. The woman, he supposed, up for punishment.

As an intensely practical man, the fleeting appearance of the woman in the mirror shook him badly. Shit, that kind of crap was for late-night horror movies on TV. He hooked another Scotch.

He stared at the mirror again—harder—and, for an instant, the apparition appeared again. Christ, it kind of looked like Angie Psalter. Oh, man, oh, man, he was in trouble. Reliable old Hardy Remarque seeing things in mirrors that weren't there. He was going around the bend, he decided, but then, the whole town was going crazy. It was that damned Bible salesman from Cheboygan again, he could feel it in his bones. The man was back, maybe, trying some new kind of scam. Shit.

He felt the raw liquor begin to warm his stomach. Thank God, at least poor little Peter Berringer's death had been an easily explained, proven accidental one. He'd read the state Police reports himself just this afternoon. Thorough bunch. No one would be hearing *Peter's* voice.

The sense of foreboding descended around him like a cloud; a shattering thought crossed his mind.

Or *would* they?

Chapter Eighteen

They're just beginning to put up the Christmas stuff in the store windows of St. Max. Later than most places, I guess. Hell, at Marquette they'd barely get the dishes cleared off the table from Thanksgiving before the whole town would be blazing with Christmas junk. In St. Max the displays never really amount to much at best; decorations go up in Nate's Pharmacy and Eddie's Market and DeRham's Drygoods, and that's about it. Tacky.

This year I thought about hanging a string of colored lights above the Tenniel's sign, but decided it would only upset the customers. To die at Christmastime, particularly if you're still a kid, seems cruel enough as it is.

Funny, this morning I caught myself hoping that the Voice wouldn't pull anything funny until at least after New Year's. People, I told myself, ought to be happy at Christmas, not getting themselves killed. Some lover. I mean, if the only reason I can think of for not wanting the Voice to go after Angie is that it's Christmas, I'm one hell of a lousy Santa Claus.

Christmases have never worked out very good for me, anyway. When I was a kid myself, I used to get so excited I couldn't eat, but something always went wrong. Toys would have important parts missing. Clothes would be either too big or too small. . . . Other things would show up already busted. Once, Dad got me a set of electric trains—God, I'd wanted one of those—but he didn't discover until late Christmas Eve they ran on AC and ours was DC. Shit. It was like St. Max had it in for me, always, and wasn't going to let me forget it for one minute.

About the best I can say for Christmas is that four

days before it—the twenty-first of December—is the shortest day of the year.

> *Jorbie Tenniel—to the rock,*
> *5:15 P.M., November 30th*

The water lapped at the edge of the raft, making crazy little slurping noises against the wood. Like it was thirsty. It was a strange kind of raft, anchored off the beach in a strange place. At first he thought he could make out St. Max's beach on the shoreline, but when he looked closer he realized he must be off the shores of Lake Waloon. Somewhere in the distance he could hear Peter Berringer screaming as his bones were broken. Jorbie shuddered.

The reason the raft itself appeared so peculiar suddenly became clear to him. Nailed to an upright coffin support in the center of the raft was a long, hand-lettered list. The Voice's list. Jorbie kept trying to reach it to see who else's name was on it, but every time his hand came close to grabbing the list and tearing it down, the raft would wrench itself into a violently tilting position. Jorbie started to get mad, but a particularly angry lurch forced him to dig his nails into the wood hard just to stay aboard; he became more frightened than angry. A voice called his name, and looking over the side of the raft, he saw Angie, struggling against the waves to keep her head above the water. She pleaded for help, but Jorbie felt himself shake his head to tell her he wouldn't. When she reached up and grabbed frantically at his arm, he shook her hand loose, watching her struggle helplessly until she disappeared under the surface, still calling his name.

The list remained where it was, flapping wildly in the rising wind, permanently out of his reach. Overhead the sullen Raptors circled the sky endlessly, watching, wait-

ing for that instant of stillness that would tell them they
could now rocket down and begin tearing at their prey.

There was another violent lurch and Jorbie felt himself sliding completely off the raft. Instead of water, he
was buried almost up to his neck in sand—wet sand
shaped into some sort of wall. He struggled and, for the
first time, became aware of a muffled throbbing that
seemed to grow out of the beach all around him. He
screamed in terror as pieces of the wall began collapsing on him, threatening to bury him, but his only answer was the flapping of the list, nailed now to a small
sand tower rising above his head.

Jorbie could feel the sand in his mouth and the suffocating pressure it put on him; the ground lurched, just
as the raft had, and the walls of sand fell in on him,
covering his head and beginning to smother him. Angie
reappeared, this time standing above him, laughing and
making fun of him, teasing him as he was completely
buried by the damp sand. His screams were lost in the
muffled throbbing that came from the ground, made
inaudible by the pebbles and sand that covered him.

He woke up, his pajama top drenched in sweat and
feeling cold and wet against the bed. Jorbie sighed. It
was another of those damned crazy nightmares that had
been filling his nights with restless terror. He could
laugh at them in the mornings, but his nights were becoming an agony. The Theater of the Absurd raised to
the level of a primal scream.

He had begun to dread the night, usually his favorite
time of day.

"It was all my fault, and God, I'm sorry."

Cathy winced. "Please no. I've learned my lesson. As
far as I'm concerned, the subject of Jorbie Tenniel is
one for you and you alone. I won't comment, I won't
pry, I won't try to interfere. That's a promise."

"Gee, Cathy," Angie said with absolute sincerity. "Gee, but that's great. That's where all the trouble was coming from." She reached across the table and gave Cathy's hand a brief squeeze. "With that out of the way, the whole ugly mess between us is done with. I missed you, Cathy. Really."

Over their morning coffee break, Angie Psalter and Cathy Springer were making up for their ugly argument. They'd grown up together, they'd been best friends since either could remember, and the whole incident had been painful to both of them. Now the air was cleared. Angie was enormously relieved. Cathy was relieved too, even though she still harbored an indefinable fear of what Jorbie might ultimately do to Angie. She shrugged; her declaration of not trying to interfere troubled her, but was necessary. Abruptly she changed the subject.

"After Flan's, did you hear poor Lutetia's voice too, Angie?"

Angie stiffened; they were on the edge of another sensitive subject. But Cathy proceeded to surprise her. "Well, that's the other place where I was wrong, Angie. The voices. I'm not really sure what happened, but all of a sudden—last night, in fact—I woke up and found I believed in them. I know, I know, I used to laugh at them, but I'm not laughing anymore. I'm believing. I don't know what happened to change my mind so. Your old friend, the agnostic, gone crackers." Cathy pondered a second, then raised her eyes to meet Angie's. "Do you suppose I'm too young for senility?"

Cathy's announcement had rocked Angie. Of all people. Cathy. She studied her, sitting opposite her across the Formica, her eyes cast down, as if somehow embarrassed by her confession. Unexpected by either of them, the period bell rang stridently. Each of them returned to their own classrooms, glad that their fight was over, mystified as to the meaning behind Cathy's abrupt transmogrification.

It was a curious footnote to events in St. Max that Cathy Springer should begin believing in the Miracle of the Voices on the very same day she finally abandoned trying to persuade Angie about Jorbie. Ironic because both events pointed toward Angie's almost inevitable end: being buried alive.

It was cold today, even downtown in St. Max, which ordinarily was protected enough from the wind to keep it several degrees warmer than the areas directly on the Straits. Jorbie shivered in the raw wind and pulled his coat tighter around him; it was not a day for being outside, but he had errands to do in town and had no choice.

As he started through the door of Nate's Pharmacy, he almost ran into Edith Pardee. She looked as cold as he felt. They huddled in the warmth of the small, heated opening that led to Nate's front door. "Brr!" Edith Pardee laughed. "It's the new Ice Age, I think."

Mischievously, Jorbie smiled at her. "Saves *me* money."

Like everyone else in St. Max, Jorbie worshiped Edith Pardee. And it was clear even to Jorbie that she returned his feeling in kind. Occasionally she would rebuke him for being so shy that he held himself apart from the people of the town. "My God, Jorbie," she would tell him. "This whole town thinks you're the greatest. They really do. Like myself, they think you're bright and handsome and have a wonderful sense of humor. They love you. You're what they wish their sons had grown up to be. But you just keep hiding from them. For God's sake, Jorbie, give them a chance."

Edith Pardee had another motif she returned to time after time. "You and Angie, Jorbie," she had said one day just the week before. "She adores you. And I know you love her. But I bet you never tell *her* that—I know how hard words like that come to you, Jorbie. Promise me something: tell her. Tell her before someone else comes along and runs off with her. You make a fabulous couple."

The warmth of Nate's outer warm-room was getting to them both. Edith Pardee seemed to be studying Jorbie, as if she'd just seen him for the first time. "Oh, Jorbie, it always makes me so upset to see you still in town like this. You belong back in med school, back at Marquette, where you can really use that superb brain of yours. You're wasted here. It kills me."

Jorbie gave a small shrug and a weak smile. "Afraid there's nothing much anyone can do about *that*, Mrs. Pardee. Things happen, and there you are. I don't like it myself, not one bit, but please don't worry; I'll survive."

Edith Pardee studied her shoes for a moment, suddenly raising her eyes to meet Jorbie's. "I'm not sure I should tell you this, Jorbie, because it probably won't work out and I don't want to get your hopes up for nothing. But the fact is some other people and myself are so concerned over what we consider the almost criminal waste of a brain, we've been trying to organize a group that could hire a replacement for you at the mortuary. Then you could go back to school, free and clear. We've made a little progress, sweetheart, but it's slow, so terribly slow. People are really strapped these days. But we've got a couple of summer people and a company down in Saginaw interested, and maybe, with a little luck, we'll be able to collect enough. . . ."

What Mrs. Pardee was saying took Jorbie's breath away. The admittedly slim promise it offered was incredible. Yet, even as he thought about it, he could not escape the irony of the situation. Suddenly he wasn't sure he *wanted* to go back to Marquette. The *bonaro*. Captain Marvel's kiss. The taking of orders from his

Voice on who to kill and who to leave alone. All of these new things made his earlier dreams of Marquette, medicine, and monumental breakthroughs in medical research seem as the games of children. He stared at Mrs. Pardee, confused.

On the other hand, if he went back to Marquette, maybe he could leave the Voice behind him in St. Max. In a way, this would be a relief. The Voice was taking more and more control of him, seizing him ever more frequently, making him do things he wasn't always sure he wanted to do. For him, Marquette might be an escape. He stared at Mrs. Pardee, troubled and confused. She appeared oblivious.

"I can't promise anything, of course, Jorbie, but you know I'll do my damnedest to make it work . . ." Her voice trailed off; she saw a frightening thing happening to Jorbie as they stood there.

Without warning, for apparently no reason, the muffled throbbing began suddenly booming from Mrs. Pardee. The sound swelled and grew until he could barely stand it, digging painfully into his eardrums and making him feel faint and dizzy. All of the color had drained from his face and Edith Pardee saw him put one hand on the wall to steady himself. He looked as if he might collapse where he stood. "Jorbie . . . Jorbie . . . what's the matter . . . here, take my hand and we'll go inside and sit down . . . Jorbie . . ."

Jorbie stared at the hand as if it were the property of some alien from another planet. Nate's, the street outside it, all of St. Max, felt like it was rocketing into space to join the alien whose hand it was. Yanking himself free from Mrs. Pardee roughly, Jorbie fled down the street followed by the hounds of panic. Mrs. Pardee stared after him as he ran, a worried, troubled frown across her face.

Jorbie didn't stop until he reached his car. The deeply terrifying nightmares had already turned his nights into a hell. Now even his days were no longer safe.

Jorbie was ready for him when the car pulled into the garage. George deCarre's garage was a windowless, dirty place, cluttered with junk and piled to the ceiling with the jetsam of a lifetime. In the bay alongside the one place kept clear enough for deCarre's beat-up old car stood a fancy sleigh, not used since the days of deCarre's grandfather, decorated with faded hand-painted scenes of winters past. Like deCarre himself, there was something sad and forgotten about it.

For the last three quarters of an hour Jorbie had been tracking him, waiting for deCarre to finally head home. At the Mackinac Bar and Grill he had even bought the old man a couple of drinks. DeCarre was more than a little drunk. Today had been his last day at the St. Max Fish Cannery; as with many of his fellow workers, his job had become a victim of raging inflation. The younger ones would eventually find other work; at sixty-eight, deCarre wasn't sure he ever would.

As it grew time for the bar to close, Jorbie had left, driven to deCarre's house, and waited inside, hidden. Unsteadily, the old man climbed out of his car and pulled the garage doors shut. For a moment he stared at the old sleigh, then walked slowly toward the heavy door that connected the garage to his house. Once he heard something outside the garage—it was Jorbie locking the garage doors from the outside—and twice he stumbled, finally climbing up the short flight of steps to the inside door. He was startled when the door opened before he'd even put his hand on the knob.

"Oh. Hi, Jorbie." He studied Jorbie with confusion. What was he doing in his house? Had he asked him home from the bar? He couldn't remember, any more than he could remember being young and looking forward to a life of hard work laced with happiness. It was a kind of life that somehow had never materialized. He'd known Jorbie Tenniel since the man was practically a baby; he would never forget the terrible day on the beach when he had organized the dory full of rowers to try and find poor little Kenneth Tenniel. Or, at least, his body. "Hi, Jorbie," he repeated, still trying to understand why the young man stood framed in his door.

"Hi, Mr. deCarre. I just wanted to be sure you'd gotten home all right."

DeCarre displayed a toothless smile. Jorbie Tenniel's explanation made sense—Jorbie Tenniel was that kind of thoughtful, caring person, as anyone in St. Max could tell you—but it still didn't explain how or why he'd gotten *inside* his house, which he must have, to come out through that door. A drink. That was it, he *had* asked Jorbie home for a drink. There was only one small flaw in that explanation. "I'm afraid there's no booze, Jorbie. I forgot that I guess, when I asked you back. Stupid. No booze at all."

"I don't want a drink, Mr. deCarre. Like I said, I just wanted to be sure you'd made it home okay. You were so damned depressed when I talked to you at the Mackinac."

"Shit, I got plenty of reason to be depressed, Jorbie. Thirty years, and the cannery dumps me. I'm too fucking old to get another job. I'll have to go on relief, like the Portareeks and shades. Shit."

Jorbie smiled reassuringly. "Something will turn up, Mr. deCarre. Something always does. For all you know, something absolutely staggering could lie just ahead of you." He reached over and squeezed deCarre's upper arm. The old man was far too drunk to either hear or feel Captain Marvel's sharp embrace. Today's dose of *bonaro* was especially strong and would take effect in less than half an hour.

"You're a nice man, Jorbie Tenniel," he said somberly, suddenly feeling very sad. "A very nice man."

DeCarre's liquored breath was more than Jorbie could take. Suddenly turning, he walked upstairs into the house, closing the door and locking it behind him. He began riffling through the papers in deCarre's desk, making a melancholy pile of the old man's unpaid bills, mortgage notices, threats to cut off the power, and medical statements. Every now and then he would hear deCarre pound on the door, yelling his name, but blithely ignored it. The Voice had told him what to do, and he was doing it.

Half an hour later the intermittent pounding from George deCarre had stopped. Slipping into the garage, Jorbie found him lying on the floor a few feet from his weather-beaten Ford. His hands were outstretched to it as if his last thought had been to climb into the car and drive right through the double garage doors to freedom when God reached out a hand and struck him down. The effort would have failed anyway. While old de-Carre was talking to him, Jorbie had pocketed the ignition keys.

Gently, as if carying a baby, Jorbie picked up de-Carre's fragile body and carried it over to the sleigh, propping him up in the front seat with a Bible in his lap. Then he returned to the old Ford, checking to see that there was plenty of gas. Squinting, Jorbie put the keys back in and started the motor. A dense cloud of carbon monoxide poured from the exhaust.

Almost running, Jorbie went back into the house. This was the tricky part. Too much carbon monoxide and the Voice would be robbed of its living burial. Quickly he dialed O, then mumbled deCarre's name to the operator, telling her his life had become too much to take. The overdue bills. Fired by the God damned cannery—after thirty fucking years. Welfare and the Portareeks. Too much, too much. Jorbie let the receiver crash to the floor and walked calmly out of the house.

* * *

"Suicide," Hardy Remarque announced, feeling sure of himself for the first time since the death of Flan Tierney.

"Suicide by self-induced carbon monoxide poisoning," Dr. L'Eveque wrote on the formal medical investigation form.

"Suicide," cried crazy old Mrs. Lavin. After all, in her charts wasn't Malachi in the Seventh House of Zephaniah?

"Suicide, shit," George deCarre tried to scream over and over again. "I'm still alive!"

At first George deCarre thought the whole thing must be the product of his drunkenness. A great guy like Jorbie Tenniel wouldn't do something like this nightmare told him he had. It didn't make sense. He hadn't understood when Jorbie first locked him in the garage; that didn't make any sense either. And then there'd been that strange floating feeling that suddenly hit him, like he'd been bombed for a week instead of just a few hours. Neither did he understand what had made him suddenly collapse, although that could have been the booze, too, he supposed. Nothing would move; he could make no sound. Dimly he'd seen Jorbie come back into the garage, lift him into the sleigh, and start the Ford's motor. At least, he thought that was what he'd seen. None of it made any sense, not one bit.

But it was when he was stretched out on a table at Tenniel's with Jorbie smiling down at him that George deCarre finally had to accept the horror of full realization: Not only was all of it happening to him, but Jorbie Tenniel was behind it.

"Well, Mr. deCarre," Jorbie had said, "Back in your garage, I told you something absolutely staggering could lie just ahead of you, and, man, here it is already."

DeCarre wanted to speak to him, to scream at him, to cry out "Why?" but could make no sound. "Anyway," Jorbie continued, "at least you don't have to worry anymore about losing your job or the bills or Welfare. That's all behind you. I suppose you really ought to thank me . . ." George deCarre screamed and shrieked and pleaded for mercy, but already knew his voice made no sound and was fully aware Jorbie had somehow imprisoned him in a terrible void of silence.

The funeral was a nightmare. "He's officially listed as a suicide," deCarre heard Father Duval tell his sister, who had hurried down from Groscap after hearing what had happened. "So I'm afraid no Catholic service can be held in the church for him. Suicide, Grace," deCarre heard Duval tell his sister sadly, "is a cardinal sin in the Church's eyes." Swallowing hard, Father Duval added what he knew would be the hardest to take of all. "Nor can he be buried in sanctified ground, such as Carpas Point. You'll have to find someplace else."

Grace deCarre was a woman of few words, all of them telling. "Balls," she snorted. "All right, he can't have a service in a church. I can understand that; you don't own the damn place. Besides, I don't think George would give a rat's ass about it. But you *will* hold a service—right here in the mortuary if you have to—and you *will* say a few words—and you *will* help me find a nice place to bury poor old George, even if it isn't in your damned private graveyard."

"Grace, my dear, I'd like to help, but—" Father Duval stretched out his hands helplessly.

"You will, Father Duval, or I'll kill myself, too, and leave a note saying it was because you're so damned hidebound you wouldn't even help a grieving old woman. Murder must be a bigger sin than suicide, and you'll carry the weight of that for the rest of your life. Do we understand each other?"

Little by little, Father Duval found himself giving in.
George had killed himself while reading the Bible,
hadn't he? A service was eventually held at Tenniel's,
with Father Duval reading a few nondenominational
prayers. A weed-ridden patch of land was found just
beyond Carpas Point Cemetery and his coffin lowered
into the ground by Jorbie Tenniel and Pasteur. At
night, so no one could see what they and Duval were
doing. It was not a proper burial, Grace deCarre had to
admit to herself, but at least it would save her poor
brother from eternal hell.

His own private hell was just beginning for George
deCarre. As the effects of the *bonaro* began to wear
off, he slowly felt sensation return to his hands, his feet,
and finally, his whole body. Above him he could hear
the frozen clods of earth hitting the top of his coffin
with a dull, final sound. It had happened. He had been
buried—alive. By someone he had always admired and
liked, a young man named Jorbie Tenniel. He couldn't
believe it. But the satin-lined coffin that surrounded
him was real; the intense darkness of the grave was
real; the sound of frozen earth falling on his head was
real.

He swore and screamed and pounded the sides of the
box that held him until his fists were sore; there was no
answer. As each second passed George deCarre became more and more aware that he was going to die.
To die horribly, of suffocation, put in the ground by his
sister and by Father Duval and by the friends who
loved him.

Carefully, struggling to stay calm and not use up his
meager supply of air, his hands explored the sides of
the coffin, ripping away the satin to feel how the wood
underneath was put together. A sudden thought struck
him. In his pocket, put back by his sister Grace when

Tenniel wasn't in the viewing room, was the sturdy folding seaman's knife she'd given him years before. He'd carried it in his pocket ever since, but when they were getting him into his best suit for the burial, Jorbie Tenniel had carefully removed it. In a burst of sentimentality, Grace had replaced it. It was the only thing she'd ever given him he seemed to cherish.

At least, deCarre thought without too much enthusiasm, he had something—not much, but *something*—to use in working on the coffin top. Twisting his body from side to side, he was able to pull the heavy knife from his pocket. The thick, cold steel felt reassuring to his hands. If he could break out of the coffin and dig—

The idea was illusory, and George deCarre knew it. He suddenly began screaming, shrieking into the darkness, yelling into the silent void, pleading with persons unknown for Christ's sake to come down and get him— he was still alive, damn it, still alive and why couldn't anybody see that and do something?

The idea might be illusory, but it was, old George deCarre decided, the only idea he had. Carefully, deliberately, using strong hands that belied his age, he began carving through the top of the coffin. He'd whittled a lot when he was younger, sometimes fashioning quite elaborate pieces, and the work went quickly. The knife bit into the wood outside the satin lining, and little by little, deCarre could feel it chip away under his hands. Finally the knife was clear through the coffin into the ground. He began again, this time almost a foot away, and broke through the side as well; beyond, he could feel the cold earth that had been heaped over him in his grave.

Two more similar cuts at right angles produced a small door perhaps a foot and a half square. He pushed on it with his hands and could feel it move. God damn, he'd done it; he was on his way out. Without too much effort he'd remove the door completely and be able to dig and claw his way up to the surface through the soft earth and to freedom. And how do you like them apples, Jorbie Tenniel?

For a second he paused to collect his energy, wondering whether he should kill Jorbie himself or let the State of Michigan do it for him. Kill him himself, he decided, allowing himself a small smile of vengeance. He didn't really give a damn *who* killed Jorbie. What counted was that he would be free—safe once again. (And although there was no way for George deCarre to know it, with Jorbie dead or locked away, Angie would be safe once again too).

God damn, God damn, deCarre kept repeating to himself, the smile of success already on his face, and pulled himself together to begin the process of escape. His heart pounding with excitement, his blood pumping hard from the exertion, he tried to slide the newly made door sideways outside the coffin. He got nowhere. Not sure of what would happen, he angled the door and pulled it in on top of himself.

For a second there was no movement. Then the freshly turned earth began pouring in through the hole directly onto his face, getting into his mouth, filling his nose, and threatening to suffocate him. Panicked, deCarre shoved the little door back up against the hole, still coughing, trying to spit the dirt out of his mouth. To keep himself alive—how long would he *be* alive anyway?—he had to keep his hands pressed against the panel he had carved. There was a note of displeasure in the voice that suddenly spoke to him.

"Mr. deCarre," Jorbie's voice said clearly into his ear, sounding as if Jorbie was right there alongside him in the coffin, "that was a very stupid thing to try. There's six feet of dirt over your head, and even if you could get out of your coffin, you'd smother before you

could dig through even a foot of it. Very stupid indeed."

The frustration of the failed attempt on top of everything else was too much for old George deCarre. He
began to cry, a helpless wailing and sobbing as the full
horror of his situation once again hammered on his
consciousness. His problems with the cannery and the
unpaid bills and his loneliness all seemed suddenly very
far away, minor things, things that had bothered him
once but were so far in the past as to be laughable.

He heard Jorbie Tenniel clear his throat, apparently
about to speak again, and the misery turned to fury. He
beat the sides of the coffin again, kicking it with his
feet, pounding on it, screaming curses at Jorbie and
asking over and over again "Why? Why? Why?" As
fear and frustration swept across him he forgot—it
could have only been for an instant—to keep pressing
on the panel that separated him from the earth above,
and again the dirt poured onto his face, filling his
mouth and making him gasp for air.

"All finished, Mr. deCarre?" Jorbie asked smoothly.

"You creep!" screamed deCarre. "Why are you
pulling this shit on me? I never did anything to
you . . ."

"You did, but that's beside the point for the moment.
I'd suggest you be a little polite just now; I'm going to
make you an offer that could get you out of that hellhole you're in—free and clear, alive and in God's own
fresh air—but you're not making it very easy to be gen-
erous. . . ."

The slim ray of hope that Jorbie's statement offered,
although granted the words of a madman, silenced
George deCarre abruptly.

"Now this is how my little offer goes, Mr. deCarre,"
began Jorbie. . . .

The familiar muffled pulsing that suddenly swept

over Jorbie—great, dark waves of sound that thundered against his eardrums—was so loud he was afraid de-Carre could hear it in his grave. Although he knew it never helped, Jorbie clapped his hands over his ears, screaming at the sound, pleading with it to stop, knowing it would keep right on going until it itself decided the time to quit had arrived. Jorbie writhed and twisted under the assault, dropping to his knees and lowering his head almost to the ground as the pulsing continued to bore into his brain.

Finally, as suddenly as it began, the sound stopped. Jorbie stared emptily at the earth mounded over de-Carre; wearily he picked up the microphone again to begin spelling out his proposition.

DeCarre was going to have to say things he would not want to say, personal, threatening things addressed directly to Angie. They were things Jorbie himself did not want said to her, but the damned Voice had commanded that they be spoken. Why, for Christ's sake, did the Voice hate Angie so much? Jorbie didn't know; he knew only that he had to obey.

The doorbell at Tenniel's seemed to take forever before it was answered. Angie stood outside, shivering as the wind ripped across the Straits and howled its way through the tortured trees around the mortuary. Finally the door opened and Jorbie let her in. His greeting was mumbled, his eyes averted. Angie had a distinct impression he had forgotten she was coming and was putting up with her only because it was he who had issued the invitation. Not that she really needed to be invited anymore; her arrival was expected every night, the way you might expect the tide to rise and fall.

"You don't seem very cheerful," Angie tried.

"Tired. Just tired. Some days this grind gets to me. Sorry."

They sat in the living room, sipping some St. Emilion, but attacking it with the same enthusiasm one might feel toward a not unpleasant, but not overly zestful, medicine. It was impossible for Angie not to recognize what was happening; she sensed it the instant she stepped inside the door. The always mercurial Jorbie was in one of his dark moods, one of the darkest she'd seen for some time. Of all her problems with Jorbie, these moods troubled Angie the most. Sometimes, just for an instant, they would make her wonder if she shouldn't get out of the whole thing for good. She loved him, she knew that. But his fits of moodiness, his occasional sorties into outright violence, stirred deep fears inside her. There were things going on in his head she didn't understand, things that occasionally made her feel it might be better simply to disappear once and for all.

But then suddenly—and with no apparent reason— Jorbie would swing in the opposite direction, do something wonderful, and Angie would wonder how she ever could have thought of anything so foolish.

Angie knew. She would simply stay off sensitive subjects and stick to surface banalities when Jorbie was stricken by one of his moods. Somehow, though, she always seemed seized by a compulsion—what almost amounted to a death wish—to get at the truth, never in control of herself enough to keep quiet. Tonight was to be no exception.

Angie filled the silence with small incidents about her day at St. Etienne, small things, silly things, things easy to laugh at. Jorbie remained staring at the wall in front of him, the wineglass held listlessly in his hand. Occasionally, when pushed, he would nod inattentively.

Moving on, encouraged by a faint smile something she'd said had produced, she decided to share with him part of the conversation with Cathy. "And you'll never guess what, Jorbie. Cathy Springer. You know Cathy Springer. Anyway, this afternoon she told me she'd suddenly changed her mind and now really believed what I said about Flan Tierney's and Lutetia Losee's voices. For Cathy, that's really saying something."

As she watched Angie saw Jorbie's face go white. The fingers around his wineglass gripped it so tightly the glass finally splintered in his hand. His body trembled with some internal fury. Jorbie shot to his feet and began storming back and forth across the room, kicking the furniture like a child in a tantrum.

"Damn it, damn it, damn it!" Jorbie screamed at her. "The voices—they're nothing but a God damned lie." Angie sat there, open mouthed, transfixed. As she listened Angie realized Jorbie's voice, his whole way of speaking, had become altered in pitch and timbre; it was suddenly higher, and the words he used were those of a child.

Face white with fury, his whole body shaking, Jorbie suddenly grabbed a chair and held it above his head; Angie put her hands up over her own to ward off the blow from the chair. At the last instant Jorbie spun and hurled the chair against the wall. Splinters and pieces of wood fell to the floor noisily. Angie stared at him, trying to think what to say. She never got the chance. Sobbing like a child, Jorbie dashed out of the room; from downstairs she could hear the doors of the preparation room being slammed behind him.

A stunned Angie slowly got to her feet. It was difficult, no, it was impossible, to understand how such a seemingly harmless remark of hers could produce such a violent reaction. Fleetingly a shadow of her sometime question to herself—whether it might not be wiser to get out of the whole affair while she still could—crossed her mind. Almost as quickly as the question had come, Angie dismissed it. She couldn't give Jorbie up. Jorbie had become her whole life. Why she got up in the morning, why she ate, breathed, and existed. Without him, she would be nothing.

Her usual device of blaming anything that went wrong between her and Jorbie on herself—on something stupid she'd said or done—for once failed her. Even as she tried to make it work once more, Angie knew that in this case the fault had been entirely Jorbie's, not hers. Her longtime rationalization stripped away, all that was left was a dim, shadowy uneasiness, a hint of something evil she could neither explain nor understand.

For the first time since she'd known him, Angie Psalter realized that at moments like this Jorbie not only frightened her, he *terrified* her.

Chapter Nineteen

Dreams. Part of life since the beginning to time. Prophets in the Bible, always yakking about their dreams. Pharaohs having nightmares. Greeks and Romans—including their gods—finding omens in every dream. They even paid people to tell them what the dreams meant.

I think Galileo dreamed his way into the falling-body theory; I know Columbus dreamed the world was round instead of flat. Isabella?—Well, she just kept dreaming about good old Columbus, I guess.

Along came Freud and the whole picture changed. We dream of what we want, he says, of what we fear, of what we don't have, and most of all, we dream about sex. I don't know how Sigmund thought men were going to get any sleep; they were all supposed to be dreaming about the Wonderful Mom Machine.

I wish mine were that simple. It's the same damned dream—nightmare, anyway—repeated over and over with minor variations. I haven't a clue what it means. Everything in it is familiar enough, but I still can't make head or tail of it. Is the basic dream trying to tell me something about myself? I know that sometimes in my dreams a strange little boy and Angie get all mixed up, but God knows what the hell that means. All I know for sure is that the nightmares are getting worse, a little more frequent, a lot more intense. I wake up in a puddle of sweat every morning.

Hell, maybe the Wonderful Mom Machine isn't such a bad thing to dream about at that.

> *Jorbie Tenniel—to the rock,*
> *6:00 P.M., December 1st*

Angie hated having the cafeteria at St. Etienne become the only place she could really talk to Cathy Springer. Once they had seen a great deal of each other—in town, at dinner, at the movies—but now Angie's nights and weekends were full of Jorbie, and when she wanted to talk—really talk—with Cathy, these hurried little between-class meetings in the cafeteria were the only times she had left.

The cafeteria was not the best place to hold a serious conversation. Full, it was too noisy; empty—as it was just now—it was a bleak place, casting long shadows over anything you said.

But today there were worries pressing on Angie's consciousness; desperately, she needed Cathy's outlook on things. Jorbie's reactions of the night before had been all out of proportion. Brutal. Frightening.

Cathy sat opposite her, a little baffled that Angie should have maneuvered her into coffee in the middle of the afternoon. In the emptiness even the sound of their spoons scraping the inside of their cups played back a mournful, echoing sound.

"The coffee's worse than usual today," volunteered Cathy, well aware that something must be weighing heavily on Angie's mind. She could guess whatever it was had something to do with her God damned Jorbie.

The thought made Cathy shift uneasily. She really wanted to stay clear of any further talk about Jorbie. One conversation about him had already almost cost her Angie's friendship for good.

The spoons scraping the cups sounded deafening in the uncomfortable silence. Angie, who had been staring at the ceiling, suddenly looked Cathy squarely in the eye. "Did you know that Jorbie used to have a twin? An identical twin?"

Avoiding Angie's eyes, Cathy shook her head and looked away. No, she didn't know that.

"Well," Angie went on, "he did. A twin that was the spitting image of him, apparently. Somewhere along the line, he died. I don't know of what."

"Why don't you ask *him*?"

A shudder ran through Angie. It was a subject she could never broach to Jorbie. Not in a million years. He'd stuff her into the walk-in freezer like the boys at his twelfth birthday party. "It just doesn't seem like something you ask somebody."

"I'm surprised he hasn't brought it up to you himself."

"Jorbie's a very private person. Above everything else, I'd say, he values his personal privacy."

The subject was becoming increasingly uncomfortable for Cathy Springer. Little bits and pieces revealed out of what she realized had to be a much larger, more complicated picture. Angie's brave statements about how she and Jorbie knew everything about each other were slowly crumbling. Jorbie might know everything about Angie, but here *she* was, afraid even to ask Jorbie about something as basic as his own twin brother.

"Look," suggested Cathy suddenly, taking pity on Angie. "I have a friend—Alice Sprague—you know Alice—who works at Town Hall. In the Town Records room." Moving into an area she didn't have the slightest wish even to go near—Jorbie—Cathy volunteered to find out from Alice what Town Records had to say about the twin's death. "All you have to give me is Jorbie's birth date," Cathy explained, "and Alice Sprague can dig out the twin's records. There had to be a death certificate over there somewhere that will say what he died of, but everything's filed by date, not name. It's a real mess. But give me Jorbie's birth date and Alice will do the rest. Easy enough."

"Great, Cathy, great," Angie said, flushed with excitement. The scraping of the spoons reached a crescendo as Angie stirred away and stared off into space.

"Too bad Town Records can't explain why some things upset Jorbie so terribly, " Angie added sadly. She forced a not very convincing laugh. "The other night, well, I thought he was going to brain me with that chair instead of just throwing it at the wall. . . ."

Inside Cathy a sudden battle was raging. This oblique reference to what apparently had been a physically violent reaction from Jorbie confirmed her worst fears. Cathy desperately wanted to say something, to point out one more time that Angie's closeness to Jorbie was becoming unabashedly dangerous. But she had promised—promised Angie and promised herself—that she wouldn't try to interfere again about Jorbie. To keep Angie as a friend, it was a promise she had to keep. But my God, how blind could Angie be!

Standing up suddenly, Cathy mumbled something about having to see someone before her next class, and fled. In retrospect, it was unfortunate Cathy *didn't* say what she was feeling. If she could have brought Angie to her senses, she might well have saved her life. Instead, she ran.

Behind her, in the deserted cafeteria, Angie continued to stare into space, her spoon still stirring coffee that was no longer there.

Standing in her kitchen, just back from Tenniel's and Jorbie, Angie tried to make up her mind about having coffee. Her evening with Jorbie—it was almost four in the morning now—had left her exhausted. But it was a wonderful kind of exhaustion, the relaxed, satisfied feeling of being filled by him, torn apart by him, strained and engorged and overwhelmed by him. She wanted to sleep, yet she didn't want to shut off the flow of memories coursing through her brain. The coffee would keep her awake—to remember, to relive, to savor— Jorbie and the night, but she would stay sleepless for the rest of the night and get up in the morning looking like an albino's ghost. In spite of that, she decided on the coffee; it was a night she didn't want to have end.

She was still sitting at the kitchen table stirring her coffee, tracing the curious pattern a single drop of spilled coffee had made on the red Formica top, when she heard it. There was no question about it; one of the voices was calling her name. Angie's head snapped upright, trying to locate the source of the voice. The most she could tell was that it was coming from somewhere inside the house.

"Angie . . . Angie . . . listen to me, listen. . . ." George deCarre's voice. There was no mistaking the distinctive croaking quality of the old man, a whispered moan that was almost that of an animal in pain. Angie could hear him coughing fitfully. (deCarre's mouth had remained partly filled with earth, and with no water available, he had been unable to clear his throat.) To Angie the sound he was making was at once pitiful and frightening. "Angie, you didn't listen," he rasped. "You didn't listen to what Lutetia Losee's voice said. She told you to obey, or else you would be punished as others have been punished. She told you that there would be yet more people, others condemned to scream helplessly from below the ground. She told you that one of them would be a woman. A young woman, but an important one. A molder of minds . . . But you wouldn't listen." DeCarre apparently was seized by a new fit of coughing that shook Angie. Coughing that was intermixed with a gasping sound as he seemed to struggle to get air.

"Now, perhaps you will. Because *you,* Angie, you are that woman. A teacher, molding children's minds. Sentenced to an eternity of pain because you wouldn't listen and obey. For pretending to be what you are not. For pretending to be *who* you are not.

"I have seen and heard the others who disobeyed. Pounding on their coffins. Screaming. Gasping for air. Pleading to die. But they will not be allowed to. Anymore than you will be—you are doomed to the endless hell of screaming for help from below the ground, knowing that no one can hear you, knowing that no one can help you." George deCarre suddenly began sobbing helplessly.

"You should have listened, Angie. Now you must pay . . ."

As suddenly as it had appeared, the voice vanished. George deCarre was once again silent.

His croaked message was the first actual threat that the voices had made against anyone. (Later Angie would discover that her name was actually mentioned only in deCarre's message to *her*. When deCarre's voice was heard by others in St. Max, he, like Lutetia Losee, mentioned only that one of those to be punished would be a woman. No one else in St. Max yet knew, then, who the woman was; Angie did—and everytime someone mentioned George deCarre's voice it filled her with dread.)

In the deep dark of the very early morning, the windows black, the house dark, George deCarre's threat was a terrifying one. The shiver ran through her again. Upstairs, she heard her father moving around and could guess he was about to come down and get more to drink. Angie fled.

Our Lady of Misery was once again filled for the funeral of a child. The crowd for Peter Berringer was not as large as the turnout for Flan Tierney, but large, nonetheless. All of St. Etienne's student body was there again, led by Sister Honorée. With every day that passed, the Sister's shoulders appeared more stooped; the toll of death among her students was draining the

life out of her as well. By noon the broken body of
Peter Berringer, a boy with a beautiful voice and the
eyes of an angel, was laid to rest in Carpas Point Cemetery.

Well, not quite to rest. After dark Jorbie Tenniel
paid a visit to the new grave, driving neither the body-
wagon nor the hearse, both of which he knew were too
familiar. Instead he drove his own car, a slightly bat-
tered 1972 T-Bird. The moment he stepped out of the
car, he realized how suddenly cold it had become. Earlier, during the interment, the sun had been bright and
the wind, for once, had not been too unbearable. Now
the wind had returned, moaning around the corners of
the headstones, putting its chill hand on anyone crazy
enough to visit it after the sun had set. Jorbie wished he
had dressed even more warmly than he had.

Finding Peter Berringer's grave, even in the dark and
without a flashlight, was easy for him. In the dim, uncertain light produced by a moon partially hidden behind racing clouds, Jorbie could make it out from a
considerable distance. Once everyone had left after the
service, the earth had been neatly mounded over Peter.
From the top end of the grave—where a headstone
would eventually be placed once the earth had settled
sufficiently—to the foot, the mound was completely
covered with flowers. A carpet of carnations from his
mother and father; an enormous wreath from St.
Etienne; various sprays and floral groupings from
friends and family, distant relatives, and people who
owed his father something. Looking at the giant wreath
sent by St. Etienne, Jorbie found it ludicrous.

A silken band lettered "Good Luck" had been
placed catty-cornered across it. It must have been a
mistake made at the florist's. *Good Luck* indeed, Peter, Jorbie whispered to himself. You're about to become part of a miracle.

Kneeling on the frozen earth, Jorbie carefully pulled

aside the blanket of carnations and some of the other displays from the head of the grave, taking careful note of where each individual spray was positioned so he could replace it later exactly where it had been. His hands ran back and forth across the ground until they located two sets of fine wire protruding from the still-soft earth above the grave itself.

One set of wires he connected to his tape recorder, the other to a small microphone and headset. He checked his watch and tapped on the microphone. Almost immediately he heard Peter Berringer screaming and crying. It was the same system Jorbie had used with Flan Tierney, Lutetia Losee, and George deCarre. As each of them were lowered into their grave, the thin wires were played out and left sticking inconspicuously aboveground, to be hidden later by the flowers. Inside each coffin, and concealed beneath the satin lining, was a miniature speaker and a microphone matching the one Jorbie held in his hand now. With this device, once the *bonaro* had worn off, Jorbie could speak to those he had buried alive, and—for a while, anyway—they to him.

Patiently, Jorbie waited for a pause in Peter Berringer's screaming and crying. Finally: "Look, Peter. I know it's cold and scary down there. Terrible, in fact. But try to hang on to yourself, Pete. There's a way out of there for you. Only first we have some things to talk about."

Jorbie heard a great deal of sniffling and throat-clearing through his headset; the drowning boy had just been cast a rope. "We do?" asked Peter incredulously. "We *do*?"

"Yup. Man-to-man talk."

"You said I could get out of here . . ." Peter began, the horror of his situation overwhelming him again. He began to cry, not as loudly as before, but still loud enough to make any further conversation impossible.

Jorbie once again rapped on his microphone with his pencil to command Peter's attention.

"I said man-to-man, Peter. Men don't cry."

Jorbie wondered where this myth had ever started and who had perpetuated it. Men cried—he'd seen it at Marquette—when they knew they were going to die. Men cried—he'd seen it often enough in St. Max and the other towns of the county when they got their first look at their wives or mothers or children at the mortuary. They cried during the funerals and they cried during the interments. It was a myth no one believed but everyone accepted. A code of stoic behavior passed down, perhaps, from the Spartans, nourished by the Vikings and the Visigoths, and today hammered into the ears of every small boy over the age of six. Men don't cry, balls.

For several seconds there had been silence from Peter's end of the wire. He had heard what Jorbie said but any worry about not acting like a man was the furthest thing from his mind. He was terrified, the cold dark walls of his grave closing in on him with the blackness of the blackest night. Always in the past, somehow, his mother or father had turned up when he needed help most, to hold him, to comfort him, to tell him everything would be all right. This time, all he had to comfort him was a disembodied voice, speaking to him through a loudspeaker. Peter began to cry again, then to scream in his helplessness.

"Peter," asked Jorbie. "Can you hear me? If we're ever going to get you out of there, you'll have to listen very carefully. And you can't do that if you're crying."

"I'll try," sniffled Peter in a small voice, no longer sure he *could* stop.

"Good. Now this is all you have to do. Just repeat what I tell you to say. Not very hard. Just listen very carefully, then repeat it."

"Why? Why do you want me to say things?" Peter wasn't sure why he asked, except that talking to someone, scared as he was, made him feel a little better.

Jorbie felt himself becoming irritated. "Don't worry about why. Just do what I tell you. Men don't say 'why' all the time either. And for God's sake stop that crying. Of course, if you don't *want* to get out of there. . . ."

Peter's voice came back edged with panic. He'd say whatever he was told to say. But was that really all it was going to take to free him?

"That's all, Peter. I have the shovel right here with me to dig you up. Just say what I tell you to, and you're as good as out."

Below, in the clutching blackness of his coffin, something still worried Peter about the deal the man was offering. If he was really going to dig him up in return for saying a few things to people, why didn't he dig him up *first* and let him say the things to the people in person?

There was also a gnawing fear that the man might not carry through with his end of the bargain. But the man was a grown-up, wasn't he? You had to believe what grown-ups told you, didn't you? Alone in the dreadful darkness, offered a chance at escape, terrified, he had heard a grown-up give him his word. He had to believe him. The fact was that he'd have agreed to do anything to get out of where he was. Quickly, suddenly afraid the man might change his mind and leave him here, he made the deal with Jorbie: freedom from this excruciating hell in return for saying a few words. Crazy, but Peter knew he was too petrified to think very clearly.

"Good. The shovel's waiting. You're halfway out already." Shielding the light with his hands, Jorbie took out a pencil flashlight and studied his notes. "All right, Peter. I want you to pretend you're talking to your mother. You know, just like you were already home and she was standing right in front of you. Call her

'Mom.' Sound happy. Now, this is what you're going to say. Don't worry if you don't get it right the first time; we can always start over. 'Mom . . . Mom . . . this is Peter . . . Mom, don't cry, Mom, you should be happy for me. . . .' "

Sentence by sentence, Jorbie led Peter through his words to his mother. The section on life after death had been greatly shortened but still gave trouble. As an added fillip, Jorbie had the sobbing Peter sing a snatch of *Ave Maria* for his mother, a touch he liked so much he added it to the tape he had Peter make for Father Duval. Even Jorbie was impressed by how emotional a reading Peter delivered. Little bastard was a natural-born ham.

It had been equally easy with Flan Tierney; like Peter, Flan had been so totally terrified he would have grabbed at any chance, however slim, to get himself out of his grave. Comparing the two, however, Flan's reading couldn't be considered close to Peter Berringer's for emotional impact.

Lutetia Losee had been much more difficult to persuade. A skeptic by nature, she had doubted that she would be dug up, no matter what she said into the microphone. For one thing, unlike the children who had preceded her, she knew Jorbie could never let any of them go free. They were witnesses to his crime; they would tell the police; he would be indicted for murder.

But in the end, like Flan Tierney before her, and George deCarre and Peter Berringer after her, she had given in. She was in a state of helpless terror, without hope, and terrified she would be left where she was; she believed what Jorbie promised because she wanted to believe it as much as Father Duval wanted to believe the voices were a miracle.

"Very good, Peter," said Jorbie into the microphone. "Very good indeed. I never guessed you were such an actor."

"That's all you want me to say?" asked Peter, his voice tentative but shaking with anticipation.

"Right. I've got everything I need."

There was a short silence, then: "Can you hurry up with the shovel and dig me out now? It's terribly cold down here. I'm all over goosebumps."

Jorbie sighed. "I'm sorry, Peter. But I can't."

"You promised! You gave your word. You—"

"That's the trouble with grown-ups, Peter. You can't trust a thing they say. I'm sorry, I really am."

For a moment he listened to Peter's screaming and shrieking and pounding and crying in his headset. With a shrug, he gave the wires from the coffin a hard tug, pulling them loose for good. Carefully he wrapped them into a neat coil and stuffed them into his pocket.

As he walked slowly back toward his car, he thought about his own last statement to Peter before he had yanked the wires free for good. He wasn't sure where it had come from, he thought perhaps it was something Angie had said. No, that didn't make sense. Well, maybe it was something somebody who Angie reminded him of had said, then. No matter how hard he tried, though, he couldn't remember who. He was surprised at how deeply the statement affected him, stabbing at his heart. He shook himself to dismiss it; where it came from was incidental.

Anyway, it was certainly completely valid—perhaps even profound.

You couldn't trust a thing grown-ups told you.

Chapter Twenty

When all this started, I wasn't really sure I could get those buried people to say what I told them to. My Voice kept telling me it would be easy, and like with most things, the Voice turned out to be one hundred percent right. I'd underestimated what fear and even a slim chance of rescue could make people do, I guess.

The Voice never did tell me, though, why getting those people to say the things I made them say was so important. All the stuff about life after death bothers me somehow.

I'm not much for religion, and all this stuff about obeying or getting punished is beginning to get me down, too. The Voice knows what it's doing; I wish it would tell me.

My own best guess is that the Voice wants to build up religion in everybody's mind so later it can pull the rug on it. The Voice thinks like that. Either that, or maybe the Voice is using the miracle of the voices as a distraction. People here in St. Max can't think too much about what might happen to them if they're spending all their time trying to figure out what the voices mean, and if they're a real miracle.

I just hope that from now on Angie will stay away from the whole thing. My Voice doesn't like people messing around in its private business any more than I do.

And when the Voice doesn't like something, it just whispers in my ear a couple of times, and there you

are: face to face with Captain Marvel. Or face to but-
tock, anyway. Poor Angie.

> *Jorbie Tenniel—to the rock,*
> *7:15 P.M., December 3rd*

The eyes staring at him were his mother's, Jorbie was
pretty sure of that. He didn't know how he could be so
sure—his mother had died when he was only seven—
but he was. Shifting, he tried to see more of her. He
couldn't.

The light was coming from behind her, and she was
wearing a hooded cloak of some sort, making her more
of a silhouette than anything else. Only the eyes were
clear, shining out luminously from the total black of the
hood. To Jorbie as he stared at them the eyes seemed
infinitely sad.

Beside his mother was another figure, that of a little
boy. He, too, was dressed in a long cloak, but his eyes,
while visible, were less distinct. Jorbie supposed it was
himself, except that didn't make any sense, since he was
standing on the far edge of whatever part of the Straits
his mother stood on.

At first, when he heard a woman calling his name,
he thought it was Angie's voice, but a second later he
realized it wasn't a woman's voice at all, it was a
child's. The little boy's. "Jorbie . . ." the voice called
from some place far beyond the horizon, "Why did you
do it, Jorbie? Why? You shouldn't have killed me
. . . you just shouldn't. . . ."

Jorbie tried to answer, to explain he didn't know who
the little boy was, and that he was sure, *whoever* he
was, he hadn't killed him, but the voice vanished back
into the distance it had come from. The little boy's face,
until now shrouded in darkness, became brightly lit,

and Jorbie could see that it was changing in and out of focus; sometimes the face was that of the little boy, other times it was that of Angie. Then, as the little boy's figure retreated into the darkness, his mother's eyes once again became candescent, once more staring at Jorbie.

He tried to call out, to speak to her, but no sound would come from his voice; perhaps, he thought, this was how it felt being in the grip of *bonaro*. Like a vice, the paralysis swept over him, freezing him in position. From somewhere beside his mother he heard the muffled throbbing that always filled him with unspoken dread. It grew louder. Twisting and turning, Jorbie tried covering his ears with his hands, but the hammering and throbbing sound was too powerful, drilling into his brain, relentless and inescapable. He stretched out one imploring hand toward his mother, but her only answer was to move her head slowly from one side to the other, in a gesture of heavyhearted disapproval.

Jorbie desperately wanted to explain to her, to plead with her, but his voice remained soundless. From nowhere, the wind suddenly rose, whipping the cloak wildly around the figures of his mother and the boy. The brightness seemed to go out of his mother's eyes and was now concentrated almost entirely on the little boy's. As Jorbie watched the eyes grew larger and more intense, glowing brighter and more penetrating. Jorbie gasped, suddenly realizing the little boy's eyes had become gaping holes in torn flesh, empty sockets in a dim face. Terror swept across Jorbie, a terror he couldn't explain.

Finally, he found his voice. He screamed in panic, waking himself, drenched once again in his own sweat, wrestling with the sheets and pillows in his struggle against—*what?* Jorbie didn't know.

Fully awake, suddenly trembling, Jorbie sat in a chair puffing furiously on a cigarette. Even the fitfully rising smoke seemed haunted by a fear he could put no name to. More and more he felt pushed as if by some powerful unseen force. He threw on some clothes—the warmest he could lay his hands on in a hurry—and half walked, half ran through the darkness, down the steep slope, to the rock. The wind was high and the waves were dashing against the other rocks along the shore, sending great flumes of spray into the air far above his head. In a few minutes he was soaked through by the water dashing against the shore, the wind tearing at his wet clothes and going right through to his body. Jorbie began to shiver uncontrollably, as much from fear as from the cold, some part of him wanting to race back to the warmth and safety of Tenniel's. He couldn't. Whatever force it was that had made him come here, now, at this hour, was not yet ready to release him.

Clambering over the slippery rocks, Jorbie made his uncertain way toward the rock, finally standing a few feet from it, while the water of the Straits drenched him further, filling his sneakers with its angry slosh and taking his breath away with its frigid, penetrating coldness.

For a few seconds he stood there, silent and shivering. Suddenly he heard his own voice rise in a scream—almost a wail—mixing with the turgid thunder of the waves and carried away on the moaning wind. "Damn you, rock. Leave me alone. Get your hands off me. I don't know what it is you want. You've done enough to me already—too damned much."

Jorbie stared at the water surging against the rock, breaking into ominous splinters of gray foam as it struck; he moved farther out onto some large, flat stones, cupping his hands so that he could lower his voice and still be heard. Starting to shiver again, he felt as cold and wet and frightened as he could remember.

"I know your secret, rock. I've known all along, ever since this all began. The Voice—the Voice lives inside you. You're trying to destroy me, both of you. Little by little, you're trying to take me over. Making me kill people I don't want to kill. Between you, you make up that list of who's next, the Voice tells me, and I have to do it. You bastard. I know it's only a matter of time before you make me kill Angie—bury her alive—and, damn it, I don't want that.

"Any more than I wanted to when you made me kill that little boy from the dream, whoever the hell *he* was. Please, please, for Christ's sake, let me go. Destroy me if you have to. Kill me if you have to. But leave me alone, sweet Jesus, let me go. . . ."

Half kneeling on the flat stone he'd been standing on, Jorbie let the water surge around him, sometimes almost seeming to cover him as he waited, listening. He received no answer except the moan of the wind and the crash of the waves.

Angie waited in the heated space just outside the door of Nate's Pharmacy, her eyes constantly checking down the street to her left. Even with the artificial warmth provided by the heat bulbs above her, it was cold in St. Max today; the lights inside Nate's burned brightly in the gathering darkness, and Angie wanted desperately to go inside. She had told Cathy, though, she would meet her here, outside, and since it was Cathy who was doing *her* the favor, Angie decided she owed her the courtesy of being where she'd said she would be.

She checked her watch. She would be late getting to Tenniel's, but she had called Jorbie earlier and warned him of that. She hadn't really expected to be anywhere near as late as she could see she was going to be, but Jorbie had sounded in extremely high spirits and hadn't even asked her the reason for the delay. It was these moments—when Jorbie was in his high moods—that Angie existed for. A subtle burning inside her reminded Angie there was also something on the purely physical

side that she existed for, and the realization made her
laugh out loud. Was she what she'd heard the older
boys at St. Etienne call "horny"? She supposed she
was, Angie admitted, and laughed again.

"Standing on the street laughing to yourself? Well,
you've gone over the edge, Psalter. Off the wall. I knew
it would happen sooner or later."

Angie giggled and spun to face Cathy Springer.
"Thank God, you're here," she said happily. "Nate's
heat bulbs are better than nothing, but I was freezing
my"—she stopped abruptly in midsentence to rephrase;
her own high spirits were no excuse for boy's-room language—"that is, heat bulbs or not, I was freezing out
there."

"I liked what you almost said better. That you were
freezing your ass off. There's a lot to be said for direct,
primitive language." Cathy shook her head as she put
one hand on Nate's doorknob. "Boy, Angie, but you've
changed."

"Something to do with being happy," Angie noted,
glad to go inside and get out of the wind and cold. She
didn't notice the grim expression that fled briefly across
Cathy's face; Cathy knew what was making Angie
happy all too well, and knew the happiness had its roots
in something simultaneously terrifying and dangerous.

The soda-fountain area of Nate's was like something
out of another century. Small, round marble-topped tables. Wire-backed, wooden ice-cream parlor chairs. Ornate hanging-globe lights that must have once been fed
by gas rather than electricity. The young girl who
served as Nate's waitress seemed genuinely stricken
when both Angie and Cathy resisted her suggestions of
banana splits or lemon phosphates or hot chocolates
topped with genuine whipped cream and asked for coffee. Shrugging, the girl walked back to her counter dispiritedly.

"I wasn't at my most brilliant over at Town Hall, I'm

afraid," Cathy announced, sipping at the coffee the girl, still bristling with disappointment, had finally delivered.

"That's all right, Cathy. It probably isn't important anyway."

"To you it is. I know that. Anyway, Alice Sprague—she's my friend who works there part time—had no trouble in finding the birth records. You'd given me Jorbie's birthday, so that part was easy. But the page that recorded when his twin died—well, it was all mildewed or had water spilled on it or something—Alice showed me the page; it was a mess—so all she could guarantee was the year. Not the month or the day. Naturally, without those the death certificate couldn't be found either. Anyway, the year was 1965, which would have made Jorbie and his twin about eight, depending on what month the twin died in. I'm sorry."

Eight. Eight years old. Angie was running the age through her head to see if she could remember anything Jorbie had said about being eight. She couldn't, but then, Jorbie was as mysterious about his childhood as his father, old Caleb, was, and it dawned on Angie that Jorbie had never said anything at all. She smiled up brightly at Cathy; she knew Cathy hadn't wanted to get involved, even on the periphery, with anything that involved Jorbie. "With that year, I've got plenty to go on. The *St. Max Courier* has a complete set of back issues somewhere. I'll just look through 1965 until I find something." A thought suddenly struck her. "Did Alice Sprague give you the twin's name?"

"Not even that. On the birth certificates they were still unnamed. You know, 'Baby boy Tenniel, Baby boy Tenniel.' I'm sorry."

"Don't be, don't be, Cathy. You've been a big help." Angie surreptitiously checked her watch again. "Cathy, I have to go. It's awful, after everything you've done, but I'm late as it is. Can you ever forgive me for being so rude?"

"No, never. I'll hold it against you for life," Cathy laughed. "Go on, run along. My treat. Staggering tab, but I'm a big spender." Because she didn't want to, Angie did not see the same grim expression flicker across Cathy's face as before. Cathy Springer knew exactly where Angie was going, and the thought never failed to terrify her.

Gratefully, Angie thanked her again and pecked Cathy on one cheek, almost running down the street to get to her car. On the way out to Tenniel's she considered the weary prospect of looking through a year's worth of *St. Max Courier*'s back issues. She'd seen the room where they kept them; it was a worse mess than what Cathy described finding at Town Hall. Mr. Giradoux—he was editor, publisher, circulation director, and sole reporter—had many virtues, but neatness was not among them. She shivered slightly thinking of the dirty little storage room where the back issues were kept, filled with dirt, mouse droppings, and small crawling insects. Still, somewhere inside those issues, she was convinced, lay the secret behind Jorbie's tortured behavior. She was determined to uncover it. Quite possibly it was something even Jorbie himself couldn't remember. The idea of there once having been a double image of Jorbie returned to fascinate her. If the twin had lived, would he still look exactly like Jorbie? Obviously. Would he have the same mind, the same sense of humor, the same wonderfully mysterious spirit as Jorbie? Less certain, she supposed. Would he have the same body? Of course. The same—? Angie stopped herself in midthought. She was becoming a dirty old woman. But the thought kept reappearing at intervals during the drive, teasing her, laughing at her. With a shake of her head Angie realized the ache she felt earlier inside had returned. Okay—she was horny, as her older pupils would have said.

She shivered again, this time from the cold inside the car; some day she'd have to invest in a gas-heater for it. The car was just becoming warm when she swung into the long drive that led in to Tenniel's, following the deathly pale beams of her headlights as they probed among the twisted trees until her car finally pulled up in front of the house itself. The place was brightly lit and looked warm and cheerful. Here was her happiness. Here was her warmth. Here was her safety.

Jorbie had been working on the freezer's compressor, and finally had the machine adjusted to his satisfaction, when he realized Pasteur was standing behind him, watching him work, and holding something fuzzy cradled in his hands.

Standing up, cleaning his fingers on a small piece of cloth, Jorbie had turned toward Pasteur with a small, sarcastic smile. "What the hell is *that*, Pasteur? You playing with dolls now?"

"It's one of them hamsters, Mr. Jorbie. The cage out there is getting real crowded, see. This poor li'l feller just got pushed away from the feed trough too often, seems. Fell over dead."

Pasteur had stroked the lifeless fur of the dead hamster and looked at Jorbie sadly. The death of any animal affected him; the hamsters, left over from the time when Jorbie was experimenting with dosage levels of *bonaro*, were his particular passion. ("They can recognize me, honest, Mr. Jorbie," he had once told him. "They run over to the feed trough soon as they see me coming.")

"Too crowded, uh?" Jorbie snickered. "That's because they fuck too much. Fuck themselves stupid. All hamsters do." Jorbie gave a mean laugh. "Okay, just leave it over there on the table; I'll do something with it."

A pleading look crept into Pasteur's expression. "Mr. Jorbie, could *I* bury it? Please? Like he was a special friend of mine?"

"For all I care, you can eat the damned thing." Amused, he'd watched Pasteur trot out of the room with the hamster's body still cradled in his arms.

Jorbie had forgotten the hamsters were still even in the makeshift lab. Once, they'd been important; now, they were superfluous. Someday, though, they might become important again, but for the moment . . .

Quickly he had walked out of the preparation room and into the old lab, trying not to notice the peculiarly sour-sweet stench any room with a large cage of small animals always has. The hamsters eyed him with misgivings, their endless succession of squeals and chirps slowly fading into silence.

Long ago Jorbie had given the original set names, chosen from among the citizens of St. Max. To make them easy to identify, a splash of indelible dye had been painted on their ears, matching a color-coded list of names fastened to the outside of the cage. He never quite understood why he'd chosen most of the names he had. There was Hardy Remarque, Dr. L'Eveque, Sister Honorée, Angie Psalter, Lutetia Losee . . . and on, and on.

Studying them, Jorbie had to agree that Pasteur was right; the cage was crowded. One of the animals—the list indicated it was Cathy Springer—was trying to use the exercise wheel but couldn't; too many other hamsters were jammed tightly against it. With a shrug, Jorbie decided it was time to thin them out.

Reaching inside, Jorbie seized the hamster named Flan Tierney. He didn't know why there should have been a hamster named after Flan, but there was, and he held the animal firmly in his left hand while it struggled and squirmed, trying to escape. "Hi, Flan, we meet again," Jorbie had whispered, and then took his right hand, grabbed the hamster's head, and twisted it until there was a small but clearly audible snap. The hamster went limp. Flan Tierney had suffered his second death.

The next victim was pulled out of the cage after another consultation with the list of names. Carefully, Jorbie had matched the vibrantly purple ears of one animal with the list's indicated color. Jorbie held the hamster directly up in front of his face. "Well, Lutetia," he had said, "you always *did* look good in fur . . . in fact, I might say you never looked better than you do right now." Once again, he turned the hamster's neck, twisting it around with his right hand. *Snap-crunch*. Because he pulled the head back the same time as he twisted, Lutetia's neck gave a far more satisfying *snap-crunch* than Flan Tierney's had.

To Hardy Remarque, a man who filled him with anger, he made the neck-twisting a slow and agonizing process, his eyes shining as the hamster struggled painfully under the pressure, so terrified it peed all over Jorbie's hand. Jorbie swore. Just like Hardy, always pissing all over him.

Jorbie could feel his heart beating faster and a flush of frenzy coming over him as he moved from animal to animal. He was going much faster now, either because he was becoming more adept or because of what seemed a rampaging fever. *Snap-crunch*: Peter Berringer. The hamster named Peter was definitely not singing today. *Snap-crunch*: George deCarre, *snap-crunch*: Jorbie's eyes stared at the dead hamster in his hand. Even before he looked at the list, he knew he had just killed Angie.

A puzzled look came across his face. He hadn't intended that. Yet he had done it, as surely as if the Voice had whispered the command in his ear. He shrugged and winnowed down the rest of the hamsters, choosing ones with names he didn't care about. To any interested ob-

server the names he chose would have made a fascinat-
ing study. When he had finished, Jorbie put all but one
of the dead hamsters in a large carton, which he would
carry down to the Straits of Mackinac and let drift
away.

The remaining hamster he had carried very gently
downstairs into the mortuary's boiler room, pulling
open the door of the oil burner and cremating the small
animal in the searing blast of heat from the giant burner.

It was the hamster named Angie, and Jorbie felt she
deserved a more dignified fate than being eaten by the
crabs and the fish and the bottom-crawlers of Lake
Michigan. That had happened to someone he knew
once, although Jorbie, for some reason, couldn't remember who.

When he was all through, Jorbie had been exuberant,
almost euphoric. He could feel it in his step as he
walked back upstairs; he could hear it in his voice when
he had talked to Angie.

Maybe, he told himself, he just didn't like hamsters—
any hamster.

Jorbie lived up to the mood his voice promised over
the phone. He was exuberant. The moment Angie
walked in the door, he folded her into his arms and
began talking very fast, like an excited child. In the living room the fire blazed brightly: Angie noticed some
of the candlesticks along the far wall were flickering
with cheerful, warm promise.

Hesitantly, Jorbie fielded a suggestion. "You know,
Angie, let's not get into sex tonight. Okay? I'm tired,
but something else. It'll be more fun just sitting in front
of the fire after dinner and talking. I love to talk."

Although disappointed in one way—the ache inside
her had grown progressively ever since she'd set foot
inside the front door—Angie was flattered. Every
woman's secret fear about an affair is that she is some-

how being reduced to a sex object; Jorbie's suggestion had just exorcised that worry for Angie. Still . . . the ache . . .

Angie had no way of knowing that Jorbie's sudden love of talking sprang largely from his increasing fear of silence, any silence that might allow the muffled pulsing to intrude on his consciousness. The sound haunted him, the fear of it following him wherever he went, night or day.

And they *did* talk for a while, Angie pulling back several times from an almost compulsive desire to ask Jorbie about his twin. She couldn't seem to erase the subject from her mind. Yet she was in control of herself enough to know that bringing it up could easily lead to another of his frightening mood-swings or outright violence. She found the talking increasingly difficult, possessed on the one hand by wanting desperately to bring up what she knew she shouldn't, and on the other, by the ache inside her that was beginning to tear her apart.

For the first time Angie deliberately and openly played the aggressor, the last vestiges of the Victorian novel melted away. In the middle of a sentence Angie reached over and put her hand on Jorbie's crotch, moving it slightly, and then leaned across to kiss his ear. For an instant Jorbie stared at her with amazement, then the slow, expert movement of her fingers produced the swelling she so desperately needed.

Jorbie's desire to talk vanished. On the couch in front of the blazing fire, they quickly melted together. Impatiently, she turned off the light and tore off his clothes, leaving his trim, gleaming body illuminated only by the flickering gold of the fire. Jorbie still appeared surprised, but he was excited and breathing heavily, responding to the movement of her hands up and down the entire length of him, probing, exploring, finding. Angie's clothes joined his in a puddle on the floor.

The thing surprised him when it happened again.

Christ, at a moment like this. But it was a sensation he'd been experiencing more and more strongly lately. And more frequently. For no reason he could think of, Angie kept reminding him of someone, someone from the long-distant past. The way she spoke, the way she laughed, the way she moved.

It was an eerie feeling. To rid himself of it, he threw himself back into the business of making love with all the energy he could summon.

Abruptly, as if he'd just thought of it for the first time, his hands came alive and began running over her, once again finding that spot inside her that, until Jorbie, she had barely known existed. There was something marvelously primitive, almost savage, about making love this way, Angie decided—suddenly, without preparation, on a chance couch instead of the calculated formality of a bed. A noise somewhere inside the house brought to it, however, a twinge of nervousness, in itself exciting in its dangerous implications.

"What do we do," Angie hissed, "if someone walks in on us?"

Jorbie laughed softly. "Dad can't get down the stairs. There's a couple of bodies in the freezer, but Christ, if *they* walk in, well, hell—they'll find us both right here in the morning, stiff as boards. Simultaneous massive coronaries."

Angie couldn't help laughing; the picture he painted was ludicrous. The laughter quickly transformed itself into a moan as she felt Jorbie thrusting inside her, moaning himself, pushing her so deep into the cushions of the couch she felt her body was surrounded by a sea of eiderdown.

The only trouble with a couch, Angie discovered later, was that after it was over, you couldn't lie there and snuggle. The air on your body suddenly felt cold: you became aware of your own nakedness; your lover seemed nervous, almost guilty. "We'd better get upstairs," Jorbie said, apparently feeling the same thing. "I told Dad we'd have dinner with him in his room."

"Oh, Jorbie, my God, but I love you," Angie whispered as Jorbie climbed back into his clothes.

He turned and kissed her, mumbling something she couldn't quite hear. Angie assumed he had returned her statement in kind, but wished just once Jorbie would tell her clearly, distinctly, and without equivocation.

"*Officers and Gentlemen* was very good, Angie. I'm afraid we've about done all of Waugh, though; I don't know where we go next."

"Maybe Graham Greene. He has some wonderfully light stuff sprinkled through his work. I'll check it out."

Angie was sitting in the chair she usually took, toward the bottom of Caleb Tenniel's bed. He liked her there rather than in one of the closer ones, he said, because he could keep her in full view the whole time she was in it. "It's quite a sight," he had once commented. Jorbie was back downstairs, doing something with a sauce for the fish, which he had told them was a Great Lakes version of red snapper. No, he wouldn't listen to any suggestion of help from Angie.

A question—the question that Angie could not force out of her mind—was making her restless. Caleb had always been highly evasive about Jorbie's childhood. But, with what was almost a death wish, Angie seemed unable to control herself any longer. This was the perfect moment for it. "Caleb, I know it's not something you probably want to go into, but Jorbie's twin. What happened to him? Jorbie never mentions him. All I know is that he died."

At first Caleb stared at her in surprise, the glass in his hand beginning to tremble a little. The shocked state was finally replaced by a resigned sigh. "Kenneth? He drowned. In 1965. It was tragic."

"But why doesn't Jorbie ever mention him? An identical twin, after all—"

"No one *ever* mentions him. My God, Angie, that was almost twenty years ago."

"Did he talk a lot about it then? I mean, right after it happened."

"At first. He was heartbroken. Identical twins like that, you know, are almost two parts of the same person. Act alike, dress alike, hell, even *think* alike. Sometimes it was hard to believe. But we had fun, my God, we had fun." Caleb smiled to himself, apparently living some scene out of the past. Suddenly his face turned angry-looking, as if he'd remembered something he wished he hadn't. He shook his head as if to get rid of it, and turned back to Angie.

"After a while, though, Jorbie just stopped talking about him at all. It was all locked up inside him. I left it at that. Jorbie hasn't mentioned him to me since a couple of months after the accident. Nor I to him. It seemed better that way. . . ."

Something in what Caleb had said was bothering Angie deeply. She wasn't being told something. Angie wanted to ask more, to find out what Caleb was hiding from her, but she could see Caleb growing increasingly nervous, as if he feared being caught discussing a forbidden subject. Even from where she sat, Angie could see a small line of perspiration rimming his forehead just beneath the shock of flowing white hair. She didn't mean to be cruel to Caleb—since Jorbie, he had become a highly important part of her life—but there was one final question Angie couldn't resist. "Are you sure he even *remembers* it, Caleb?"

"That's a God damn ridiculous question, Angie, and you know it. Of course he remembers it. He found the body, for Christ's sake. He just doesn't want to talk about it. And neither do I." It was the first time Angie

had ever seen Caleb angry; it was the first time he had
ever spoken to her crossly. His face had reddened, and
he suddenly took the wineglass and drained it in one
swallow.

"I'm sorry, Caleb. I really am. I just had to know."

"Now you know." There was a note of genuine bitterness in his voice, and his eyes burned into her angrily. "Could you get me another glass of Pouilly
Fuissé?" he asked suddenly, trying, Angie suspected, to
change the subject. Suddenly an afterthought appeared
to come to him. "Don't *you* ever mention it to him either, Angie. I tell you, it's better left alone."

Angie didn't agree. Caleb was hiding something, she
decided, not only from her but possibly from himself as
well. But she didn't want to get Caleb angry again. She
shrugged and was on her way to the door when Jorbie
appeared with the Great Lakes red snapper.

The Pouilly Fuissé was as good as wine can be; the
snapper was superb, but it all seemed suddenly flat and
tasteless to Angie. There are some things in life, she
suspected, you can't hide from forever.

Later, after dinner was over and she and Jorbie had
spent their ritual half hour in front of the fire, they
softly climbed the stairs to his bedroom. Twice, Angie
found herself on the verge of asking Jorbie a direct
question about his twin—damn, Caleb had mentioned
his name, but he'd mumbled it, and it had gone right
past Angie—but each time she had smothered the impulse by initiating sex. Perhaps, Angie told herself, she
had found the solution to not asking Jorbie questions
that could set him off: reach for his balls.

But after the third time, with Jorbie now barely able
to speak and half falling asleep from exhaustion, and
the burning inside herself well quenched, she felt the
impulse returning and was unable to resort to her new
system. She knew it was wrong, she knew it was dan-

gerous, and she struggled to keep herself from speaking, but the words crept up on her and she found herself saying them anyway, as bluntly, as matter-of-factly, as if she were asking him the time. "Jorbie, sweetheart, why don't you ever talk about your twin?"

Jorbie raised himself slightly off his pillow and fixed her with a curious eye. He gave her a lopsided smile, looking at her sadly, as if he thought she might have lost her mind. "I never had any brothers or sisters at all."

"Your father says you did. The Town Records *show* you did. He died in 1965. You can't have forgotten. . . ."

Jorbie was sitting all the way up now. His face quickly filled with fury, his expression grew ugly, and he appeared to Angie to have gone a little insane. "You're crazy!" he screamed at her. "Stop lying to me!" His hand rose off the bed and slapped her across the face so hard she knew by tomorrow she would have a beauty of a black eye.

Still naked, Jorbie was out of bed, standing over her. "Damn you, why do you keep on doing it? It's unfair, unfair, unfair! You're spying on me again, making up lies about me, that's what you're doing." His voice had soared to the same high pitch it had assumed the other night, the language again becoming a child's. "Spying," he yelled. "Making things up, that's what. So you can tattle. I know how you work."

Angie was shocked at his reversion to the childish.

He stood by the bed, looming over her, his face turning dark in his anger. He was behaving so irrationally Angie found herself frightened. "Jorbie," pleaded Angie, trying reason, "I'm not spying on you, sweetheart. I'm not making things up. You just have to face—"

"Shut up, shut up. Lies, lies, lies!" For an instant his eyes burned into hers. Not sure of what he might do next, Angie instinctively shrank into the pillows.

"That's right. Try to hide, scaredy-cat. You can't hide from me. Scaredy-cat tattletale liar!" He suddenly spat in her face, then spun, picked up his clothes, and raced from the room.

She lay where she was, too stunned to move. In a curious way, Jorbie's denial of having a twin brother was the most frightening thing that had happened yet. Because, it showed that somewhere just below the surface, there ran an ominous vein of madness. Downstairs, she could hear the front door slam as he rushed out into the night.

It was a pity Angie Psalter didn't rush out of Jorbie's life with the same urgency.

Chapter Twenty-one

I don't suppose there's an undertaker alive who hasn't looked at someone on his slab and wondered what it would be like if—well, what is pretty obvious. I heard once that a certain number of them stop wondering and decide to find out for themselves, sometimes turning it into a full-scale pastime. See, when you work around bodies all day, you get over your initial qualms pretty fast. A body is just a lump of flesh, only some lumps are more attractive than others.

I only came even close once—when I was maybe seventeen or so. There was this girl on the slab from Charlevoix, about sixteen, I guess, killed in an automobile accident down in Traverse City. Not a mark on her, except one small bruise on her upper neck.

I stood staring down at her for a long time—she was damned attractive, that girl—thinking maybe I would. Hell, the girl wouldn't mind.

But something stopped me. I ran my fingers over her a little, but that was as far as I went. Finally, I swore at her a couple of times and pulled the sheet back up over her head.

Funny, I hadn't thought of that thing in years until I dreamed about it the other night. Out of nowhere. Only instead of the girl from Charlevoix it was Angie on the slab. And the Voice kept telling me that was where she belonged, and Angie kept arguing with me, saying she was too close to me for me even to consider putting her there. And that, hell, I could sleep with her anytime; I didn't have to kill her to get all of that I wanted.

Too close to me. Maybe that's the problem right there. I've let Angie get too close to me. It's getting worse all the time, damn it. Pretty soon she'll be so

*close she'll know all about me. Then, the next time the
Voice tells me to get rid of her, I won't have any
choice.*

*Angie will be planted somewhere out at Carpas
Point, right next to the girl from Charlevoix. It's only
fair; they both tempted me into doing things I really
knew better than to do.*

> *Jorbie Tenniel—to the rock,
> 5:20 P.M., December 5th*

The first thing Angie heard that morning, a Saturday,
was the strident ringing of the phone downstairs. Damn.
She hoped her father wasn't up yet. He was. She raced
into the kitchen just in time to hear him swearing angrily at Jorbie, yelling at him to keep his fucking cold
hands away from his daughter. Her father spun on her.
"That was your friend, the ghoul. Well, I told him!
Maybe he'll keep his ass out of your life from now on. I
heard what time you got home last night, Angie. Three
o'clock, for Christ's sake. Bad enough you turn into the
town lay; you got to pick the local grave robber to fuck
around with. I know what you're doing, damn it. I'm a
drunk, not a stupid jerk."

Tight-lipped, Angie sat in the kitchen, waiting impatiently for her father to go to the bathroom. It was a
morning ritual with him that even his state of perpetual
drunkenness had not changed. Muttering, he finally
picked up a magazine and headed across the hall.

Angie dialed Jorbie. "Hi," he answered cheerfully. "I
wasn't sure you'd be speaking to me this morning. I
talked to your father; he sounds as pleasant as I can be
sometimes." There was a short pause while Jorbie
shifted his mood from lightness to solemnity. "I'm sorry
about last night. Or this morning, or whenever it was. A

real twenty-four-karat bastard. Sometimes I have a foul temper. Awful. Can you forgive me, Angie?"

"I don't know." The words had just slipped out. They were what she felt, but Angie was as surprised to hear them as she supposed Jorbie was. She'd seen herself in the mirror, and the predicted black eye had materialized; she'd have to wear dark glasses for a couple of days to avoid the eye becoming a topic of conversation, and dark glasses in St. Max in the middle of winter would in themselves raise a good deal of headshaking curiosity. The changing moods, the outbursts, the violence were becoming more frightening to Angie; to these Angie could now add what was perhaps the most frightening element of all: Jorbie's denial of his twin's existence. Less spectacular on the surface, this aspect of Jorbie's behavior was a powerful indication of his growing dementia.

As for herself, Angie had a growing sense that with Jorbie some vague danger was closing in on her, moving in to threaten her like the walls of the suddenly claustrophobic kitchen she was standing in at that particular moment, talking to Jorbie.

Some distant voice of reason told her to get out of the whole thing. But even as she thought about it, Angie found herself beginning to waver, remembering the wonderful times with Jorbie, the closeness, the laughter, the feeling of being loved and wanted, and the glorious physical expression of it all.

Over the phone Jorbie's voice sounded suddenly small and hurt.

"Well, it's up to you, of course. But"—there was a long silence during which Angie could hear his breathing— "Oh, never mind. . . ."

A sudden panic swept over Angie. What did Jorbie mean? Maybe it *was* all over and she'd just said the words that finished it. The worries and dangers and unpleasantness she sometimes associated with him quickly receded into the background; all she was left with was a sudden desperate fear she would lose the wonderful side of her life he represented. Angie knew she should stay calm and keep sounding a little distant, but, as in the desperate things she sometimes said that sent him into wild but predictable furies, she couldn't control herself. "What I mean is, yes, of course, I forgive you, Jorbie. What I don't know is why sometimes you have to act so violently." It was a lame retreat from a position of strength. Angie knew it, and wished she could somehow have been firmer with him, but couldn't.

"All I can say is to repeat I'm sorry, Angie. I don't know what makes me act that way. Your father, at least, has booze as an excuse."

"Don't worry about it." Angie almost despised herself for those words. The weakness of the totally dependent.

"Anyway," said Jorbie, "I'm glad we're back being—what?—lovers again." It was as calculated an attack as some of the devices he used with Pasteur, and Jorbie knew it, hating himself a little for how he was manipulating Angie. In his own way, he knew, he did love her.

Calculated or not, the word "lover" sent Angie into a fit of happiness. It was as close as Jorbie had ever come to saying outright that he loved her. Without realizing what she was really doing, Angie pressed to capitalize on her new advantage.

"Maybe we could meet for lunch—it's Saturday—and go to a movie and get the taste out of our mouths. You know . . ."

"Oh, Jesus, Angie, I'd love to. But I can't, though. Too damned many things to get out of the way. Here and downtown. Could we make it tonight for dinner? I know, there's not much kick in that for you—coming here again—but it's the best I can manage."

On one point Jorbie had been completely honest in what he said to Angie. No, he couldn't meet her for lunch; he had too many things to get out of the way. Only a more fitting word than "things" would have been "people."

From one standpoint the incredible regularity of Hardy Remarque's daily schedule was an advantage: People almost always knew exactly where their police chief would be at any given hour, and if they needed him, could count on finding him there. 8:00 A.M., coffee at Nate's Pharmacy. Before leaving, he would telephone Mae Evers and check in for the day. 8:30, his tour of the streets on foot. 9:00, a cruise around the outlying neighborhoods in the police car. 10:00, his office. 11:00, coffee again at Nate's. Before he left, he would again telephone Mae Evers and check out for lunch. 12:00, lunch at the Mackinac Bar and Grill. 1:00, another tour of the streets. Et cetera.

Jorbie Tenniel knew the chief's routine as well as anyone else. It had always amazed him that, short of a blizzard or summer downpour, Hardy Remarque could stick to his schedule with such incredible precision, as unchanging as the revolutions of the strike wheel on some giant clock. Jorbie had smiled; he could use the chief's monotonously rigid pattern to his own advantage.

This was not a mission that the Voice had commanded him to perform; Hardy Remarque's name had not been whispered in his ear. But disposing of him had become a necessity; the man, only mystified at first, had now become suspicious. Jorbie had never liked Remarque; he tolerated him. But what made his decision to eliminate him necessary had come in a telephone call from Remarque that Jorbie received before leaving Tenniel's.

"Jorbie? Hardy Remarque. Hope I'm not interrupting anything."

"No, nothing at all," Jorbie had smiled into the receiver.

"Look, Jorbie, I have to ask you to keep this quiet. But tell me, have you heard yet that little Peter Berringer's voice was heard last night too?"

"No, I hadn't. I suppose I will, though."

"Damned right you will. This town's on fire with the story. Whale Berringer, his wife, Father Duval, a brother in Charlevoix—they all heard it. Same kind of stuff as with Flan Tierney and Lutetia Losee."

"I'll be damned." Jorbie had to force the surprise into his voice; inside, he wanted to howl with laughter at Mr. Regularity, Hardy Remarque.

"And the reason I'm calling you is because of where you fit in St. Max's structure. See, I could buy two somewhat mysterious deaths—Flan's and Lutetia's—I didn't like it, but I could go along. I was already damned suspicious, but no one else seemed bothered. Three is too much, particularly with all this crap about the voices loaded on top of it. Either someone is pulling a big scam, or we've got an old-fashioned murderer running around loose. Either way, I want to get to the bottom of it. I wanted to do an autopsy—a real one, not one of Dr. L'Eveque's—on Lutetia, but I was too late getting to you. That's what I want to prevent happening again. If someone suddenly dies, I'll call you, and instead of draining the body and filling it with formaldehyde or whatever it is you do, I want you to hang on to it until I can get it taken down to Saginaw for an autopsy by the coroner there. I've already talked to him, and he's all set. But it won't do any good if you've already drained the body. Is that okay with you?"

"Sure, Hardy. I'll hang on to as many bodies as my freezer will hold. After that, I'll have to start kicking them out to make room for paying customers."

Hardy Remarque had not laughed, or even chuckled. Square. But Jorbie already knew that. Remarque's answer was as square as he was. "I'd appreciate it, Jorbie. I really would. There's something fishy going on here."

"You're so right," Jorbie said mostly to himself. Then he had returned to his innocent act. "Peter Berringer's voice heard too. I'll be damned."

After a brief further exchange, Hardy Remarque hung up. Jorbie sat and stared at the wall. People snooping. Angie prying. Hardy Remarque talking about autopsies. He had to act; his plan for Remarque had been in the back of his mind ever since Dr. L'Eveque had let it slip that Remarque was suspicious.

"Dark glasses in the middle of winter?" Cathy Springer stared at Angie, leaning from side to side, trying to get a look beneath the edges of the lenses.

Angie tried to shrug it off. "Oh, I'm on the way to the *Courier* office to look through their 1965 back issues. You know the light in there. Fluorescent. Every time I've tried to read small type under fluorescent light anywhere before, I've gotten a headache. My eyes."

"Baloney, Angie. Who are you trying to kid?" Cathy had finally spotted the edge of the dark bruise under Angie's right eye. "You've got a shiner. A beaut." She paused for a moment, caught between her wish not to get herself back in the middle and her genuine concern for Angie. She made her choice. "I don't even have to ask you how you got it."

The note of open hostility in Cathy's voice was obvious to Angie. She could feel her defenses going up. "It was an accident, Cathy. A stupid accident. Something real silly. You'd laugh if I told you. But it made Jorbie feel simply terrible. He called this morning to apologize again."

Inside, Cathy exploded. Somehow she had to make Angie face reality, whatever the risk to their friendship.

Shaking her head, Cathy pointed sourly to the bruise behind the glasses. "Look. This time it's only a black eye. God knows what it'll be next. Promise or no promise, I've got to give it to you straight, Angie. That man is dangerous. Nuts. A terrible threat to you." Cathy stared into Angie's blank expression, aware that what she was saying wasn't getting through. "Oh, shit. Maybe you get some kind of kick putting yourself out on a limb, taking your life in your hands. I don't know."

Angie merely smiled.

A little after ten thirty Jorbie walked into Nate's Pharmacy. He walked directly back to where Nate himself stood, behind the long counter where the prescriptions were filled. "Nate, you got a small deVilbis atomizer back there anywhere? I need one for some makeup work."

"Sure thing, Jorbie. Let's see. This too big or too small?"

Jorbie pretended to study the atomizer Nate held up over the countertop. "Just right. How much?"

"Two ninety-five. Plus tax."

"Christ, I can remember when they went for half that. But I got to have it, so there we are."

Nate laughed; Jorbie had always liked him. Unlike many of the people in St. Max, he didn't take himself and everything that happened so damned seriously. "Hell, Jorbie," Nate said. "I can remember when I could sell a Coke for a nickel and a hamburger for a quarter. I can't even give 'em a stick of gum for that these days."

Jorbie pocketed the atomizer and a few minutes later slipped into the men's room, off to one side of the old-fashioned ice-cream parlor. There, he filled the deVilbis from a small vial—it was the same vial he'd swiped

from the refrigerated safe at Marquette's labs the day
he stole his supply of *bonaro*—and put it carefully back
in his pocket. With great thoroughness, he rinsed his
hands with a powerful antiseptic, carried in a bottle he
had tucked away in his overcoat pocket. On his way out
he studied a twisted bunch of wires that ran along the
ceiling molding. It was just as he thought: They ran
down the wall behind Nate's magazine counter before
disappearing into the wall. This counter, stuffed with
comic books and an occasional dog-eared copy of *Playboy* and other minor erotica, was a sort of reading room
for the town's older children, some of whom were already drifting in.

Quickly, Jorbie reached over the rack and cut the
bunched wires with a finely sharpened pocket knife.
That should do it.

Out on the street, Jorbie stepped into the phone
booth outside Nate's. It was presumably heated by an
electric element and fan in its ceiling, and another in its
floor, but was rarely used in cold weather. Most people
simply drifted into Nate's and used his. Taking out the
deVilbis atomizer, Jorbie thoroughly sprayed the telephone mouthpiece and dial, then quickly stepped out,
shutting the folding doors behind him. Shivering a little
from the cold, he walked a few steps up the street and
shrank into the doorway of Pete's Market to watch.

At eleven, precisely on schedule—was St. Max's police chief ever even just a few minutes late?—Hardy
Remarque strode briskly into Nate's Pharmacy. Everything was ready for him; Jorbie had set his deadfall
with great care, using Remarque's inflexible schedule to
maximum advantage. By that schedule, the first thing
Hardy Remarque would do was use Nate Lavin's
phone to check in with Mae Evers. Only today, he
would discover Nate's phone wasn't working—Jorbie
had cut the wires.

Later, no one would think anything of the wires. It must have been one of the kids, someone would say, and that would be that.

Hardy Remarque, frustrated by not being able to use Nate's phone, would take the obvious step; he would walk to the street and use the one in the phone booth outside. Talking into it, he would inhale what Jorbie had sprayed on the mouthpiece: spores of pulmonary anthrax, left over from his investigations into the disease two years earlier.

The agony of the kind of death pulmonary anthrax produced was a little strong, even for Jorbie. He had waited for his Voice to whisper Remarque's name in his ear, but the Voice would not cooperate. Being given the Captain Marvel treatment and then buried alive might or might not be worse than death by pulmonary anthrax, but it was certainly tidier.

The disease struck first with a high, flu-like fever—perhaps twenty-four hours after exposure to the spores—that progressed rapidly to open, running sores, agonizing pain, delirium, coma, and finally, an inevitable but deeply appreciated death. Fitting, Jorbie thought, for those who snooped and pried, trying to uncover the secret he shared only with his Voice. Jorbie could feel his adrenaline pumping with excitement as he peered around the corner of his hiding place, waiting for Hardy Remarque to storm out of Nate's and angrily march into the phone booth—and eternity. But someone coming down the street forced him to pull back sharply, leaving only one eye exposed.

Walking toward Nate's, carrying a clipboard under her arm and looking worried and sad, was Angie Psalter. Jorbie's heart jumped. My God, what if *Angie* had a call to make and used that phone? He couldn't very well rush out to warn her. Yet, in his own way, Jorbie knew he loved and needed Angie almost as much as she did him. She couldn't go into the booth, damn it, she couldn't. Damn, damn, damn. Where the hell was Remarque? Why was his usually inalterable schedule not running true to course?

In his plan, no one was to use that phone *except* Hardy Remarque. Damn it, his changed timing was endangering innocent people. (To prevent anyone from using the phone *after* Hardy Remarque, Jorbie had a plastic bag of dogshit, kept warm in a thermos-locker, stashed in his car. As soon as Remarque had placed his call, Jorbie would take a deep breath, hold it, and smear the mess on the floor's heating element, using a shoe to make it look natural. With the door shut and the heating element on, anyone stepping into the booth would gag on the smell. It would make the booth unusable long enough for the short-lived spores to become impotent.)

Fascinated but horrified, he watched Angie draw close. Outside Nate's she hesitated, looking in through the window, and, at one point, turning to look toward the booth. Jorbie groaned. If he'd had any idea of what Angie had been doing, or what she planned to do next, he would have groaned even louder.

"Let's see, let's see. Somewhere over there, I think." Crotchety old Mr. Giradoux had said it to Angie's face, but she could see he was really saying it to himself. Following up his words, Giradoux had led Angie over to several piles of back issues stacked haphazardly on rickety-looking tables in the storage room. The place was presumably heated, but not very efficiently; Angie felt herself begin to shiver the moment she followed him into the room. It was every bit as dirty as she remembered, and every now and then you could hear mice or rats scurrying across the disintegrating paper. "1965, 1965, 1965." Giradoux had muttered, almost as if enough repetition would conjure up the correct stack on demand. "Ah, here they are. 1965."

"Great," Angie said, sweeping something that hung from the ceiling away from her face.

"I'm sorry they're not in better order. They're in *no* order, I'm afraid. Just the way you see them. But all of the issues are there. I'm afraid you'll just have to wade through them, Angie, until you find what you want."

Humming, Giradoux had left her. Angie stared at the pile of 1965 issues dispiritedly. Instead of the fluorescent lights she'd told Cathy about, the room was lit by two single one-hundred-watt bulbs, hanging from the end of long cords, and swaying slightly every time Angie moved in any direction. With a sigh of resignation, Angie had dragged a small straight-backed chair over to the table and began going through the year 1965, slowly, carefully, trying to ignore the dirt and grime the copies left on her hands.

In the end, Angie decided she had been lucky. She had arrived to start searching at eight thirty; she found what she was looking for shortly before ten thirty.

It was all there, in a much more prominent position than she had expected—the front page. The story of the twin's drowning had been big news then; a similiar event today would have been too. All of the details were reported in depth. The boys building the sand castle on the beach; the boys swimming to the raft where the older boys were; the fact that Jorbie was a good swimmer, while his twin was not; the middle-aged swimmer's futile effort to save the child; a man who had organized the launching of the dory in another useless effort to rescue the boy; the lay teacher from St. Etienne who had comforted Jorbie and finally taken him home. The name of the teacher startled Angie: Edith Pardee. It shouldn't, Angie realized. Like herself, Mrs. Pardee had been a lay teacher at St. Etienne.

There were a lot of other names mentioned as well, Angie discovered. Some were familiar, some were not.

Actually, if Angie had studied the *Courier* article calmly and rationally, she'd have realized that *all* of the names were familiar. Familiar and part of a frightening pattern.

Flan Tierney and Peter Berringer were both sons of boys who had been on the raft that day: Hank Tierney and Whale Berringer. Lutetia Losee was the wife of the swimmer who failed in his effort to save the drowning boy: Quentin Losee. The man who had launched the rescue dory was St. Max's recent "suicide": George deCarre. With the exception of deCarre, all of these people were recently dead and represented only by their voices calling from the grave.

If Angie could have put all of this together, it would have been obvious that someone was deliberately killing, one by one, everyone involved in the drowning. Then they were using the Miracle of the Voices to distract the townspeople from recognizing the horrible pattern formed by Jorbie's roll call of the dead. Worse, there had been a lot more people on the beach that September afternoon; the Voice still had many left to dispose of.

It had been so long ago Angie didn't remember it—she was about five years old at the time—but she herself had been on the beach the day of the accident, playing in the sun with her kindergarten class from St. Etienne.

In retrospect, it is sad, but Angie simply didn't see the obvious when she read the article. Many things might have turned out differently if she had. Angie had not yet tied the rash of other deaths in St. Max to Jorbie and herself—her capacity to avoid facing the reality of the jeopardy she was in sprang from her need and love for Jorbie—but she couldn't help but be aware that in Jorbie's mind some dangerous connection existed between the drowned twin and herself.

And some of the things Jorbie had said to her over
the past month—how much she reminded him of someone from the past, although he could never remember
quite who—coming on top of Caleb's strange, angry behavior about the never-mentioned Kenneth, disturbed
her deeply. "Disturbed" was far too mild a word.
"Scared speechless" would have been more appropriate.
An ominous shadow that somehow connected her and
Kenneth and Jorbie, a dark cloud of inexplicable fear
that had suddenly mushroomed in her brain.

She shuddered. Above her head, the single bulb
trembled. As she thought she felt something brush
against her hair, she reached up and fitfully ran her fingers through it. Looking at her hand, she discovered it
had been a cobweb and shook her fingers in panic to
rid herself of it.

Or was she making another futile effort to rid herself
of Jorbie?

Leaving the *Courier*, Angie checked her watch and
headed up the street. She had to talk to someone; what
she had learned was something she could not keep
locked up inside herself. Cathy. It was a Saturday, and
she would call to see if Cathy could have lunch with
her. Angie knew that Cathy Springer did her best to stay
away from any talk with her about Jorbie, but she
would appeal to her, explain to her that this was something crucial, and beg her to hear her story.

Angie checked her watch again. If she called Cathy
now—within the next few minutes—instead of waiting
until she got home, she could probably catch her before
she went out. Nate's. It was just up the block. The
phone in Nate's was terribly public to say what she had
to say, but she didn't really have much choice.

Outside Nate's she peered in through the large glass
store window. Toward the rear, the phone in his hand,
Hardy Remarque appeared to be arguing with Nate,

shaking the phone at him angrily. Shrugging, she went inside just as Hardy Remarque hung up the receiver in disgust.

"Can I use your phone, Nate?" she asked quietly.

"Nobody can use his phone, for Christ's sake." Hardy Remarque turned to her, still seething over something. "The damned thing's dead as a beached flounder."

"Oh c'mon, Hardy, it's not the end of the world," soothed Nate, smiling slightly and trying to make amends for his failed equipment. Nate put a coffee on the counter in front of Remarque. "On the house, Hardy. I can't have you telling people my store's falling apart."

"Oh, hell, Nate . . ."

Swearing under his breath, Hardy Remarque sat down and began gulping his coffee. Angie slipped out the front door and headed for the booth, a few feet to the left and across the sidewalk from Nate's entrance. She *had* to catch Cathy; her need for someone to talk to was desperate. Change. Why did you never have the right change when you needed it? She rummaged through her purse and finally found two nickels, one stubbornly hiding under her lipstick and compact. She had one hand on the folding door of the booth, when she heard a sudden voice call her name. Startled, she turned around in bewilderment.

Up the street, Jorbie watched, bewildered and angry. Angie showed every intention of going inside the booth and receiving the dose of anthrax spores intended for Hardy Remarque. He didn't want Angie dead. Yet, a chance throw of the dice was making it look very much like she was shortly going to die—with himself her accidental executioner.

This was one of the most selective oddities of Jorbie's illness. In most cases he was perfectly aware of the people he killed—of the Flans, the Lutetias, the Peters, the George deCarres. He did these things, he told himself, because the Voice commanded it.

But in the case of Angie he was badly confused. Since Kenneth had been erased from his brain, those violent moments where he screamed at her, calling her "Kggggdy" in his child's voice, had to be similarly erased. As far as Jorbie knew, those incidents never happened.

This fact only increased Angie's jeopardy. Jorbie's conscious might not want to bury her alive, but the Voice could easily make him do just that, making him believe he was burying not Angie but Kenneth.

Slowly he came partway out of the doorway of Pete's Market, wanting to act but unsure of what to do. Perhaps he could trot down the block and get her away from the booth.

"Angie? Angie, I know it's an imposition, but could you let me use the phone ahead of you?" Remarque pleaded. "I'm behind schedule calling Mae."

Angie hesitated; the call to Cathy had to be made. Then she broke into a grin. "Sure, Hardy. I'll wait inside where it's warm. No trouble at all. Really." The statement was, of course, a lie; her call to Cathy was again being delayed. She smiled at Remarque, turned, and headed back toward Nate's Pharmacy.

Jorbie exhaled a great sigh. Angie had been saved by a twist of fate, the same fate that had just doomed Hardy Remarque. Relieved, he pulled back into the doorway of Pete's Market, but a new voice brought him back out around the corner again. It couldn't be happening.

"Sorry, Angie," said an agitated Nate Lavin, coming out through the door of the pharmacy and running straight into Angie, on her way in. "It isn't my day."

Angie turned to stare as Nate seized Remarque by the arm, already halfway into the booth. "Hardy, you old bastard. Can I use that phone first? I got a prescription here for old lady Evers—Dr. L'Eveque said it was urgent—but old Doc's hand shakes so badly there's a lot I can't make out. If he gets out to lunch, I won't be able to reach him until late afternoon, and the Evers woman needs this stuff now. That damned phone of mine. Crazy kids. I know you got a call to make but . . ." He left the sentence to dangle in the chill St. Max air.

Hardy Remarque looked at Angie and laughed. "Looks like we both got knocked out of line, Angie." He turned to Nate, still laughing. "Sure, sure, Nate. Medicine before law. Go ahead. Mae can wait. We'll be inside. Anyway, it's warmer." He opened the door for Angie and they went back inside.

Jorbie's heart sank. Nate Lavin was one of his favorite people in St. Max, one of the few he genuinely liked and respected. But there was nothing he could do. As if watching an accident happening that he could do nothing about, he saw Nate step inside and call his number. A few minutes later he started out of the booth, but the phone rang abruptly, and Nate stepped back inside. At the pharmacy door, he stopped Remarque on his way out to use it. "Mae just called and left you a message. She said she'd gotten a call that the old Loring place— you know, the summer people from Milwaukee—was broken into last night. The caretaker's having a fit. Mae said you can call her on the car radio on your way out there. The man's threatening to call in the state cops, she said."

Jorbie saw Remarque swear and head for his car, Nate waving cheerfully at him from his doorway. Damn, but it wasn't fair. In about twelve hours Nate would get a headache. After that, agony. A man he liked and respected. Hardy Remarque would get away scot-free. The bastard. The stinking bastard. Nothing in life was fair; you killed the people you liked or loved, and the people who deserved to die got away without a scratch.

Jorbie's observations on the unfairness of life came to an abrupt end. Out of Nate's door strode Angie, headed once more for the lethal phone booth. Jorbie groaned. There was a look on her face that told him this time, nothing would stop her. In this, Jorbie was completely right; Angie had had enough of people cutting in line in front of her and was determined to get hold of Cathy Springer no matter how rude she had to be.

Determined, Jorbie stepped all the way out into the middle of the sidewalk. By accident, he'd already killed one person today whom he liked; he was damned if he'd kill someone who, well, in his own way, he loved. He watched Angie put one hand on the folding door of the booth; she was having trouble getting the door to open. Finally, the door gave and folded inward.

His hands raised to his mouth, Jorbie was about to shout a warning to Angie. His resolve faded as he thought of trying to explain his behavior later. The Voice, the damned Voice, somehow was behind all of this, Jorbie told himself. Instead of ordering him to do things it knew he didn't want to do, the Voice was sneaking behind his back, getting him to do what it wanted by subtle manipulation—making things look like accidents. Damn the Voice; he was its slave.

The hands that had been raised to his mouth were allowed to slip halfway down his face in a gesture of horror as he watched Angie pulling her coat tighter around herself to squeeze through the booth's narrow opening. No, Jesus, no, he whispered helplessly.

Three sudden blasts of a car horn made both Jorbie and Angie look up. "Hi, Ange!" yelled Cathy Springer from her car as she pulled it to the curb. "Calling your bookie?"

Angie laughed and ran around to the driver's side of the car, laughing and chattering about lunch. A few moments later Jorbie saw her climb into the car with Cathy and watched them drive off.

Jorbie was enormously relieved. Even in the frigid wind of a St. Max noontime, he could feel the dampness on his body of nervous perspiration. It had been close, very close. And he was still sickened by what he had done to Nate and almost done to Angie.

With a sigh of disgust, Jorbie pulled the warm plastic bag of dogshit out of the thermos locker. It pretty well summed up how he felt about life at the moment. But at least it would stop some poor other innocent bastard from dying by mistake.

Chapter Twenty-two

Besides the kitten I had as a kid—the one I had to drown—one year, some summer people offered me their dog when they were leaving at the end of the season.

Well, every American boy is supposed to have a dog; the Reader's Digest says so. I accepted right off, all excited. But like everything else in my life, the idea was right but the details impossibly wrong. See, the summer people hadn't told me their dog—his name was Wolfgang—was a God damned Mexican Hairless Chihuahua.

He was real cute, that dog, and I got to like him an awful lot, but I never dared let anybody know it. My friends would have laughed their balls off. For a while I thought I was going to have to drown poor old Wolfgang, too, but things sort of took care of themselves.

Winter came, and one night I forgot to let him back into the house. Poor Wolfgang stood outside until he froze to death. In the morning, I remembered he was still outside and went to look for him. God damn, there he was, right by the door, still standing on those crazy, spindly legs of his, but frozen stiff as the body we had down in the freezer.

In a way, it's sort of like what I did to Nate Lavin. I liked him a lot—a hell of a lot—but there's a lot of bigotry in a town like St. Max, so I never dared let anyone know I did. Then came the accident with the pulmonary anthrax spores, and I killed him. I didn't mean to, but I did. My fault again.

Is that how it will eventually turn out with Angie? Buried alive by a guy who didn't want or mean to? I

*couldn't blame her for feeling pretty sore at me if it
does.*

> Jorbie Tenniel—to the rock,
> 7:14 A.M., December 5th

The Sunday service at Our Lady of Misery always drew
a pretty good turnout; Father Duval was very active in
keeping people coming to Mass regularly. But Angie
noticed today the Sunday Mass seemed more heavily
attended than usual. On the surface, people looked
pretty much as they always did, but she could feel an
undercurrent of confusion and bewilderment running
through them.

It was, Angie decided, the effect of the voices—
Flan's, Lutetia Losee's, Peter Berringer's, and now,
George deCarre's—one filled with the doom of some
unidentified woman in St. Max. It was something most
of the people there didn't discuss openly, but a subject
clearly occupying everyone's mind.

It was as if they all expected Father Duval to vault
out from behind the altar and give them the definitive
answer. By now, Duval had reached the conclusion that
the voices were indeed a genuine miracle, but stayed off
the subject; he was still hewing to the party line laid
down by his Bishop in Detroit. Increasingly, he found
difficulty in accepting the bishop's orders, but was con-
stitutionally unable to fly in the face of so awesome a
figure.

Sitting toward the rear of the church, Angie kept
scanning the area near the altar for Jorbie. He was not
there. Nor was he seated farther back in the pews.
Once, she thought she recognized the back of his neck,
making her heart leap, but the neck's owner turned out
to be Miles Overing, a youngish mechanic from Gros-

cap. Angie was baffled. Usually, for business reasons, if nothing else, Jorbie came to Sunday Mass. Today he had not.

After church Angie came down the broad flight of stone steps to the street as quickly as she could. There was someone she wanted to catch. It was only a matter of minutes before she saw him, and Angie made a point on almost running headlong into him in the crowd gathered at the bottom of the church steps.

"Hello, Hardy," Angie said, pretending to be a little surprised to run into him. "You're looking well today."

Hardy Remarque grunted. But the new look that had swept over Angie in the last month made him realize how suddenly attractive she had become. He felt a surge of warmth and produced a smile. "*You're* the one who really looks good, Angie. By God, you seem to grow better looking every time I see you."

In spite of knowing this was transparent flattery, Angie felt a glow inside herself. "Which way are you walking, Hardy?"

"Just a few blocks toward downtown. My car's there."

"Good. So am I." Angie's answer was a lie; her own car was parked in the opposite direction. The lie to Remarque had been as carefully planned as running into him.

They walked together down the sidewalk, talking about not much of anything, pleasantly, animatedly. Suddenly from Angie: "Hardy, did you know Kenneth Tenniel? You know, Jorbie's twin brother. He drowned in 1965."

Hardy Remarque rubbed the side of his face, trying to put things together in his memory. The question had come at him out of nowhere, but Angie was determined to find out if the old chief knew anything about Jorbie's twin or the accident that killed him. "1965," Remarque repeated once or twice. Slowly the pieces fell together in his mind. "That was the year the county sent me to Saginaw for advanced training. I wasn't here, and I can't remember the name of the man who stood in for me. I remember hearing about the accident a little, though, but not much. The boy is still very clear in my mind: a dead ringer for Jorbie. But, hell, I don't even remember his name now."

"Kenneth. You don't remember anything funny about the drowning or anything like that?"

Remarque studied the sky, looking for an answer. "Angie, that was a long time ago. I just don't remember."

"Damn."

Remarque looked at Angie and laughed. "Why don't you just ask Jorbie? I hear you see plenty of each other." He smiled again, this time conspiratorially. "Incidentally, I think that's just great too. You deserve the best; Jorbie deserves the best. Hell, you seem so close—like you're made for each other. That doesn't happen too often these days."

Angie loved the compliment, filled, as it was, with overtones of a closeness she'd never before known. Her question, however, left Remarque curious. "What made you ask?" he said suddenly.

"Oh, nothing. I was just wondering."

Hardy Remarque's face abruptly turned grim. "Lots to wonder about in this town these days. Those damned voices. Someone's pulling something on us, I think. Well, I got plans to get to the bottom of them."

For no reason, Angie abruptly felt herself afraid. She said little more until she waved after Hardy as he climbed into his car.

Hardy was right; there was a lot to wonder about in St. Max these days.

* * *

Almost exactly on schedule, Nate Lavin had come down with what was at first thought to be flu. He woke early Sunday morning, his mother, crazy old Mrs. Lavin, told people, with a splitting headache and a high fever. But he'd taken some pills and told her that he felt a little better.

By Sunday noon it was clear this was illusory. Dr. L'Eveque was summoned, examined Nate, and noticed the first of the boils on his legs. L'Eveque had been through this two years ago and knew what the symptoms meant: pulmonary anthrax. Only this time, he was going to play the disease by the book.

Mrs. Lavin was ejected from her own house, carrying her Bible charts and reference books, and Nate's home was put under quarantine. A special nurse was sent for from Saginaw to take over his care. On the front door a large sign was posted warning people to stay out. Outside, Mrs. Lavin marched up and down, stopping anyone who would listen to show them how the third aspect of Hezekiah was in conjunction with a rising Deuteronomy, so no one should be surprised. She just hadn't guessed the victim would be her own son.

When L'Eveque ran into Hardy Remarque on the street, he suddenly dragged him to Nate's house, breaking the quarantine he himself had just decreed. "See," he yelled at the startled Remarque, throwing back Nate's bedcovers suddenly. Remarque gasped.

From his toes to his upper waist, Nate's body was covered with frightening running sores. The sores themselves were an angry, deep red, each capped by a purplish-white pustule. Above the sores, extending from his chest to his hairline, Nate's skin had a mottled look, deeper red blotches indicating where the next wave of sores and boils would appear.

Nate Lavin had already reached the delirium stage and was muttering and screaming incoherently, his eyes sometimes suddenly opening and seeing something in the room that terrified him. Mixed in with the mutterings and shouts for help were names of various prescriptions he'd filled, some of them many years before, along with sudden, mumbled snatches of the kaddish.

Dr. L'Eveque slowly pulled the covers back up over Nate and turned to face Remarque. "That's what pulmonary anthrax looks like, you stupid bastard. A while back you accused me of letting a new epidemic of this stuff happen in St. Max. Of covering it up. Look at that poor man. Look at those festering sores. Did you hear anything about that kind of thing with Flan Tierney or Lutetia Losee or Peter Berringer? Did you? Hell, no! Next time, get your facts straight, damn it."

Hardy Remarque fled; the sight of Nate Lavin was too terrible to spend any more time with than you had to.

The slow, agonizing death that Jorbie had originally planned for Remarque, one that had been diverted by accident to Jorbie's friend Nate and had come within a whisper of striking Angie, represented an exquisite agony of suffering.

At the mortuary, Jorbie was suffering too. He couldn't shake the awful responsibility of what he'd done to his friend, Nate Lavin. He had sentenced him to death, while his real target, Hardy Remarque, was waltzing around St. Max, causing more trouble.

On top of this, the Voice had been whispering in his ear again. Of the two assignments it had given him for today, one Jorbie agreed with completely: Linda Crane. Jorbie's unconscious was too blocked to understand that Linda Crane was yet another child of one of the boys on the raft, Moon Crane. Instead, he believed the Voice was seeking vengeance for something completely unconnected with the incident.

Linda Crane, he told himself, had absolutely no business writing what she had written; the Voice was certainly right about that. He read it again to make sure.

She had written a long letter to the Editor of the *Courier,* appearing today. To Jorbie, it was not hard to see why the Voice apparently considered it a personal insult. The more he read, the more furious he got.

"Have you read this?" he screamed at Pasteur, shaking the paper in his face. Pasteur stared at Jorbie blankly.

"Well, no, Mr. Jorbie. I been busy, and—"

"Look at it, look at it!" Jorbie shrieked. "Some snot-nosed kid wrote a letter here that says the voices are a miracle—damned little bitch calls it 'The Miracle of the Voices'—and says they are final proof of life after death. Proof, my ass!"

Jorbie stalked up and down the room while Pasteur continued to stare at him with a vacant look. This was one of those moments when he wished he could disappear into the floor before Mr. Jorbie noticed he was there and turned his awesome fury on him. "Mr. Jorbie," he began, knowing that the next best thing to disappearing was to annoy Mr. Jorbie enough so he'd finally yell at him to go away.

"Get your ass out of here and leave me alone. I got some thinking to do," Jorbie bellowed.

Instead of feeling hurt, as he would usually, Pasteur was pleased with himself. His strategy had worked. Shaking his head to appear upset, he gratefully left the preparation room and worked outside. He didn't outsmart Mr. Jorbie like this very often, he knew, but it always gave him an enormous sense of satisfaction on the few occasions he did.

Jorbie checked his watch and walked quickly down the street. Linda Crane, he knew, had an after-school job at Nate's Pharmacy; she was about due for work.

Jorbie had been afraid that Nate's might be closed, but the rumor he'd heard that a cousin of Nate's from

Saginaw, also a pharmacist, had come to fill in for him temporarily turned out to be true. From down the street, Jorbie could see a steady line of customers going in and out of the place; the phone booth had been locked and a sign hung outside, declaring it out of order.

It felt odd walking into the drugstore and seeing someone else behind the counter, but it didn't seem to be affecting business. Jorbie didn't like using this place, even though there was a certain justice for Linda Crane in its selection.

He saw her immediately. She was an attractive little thing, fifteen or so, wearing a short blue uniform and waiting on the tables. There was something about the girl that immediately reminded him of Angie. Jorbie caught himself, aware that recently an awful lot of people had been reminding him of Angie; it didn't occur to him that most of the people who did, either had been or were about to be recipients of Captain Marvel's deadly embrace.

Down the counter, Jorbie studied her movements for a few moments, once nodding to her pleasantly when she looked toward him. Close to the spot where Linda came to give her orders was a chromium rack on which hung bags of potato chips, placed there so the counter customers could get them themselves to go with whatever they were eating. The next time Linda came up to the counter, Jorbie was at the rack, pretending to have trouble unattaching one of the potato-chip bags. Linda laughed lightly and began helping Jorbie with it. The sharp metallic sting of Captain Marvel's needle injecting the *bonaro* into Linda's left buttock was apparently not noticed by Linda, but Jorbie's hand *was*. Linda stared at him with reproach. As she stared, anger filled her expression. There was no way Jorbie could explain it to himself, but as he tried to stare the girl down her face seemed to change; it was no longer the face of Linda Crane, but of Angie Psalter, her expression as angry and reproachful as Linda's had been. He was thankful that the image of Angie did not confront him very long. As quickly as it had appeared, it disappeared, leaving him once again staring at Linda Crane.

"That's not nice, Mr. Tenniel. We get old men in here who try that sometimes, but I never would have guessed you for it. . . ."

Jorbie felt himself blushing. A very aware and outspoken little teen-ager still faced him. "I don't know what you mean," he began hesitantly. Linda shook her head and walked away, heading for a table with a full tray. Damn her, thought Jorbie. Why the hell should I care what *she* thinks? She had infuriated him with her letter in the *Courier,* she had changed faces with Angie right before his eyes, and now she had insulted him by lumping him with St. Max's dirty old men. Inside, Jorbie seethed, consoling himself with the thought of what he had planned for Linda Crane. No one was to hear *her* voice.

Angie was seated at the upright in St. Etienne's auditorium. She would play a few bars, and then struggle to get the school choir to follow her through the parts of Handel's *Messiah* they were doing. It was to be the endpiece for the Christmas program at St. Etienne. The choir wasn't being very helpful today, giggling and whispering among themselves, and Angie found herself growing angry and shrewish sounding. "Look," she said finally. "It's *you* who're going to be standing up on the stage singing *The Messiah*. Do you really want your parents and friends to think you can't sing it any better than you're doing today? It's terrible!"

The giggling stopped and the children's faces struggled to appear sober and concerned. Wearily, Angie sat down at the upright and began again. Kids.

* * *

In Alpena, Edith Pardee sat at the upright in the living room of the Clausens'. George Clausen, just eleven, was usually a reasonably good student, a boy who practiced faithfully, but today his mind was on anything else but the third book of Diller-Quaille. Mrs. Pardee tried to remain patient—giving piano lessons across Mackinac County was something she depended on to supplement her late husband's pension—but was having a harder and harder time with her pupil's high spirits. Whenever she tried to bring George Clausen back to earth, he would giggle, filled with some private joke of his own. Probably, Mrs. Pardee thought, something dirty he'd heard today in school. Finally, George began giggling so hard he fell off the hard, round piano stool and landed on the floor, screaming with laughter. Mrs. Pardee looked at the clock on the mantel. Close enough so she could declare the lesson finished; maybe George would be in a more receptive mood next week. She sighed heavily, putting her books away, and hopefully gave George his practice assignments. George giggled. Children.

Coming out of the Clausens', Mrs. Pardee turned left and started down the street to where her car was parked. It was cold, and the afternoon's lessons had depressed her; some days she felt her pupils made no progress at all, and this was one of them.

Across the street from the Clausens', Jorbie scrunched down in the carseat, one pale, unhappy eye on the front door. Every now and then he would start up the motor to heat up the car; in this kind of cold it lost its warmth quickly. She should be coming out the door at any minute; her hour with George Clausen must be just about up.

It was going to be a mission for Captain Marvel that Jorbie bitterly regretted. One that he would have done anything to avoid. Mrs. Pardee had always been particularly kind to him——the group she was trying to put together to send him back to Marquette was only one example. He had argued with the Voice when it first whispered her name in his ear, pleading with it not to make him carry out the sentence, but the Voice had remained immovable. It wasn't fair, damn it. Mrs. Pardee was too nice and had been too kind to him to deserve this sort of treatment; it saddened him, even sickened him, but the Voice left him with no choice. Jorbie had driven to Alpena just after he had taken care of Linda Crane; the trip here was an unwilling response to the Voice's command.

The sound of the Clausens' front door being opened made him turn off his motor. Mrs. Pardee, looking, Jorbie thought, angry and discouraged, strode briskly down the street. For her, she was walking unusually fast; something must be bothering her. Jorbie realized that if he was to reach her, he'd have to change his plans. Already she was in her car fiddling with the ignition keys.

Hating himself, Jorbie darted across the street and rapped on the driver's window. She looked up in surprise, then saw who it was and rolled her window halfway down. "Jorbie Good Heavens. I thought I was being attacked by rapists."

Holding on to the car door, Jorbie listened to her laugh and hated himself even more. "No, just me. I saw you from across the street and wanted to say hi."

A look of curiosity clouded Edith Pardee's handsome face. "Whatever are you doing on a back street of Alpena, for Heaven's sake, Jorbie?"

"Business," he answered simply, and shrugged.

"You certainly look better than the other day, Jorbie; you scared me to death."

"Oh, that. Nothing to worry about. But thanks for your concern anyway." Jorbie feigned a shudder of cold; inside, he was burning up with the nervous strain of what he had to do. "Anyway, we'll both get pneumonia if we stay here much longer. You must be freezing. Take care of yourself, Mrs. Pardee; nice to see you."

He reached in through the window, smiling warmly, and gave Mrs. Pardee an affectionate squeeze of the shoulder. Then, waving, he went back across the street to his own car.

Edith Pardee watched him. Such a terribly nice boy, she told herself. Four hours later Edith Pardee was dead to all purposes.

Muttering to himself and still cursing the Voice, Jorbie climbed into his car and watched Edith Pardee drive slowly around a corner and disappear into eternity. His affectionate squeeze of her shoulder had provided Captain Marvel with his opportunity; Jorbie had too much respect for Mrs. Pardee's essential dignity to wait until he could inject the *bonaro* into one of her buttocks, the location he'd used for most of the other victims.

With a grunt, he suddenly remembered the rest of his mission, and started his car to race back to St. Max. There he would await Hardy Remarque's inevitable call about Linda Crane.

He had made very sure the call would come.

By the time he reached the mortuary, three full hours before Edith Pardee's collapse, he discovered Linda Crane was already in an ambulance and on her way to the coroner's lab in Saginaw. Jorbie had made absolutely no effort to disguise Linda's death as an accident, thus insuring a demand for an autopsy from the already suspicious Hardy Remarque.

She had earned it, Jorbie convinced himself, by her letter to the Editor. More significantly—and something

Jorbie *couldn't* see—she had earned it by being the daughter of one of the boys on the raft the day of the drowning.

Jorbie smiled faintly at the thought of what lay in store for the fifteen-year-old. He wished he could be there.

The autopsy of Linda Crane was a sadist's delight. Apparently dead, but fully capable of hearing, seeing, and thinking, Linda felt herself being lifted up onto the coroner's examining table. He was a slender, middle-aged man graying slightly at the temples, who stared at her naked body as dispassionately as if he were studying a side of beef for proper marbleization. In front of him was some sort of microphone on a folding extension arm that, from what he said to his assistant, Linda could guess was attached to a tape machine.

"Deceased, white female, approximately fifteen years of age. Weight, 105 pounds, height, one point six meters. Body shows no abrasions, contusions or other indications of damage. Sphincter, normal and untouched. Anus to be examined later. Vaginal opening"—if Linda could have blushed, she would have as the doctor spread apart the lips of her vagina and peered into it with a powerful light—"labia show no damage or evidence of recent penetration." The coroner pressed a button on his microphone, presumably turning the tape machine off. He looked over at his assistant and laughed. "Poor kid doesn't look to ever having gotten laid. Too bad; she'd have been one nice piece."

"Fifteen's pretty young, Larabee. Particularly in a hick town like St. Max. Besides, she's got a nice, big juicy mouth. Today's kids go in for stuff like that a lot, I understand."

The coroner sighed and pulled the microphone back toward him, switching on the little button again. Linda's heart rocked with horror as she heard the coroner's next sentence; she wanted to cry out, to scream, to protest, but could find no way to produce a sound.

"I'm going in now. I shall make an incision from the sternum to the navel to begin with, looking for any signs of altered organ sizes or unusual coloration."

Calmly, the assistant handed a scalpel across Linda to Dr. Larabee, the coroner. Whistling softly, the pathologist cut an incision down Linda's front, from the bottom of her rib cage to just above her navel. Dr. Larabee and his assistant pulled the incision apart with their hands; the knives cut, the scalpels sliced; the doctor hacked his way through her muscle wall to take a look at her interior organs. Linda felt dizzy and faint; she could feel no pain, but why couldn't these men see that she was still alive, that she was still Linda Crane—as she had been all her life? Filled with hopes and dreams of the future, not just an inanimate mound of flesh to cut into pieces at their whim.

"Organs *appear* normal, but you never know." He turned to his assistant. "Jars?" he commanded, and then turned back to the mike, his scalpel in midair. "Both kidneys are being removed now for examination in toxicological lab." Grunting slightly, Dr. Larabee cut the tubes connecting Linda's kidneys to her bladder and dropped them into the jars held out to him by his assistant, one kidney in each.

Linda's mind began floating in space; the doctor's voice seemed to come from a great distance, although she was able to hear clearly the wet squish that was made as various small organs were removed from her and dropped into similar containers. She heard herself screaming in agony, but knew this to be impossible. Regardless of how hard she tried, she couldn't force a single sound out of herself. The coroner droned on into his microphone; the knives cut; the scalpels sliced; one part after another of her was placed in jars for examination in the coroner's toxicological laboratory. Linda became unsure of whether she was conscious or whether she had slipped off into some sort of brutal nightmare. Finally:

"Stomach is being removed now," droned the coroner, "and will be sent to tox lab for complete work-up: will check out possibility of poison ingested either through the mouth or inhaled by lungs. After that—"

Linda knew that her intestines had been pulled loose in her stomach cavity and heaped on her lower abdomen to make the removal of her stomach easier. She saw the scalpels descend into the gaping cavity, and heard Larabee's causal, droning voice describe what he could see. "So far, organs appear nor—"

She never heard the end of his sentence. For a second she could still hear the voices, as if at a great distance, then no more.

The autopsy itself had killed her.

Chapter Twenty-three

Suddenly, a lot seems to be going a little wrong. The pulmonary anthrax spores that were supposed to knock off Hardy Remarque wound up killing Nate Lavin. I like Nate, a damned bright man with a great sense of humor. The town was stand-offish about him—something I can identify with pretty easily—but I personally never held anything against him just because he was Jewish. In fact, being Jewish is probably why he was damned bright. Well, he isn't bright just now; I screwed the whole thing up real good.

And that bastard Hardy Remarque is still walking around alive. My Voice wasn't any help on him at all. I'll have to wait a little and then take care of Hardy the Punctual.

Linda Crane? That's the one thing that did go right. Both my Voice and I agreed she had to go. The agony of her autopsy, still alive but in a state of suspended animation, should have taught her a thing or two. Excruciating. Wonderful.

But worst of all was the Voice's command that I Captain Marvel Edith Pardee. I argued but got nowhere. I'm not big on conscience, but that one really bothered me. Jesus, a great lady like that.

It's the kind of thing that really worries me. All the time. For instance, I know in my bones it's only a matter of time before the Voice creeps up on me and suddenly whispers Angie's name in my ear. Christ, how would I handle that? Fight? Give in? I don't know.

Sometimes I wonder if my Voice is as infallible as I think. Infallible or not, there's nothing I can do about it; disagreeing is hopeless.

*It would be like a priest telling the Pope he had his
funny hat on backward.*

> *Jorbie Tenniel—to the rock,*
> *11:53 P.M., December 7th*

"God damn, but I'm sorry this had to happen. It wasn't
my fault; it's just the way the shots were called. I fought
back about it, but I couldn't get anywhere. Once my
Voice tells me what I have to do, that's it. But you—
Christ, of all people *you*."

Jorbie stood beside the slab in the preparation room,
his face saddened and drawn. He was talking to Edith
Pardee; unlike the others who'd been on the slab earlier, Jorbie meticulously kept the sheet drawn up to
cover everything but her face; this little touch of mod-
esty, unusual for Jorbie, was, he felt, the least he could
do. A sign of his respect.

In the squeezed corner landing across the room, hidden from sight, Pasteur crouched. He didn't want to be
here; he knew how Mr. Jorbie reacted to any suggestion
that he was spying on him. Mr. Jorbie was talking to the
dead again, and if he discovered Pasteur here, he would
assume he was spying on him. He didn't want to be here,
but there was nothing he could do about it; if he tried
to go up the stairs, Mr. Jorbie would know he'd been
there and heard him. Pasteur pressed himself against
the wall and tried to hold his breath.

"Look, Mrs. Pardee, if there was any way to make
this easier for you, I would. But there isn't." Jorbie was
speaking again, sounding almost as if he were about to
cry. "God, I appreciate how nice you were to me all
these years. Kind, thoughtful, really wonderful. And
when I think how you were trying to get those people
together and send me back to Marquette, well . . ."

Jorbie had to blow his nose; he *was* beginning to cry a little, and it embarrassed him. Earlier, he had taken Edith Pardee's hand out from under the sheet and was holding it. Almost angrily, he stuffed her hand back where it belonged. "Damn, damn, damn. It isn't fair. Having to do this to you plain isn't right. But if you can manage it, try to understand the decision wasn't mine, it was my Voice's. I can't fight that Voice. And—Christ, this is asking an awful lot—if you can, try to forgive me a little. I'm sorry, Mrs. Pardee. I really am." He had more to say, but the muffled throbbing began to beat in his ears, and it was some minutes before he could even think clearly again. This time the throbbing seemed to be whispering something in time with its pulsing: An-gie—An-gie—An-gie.

Edith Pardee's pale blue eyes continued to stare at him; Jorbie couldn't stand the unspoken disappointment that lay behind them and walked away from the slab, first carefully tucking the sheet up under Edith Pardee's chin like a mother getting her child ready for sleep.

When he realized Jorbie was about to leave the preparation room, Pasteur, as quietly as he could manage, crept halfway up the stairs, hoping Mr. Jorbie's voice would drown out any sound he made. Below, he heard him moving about, and made a lot of noise to let him know he was coming down. At the bottom of the stairs, he smiled and mumbled something; Mr. Jorbie barely acknowledged him.

"We have to get the crematorium fire going," Jorbie said suddenly. "They're bringing up a body from Saginaw late this afternoon." Pasteur nodded. It was not a job he liked. The process of reducing people to ashes had always disturbed him. He kept thinking he smelled something funny when the gas was going, and once or twice, swore he had heard someone screaming when they were slid into the oven. Mr. Jorbie had told him he was nuts, but Pasteur wasn't all that sure. Together they walked out of the main building of Tenniel's and headed for the crematorium, perhaps three hundred yards farther along the slope leading to the Straits.

On her slab, Edith Pardee's eyes stared at the ceiling, unforgiving.

"Stop beating around the bush and say what you mean, Angie. You sound like a schoolgirl trying to tell her mother she's just had her first kiss."

Angie raised her eyes and stared hard into Cathy's. "I'm pregnant."

From Cathy, a stunned silence. She wasn't sure why Angie's announcement should stagger her so; with Angie being screwed regularly by Jorbie, it actually would have been more surprising if she *hadn't* eventually gotten knocked up. But, my God, Angie of all people. . . . Cathy shifted uncomfortably as Angie's eyes continued to burn into her; something had to be said even if it was something silly. "Well, that's certainly not telling your mother you've just gotten your first kiss." Cathy laughed nervously; the eyes kept staring at her. Finally from Cathy: "What can I say, Angie?"

Angie shook her head, looking as helpless as Cathy felt. The two of them were having an unusual lunch at the Mackinac Bar and Grill in St. Max. Today had only been a half day at St. Etienne; there were always a lot of these days off in the last weeks of school before Christmas vacation began. Cathy had planned it as a little celebration; they were even sharing a bottle of wine. All of that was before Angie had dropped her bombshell. Cathy struggled now to find something positive to say. "Are you *sure*?" Certainly not very positive, Cathy told herself, but at least it bought her some time.

"Positive," answered Angie miserably. "I thought so anyway, so I bought one of those home-test kits down in Traverse City. I did it three times. All positive."

Cathy took a deep breath; reality must be faced. She took a sip of wine, and, for the first time, stared back at Angie. "All right. The answer's simple. Abortion. Go down to Saginaw and get rid of it. Not even very expensive anymore."

"I don't think I could bear that, Cath. I was raised a Catholic, I'm still one, even if not a very good one. I just don't think I could."

"You *have* to, Angie. You can't limp around town until it gets far enough along to show. You just have to."

Stubbornly, Angie shook her head. "It's not that simple. It would fly in the face of everything I've ever been taught and everything I've ever believed in." There was more to it than Angie was saying. Part of her was thinking of a child—Jorbie's child—a boy, she was somehow sure. And with a son, Jorbie suddenly realizing he wanted to marry her. Actually, all of this was to be settled well before the boy was born, Angie told herself. The idea was something she could never admit to Cathy, a wild fantasy—or was it really so farfetched, she wondered. She couldn't let Cathy in on it; she had a hard enough time making herself believe it, but the idea had been preying on her mind ever since the home-test kit proved what Angie already knew. She looked up as Cathy poured them both some more wine—they had not intended to finish the whole bottle of California white, but it looked as if they would.

"Angie," Cathy spoke very carefully, her eyes studying the clear amber liquid in her glass. "At least you have to *tell* Jorbie what's happened. I mean, I can understand how you feel about an abortion. And you certainly know how *I* feel about Jorbie. But you have to tell him. It's *his* responsibility, after all."

Slowly, Angie shook her head from side to side. "I can't do that either. Not right now, anyway. Jorbie's under a great strain of some sort. He gets a lot more deaths in the winter anyway, you see. And then, there's a lot extra happening in St. Max. Poor Edith Pardee. Jorbie loved that woman. It was an awful shock to him."

"No more of a shock to him, Angie, than those tests must have been to you. My God, you've got to get off your ass and do *something*."

"I know, I know. But now isn't the right time. I have to wait until the moment's just right."

"Okay, Angie, but force yourself to tell him, damn it. Don't just find excuses to put it off. You've only got so much time."

Angie nodded uncertainly and forced a smile for Cathy. On one point, at least, her friend was completely correct. There was only so much time. Subtle changes inside her body were conspiring to produce a child, a boy, hers and Jorbie's baby. This afternoon—she had mentioned to Jorbie she was free and he'd suggested she come out to Tenniel's—she would see how things went this afternoon. Maybe, maybe—a terrible sinking feeling swept over Angie. Would there ever *really* be a right time to tell Jorbie?

That afternoon when she got to the mortuary, she found Jorbie wasn't there. From somewhere outside, Pasteur came panting up, his face flushed from running. The giant creature—Angie had caught fleeting glimpses of him several times before, and even talked to him once or twice—always upset her. He was harmless, Jorbie had assured her, but there was something about his desperate efforts to please that always unsettled her. Obviously, Jorbie had told this man, Pasteur—what a cruel name for him!—to be nice to her, and the poor creature was trying his best.

"Mr. Jorbie's out at the crematorium, ma'am. He

saw your car and sent me back to guide you out. He's all busy." Pasteur appeared to search his mind for something else Jorbie had told him to tell her. He smiled at her—too hard, she thought. "Oh, something else, ma'am. He said to say to you there was no one being burned yet, so it was okay, and not to be skeered."

Numbly, Angie followed Pasteur along the narrow path toward a low stone building without windows. It looked a little like a secret atomic plant of some sinister sort, walled off from the outside world. Inside, she found Jorbie. Today there was nothing walled-off about *him*; he was exuberant. In spite of the cold outside, he was dressed only in shirt sleeves, a concession, she supposed, to the suffocating heat of the main chamber. "Hi," he bubbled cheerfully, giving Angie a warm kiss. "Afraid it's on the hot side in here already. You should feel it later. We're just warming it up at the moment; have to heat up the fire brick and the concrete of the oven itself. When it's about time for the body, we turn up the gas and really send the heat up. There's this body coming up from Saginaw, you see, and . . ."

Enthusiastically, he showed Angie around. There was a glass-walled room in one corner of the chamber, behind which relatives could observe the moment of cremation without being felled by the heat. At one end of the chamber the wall was yellow fire brick, with a heavy iron door—to Angie it looked like the door of an unusually large baker's oven—set low in its center. Leading up to the door was a chromium track made up of rollers on which, at the moment, rested two pairs of heavy asbestos gloves.

"See, we put the body on the rollers. Pasteur or I swing open that door and the body goes in. A couple of hours later, nothing but ash. Very clean, very simple. Of course"—Jorbie turned toward Angie with a conspiratorial grin—"I'm glad more people don't go in for cremation. With regular funerals, we make an awful lot on the markup of coffins. Especially the fancy solid-mahogany ones."

Angie was thunderstruck. "You put them in—in *there*—without even a coffin?" she asked incredulously.

"Of course there's a coffin. State law. But usually a very simple, inexpensive pine one. Tough on us, but there's a certain logic. No one wants to pay for a real fancy casket when they know it's only going to be a heap of ash a few hours later."

Angie was unable to share Jorbie's enthusiasm. The crematorium, with its gleaming tiled side-walls, was better than an open grave in Carpas Point, she supposed, but there was something mercilessly efficient-seeming about it. At the same time, a touch of macabre insanity underlay the procedure. As if a mad baker might suddenly appear from the glass-walled viewing room and begin shoving gigantic cookies through the open oven door.

Jorbie had put on a pair of asbestos gloves and was heading toward the oven, but Angie called after him. "Jorbie, can we get out of here? It's too hot for me; my God, I feel like I could faint." She studied him for a second; he seemed neither pleased nor upset. "And I don't like seeing this-kind of stuff; it gives me the willies. You know that."

Jorbie shrugged and pulled off the gloves, tossing them back on the gleaming chromium row of rollers. Once they were outside and heading back toward the main building of Tenniel's, Angie realized how silent it suddenly seemed. Inside, there had been a constant roar—from the gas jets, she supposed—that she had barely noticed until she could not hear it any longer.

They walked along slowly, chatting. Later, Angie couldn't remember about what. She could remember deciding this wasn't the time to tell Jorbie about the baby. His son. Angie didn't know why she was so sure it would be a boy; she just was.

As they neared Tenniel's, Angie almost tripped over a deep hole, perhaps two feet around and four feet deep, dug outside the door to the mortuary. At one end, stuck into the ground, was a wooden stake with some numbers written on it. When Jorbie had first explained how the undertaking business worked, he'd said a marker like this was used to mark where a grave was to be dug at the cemetery; the numbers were coded to correspond with the deceased's name and the date of the interment. "Is that somebody's *grave*, Jorbie? I mean, you don't bury people's ashes right here, do you?"

Jorbie laughed. "I wish we could. And charge people for it. But there's another state law. Only in a certified cemetery."

A sudden shudder she could not explain ran through Angie. It was as if the curious, shrunken grave with its coded stake was of some great significance to her, but an importance she could not fathom. The shudder ran through Angie again.

"What is it, then?" she asked, her voice filled with uncertainty.

The strange look that sometimes came into Jorbie's eyes when he was about to lie did not escape her. "Grave for a midget?" he asked weakly, smiling, and then turned serious. "It's for Pasteur's dog, Alfalfa. Sick as hell. We're just waiting for him to die, poor damned animal. But Pasteur wanted a grave for him, just like a person's, and asked if he could dig it here. That's it."

The lie was terribly transparent. Angie had seen Alfalfa earlier, running alongside Pasteur and looking far from any signs of dying. Another point was just as troubling. Alfalfa was a German shepherd. To fit in a grave that small, he would have to be buried standing up. For reasons she couldn't understand, Angie found herself wishing she could know what the coded writing on the stake meant.

Together she and Jorbie walked into Tenniel's. It was warm inside, but Angie felt a sudden shiver run through her. This time, it was not as if someone had walked over her grave, but as if someone had tripped over it and fallen in.

Chapter Twenty-four

Dad had the crematorium built when I was about thirteen, I guess. At first, I went ape over the place. The gas hissing, the shiny chromium rollers, the great big heavy iron door. It was about the only new thing Tenniel's ever had.

Dad was less enthusiastic. Even though it was the only crematorium in the area and got customers from as far away as Saginaw, he saw early in the game it was going to be a losing proposition. He'd overestimated the number of people who'd want to be cremated, I suspect. Amortization of the construction cost alone was going to take forever.

I was too young to understand anything like that. I couldn't keep away from the place. A friend of mine, Punky Dureau—he was a real nut-case, Punky—used to try to be there whenever it was in its warm-up stage. Once, we tried to toast marshmallows in the oven, but it was so damned hot they caught fire in seconds. Another time, we used hot dogs; they worked a little better, but you could only stick them inside for an instant, and even then, they came out all burned and shriveled up. We ate them anyway, just because there was something so crazy about the idea.

Angie, naturally, couldn't stand the place. I can't see her holding a weenie roast there like Punky and I did.

I hope Angie doesn't get too nosy about Alfalfa. That was a real stupid lie I told her, because that dog's always roaming around the place, and she'll see him, and know I lied. The only solution is to take poor Alfalfa out in back some day when Pasteur's not around and shoot him.

*He sure as hell isn't going to wind up in that little
grave beside the side door. That, my Voice tells me, it
has other plans for. Christ, I hope not Angie.*

> **Jorbie Tenniel—to the rock,
> 7:00 A.M., December 9th**

The day continued in the same confusing way it had
started. Jorbie told Angie he'd have to be gone tonight—he mumbled something about seeing an old
friend over in Alpena, but it didn't ring any truer than
his mysterious yarn about Alfalfa—so Angie had to settle for the couch late in the afternoon. It was not one of
their better times; Angie felt nervous about this sort of
thing during the day, and kept having a senseless feeling someone was probably watching them. Stupid, she
told herself.

Actually, not all that stupid. Pasteur had an eye
glued to a crack in the living room wall, and stood with
his mouth hanging slightly open. He'd heard about how
love was made, he'd seen grotesque drawings on men's
room walls, he'd even leafed through a book of dirty
pictures once. But this was different. He couldn't take
his eyes away from the crack, guilty as he felt to be
spying on Mr. Jorbie. The sight of Angie's lithe young
body thrashing and scrambling beneath his, Mr. Jorbie's breathy groans and the escalating movement of his
buttocks, the passionate sighs of the girl, riveted him
where he stood.

He could feel his body responding, and without even
realizing what he was doing, unzipped his fly to make
his thing coordinate with their movements. From nowhere, he suddenly heard his mother's voice screaming
at him, telling him for Christ's sake to stop playing with
himself. Ashamed and guilty, he put it back. Jorbie and

the girl appeared to be through now anyway, lying there on the couch, spent.

Still breathing heavily, the images racing through his brain again and again, Pasteur silently crept away. My God, he told himself, if Mr. Jorbie ever knew what he'd seen—would his mother tell him? No, she'd been dead for almost eleven years—he'd go into such a towering rage he'd probably kill him.

Pasteur wondered if Mr. Jorbie was capable of anything like that. He was afraid he was—he himself had even helped with Peter Berringer—but the idea was so awful Pasteur forced it out of his mind. It came right back, even stronger than it was before. Mr. Jorbie was doing some very peculiar things. Not just talking to the dead 'uns, although that was plenty damned strange in itself. But Pasteur was aware—he wondered if Mr. Jorbie knew that, or just thought he was plain stupid—that Mr. Jorbie was doing something real strange with some of the dead he was burying. With Flan Tierney, with Mrs. Losee, with Peter Berringer, with Mr. deCarre, and now, with Mrs. Pardee. Maybe others, he wasn't sure.

Usually, one of the first things they did when they got a body was to drain out all the blood and replace it with embalming fluid. They hadn't done that with those people, none of them. Each time, Mr. Jorbie'd told him he'd already drained them—the night before, he said—but Pasteur didn't believe him.

He couldn't overlook that electric blanket, either. Mr. Jorbie had folded it neatly and hidden it in the freezer where he thought he wouldn't find it. Well, he had. What did he use an electirc blanket in a freezer for? It hadn't even been hidden very well. Christ, Mr. Jorbie must think he was blind as well as stupid.

All of these things troubled Pasteur, but he couldn't even begin to make sense out of them. He wished there was someone he could talk about these strange things with, but he had no friends. Not in town, not anywhere. Besides, no one ever seemed to believe much of what he said anyway.

Shaking his head, wishing he was smarter so he could understand, Pasteur slowly walked out of the door and into the night.

There is no place on earth more forlorn than a school building empty of its children. At night, it is even worse. In the dim gloom of empty hallways and vestibules, frail lights cast long shadows over abandoned desks and chairs and silent statues. The sound of someone walking the halls echoes hollowly, and there is a muffled whispering sound, as if the absent children were laughing and playing somewhere far in the distance, unable to wait for tomorrow so they could return.

This lonely walk was one Sister Honorée took every night. She lived in a small house overlooking the Straits and abutting St. Etienne, but the walk was not to inspect the school building. Rather, it was because the school's chapel was where she made her evening prayers every night before going to bed.

Tonight, the darkened chapel, lit only by a single one-hundred-watt bulb behind the altar and the two candles the Sister had lit on coming in, struck her as particularly lonely, the flickering shadows making the vacant eyes of the Virgin Mother high above the altar look sadder than usual.

Sister Honorée had just knelt on the cushion of her pew in the front when her head snapped suddenly upright, her eyes wide. From somewhere—the echoes made it impossible to know whether it came from behind the altar or from beside it—she could hear a voice speaking to her.

"Sister Honorée . . . Sister Honorée . . . can you hear me, Sister Honorée? It's Edith Pardee. . . ."

Automatically, Sister Honorée crossed herself, her fingers nervously wrapping and unwrapping themselves around her rosary. She had believed in it when few others had; now the Miracle of the Voices was happening to *her*. Yet there was something about this voice from beyond the grave that frightened her. Uneasily, she stared at the statue of the Blessed Mother, as if this holiest of all the saints could somehow explain the voice of Edith Pardee and make her less frightening. Impassively, the statue stared back, the blank wooden eyes lost in the dark above the altar.

"Sister Honorée, the last time I talked to you was to ask your help raising money to send Jorbie Tenniel back to med school." Edith Pardee sounded suddenly weary and disappointed. "For some reason," she continued, "you said you couldn't. Well, Sister, I forgive you. And forgiving, after all, is the cornerstone of our religion, isn't it?"

Almost without realizing it, Sister Honorée found herself nodding agreement. She could remember the conversation Edith Pardee was talking about—there had been just the two of them, in her office at the school—but she had had no choice but to turn the poor woman down. Against diocesan policy. No one else had known about their talk. She was able to recognize Edith Pardee's voice, and the allusion to the chat confirmed what she already believed: the dead Edith Pardee had indeed come back among the living. Automatically, Sister Honorée crossed herself again.

"I forgive you, Sister Honorée," Edith Pardee repeated in the same cheerful tone she always used, "and I have a mission for you. It is a mission you must obey, Sister, obey to the letter. If you do not, you will be punished . . . as others who do not obey will be. . . ."

Silently, Sister Honorée nodded. To her, such an instruction was unnecessary. No threat was needed.

"I know you believe deeply in the Miracle of the Voices, Sister. There are some in St. Max who still do not. And some who merely may be afraid. I want you to be my messenger, Sister Honorée, to all of them, to the world.

"You have heard before, both from myself and from other voices, that there is a woman in St. Max who must be punished. Conceivably you have even wondered if that woman could be yourself, Sister; it is not, although it *is* someone you see every day."

Sister Honorée heard Edith Pardee suddenly begin to cry, getting control of herself only slowly. It was a problem Jorbie had had a good deal of trouble with during his taping. Mrs. Pardee must have figured out whom he meant when he came to the part about the woman—Angie—and each time had started in crying. Jorbie had loathed the whole session. He hated it because it involved Mrs. Pardee; he hated it because it involved Angie. Never before had the Voice been so specific in what he must say, and Jorbie realized this was because the Voice was probably trying to trick him somehow into killing Angie. The damned Voice was like that.

"About the woman," Edith Pardee began again to Sister Honorée. "The message you are to give the town is about her. Find her, find the woman. Find her and destroy her, then she can be punished as she deserves— screaming endlessly in her grave. In return for this, those who are now being punished will be forgiven. The rash of unexpected deaths will stop. In fact, there will be less death than usual. But *only* if you find the woman, find her and destroy her."

Mrs. Pardee cried a little again, then spoke firmly to the Sister. "Do you understand the message you are to give the town, Sister Honorée? Tell them. Tell them all. Do not hold back. You must obey . . . obey. . . ."

Edith Pardee's voice faded into nothingness, with a final, whispered "obey . . ."

Sitting bolt upright in the pew, Sister Honorée found herself shivering. She would obey, she would obey without question. She had not only heard a voice, she had been chosen to be the messenger for the Miracle of the Voices. Finding and destroying the woman bothered her a little, but the promise of forgiveness and an end to the many deaths sent an electric shock through her.

Her heart almost bursting with the thrill of it, Sister Honorée rose from the pew and walked briskly toward the doors. *She,* chosen for so great a message! It was a message the world must know, a message she must give to it. Her eyes fell upon a long heavy rope that disappeared into the ceiling. They would be told.

Sister Honorée was not left the sole messenger from Edith Pardee for very long. At around eleven, St. Max had been startled to hear the chapel bell of St. Etienne suddenly come to life. The Sister had promised to tell the world and she would. Sister Honorée was too weak to manage the bell rope on anything heavier than a single large bell, but its ringing was nonetheless awesome, bursting across the hills around St. Max and thundering out across the waters of the Straits of Mackinac.

Telephoned by someone living near the school who was worried that Sister Honorée was in some kind of trouble and calling for help, Hardy Remarque dragged himself out of bed and drove to the school. Hearing why the Sister was ringing the bell in the middle of the night, Remarque shook his head and groaned inwardly. His earlier assessment had been correct; the town was going nuts.

Back home, both Hardy Remarque and Father Duval began getting telephone calls. Edith Pardee's sister in Alpena had also heard her voice and the promise:

find the woman and destroy her and the plague of deaths would end. The sister experienced the same electrifying shock as Sister Honorée and the others who heard Edith Pardee's promise that same night, but who, she asked, was the woman? Father Duval, Grace Lutece—Edith Pardee's niece in St. Max—Angie Psalter, Cathy Springer, and, at least according to him, Jorbie Tenniel—all of them asked themselves the same question. A handful of Edith Pardee's close friends also heard her voice the same night, only much later.

Father Duval could contain himself no longer. In spite of the bishop's orders, Duval finally took a firm stand. To anyone who asked—to anyone, in fact, who would listen—he said that in his opinion, the Miracle of the Voices was genuine. Proof of life after death. Now that both he and Sister Honorée had heard the same voice and the same message, even the most cynical could no longer disbelieve it. No, he told anyone who asked, he didn't know who the woman was either.

Later that night Father Duval called the bishop. One of the dead, he reported, now had told both him and Sister Honorée that the explosion of unusual deaths in St. Max would end, and the already dead be forgiven, if the town would find and destroy the woman the voices had lately been talking about. God's Mercy, he said, God's vengeance.

Like Hardy Remarque, the bishop groaned. It was all too much. That whole town was going crazy.

Jorbie was not at home when Dr. L'Eveque called to report the death of Nate Lavin and to ask that the body be taken to Tenniel's. Instead of Jorbie, he found himself talking to Caleb, who had an extension beside his bed.

"I don't usually go for that old bromide about death being merciful . . ." L'Eveque said.

"Terrible," Caleb agreed.

"Mrs. Lavin said a rabbi is coming up from Saginaw. She also said Nate has to be buried within twenty-four hours. Is that going to give Jorbie a problem?"

"Shouldn't."

"Good. See you on Wednesday, Caleb."

Wednesdays were when L'Eveque paid his weekly visit to Caleb Tenniel. There wasn't anything he could do about the paralysis, but he could make sure that the rest of Caleb stayed healthy and that he wasn't sinking into a dangerous depression—a lot of paralyzed people did that—or developing bed-sores or something. A thought slipped through L'Eveque's mind. Twice now, he'd seen Angie Psalter there when he'd come. There to visit Jorbie, he supposed. The thought pleased him. L'Eveque had always been genuinely fond of young Jorbie; with his own hands he'd brought him and his twin into the world. Bright, handsome, good sense of humor. And Angie had had such a sad, difficult life— her father and all—that it was good to know she had finally latched onto someone as splendid as Jorbie. She would be good for Jorbie, too, he thought; the boy had been so shy ever since the drowning of his twin.

For a second, L'Eveque thought of speaking to Angie about him, encouraging her to keep working on Jorbie. No, doctors were pain in the ass enough without having them make suggestions about your personal life. But Jorbie was certainly the type of man someone like Angie deserved.

Sadly, he took Nate Lavin's file folder out of the file case and slipped it into his "Deceased" cabinet. Too bad. Nice guy, Nate.

* * *

Jorbie had had an exhausting morning. The tenets of the Jewish faith required Nate Lavin to be buried before sundown of that day, so the leisurely pace he usually followed in preparing the dead had to be squeezed into a few hours. There were his own plans to fit around this as well; the Voice was keeping him busy. In midafternoon he was finished and went upstairs to tell Caleb that the funeral would be late this afternoon, and that he had some other things to do after that. "I'll bring you up a cold dinner, if that's all right with you, before I leave."

Jorbie had noticed it when he first came into the room; there was something strange going on with his father. Caleb lay back, brushing the hair out of his eyes, and studied him, as if staring long enough would provide the answer to some unasked question.

"Sit down a minute, Jorbie. We have to talk."

Uneasily, Jorbie sank into a chair. He and his father rarely spoke of more than surface things, but something about the way Caleb was acting warned him this time was going to be different. The hair was brushed away from Caleb's forehead again, this time angrily, as though the errant white tangle was somehow responsible for whatever was bothering him. His pale eyes fixed themselves on his son. "Jorbie, I don't like interfering in your life. I know what a sacrifice you made—giving up medicine and all—to come home and take care of me and this business, and I appreciate it. More than you'll ever know. But that doesn't mean I can close my eyes to what's going on."

Upset by how much Caleb might or might not know, Jorbie opened his mouth to speak, but his father held up his hand to silence him. "I use this a lot, you know"—his same hand lifted up the phone receiver and carefully replaced it—"so I'm not entirely in the dark. I know all about the Miracle of the Voices. I know all about the strange deaths in St. Max and the other towns near it. . . ." Hands shaking visibly, his eyes never leaving Jorbie's face, Caleb took a swallow of water from the glass beside him on the table. "What worries me," he continued, "is that all of the deaths somehow seem connected to Tenniel's. The dead people whose voices get heard are people *we* buried; ones that die someplace else don't get heard. I can't explain it, Jorbie, but there's something strange going on that we're a part of . . . and it frightens me. Frightens me badly."

Feeling trapped, Jorbie spread his hands to show he had no explanation. Beneath his shirt he could feel small rivulets of sweat gathering under his arms and threatening to run down his body. He wasn't sure, but he thought that muffled pulsing was about to assault his eardrums again.

"I know about how you and that awful man, Pasteur, leave for places in the middle of the night. I can hear you go. I know something is terribly wrong somewhere, and it scares me to death. Those voices—they keep referring to punishment. It's been a favorite theme of yours since you were a little boy. You always used to use it a lot, demanding that I punish Kenneth, someone we haven't talked about for years, although maybe we should have. My God, Jorbie, are you somehow mixed up with those voices people keep hearing? Did you—*could* you—have let him drown on purpose? To punish him? It terrifies me to think that—"

Caleb never got to finish his sentence. With a crash, Jorbie had leapt to his feet, knocking the chair he was sitting in over and pacing angrily up and down the small area of clear space in Caleb's room. Furious, he waved his arms in the air, his face a combination of anger and self-pity. "Damn it," he yelled, spinning to face his father, "Everybody in this lousy town's always prying into my business. Everybody. Hardy Remarque, everybody. Especially Angie. And now *you.* Jesus Christ!"

Caleb watched his son with growing horror, seeing him suddenly appear to shrivel in size. Jorbie stopped his pacing and stood stock-still, his head hanging down, each hand nervously caressing the opposite forearm in a pose of misery, like a little boy asking for something he knows he can't have. Even his voice rose to a little boy's pitch, a hurt tone mixed in with the anger it expressed. "You always liked Kenneth more than me, Daddy," Jorbie piped. "Always. You kept holding him up to me, telling me how wonderful he was and why couldn't I be more like Kenneth, you said. That's because you believed Kenny when he lied about me, Daddy. You believed him and you didn't believe me. Well, I took care of Kenneth and I can take care of all of you and stop the lying and the way people spy on me and pry into my things. That Angie is the worst of all of them. Well, I can take care of them, Daddy, I can. All of them . . ."

Caleb stared at his son, not knowing what to say or what to do. The strange, child's voice Jorbie'd used and the petulant look of fury in his face—how were you supposed to react to things as crazy as that?

So many terrifying thoughts were racing through Caleb's mind he found he was trembling. Had Jorbie really killed Kenneth, as he implied? He knew there had always been a fantastic level of jealousy between the twins, and he'd already had his own suspicions. Then, there were the voices and their constant threats about punishment. He was sure Jorbie couldn't be making the voices, yet—another terrible thought came to Caleb. If Jorbie *was*, that meant—the idea was too horrible to even consider.

He should do something; my God, Angie was in danger. She might be next on his list. As with Kenneth, Jorbie had just accused her of spying on him. He should tell the police, tell someone, but Jorbie was his son . . .

Pulling himself up in his bed, Caleb tried to say something, but Jorbie didn't give him a chance. For a second, Jorbie stood where he was, looking surprised. Even if he couldn't remember too much of it, he was baffled by what he'd heard himself say. It didn't make sense.

"Jorbie," Caleb began, as puzzled as his son, "maybe you've been working too—"

His eyes filled with tears, Jorbie stared at Caleb for a second, and, shaking his head back and forth in confusion, fled from the room.

His own eyes suddenly moist, Caleb listened to the slamming of the doors as Jorbie fled the house. He was terrified for Angie, he was terrified for St. Max, he was, he supposed, even terrified for himself. If Jorbie weren't his son . . .

The funeral that evening of Nate Lavin was a miserable affair. A light rain was falling, and not one of St. Max's citizens understood a word of what the rabbi was saying. Toward the end of it Angie slipped over toward Jorbie. "I'll be late tonight, Jorbie. All of old Mrs. Lavin's relatives are leaving right after the funeral. She's going to be terribly alone, so I'm going to sit with her a couple of hours. Poor thing."

Inside, Jorbie was relieved. Mrs. Pardee was due to speak again tonight, which required travel to Alpena and other places. Since early morning he had fretted over how he would explain where he was to Angie. She had just solved the problem for him. Jorbie smiled at her warmly. "Don't worry about being late; I've got some things to do myself."

Almost without anyone noticing it, the funeral was suddenly over. Quickly the people of St. Max drifted away, leaving only Angie and Jorbie and the two grave-diggers.

Apparently Jorbie didn't realize how close behind

him Angie was standing. For a long time he stared down into his friend Nate Lavin's grave. "I'm sorry, Nate," he whispered when he thought no one could hear him. "It was my fault and I'm sorry. *Shalom*."

He was startled when he turned around and almost crashed into Angie. Together they walked to his car in silence. A crazy thought had just raced across Angie's brain. If something terrible happened to *her*, would Jorbie finally say what she'd been waiting to hear him say all along, or would he just whisper "I'm sorry" into her grave.

And what did he mean, "I'm sorry, Nate; it was my fault"? Would whatever happened to *her* be his fault too?

They were good questions.

Chapter Twenty-five

My God, the Voice has been busy, whispering into my ear day and night. I agree with some of the names it gave me—say, Hardy Remarque—but some of the others I have a lot of trouble understanding. I asked the Voice to explain, but it just laughed at me. That's one thing I can't stand—being laughed at.

I remember as a kid how, when the other boys wanted to be mean, they'd laugh at me because of Dad's business. Asking if the bodies were even dressed below where you could see them in the coffin and stuff like that.

Real funny.

Only some of them aren't laughing anymore. I helped them discover just what being buried is like. Come to think of it, Angie is the only person I know who would never laugh at me about anything. I hope not, anyway.

The Voice doesn't like being laughed at any more than I do.

> *Jorbie Tenniel—to the rock,*
> *3:13 P.M., December 8th*

The two and a half hours Angie spent with Mrs. Lavin—was it really only two and a half hours?—were sad, painful, and infinitely depressing. That the old lady was crazy was beside the point. Suddenly, left alone in the house she had shared with Nate, she faced the realities of a lonely old age. For a while she talked to Angie about perhaps moving to Saginaw or Grand Rapids, but decided her relatives there really didn't want her. If they had, they would have brought it up today.

Angie didn't know what to say. Mrs. Lavin was right. And while she was acting sane enough now, Angie knew it was only a matter of time before she plunged back into her Bible charts and predictions. St. Max had a hard enough time putting up with them; no relative would.

Mrs. Lavin suddenly reached out and patted Angie's hand. "You're being terribly sweet to me, dear, and I was so little help to you when you came to see me last time. To ask about the Tenniels. Jorbie Tenniel, particularly. Well, I did it on purpose; you see, I was trying to avoid the subject. You know, dear, people think I'm a little crazy, I guess, with the Bible Prophecies and Predictive Charts and everything." Mrs. Lavin gave a rasping little laugh, studying Angie's face.

"And maybe I am." The laugh again, only there was a new, almost sinister note to it. "But I've seen a lot of strange things here in St. Max over the years, and I have a sort of intuitive sense about people. I've always had one about Jorbie Tenniel. A bad one, I'm afraid. Nate was three years older than them, but Kenneth and Jorbie were so terribly bright they were all very close friends as children. But even Nate was a little scared of Jorbie. I don't know whether he knew something about him or what, dear. Then last week, when he was raving, talking to people who weren't there—before they threw me out of my own house—I heard him mumbling about the drowning—like it happened yesterday—"

Mrs. Lavin, her eyes half closed, was looking both sleepier and more sinister by the moment. She leaned forward, her eyes down to exhausted slits in her tired, haggard face, and squeezed Angie's hand. "I don't need a Predictive Chart to know you're in terrible danger. Be smart, child. Get away from Jorbie while you can.

There's something wrong there, and always has been. Get away dear, while you can. . . ."

But Angie couldn't get away. She loved Jorbie too much.

The wind was up in the Straits. The waves that thundered against Jorbie's rock seemed unusually high, the crash of each wave a dull, shuddering sound followed by a hissing withdrawal, filled with menace. Jorbie stood not far from his rock, trembling from the cold, his eyes trying to adjust to the early darkness of the winter night.

Uneasily, he pulled his parka tighter around his body; the wind laughed at him, biting through the padded cloth and boring into his skin. Ordinarily he came to the rock in winter only rarely, but the Voice had been whispering things he didn't want to hear. He felt the only solution was to face it head on.

"Voice! Voice, I know you're there," he yelled across the foaming waves. "You're in the rock—*my* rock—you can't hide from me there. You whisper things in my ear, ordering me to do what I don't want to do. But I do them, because you tell me to. Well, look. I've done what you told me to without ever asking a question, only now I want something in return. Now I'm asking—pleading—for just one little change in your orders—one damned stinking little change, that's all. I'm pleading with you, Voice. Can you hear me?"

A giant black wave hurtled high in the air, splashing Jorbie with an icy spray that seized him like a giant fist. He flinched, wiping the water from his eyes, and waited for an answer. None came. Jorbie swore loudly and went ahead anyway. He was sure the Voice could hear him.

"That change. You owe it to me. It's about Angie Psalter," he yelled into the darkness. "You've ordered me to kill her. That's not fair, damn it. I like Angie, I *need* Angie. For Christ's sake, maybe I even love her, I don't know. I'm not just pleading, Voice, I'm begging. Please don't make me go through with it. Shit, I *need* her, I tell you. Why do I have to kill her? *Why?*"

The only sound was the crashing of the waves and the shriek of the wind. "Damn it, I know you can hear me. I know you can hear every fucking word."

Abruptly, the wind dropped and the waves died down a little. Jorbie braced himself to hear the Voice whisper into his ear. Instead he heard a little laugh, a child's laugh.

"Point your finger at the sky?" the child asked, speaking as if from a great distance. "Cross your heart and—" Jorbie couldn't place where he'd heard it or who had said it. Kenneth? Angie? Himself? From the same distant void came the sound of another voice, an adult's, angry and accusing.

"You're a terrible man, Jorbie Tenniel. You put me in that dreadful grave, and then you promised to let me out if I did what you told me to. But you didn't. You're a mean, lying, wicked, evil, terrible man, Jorbie Tenniel. I used to admire you, I used to like you, but then something went wrong with you. . . ." Lutetia Losee, Jorbie was sure of that much. He could remember some of the things she'd screamed at him when he told her he wasn't going to dig her up. Before she'd begun to shriek incoherently and pound on the sides of her coffin. The sound of the distant voices began coming faster, sometimes more than one person talking or screaming at the same time.

Peter Berringer singing "Tender Shepherd" . . . then screaming as his bones were broken, one by one. Flan Tierney crying and wanting to know why Mr. Tenniel was being so mean to him.

"I didn't expect it from a man like you," Linda Crane reproached him, laughing the laugh that reminded him of Angie. "There's a lot of dirty old men in St. Max, but I never would have expected—"

The wind that had dropped a few moments earlier began rising again. Over the thunder of the waves Jorbie heard something that always terrified him. There was no mistaking it: the muffled throbbing, growing louder and louder until it pounded against his eardrums like a jackhammer. The distant voices came back too, but much louder and going much faster than before, one voice talking on top of the next.

"Point your finger—"

"I've formed a group and we're trying to send you back to med—"

" 'Tender Shepherd' . . ."

"You *did* have a twin, Jorbie. Your father says—"

"Point your finger"—"Why are you trying to bury me?"—"I can't swim as good as you, Jorb, and those older boys on the raft"—twin twin—"You gave me a black eye and"—twin twin—"I'm not spying on you, I'm in love with"—twin twin—

The voices were all chanting at once, a choir of rhythmic demons. Over it, the muffled pulsing became unbearably loud, forcing Jorbie to cover his ears, his whole body a twisting spasm of shaking. "Stop it!" Jorbie screamed over the din. "Stop it, Voice. I know all your tricks, damn it. Tell me I don't have to do it to Angie. For God's sake tell me . . ."

For a second there was total silence. Even the wind and the waves became deathly still. Then, suddenly, all of the voices began chanting in unison: "Kill her! Kill her! Kill her! Kill her!" Out of the water rose a mountain of black water fringed with white foam. For a second it hovered. Slowly, unstoppably, it came down, the Lord Justice lowering the black cap onto his judicial wig. The towering wave crashed with dreadful finality, sending sheets of frigid water across Jorbie.

A sudden sharp pain in his ankle made him look down. Half a dozen crabs, torn out of their winter homes by the unusual pounding of the waves, were clinging to his trouser legs and his socks, nipping his flesh, trying to burrow themselves inside him.

Jorbie screamed. He suddenly remembered Kenneth's body washed up, eaten by the crabs. Stumbling and clawing, he fled across the beach and scrambled up the rocks. He had tried and he had failed to save Angie.

Sentence had been passed.

Looming up suddenly into the glare of her headlights, Tenniel's looked unusually dark and forbidding. Never exactly a cheerful place, there was something different about it tonight, an air of the grim and unfamiliar. Studying it, Angie realized one reason was that very few lights were on; usually the house blazed. She could see a few lamps burning, but very few. Lights, she told herself, and laughed. How can you be so influenced by little things like that? She walked briskly up the path and let herself in when no one answered her ring. Jorbie had said he might be late; he was living up to his promise.

Almost the first thing Angie did was switch on every light she could find the switch for. It helped a little, but the house seemed determined to remain gloomy and forbidding, as if its ancient wood were trying to give Angie some sort of warning. Silly.

Caleb. She would go upstairs and see Caleb. He was usually cheerful, always good company, and might help her shake her crazy feeling of foreboding. In her shoulder bag she had another book for him anyway.

Her foot had barely touched the first step of the stairs when, from below, down in the preparation room, came a little thump. In her present state the sound made her jump. A moment later she found herself wondering. Jorbie? Could Jorbie be down there? She still hated even the thought of the preparation room, but that, she knew, was childish. The way to rid yourself of foreboding is to face it and overcome it. Like getting right back on a horse when you've taken a fall. She walked the short distance across the hall and called down the darkened stairs. "Jorbie? Is that you, Jorbie?"

No answer. Taking a deep breath—she wasn't sure why she was willingly going down into this area, a place she ordinarily avoided at any cost; perhaps it was a simple determination to overcome her fear of the area. She found it even stranger that she should make such an effort to come down the stairs noiselessly, like a spy.

Coming around the corner, she was surprised to see it was not Jorbie—it was Pasteur. He was taking some things—Angie couldn't see what they were—out of the "private drawer" in Jorbie's desk. Jorbie had kidded her once about this drawer, explaining why it was always kept locked. "All my darkest secrets are hidden in there," he had joked. "Also, a set of books for Tenniel's the IRS *doesn't* get to see."

For some reason Pasteur suddenly spun and saw her standing by the landing; some noise must have alerted him. Guiltily he slammed the drawer shut, carefully locking it and pocketing the key. Saying nothing— Angie tried to start a conversation, but he ignored her. Without even looking at her directly, he half trotted out the side door, carrying two leather cases with him that might or might not have been tape machines. Outside, through the window, Angie saw him climb on his bike, heave the two cases onto a heavy aluminum carrying rack, and pedal his bicycle furiously until he disappeared down the long drive.

It was strange, she thought, as the whole evening was turning out to be strange. Earlier, crossing from her car to the front door, Angie had thought she saw a shadowy figure step off the path and vanish into the bushes as if to avoid her. For a moment she could have sworn it was her father, but the light was very poor, and besides, her father here made no sense anyway.

Upstairs in his room, Caleb seemed less than cheerful. He accepted *Travels with My Aunt* by Graham Greene without enthusiasm and with none of the usual excitement he greeted any book she brought him.

"It's pretty funny, I hear," she prompted.

Caleb looked pale and kept nervously pushing the shock of white hair back off his forehead. "Anything you bring me is great, Angie." There was a listlessness about the way he spoke, a distracted waver in his eyes. Angie decided to try another tack.

"It's a kind of crazy night," she said with a little laugh. "When I was coming up the front path, you know, I could swear I saw my father jump out of my way and disappear into the bushes." She laughed again. "I guess I'm getting to the age where I see things."

There was no smile on Caleb's face. "It *was* your father."

A wave of shock rolled across Angie. Her question was automatic. "Was he drunk, or what?"

"Not falling-down drunk, but he'd had a few, I guess."

"He's always had a few."

"I suppose you're right." Caleb brushed the hair away again, and tried to change the subject. "This hair. I've got to get the barber out here again."

"What did my father want?" Angie wasn't ever this easily turned away.

Caleb sighed. "He was upset, he said. You spend so much time out here you weren't cooking his meals and were probably cooking Jorbie's and mine instead. I don't know whether he expected me to pay him for that, or what."

"That's not true. Jorbie always does all the cooking. You know that. Besides, my father is usually passed out by the time I eat. I just leave stuff in the refrigerator for him; I still do that."

Caleb shrugged. His eyes turned toward Angie, a

sense of agony burning in them. "That was just his opening, I think. There was something else."

"Yes?"

"Angie, my dear, you're pregnant, aren't you?"

She could feel the room collapsing around her. Tenniel's crashed to the ground, a flattened heap, destroyed by her. Angie raised her eyes to meet Caleb's. He'd asked a question; he deserved an honest answer. "Yes. But how——?"

"Your father. Apparently he found some pregnancy test boxes in the wastebasket. The rest—Jorbie—wasn't very hard to figure out."

Angie moved from her usual chair and sat on the edge of Caleb's bed. It was out now. And perhaps this wonderful man—he didn't appear angry, only sad—could help her figure out what to do. "Caleb, Jorbie is the father, of course. But I don't know what to do. It's not fair to make only him feel responsible; *I'm* responsible too. I love him, my God, but I love him, and I just want to do what will make him happy."

"Everyone always has. Maybe he's spoiled. Maybe that's part of the problem."

Caleb's response was so curious, for a second Angie was thrown. Then she went back to what she'd been talking about, avoiding the suddenly panicked look in Caleb's eyes. "I have to tell Jorbie about it, I guess. He doesn't know yet. Maybe he——"

From Caleb came a groan, one so sharp Angie dropped his hand to see if something had happened to him. "My God, Angie, don't tell Jorbie," Caleb pleaded. The tangle of white hair was brushed aside once again; to Angie it looked as if Caleb was beginning to cry. Once, he tried to speak, but no words came out, just a strange sound.

"Caleb?" Angie asked anxiously.

"I'm all right, Angie," he answered with a deprecatory wave of his hand. "Just give me a second."

Angie watched, wondering what was affecting Caleb so deeply, as he adjusted his pillows, cleared his throat, and blew his nose a couple of times. He made an effort to force a smile, but it was a failure.

"Angie, dear, there's something I've been wanting to talk to you about for several days. Today something happened that makes it imperative I stop putting it off and talk to you right now. Not just the baby, you see, although that adds its own note of urgency too. Don't tell Jorbie you're pregnant, Angie. Don't tell him anything. Frankly, if you've got a brain in your head, you'll stop seeing him at all. I love Jorbie; he's my son. But I'm also a realist. Something's gone wrong with him. Something's happened. The Miracle of the Voices. Somehow, he's tied into them. Other crazy things . . . I don't know quite how to put this, but he's just not rational anymore. And worse, I'm afraid, he's dangerous. To you in particular."

Caleb cleared his throat, his eyes searching the ceiling as if trying to find some easy way to say something that was difficult or embarrassing to explain, his hands clutching the sheets as if he expected some awesome force to sweep in through the window and seize him. Finally the eyes lowered and fixed themselves on Angie. "This is terribly hard to explain, Angie. Maybe impossible.

"It's difficult, I guess, for any father to face that his only son is badly unbalanced, maybe dangerously so. No matter how wrong you know it is, you can't help blaming yourself. I should have forced Jorbie to face Kenneth's death, I know that now, and maybe that's where the trouble started. You see, Jorbie never let anyone get close to him after that. Until you came along. He got very close to you, and I'm afraid it terrifies him because the closeness reminds him of his closeness to

Kenneth. That puts you in terrible danger. He's got you and Kenny all mixed up in his head . . . and after what he did to Kenneth . . ."

"I'm sorry, Caleb. I'm not following. What did he do to Kenneth?"

A dreadful expression of pain crossed Caleb's face. "He killed him, I think. Deliberately. He let him drown, or *made* him drown. I've wondered about it for years. Now, I'm sure. . . ."

Angie was thunderstruck, and began to have trouble speaking herself. "Caleb, I—"

"I know you love him, Angie. I've told you how much you've done for him before, bringing him out of that crazy shell of his. But for the moment, at least, he's just not a safe person to be around. You know how fond I am of you, how much I love you. Leaving is going to hurt you like hell, Angie, I know that—your leaving is going to hurt *me*, too—but get away from Jorbie while you still can. While you're still in one piece. Otherwise, he could—Oh, Christ—"

By now the tears were running openly down Caleb's face. Taking hold of his hand again, Angie squeezed it as hard as she could—she wasn't sure if this gesture wasn't as much for herself as it was for Caleb—but one decision she had made the instant Caleb started speaking. "I can't give up Jorbie, and that's that." Her eyes locked with Caleb's. "I appreciate what you're saying, but I can't—I *won't* walk away from him. I need him too much, Caleb. . . ."

"Damn it, Angie, it's as hard for me to say as it is for you to do. But you have to. He'll destroy you. It's not his fault; there's something wrong in his head. Maybe I should have—hell, maybe I—oh, I don't know. All I *do* know is that something's wrong, and that he's dangerous for you. For Christ's sake, realize what you're up against and clear out of his life."

"No. I won't do it, Caleb. I'm going to get to the

bottom of whatever it is that's shaking him up and help
him."

For the first time, Caleb became angry. "Jesus
Christ, Angie, you're not thinking straight. You're
being stupid, and you're not a stupid girl. I tell you I
know it's going to hurt like hell, but you plain don't
have any choice. Get out of his life—go away—do anything, but—"

"No." There was more conviction in Angie's voice
than in her heart.

"How the hell do I convince you—"

"I won't go, Caleb."

The vehemence of her own words startled even Angie, partly because something inside her knew that
Caleb was probably right. She had, at different times,
thought of running away from Jorbie herself, but hearing someone else say it only made her resistance soar.
This was the second time today, after all, that she had
been given this same urgent advice: first, in a mystical
approach, from crazy old Mrs. Lavin, and now, in a
coldly practical manner, from Caleb.

What Caleb was saying was perfectly logical, she
knew that, but she simply could not face accepting it.
Jorbie had been completely rational when she first met
him, she told herself, and okay, so something had gone
a little wrong—temporarily. But Jorbie would get over
it. One day soon he would suddenly turn to her, laugh,
and offer some perfectly understandable explanation of
this whole trying, terrible period. Everything would be
all right again.

The painful fear that was gnawing at her suddenly
returned. The hell with it. Jorbie was fine. In spite of
everything, she believed this because she wanted to believe it, because she *had* to believe it, in spite of some
distant inner voice that kept screaming at her to get out,
to run away while she could, to leave Jorbie once and
for all.

"Damn it," she repeated, staring Caleb directly in the eye. "Nothing you say can make me. I won't go."

Their voices rose higher; they were shouting at each other now, and the more Caleb shouted, the more Angie became determined to stick with Jorbie. At one point Caleb grew so furious he threw his water glass against the wall, something that almost reminded her of Jorbie. But Angie stood her ground; she would not give in. Caleb was wrong. Jorbie would not hurt her, not *really* hurt her. Or would he? No. Never.

"I won't walk away," Angie said, trembling all over, but trying to keep her voice as calm and reasonable as she could.

Caleb threw his hands in the air and looked away. Even though Angie could not see his face, she knew he was crying again. From downstairs she heard the door slam; Jorbie, probably. She leaned over and kissed Caleb on the side of his face. "Don't be mad with me, Caleb, *please*."

There was no response. Softly, Angie walked from the room and went slowly down the stairs to the main floor.

On the ground floor, coming from the basement preparation room, she heard more noises. This time it *had* to be Jorbie. But on the outside chance that it was Pasteur again—she was determined he not see her downstairs—Angie slipped off her shoes so she could creep down the stairs without Pasteur's knowing she was there.

Damn, it *was* still Pasteur. Back once more. Back in Jorbie's private drawer again, taking out a succession of small, flat boxes and carefully stacking them in a larger carton. In the back of her mind a sudden question arose. Was Pasteur stealing things from Jorbie? Had Jorbie really given him the key to the drawer or had Pasteur stolen it? It seemed unlikely that Jorbie would let anyone rummage through something as secret as his private drawer. She leaned out farther, but her arm brushed against a bottle by the landing and it crashed to the floor.

Pasteur jumped, staring at her with a stunned, guilty look. Once again, he said nothing but grabbed the carton and fled out the door. For a considerable time Angie stared after him, and then slowly moved her eyes to the desk. From the middle drawer of the desk, the key still dangled. In his panic to leave, Pasteur had forgotten to relock the drawer or take the keys.

Shaking her head slowly back and forth, Angie stared at the key, her eyes drawn to it by a force she could not battle. Slowly, she walked across the room toward the desk. Ordinarily, Angie would never have dreamed of going through someone else's private things. Particularly things from a drawer so private it was always kept locked. And more particularly, with things belonging to someone like Jorbie, almost paranoid in his emphasis on privacy.

But Angie's need to fathom what lay behind Jorbie's recent strange behavior was even stronger than her respect for his privacy. Perhaps in the drawer was hidden some clue to the changes that seemed to be flooding across him. If she could uncover some hint of what was troubling him, possibly there was some way she could help him come to terms with it. At best, it would be a long and complicated process; none of it would be easy. But one place to begin might be to see what was in that drawer, its key glistening in its lock like the fascinator light in a hypnotist's office.

Angie set her jaw. Slowly she pulled the drawer open. At first, the interior didn't promise much. A lot of papers, and more of the same flat little boxes she'd seen Pasteur load into his carton. She picked one up and studied the printing on it. Tape. 3M recording tape.

Her eyes moved down the box to a small piece of adhesive stuck to its center. As she read her heart stopped, good intentions replaced by a growing dread. Almost frantically she picked up the next box, and the next. It was all there, all of it. She could avoid reality no further.

Printed on the adhesive tape stuck to each box, written in Jorbie's meticulous hand, was the name of one victim after the other of St. Max's mysterious rash of deaths. Inside these boxes was the Miracle of the Voices—how Jorbie had the dead speak from beyond the grave. On tape. The room swam around her; her head filled with the names—listed in the *Courier*—of the people on the beach the day of Kenneth's drowning, and more became clear. Turning, Angie could stay in this room with what she had discovered no longer; she raced for the side door and stepped out, turning her ankle on the uneven ground outside.

As she rubbed her leg Angie reconsidered what she had been planning to do: race for her car and get away from here as fast as she could. No, she could not. It was wrong to run away like that. She owed it to Jorbie to face him with the tapes. There might well be some perfectly simple, logical explanation for what she had found. Maybe he'd made recordings of the voices in various houses, perhaps he'd—

She couldn't even pretend she was acting rationally, but slowly she turned around and hobbled back to the house, opening the side door and walking softly back into the preparation room. There was no sound from upstairs. Once again she walked over to the drawer, putting back the pile of tapes she'd pulled out last time. One by one she took them out again to make sure of the names. Details from the story in the *St. Max Courier* flooded her mind. It all fitted; it all made sense. Caleb had been so terribly right.

What was she *doing* back in here? Facing Jorbie with the tapes was one thing, but her heart shriveled as she realized that, hard as she might try to avoid the reality, she would be facing the man who somehow had been behind all of the deaths.

Angie wanted to scream out, to curse God and the world for the unfairness of what was happening to her, but knew, even if she tried, no sound would have come. The echoing steps of someone coming down the stairs sent a new wave of fear through her. From the whistling she knew it was Jorbie. She wanted to run out the side door, but could see a dim shape she knew was Pasteur doing something outside. With her hip she closed the drawer shut.

She was trapped. But maybe with the drawer closed again, she could bluff her way through it.

The whistling stopped. He was coming into the room. Angie froze.

Chapter Twenty-six

It's getting damned close to Christmas and I suppose I ought to be figuring out what to get people. Especially Angie. I'm lousy buying presents; I can think of a dozen things for people in July, but December comes along and I draw a big blank. Maybe it ought to be jewelry for Angie; women always like that, even if it always does cost too much.

Angie. From the way things are going, she may not make it to Christmas. The Voice is making that pretty clear—all those people from the past yelling "Kill her, kill her, kill her!" Hell, you can't make it any clearer than that. I don't want to sound callous, but maybe buying Angie jewelry would just be a waste of money. Damn it, I don't want to have her go so soon, Voice or no Voice.

The thing's tough to figure. I think she's the one person I'm going to tell the Voice I plain won't go along with. I don't know whether I'll get away with it, but it's worth the try.

If I can pull it off, great. If not, well, hello Captain Marvel, bye-bye Angie. . . .

> *Jorbie Tenniel—to the rock,*
> *5:22 P.M., December 8th*

Jorbie walked into the room and winced with surprise when he saw Angie standing there. When he had driven up to the house and seen all the lights on, he had thought she was probably upstairs with Caleb. He knew how much she hated this part of Tenniel's, which made finding her here even more troubling. Frowning, he walked farther into the room.

Inside Angie the old passionate emotions flickered only a second, then disappeared, unable to overcome the sudden dread of what she'd seen in his drawer.

"What are you doing here?" Jorbie demanded. His voice sounded cold and hard, but a lopsided smile slipped across his face, as if he were struggling to appear pleasant.

"Oh, I thought I heard a noise down here, Jorbie. I was on my way upstairs to see your father when I heard a funny sound. It was only Pasteur. But I thought it might be someone trying to break in or something. . . ." Angie could hear her heart beating furiously; her lie sounded weak and she knew it. Desperately she hoped her heart wasn't making so much noise Jorbie would hear it and see through her lie. "There's been a lot of break-ins around town," she added lamely.

Jorbie took a deep breath. Angie couldn't tell whether or not he'd accepted her story, but she could see hints of cold fury in his expression, the look he frequently got before one of his outbursts. Maybe it was her sheer proximity to his secret drawer; the tapes were out of sight, the drawer was closed, but the look remained.

Suddenly, Jorbie shrugged. "Did Pasteur say where he was going?"

"No." Angie had answered quickly, probably too quickly, she thought. But she'd gotten away with it. Jorbie no longer had to struggle to sound pleasant, and the look of fury had faded. She felt the small, invisible muscles inside her body relax a little; she'd actually gotten away with it.

Not quite. Angie had forgotten that she still held one of the small flat boxes of tape in her hand, the one she had gone back into the drawer to look at again. It was

Edith Pardee's. She'd simply been unable to believe Jorbie would do anything to someone he was as fond of as Mrs. Pardee. Slowly she moved the hand with the tape in it around to one side, trying to get it behind her.

Apparently, realization of what was in her hand hit Jorbie the same instant it hit Angie. His face went white, his whole body began trembling, his mouth was wide with the anger inside him. From a shelf he grabbed a bottle and flung it across the room. The crash was followed by the sound of small shards of glass striking the floor in a disorderly rain of broken fragments. The suddenness of it made Angie take an automatic step backward, her heart once again pounding against her ribs. Still rooted where he stood, Jorbie began screaming at her, his voice raised to the strange, high pitch of a furious child's.

"I've told you a thousand million times, Kenneth, not to mess around with my things. I have, Kenneth, I have, I have, I have! You're always snooping and spying and tattling to Daddy about me . . ." Jorbie began moving forward, his dark hair falling down across his face like an angry little boy's. He stared deep into Angie's eyes, speaking more softly, but so angry his voice shook unevenly.

"People always like you more than they like me, Kenneth. That's because you lie to them about me. Awful stories, *dirty* stories. You tell them I'm mean and nasty and they believe you. I don't lie about you, Kenneth. Never. And I get better marks than you do and I'm better at softball and swimming and touch and they still like you better. It's not fair. It's not fair, not fair, not fair!"

Angie couldn't speak, but even if she'd been able to, she wouldn't have known what to say. What *could* she say? What could anyone? Jorbie swallowed and moved even closer to her. Helplessly, she backed away, flattening herself against the wall. His face writhing with fury, he moved after her, standing so close she could feel his breath hot against her face. He swallowed again, as if having trouble breathing. For no apparent reason, when he began speaking again, he had changed tenses, something that at first baffled, then, as the meaning sank in, terrified.

"I hated you, Kenneth. That's why I made you swim out to the raft. That's why I left you all by yourself on the other side of the raft, Kenneth. That's why, from my side, I undid the rope you were hanging on to. I knew that without the rope you'd panic and sink. Big sissy, big sissy! I killed you, Kenneth. But now you're back. Snooping again. Spying again. Going through my things again. Waiting to tattle on me to Daddy. Well, I killed you once, Kenneth, and I can do it again."

Dimly, almost frightened into unconsciousness, Angie realized that, to Jorbie, she had finally *become* Kenneth. "I'm not Kenneth," she began, but he slapped her across the face so hard she was knocked off her feet. He yanked her upright and began dragging her toward the far corner, twisting her arms behind her. "I'm not Kenneth," she screamed at him. "I'm *not* Kenneth! Can't you understand that, Jorbie? For God's sake, stop this and let me go. I'm not Kenneth!"

For a moment Jorbie stopped in the middle of the room, turning her around so he could see her. He stared at her with disbelief. The trembling stopped, the grip on her arm loosened a little, his voice returned to normal. In spite of her growing panic, for a second Angie thought Jorbie was going to become himself again and let her go. But Jorbie's instant of rationality was a short one. Shaking his head as if he knew what she had been thinking, he tightened his grip again and began dragging her back toward the desk. Jorbie's voice suddenly sounded old and tired, almost defeated.

"It doesn't matter if you're Kenneth or not. You've

seen the tapes. You know what I've done. That little bastard, Kenneth, always causing trouble. A stuck-up pain in the ass. Everybody mooning over him, always saying how wonderful he was, always ignoring me. Well, I fixed that. I knew he was a lousy swimmer."

Suddenly, Jorbie's voice broke and he started to cry like a little child. "I'd forgotten there ever *was* a Kenneth or that he died or that I killed him or anything until one night last week, after we'd been to bed.

"Now you're going to have to die. But then, so are a lot of people. On the tapes I said they'd be punished— and they will be. I'm punishing them for letting what happened happen. And for the way they ignored me and didn't obey when I told them what to do . . . and for the kind of evasive shit they always handed me and all the lies they told me. Fucking bunch of creeps, every last one of them. Okay, now they're going to get it. Just like you will.

"My Voice tells me who to kill, because I can't always see it clearly, but I've already taken care of quite a few. I have a plan—my Voice told me the way—for the rest. How, is something you don't need to know." He gave a tight little laugh. "That whole bunch of creeps is trying to figure out who the woman they're supposed to destroy is . . . You know it's you. Well, now they're waiting for Edith Pardee to speak again and tell them who the woman is. It could be quite a wait.

"You know what Edith Pardee *really* said?"

Roughly, Jorbie slammed a tape recorder on top of the desk and put the Edith Pardee tapes on. It was a piece apparently made after he'd told her she wasn't going to be dug up:

"No, no, no! Jorbie, no! You can't leave me down here. I've never done anything to you," Edith Pardee's voice screamed. "For Christ's sake, Jorbie, you can't leave me down here to die. Please no, Jorbie, *please*. I said what you told me to. You promised. You did, Jorbie. I didn't believe you, but I said what you told me to. Oh, shit, you little bastard let me out, let me—" Edith Pardee's voice suddenly fell apart from rage, terror, and frustration. On the tape you could hear her screaming and crying and shrieking, her hands beating the sides of her coffin in a futile effort to get out.

Jorbie pressed the button to stop the machine, and twisted Angie's arm, shoved her against the wall. "That's what Edith Pardee really said. Not what I let people hear on the tapes. Life after death, my ass. Burial *before* death is what."

Apparently exhausted, Jorbie sank into a chair near the desk, letting go of Angie. For a second, Angie measured the distance to the side door with her eyes. Jorbie didn't miss the look. "Don't try it. You're not going to be buried alive like the rest of them, anyway. My Voice and I got something special cooked up for you. For once, I wasn't going to listen to my Voice. I told it I wasn't. But it got to me in the end. People have to be punished. You, too. I don't have a choice."

She felt the hand tighten around her arm again as he dragged her over to the window. "Remember Alfalfa's grave?" Dimly, in the light coming from the preparation room, Angie could see the stake with the coded numbers on it, and beyond it, the strange miniature grave. "Give you any ideas?"

Numbly, she shook her head. Looking at him, Angie fully realized what she should have known all along: Jorbie was quite insane. Can you reason with an insane person? She didn't know, but she did know that she'd better try something—anything. She decided sarcasm was the best route; it was an approach he was always vulnerable to. Flattery or affection he'd have seen right through. She reached back to something he'd said earlier, something about why he had to punish so many people, presumably including himself.

"Those *people* have to be punished, Jorbie? *That's* why you think you've done all this?" Angie forced a laugh. It was contemptuous, but somehow weak. "Balls. You've been punishing yourself. Not because those people lied to you or did anything to you, but because of what *you* did to Kenneth. Killing your own twin. Very nice. Really brave." A vacant, haunted look had come across Jorbie's face; she was reaching him, Angie decided. Finally.

"You said you didn't even remember you ever had a twin until last week. Of course not. The guilt hurt too much. Think of the people you killed. All people that made you feel guilty. All people you decided were part of Kenneth's drowning, one way or another. The kids— Flan Tierney, Peter Berringer, Linda Crane—children of the older boys on the raft that day. Mrs. Losee— wife of the man who tried to, but couldn't save, Kenneth—Quentin Losee. George deCarre—the man who launched the dory to try to help. Edith Pardee—the woman who took care of you after the accident and drove you home. You weren't punishing people who'd done anything except tried to help. You were punishing yourself because you killed Kenneth . . . taking a terrible revenge against yourself . . ." Angie heard her voice break. She couldn't keep the charade going any longer. "Oh, Jorbie . . . I loved you so much . . . so terribly, terribly much . . ."

He stared at her, fastening his hand even more tightly around her wrist. Angie tried to plead with him, crying and searching his eyes for some sign of a familiar emotion. But instead of helping, her speech seemed to have made him disappear back into his childhood again.

The voice was once again a child's voice. "Stop bawling, Kenneth. What a big sissy. Men don't cry. I don't. Why are you such a big baby anyway? Maybe that's why you're always whining and tattling to Daddy—

because you can't beat me any other way. Well, I'm going to fix *you*, Kenneth Tenniel."

With a sudden sideways lurch, Jorbie grabbed her and threw her to the floor. His pockets seemed to be full of short lengths of leather thong, and he wrapped one of these quickly around Angie's wrists, fastening them so tightly her arms ached; she wondered if the blood supply to her hands had been cut off. Jorbie's voice had suddenly returned to his normal one and was almost coldly matter-of-fact. A dentist about to begin painful drilling. "I'm sorry about this, Angie. But the tapes—you shouldn't have sneaked down here and gone into that drawer. I loved you, Angie, I really did, if that makes you feel any better." He dragged her over toward the corner of the preparation room and began kicking at something, trying to move it with his foot while his hands held onto Angie. "Under these circumstances," he added calmly, "I don't suppose it does."

Finally, Jorbie let her gently down on the floor, to free his hands. From underneath the bottom shelf he pulled out a pine coffin and took off its unfastened top, laying it to one side. Another length of thong was produced and Angie's feet were firmly tied at the ankles. "Hate trussing you up like a Christmas turkey, Angie, but—well, it's the closest you'll get to seeing Christmas anyway." The calm, detached way he was speaking was somehow worse than his earlier screaming.

"Upsy-daisy!" Jorbie said suddenly, and picked her up with a grunt; when he lowered her back down, it was into the coffin. More lengths of thong were produced and he fastened her ankles to a hook in the coffin's bottom, ran a strap across her waist to fasten it to the bottom, and another across her neck. She was unable to move; even a wiggle was difficult.

To Angie, all of this had been so sudden and strange she had said nothing; her eyes had bulged with fear, she had groaned in response to the various painful tighten-ings of the thongs and straps, but she had remained silent, too stunned to speak. The meaning of what Jorbie was doing to her—had he made love to her only two days ago, or had it been years before, in another lifetime?—hit her with its full impact.

She began to scream, trying to thrash against the restraints, the tears cascading down her face, pleading with Jorbie. "Jorbie, stop, my God, stop whatever it is you're doing! I love you, I love you! Don't hurt me this way. It's a joke, I know, but you're carrying it too far. For Christ's sake, Jorbie, stop, please stop!"

Jorbie remained above it all. "Sorry, no joke. Just like that little bastard brother of mine, Kenneth, you had to pry into my things. He had to die; now you do, too. Besides, it's what the Voice wanted all along."

Angie's voice rose to a shriek. "You can't kill me, Jorbie. A baby. I'm having a baby. *Your* baby. You can't!"

For a moment, Jorbie stopped and stared at her, his face filled with a sudden, curious sense of wonder. It was a strange look, one barely filled with near excitement. But quickly a frown crossed his face, and he slowly shook his head back and forth as if dismissing any temptation to become interested. "A baby?" he asked in his calmest voice, so matter-of-factly he could have been reacting to the news it was raining outside. "Well, good. When *you* go, the baby goes. Two for the price of one, so to speak."

The thought of her baby dying at the hands of an insane father triggered Angie's most basic feeling of terror. She began screaming and shrieking, heaving her body so hard the whole coffin banged against the cement floor.

"Easy, Angie, easy. It's not polite to scream at people like that." A gag was forced deep inside her mouth—Angie's lips ached from the pressure of the heavy material—and tied with another of the leather thongs. Standing up, Jorbie, hobbling a little from cramped leg muscles, walked to the door. "Pasteur!" he shouted, and Angie could hear the giant assistant, apparently told to wait outside earlier—outside in the bitter cold of a Michigan December night—stepping just inside the threshold and the door closing behind him. She could hear his hands rubbing together and his feet stamping on the floor to get warm.

In a soft voice Jorbie was telling Pasteur what he wanted done. Unusual for him, she could hear Pasteur arguing, disagreeing and telling Jorbie they shouldn't. Fear again swept through Angie. Shouldn't? Shouldn't *what*? Desperately she tried to make enough noise by rocking the coffin, but it wasn't very successful. She tried moaning, and the sound was louder, but when Pasteur's voice at one point stopped to try and pinpoint the noise, she could hear Jorbie pulling him up short and telling him to get on with what he'd ordered.

Cursing and grumbling, Pasteur left; she heard him slam the door unnecessarily hard behind him. A few seconds later Jorbie stood above her, gazing down, shaking his head sadly. "Sorry about Pasteur's language. Very hard to get good help these days." He disappeared a moment, then returned with a hammer and a handful of nails, some of which he held between his teeth. Angie pleaded with her eyes and again tried to move her body. She received the same sad shaking of his head Pasteur had. From behind him, Jorbie produced the coffin cover, made of what appeared to be three widths of plain pine planking. Just before he put it over the coffin, shutting out all sight, he reached down and touched her nose affectionately, wearing a slight, bemused smile. It was a gesture one might make to a child, reassuring it of one's love, yet keeping yourself removed from anything more involving than a patted bottom or a touched nose.

The sound of Jorbie's hammering driving the nails into the lid was, inside the coffin, deafening. Above her she could hear Jorbie whistling through his teeth. When he was finished, silence. Angie strained against the thongs and the straps, but couldn't seem to make any progress. The strap across her trussed wrists, though, seemed to be looser than before, so she concentrated on that.

Still sounding maddeningly calm, Jorbie's voice came through the thin wood; it was so close, he must have been talking almost directly into the planking.

"I know you can hear me, Angie. And I just wanted to tell you—without making a joke out of it—that yes, I did love you. I really did. But even worse than snooping and finding the tapes, you suddenly made me remember Kenneth. I said I was planning to refuse what the Voice had ordered me to do—this—and I was. But then you made me remember Kenneth and I realized the Voice had been right all along. I love you, and I'll miss you, and I'm sorry." There was a long pause, and then Angie heard him crying, not saying anything, just sobbing bitterly, like a child when a favorite toy is suddenly broken or lost.

Inside, Angie realized if there ever was a moment to play on Jorbie's sympathy, it was now. Maybe she could make him feel so bad he'd let her go. She moaned as loudly as she could and rocked the coffin. The sobbing had stopped, but she heard Jorbie walking away. All the effort had accomplished was to loosen the strap around her wrist a little more.

Pasteur's voice was back in the room. He was still arguing with Jorbie, but at first Angie couldn't make out the words. As the argument grew they became louder and clearer. "Damn it," Jorbie shouted, "stop arguing and do what you're told. Pick up your end of this thing and shut up."

"You can't," Pasteur bellowed. "You can't do that
to the nice lady. It's wrong. It's awful, Mr. Jorbie,
please . . ."

"Pick it up!" Jorbie roared, and with a groan Pasteur picked up the other end of the box and started
walking out the door with it. Angie could hear it open
in front of them and slam behind them. The sound of
the wind beat against the wooden sides and she knew
she was outside being carried somewhere. What was it
Pasteur said Jorbie couldn't do? A terrible suspicion
grew inside her.

No. Angie had to agree with Pasteur. Jorbie—or
Kenneth or the Voice or whoever he was being just
now—couldn't do *that* to the "nice lady." Nobody
could.

The full realization hit her with jackhammer force.
Jorbie could.

Chapter Twenty-seven

AUTHOR'S NOTE: December 9th was the first day in almost twenty years that Jordan E. Tenniel (Jorbie Tenniel) had not visited the rock, standing a few feet back from it, and watched the waves dashing off its rough surface, speaking to it as you might an old friend.

There was a reason.

Lying in his bed, listlessly trying to read, Caleb Tenniel turned uncomfortably and tried to find a position that was both comfortable and gave him enough light to read. Finally, he slammed the book shut in disgust.

It was not *Travels with My Aunt* that was upsetting him. Once again he had found himself aware that something was going on in his own house, something he could neither see nor fathom. Coming from downstairs he had heard the faint sound of a woman's screams and knew they could come from only one person. The sound had stopped after a good deal of hammering, stopped in a sudden way that troubled him almost as much as the screams themselves had. Painfully, he threw his legs over the edge of the bed and settled into his motorized wheelchair. The electric whine had a particularly plaintive sound to it as he threw the little switch and headed out onto the landing.

From downstairs he could now hear nothing. He pressed the button again and ran the machine to the palladian window that ran from ceiling to floor at the end of the hall. The sky was dark gray and the light outside poor, but he could see that idiot Pasteur coming up the path from the right and disappearing into the side door of the preparation rooms. Stunned, Caleb's heart sank. He knew of only one thing that lay in that direction. The thought filled him with an agony of dread.

He ran the wheelchair back into his room and picked up the phone. He had never been particularly fond of Hardy Remarque, but now he knew he needed him. Desperately, as he put the receiver to his ear, Caleb began swearing. The extension wasn't working. There was a button on the main phone downstairs in the hall, and if Jorbie forgot to turn it in the right direction, his own phone went dead.

Quickly, his mind spinning with a sinister suspicion that the button had been left turned in the wrong direction on purpose, Caleb ran the chair over to the head of the long flight of stairs. He winced at the prospect. It would hurt like holy hell, but what he could guess Jorbie was about to do to Angie was so monstrous he had to do anything he could. He took a deep breath, bracing himself against the pain he knew he would suffer getting himself down the stairs to the main phone. He was so terrified of what he suspected was going to happen, he knew he had to act, painful or not.

As he waited his eyes grew a little more accustomed to the light and he could see the futility of his plan: the wire under the table on which the main phone sat had been cut; both ends were clearly visible from his wheelchair. For some time he sat there, staring down the shadowy length of the stairs. Then, his head leaning back at an uncomfortable angle against the back of the chair, he began to cry—for Angie and the terrible thing Jorbie was about to do to her, for the memory of Jorbie as a sweet and bright and wonderful child, and for his own failure to do better by either of them.

While the coffin was carried along unsteadily, Jorbie at one end, a grumbling Pasteur at the other, Angie worked at the thong binding her wrists. She was unable to tell if she was making any real progress or not.

The sudden sound of a door being opened stopped her for a moment. The coffin rocked from side to side as it was maneuvered through. The instant Angie heard the hollow roar—oh, sweet Jesus, no—she knew her worst fears had been right.

They had brought her to the crematorium. The coffin would be put on the shiny chromium rollers leading to the oven, the door would be heaved open by one of them in asbestos gloves, and she would be rolled inside.

It would not be an easy death. If she were to be exposed to the intense heat of the oven unprotected, it would be one thing. Death, fiery and immediate. But she was in a thick pine box, which would protect her for a few minutes. In her mind, Angie pictured it. The first thing she would feel would be the heat, not bad at first, but rising rapidly. Some smoke, she supposed, would seep in through cracks in the coffin, but not enough to asphixiate her. Then the box itself would begin to burn.

From inside her coffin she would suddenly see a little burst of flame, working its way through the wood and beginning to lick at her. By now the heat would be intense. In agony, she would shriek helplessly as the flames began to engulf her. Searing waves of fire. Suddenly the whole coffin would burst into flames and her clothes, her hair, *everything,* would start blazing. Somewhere along in here she would die, still screaming and thrashing against the restraints and thongs that held her helpless.

Burned alive. Burned to a cinder. Death as fiery and as final as the flames of hell.

Trying to not even think about it any further, she concentrated every fiber of mind and body on loosening the thong around her wrists.

And then what? Angie didn't even want to consider.

* * *

The roar was deafening. Angie heard Jorbie shout over it at Pasteur to turn the gas up to full. There was more arguing from Pasteur, and Jorbie had to bellow at him. It was difficult for Angie to make out much from inside the coffin, but Jorbie's shouting was so loud that she could understand snatches of what was said.

"God damn it, you cocksucker, turn up the gas and shut up. You get paid to do what I say, not to lecture me on what's right and wrong." More protests, too far away for her to hear, and another bellow from Jorbie, followed by the roar of the gas being pushed up to full.

She was on the chromium rollers, that much she was sure of. When they'd first put her there, Pasteur complaining every other minute, they'd rolled the coffin back and forth a foot or so to make sure it traveled smoothly. Struggling, Angie thought she might be making some real progress with the thong binding her hands; to her, it felt a little looser every time she twisted her wrists. The effort hurt like hell. She felt what she assumed was blood oozing from her wrists where they were bound. For the moment she put off trying to think of what she would do if she were able to get her hands completely free.

From outside, she heard the running argument between Jorbie and Pasteur growing louder and more abrasive. A lot of the words got lost as the two of them moved around the room, sometimes near and sometimes far from where she lay, but the gist was becoming clearer. Pasteur still did not want to accept what Jorbie planned to do with her.

"It's wrong, Mr. Jorbie. All wrong. We can't do it, I tell you, we can't."

Jorbie sounded increasingly furious. At first he had only seemed annoyed. Then angry. Now he was livid. "You stupid lunk. You jerk. Where the hell do you think you'd be if it weren't for me? Would anyone else hire you, Clarence? Well, unless you do what I tell you to, *I* won't either, Clarence. And I won't talk to you, Clarence. You'll be back, all alone, just like you were when I found you, Clarence."

Angie could hear the agony in Pasteur's voice. "Please, don't call me that, Mr. Jorbie. Please, don't."

"It's your real name, you motherfucker. I called you Pasteur because I thought you'd be a help to me. But no more. Just plain old Clarence, like you were when I found you. Always arguing."

She heard Pasteur whimpering. Everything of value was being stripped from him. "Please, Mr. Jorbie. Please . . ."

Suddenly, Angie was free. She could feel her hands break loose, her left hand slipping out through the suddenly slack loop of leather. Outside, the argument grew louder. She heard the clang of the oven door opening and Jorbie's order for Pasteur to begin rolling the coffin toward it. Pasteur refused. There was a lot of shouting and the sound of something metallic striking something else that made a dull noise, like concrete or insulation.

Quickly, Angie released her other hand and the strap that held her midsection to the floor of the coffin. Then she turned over on her stomach with her back pressing against the top. Apparently considering her firmly tied up, Jorbie had not bothered to drive the nails very far into the lid of the casket, merely tacking it shut. By pressing hard with her back, she was able to raise the head end of the coffin lid a couple of inches, letting her see out.

Just outside of the coffin, Angie could see a hand. In spite of the asbestos glove, Angie would have known the wrist anywhere; it was Jorbie's. Frantically the hand gripped the rope handle at the head end, straining to pull the coffin forward. Ahead lay the open oven door, which Angie could see beyond him, belching fiery clouds of flame and smoke. Jorbie was apparently not far in front of this door, standing high on the track of chromium rollers. At the other end, desperately trying to hold the coffin back, was Pasteur; he was at a disadvantage since he was standing at floor level and had to keep ducking the short metal pole Jorbie kept swinging at his head. It was a seesaw struggle, the coffin first rolling a few inches in one direction, then being hauled back in the other.

The shouting and cursing as they struggled was deafening, although Pasteur's voice still held a pleading note, while Jorbie's was full of anger and frustration. Angie pushed harder on the lid, opening it a little wider but afraid to open it all the way and become the object of the struggle herself.

One of Jorbie's wild swings connected with Pasteur's shoulder; the crunch of the metal striking bone and tissue was a terrible one. Angie heard Pasteur's howl of pain and felt the coffin jerked toward the oven, while Jorbie continued to swing at the wounded Pasteur with his iron pole.

Angie knew if she was to survive she had to act and act now. With a sudden heave of her back against the lid—one that took every shred of strength she still had—she rammed herself against the top. It sprang open, the lower end still fastened to the box, the upper end swinging suddenly upward toward Jorbie.

"You little bastard, Kenneth!" screamed Jorbie, swinging the pole at Angie with one hand, while yanking the coffin forward toward the oven with the other.

As she ducked the lethal swings of Jorbie's pole, Angie could hear Pasteur shrieking incoherently at Jorbie. Jorbie's eyes rose to see what Pasteur was doing, still trying to pull the coffin forward with his other hand in spite of Pasteur's iron grip on the other end.

Angie had no weapon except herself. Desperately, realizing that the coffin was moving ever closer to the door in this murderous tug-of-war, Angie sank her teeth into Jorbie's hand where it clutched the rope. He screamed and let go. For a second he seemed to teeter on the rollers, then the force of his pulling on the coffin caught up with him. The momentum of Jorbie's flailing body made it slide down the rollers. With a terrified cry of disbelief, he slid through the door into the oven.

Angie gasped, then screamed. A terrible shriek came from the oven. Probably only moving because of his automatic nervous system, Jorbie suddenly appeared at the oven door, wreathed in flame. What remained of his mouth was pulled back from his teeth in an agonized grimace; most of his skin had been burned off his face, leaving only raw patches of flesh showing; his clothes and his hair were blazing, and his outstretched arms reached out toward her from the oven, shaken by death spasms. To Angie it appeared a grim, unspoken appeal for help. Suddenly, with a final shuddering scream, Jorbie pitched backward and disappeared.

Panting, his body still shaking from the battle, Pasteur slammed the door to the oven shut. Slowly, he turned from staring at the door to staring at Angie. For a moment he stood speechless. Shakily, he raised his hand and pointed his finger at Angie.

"You! You made me kill Mr. Jorbie. I didn't want to, but you made me kill Mr. Jorbie." His body shook and a strange, strangled sound came from inside him. He was crying—sobbing—for the one man in the world who had ever noticed he even existed.

Angie, working herself free from the remaining straps, climbed over the edge of the coffin and dropped to the floor of the crematorium. The sight of Pasteur's desolation was so complete she tried to comfort him. "Pasteur, you didn't kill him. Nobody—"

Pasteur screamed, holding the iron pole Jorbie had

been using earlier over his head and threatening her with it. "Stop it," he screamed, as if she had struck him. "You made me kill Mr. Jorbie. Stop it!" He stared at her, then let the pole drop hollowly to the cement floor and fled from the room, slamming the outer door hard behind him.

For a moment Angie leaned against the far wall, trying to compose herself and make her breath come in a more regular rhythm. It seemed brutally cruel, what had happened to Jorbie, but what Jorbie had been doing all along while she stood innocently by was infinitely crueler. She had already dismissed from her mind that the agonizing death Jorbie had suffered was the same death he had planned for her.

In spite of everything, an awesome sadness filled her. And suddenly, like Pasteur, she found herself sobbing. To cry at the death of an evil man made little sense, but Angie could not help herself.

Her eyes seemed unable to stay away from the door to the oven. Behind it somewhere lay the charred remains of her friend, her lover, the father of her child, and the man she had planned—only a few short days ago—to make her husband.

Already out of breath before she even started, Angie Psalter struggled down the rocky, uneven path back to the mortuary. The way was unfamiliar to her, and it was a battle to keep her footing, stumbling and scrambling against the stones and holes in the path, leaving behind forever the crematorium with its grisly memories.

Inside the mortuary, planted at the top of the long flight of stairs, Caleb Tenniel and his wheelchair seemed to grow out of the floor, silent, unmoving, unforgiving. Several different times Caleb thought he heard Jorbie coming in through the side door, and his body stiffened. Jorbie was his son and he had loved him, but something terrible had happened to him, and he must be punished.

Grim, dark thoughts continued to sweep through Caleb's mind. Caleb shuddered. There was no way around it: his own son somehow killed all those people—those children, as well as Lutetia Losee, George deCarre, Edith Pardee, and God alone knew who else, and now, Angie.

Such evil could not be allowed without someone being made to answer for it, and Caleb knew that that someone was his own son. Downstairs, he could hear Jorbie moving around again. Across Caleb's lap lay the rod and staff he would use to mete out his judgment.

The sounds Caleb kept hearing were not made by Jorbie. At first, Pasteur had been in shock over Mr. Jorbie's death. Little by little, though, the shock had turned into a murderous fury. He was prepared to mete out his own judgment. In the kitchen he could find nothing but the expected knives and kitchen saws; they might be effective but lacked the touch of majesty he wanted for Angie's disposal. Then he remembered. Suddenly running, he charged down the stairs into the preparation room. It did not take long to find. The instrument he had chosen was a particularly grim piece of undertaking equipment. Occasionally a corpse, when it had gone into full rigor mortis before being positioned for the coffin, would have to have its bones broken to make it fit inside. On one end of a gleaming chromium handle the "body-arranger" had a solid chromium mallet designed for this purpose. On the opposite end from the mallet was a hatchet, for use on those occasions when a cadaver had been frozen so long ice had to be chipped away from the body. In Pasteur's clouded mind, this was the ideal instrument—Angie Psalter would be killed with a piece of professional equipment from Mr. Jorbie's extensive arsenal.

Back on the ground floor, the body-arranger in one hand, Pasteur stood in the recess of a small hall, waiting for Angie to come in the front door. He did not notice Caleb; Caleb did not see him.

The front door opened. Still shaking, Angie closed it and gratefully leaned against the wall, feeling relief surge through her at being safe once more. In the half-light it was difficult for her to make anything out very clearly.

"Jorbie?" called Caleb, waiting to dispense punishment. Caleb never received an answer. As Angie stepped forward to call back to him, a shape suddenly lunged at her, holding high some sort of shiny hatchet and shrieking at her. "You made me kill Mr. Jorbie!" it screamed, rushing toward her.

By any standard, Pasteur was a huge man. And as strong as he was large. In the dim shadows of the hall, he looked to Angie like an avenging giant, advancing toward her with a gleaming hatchet trembling above his head. It was the stuff a thousand children's worst nightmares are made of. Angie screamed, a scream that had no beginning and no end, an earsplitting shriek that tore at the sky, a cry of undiluted terror.

"You made me kill Mr. Jorbie!" repeated Pasteur, his voice a sinister moan. Once again he saw himself reduced to Clarence, homeless and alone in a hostile world, a friendless cipher. "Mr. Jorbie . . . you made me kill him . . . *you* . . ."

For a moment, frozen to the floor with terror, Angie watched helplessly as he advanced closer. Then, taking a deep breath, she spun and raced down the long connecting hall as hard as she could run. Behind her, she could hear Pasteur lumbering down the same hallway, his sinister footsteps echoing hollowly off the walls. Angie's breath came in gasps as she ran and ran. Through the living room, the deep couch that held so many wonderful memories mocking her with its emptiness. Up the little flight of steps to the next level. Into the viewing room, which, she knew, had another door on its far side. Gratefully, she grabbed the doorknob; she could hear Pasteur coming closer. Damn. The knob was sticking. Struggling with it, she suddenly remembered it was frequently kept locked to keep people from wandering into the wrong wake. Damn, damn, damn.

Angie spun, trapped. Seconds later, Pasteur charged into the room, his face electric with fury. The only thing that stood between him and herself was the body of one Mrs. William Owen, a lady in her eighties, laid out in her coffin for a funeral tomorrow that would never take place. Moaning, Pasteur again raised the chromium hatchet above his head. Angie could feel her heart pounding against her ribs. A final desperate idea occurred to her; possibly, as with many giants, Pasteur was powerful, but easily frightened.

Frantically, she began rocking Mrs. Owen's coffin from side to side. When Pasteur reached it, his arms stretched out over the coffin to seize her, Angie gave it one final heave. Slowly at first, like some great ship going down, Mrs. Owen's stiff body tumbled out and landed at Pasteur's feet, her head and torso grotesquely upside down, her feet still caught on the edge of the catafalque.

Pasteur screamed and jumped back.

Spinning, Angie shot out the door. A second later she could again hear Pasteur's heavy feet pounding behind her. She must be outrunning him, Angie decided, because suddenly she could no longer hear him.

Trembling, she turned the corner and started out into the hall. If she could just get to her car . . . safety.

But when Angie got to the doorway, a looming shadow suddenly filled it. Pasteur had come around some other way. His roars of fury broke over her in waves as he flung himself at her, knocking her to the floor, the hatchet spinning over his head. Again and again the chromium hatchet—really a small ax—swung at her head as he tried to pin her to the floor. Again and again it missed, biting into the wood instead as she twisted and turned. A shower of destroyed wood flew into the air each time the body-arranger tore into the floor.

Grunting, Pasteur began moving his body to cover more of Angie and stop the movement of her head and shoulders; his weight alone was beginning to make breathing impossible. And she was frighteningly aware that once he had her pinned down enough so that she could no longer duck, the finely sharpened hatchet would rip not into the floor, but into her.

Suddenly raising her knee between his legs—it was instinct, not training, that led Angie to this age-old but still brutally effective maneuver—Angie was able to slip out from beneath Pasteur's giant hulk and stagger to her feet. Pasteur dove for his weapon, dropped in his sudden agony. He had just reached it, risen, and was beginning to move toward her again when a thundering roar came from upstairs. Caleb had fired one barrel of his .30-30. Pasteur sank to his knees, staring at Caleb with disbelief. Automatically, Pasteur turned back toward Angie and began crawling toward where she stood, the hatchet still raised. Again the .30-30 roared. Pasteur reeled backward from the force of the blast, pitched to the floor, and was suddenly silent.

"Angie! Angie, are you all right? Angie? . . ." Caleb never got to finish his question. Straining to find Angie in the dimness of the hall and see if she had survived Pasteur and the .30-30, he had moved the wheelchair forward about two feet. It was, perhaps, two inches too far. For a moment the chair teetered on the edge of the first step as Caleb frantically put the motor in reverse and tried to pull the chair back.

He was too late. The chair careened down the long flight of stairs. For the first few moments it remained upright, as if it had been expressly designed to negotiate stairs like these. Possibly one quarter of the way down, it took a sudden bounce and flew end over end, Caleb clinging to it with his hands, until it landed in a heap of chromium and flesh at the bottom of the staircase.

Staggering, Angie stumbled her way across to him, calling his name, and trying to separate him from his wheelchair. She saw his eyes, staring at her sadly from a head that was twisted at an improbable angle. It did not require a doctor to tell her that his neck was broken. She found his hand, wanting to see how much pulse he still had; she could find none, but the hand grabbed hers for a moment and squeezed. Then Caleb's whole body went limp and the eyes stared not at her, but into space.

Caleb Tenniel was dead.

"Try to eat something, dear. Please, can't you just *try*?"

Mrs. Lambert up until now had fussed very little, but restraint was becoming difficult to maintain. The poor girl had to eat sometime.

When Angie had rung their doorbell, the Lamberts had done everything they could for her. Mr. and Mrs. Lambert only knew Angie slightly, but with their open, good-hearted natures, hadn't even asked the incoherent girl a question before taking her into their home.

When Angie, like Caleb before her, had discovered the main phone-line was cut, she staggered to her car and drove until she came to the first house that had lights on. It was the Lamberts'. From there, she had tried to make the necessary calls.

Hardy Remarque had stopped by on his way to Tenniel's, but found Angie almost incoherent. A little of what had happened came through what she said, though, and the saddened Remarque gave Angie a warm squeeze on the shoulder, asked her if there was anything he could do for her, and then climbed into his car and drove quickly to the mortuary.

A little later, Dr. L'Eveque, also on his way to Tenniel's to meet Remarque, had offered her sedatives and sympathy. She had refused the sedatives, but cried softly as the old doctor tried to comfort her. Cathy Springer, L'Eveque said, had not been located yet, but messages had been left and it was only a matter of time before she arrived here to help her.

The Lamberts had left Angie alone in the living room so L'Eveque could talk to her in private. The second he was out the door, Angie followed, watching L'Eveque's taillights going down the road toward the mortuary until they were finally swallowed by the frigid darkness.

Angie walked slowly back to her own car, dreading the thought of returning to her house. Everybody had been kind, terribly kind, but already Angie could feel an empty loneliness settling upon her.

She was back where she started. No longer could she tell herself that she was wanted and needed and loved. Perhaps, in time, someone else would come along, but she doubted it. No, with Jorbie gone, she would be alone forever, a permanent outcast.

Something inside her moved.

It was the baby. *He* needed her. Eventually he would love her. But not here in St. Max.

By morning, she was gone.

L'ENVOI

It was unusually hot that day, the brilliant sun of the Florida Keys blinding to her eyes even in early morning. In the eight and a half years since Angie had moved here from St. Max, she'd slowly grown used to how, along the shimmering beaches of Matecumbe Key, the virtually constant blueness of the sky merged one day into the next.

On the porch of the Matecumbe Beachcomber, the area's lone hotel, Jarvis was sweeping the sand off the steps and onto a street already covered with more sand. Jarvis wore overalls and a wide-drooping straw; he was as black as a mussel-shell, with teeth that picked up every glimmer of sunlight and almost blinded you. "Miz Angie," Jarvis said, giving his straw a small, respectful tug.

"Hello, Jarvis. Another beautiful day. . . ."

Angie wished she knew what Jarvis's last name was, but no one in town appeared to be able to supply it. Or care. After all, she had decided years before, it *was* the deep South. Tourists could come and go, Northerners could move in—as they had in increasing numbers over the last few years—but it was still as old-Southern as Spanish moss and plantations and Robert E.

Another voice from the steps suddenly called. "Angie! Angie?" It was Desmond Raleigh, the Beachcomber's owner, an old man whose hands were covered with benign cancers and whose face was weathered until it looked like a bronze prune. He stood facing Angie on the bottom step.

"Angie, last night I looked at Harley's report card—

he's my grandson, you know—and my, Angie, what a job you've done with that boy! What used to be Fs are all Bs. Thank you, m'love, thank you."

Angie never knew quite how to handle the praise parents kept heaping on her head. If she saw a student in trouble, she'd take him aside and tutor him until he wasn't in trouble any longer. It was something Matecumbe Key's parents never failed to appreciate.

Angie was still a teacher, although Matecumbe Key was a far, far different place from St. Max. They had taken her to their hearts, their welcome as easy and relaxed as their life-style. Every morning—except Saturdays like today, and Sundays—she would board the *Keyrake*, the tiny town-launch that would take her—and about a third of her pupils—to Islamadora Island where the school was, and deliver them almost to the school's doorstep. The other two thirds of the pupils lived on the island itself.

Islamadora Consolidated Grammar School was modern, efficient, and very nearly made for her kind of teacher. The children were tanned and blue-eyed and unbelievably healthy. As students, they responded to everything quickly, and seemed as fond of her as she was of them.

As Angie walked into Eric's Food Store to pick up some Cokes for lunch on the beach, the twins began yelling for Fritos. The twins, Cay (for Caleb Tenniel II) and Springy (for Springer Tenniel—named after Cathy Springer in St. Max)—should not have have been the surprise to her that they were. Twins, as the doctor had pointed out just before delivering them, ran in families. Genes, he added.

"Please, Mom," pleaded Cay. "If no Fritos, then Peanut Butter Bits."

"Or Munchies," threw in Springy, always the quieter of the two.

"No," said Angie firmly. "And I mean it. You guys do enough to your teeth with Coke without adding the other junk." Ignoring the chorus of wails and pleadings, Angie shook her head.

Defeated, Cay and Springy looked at each other. An idea struck in unison. "Fris-*beee*" they screamed, raced out the door, and began throwing the Frisbee from one side of the street to the other.

From behind her Angie heard a gentle laugh. Turning, she faced Eric Delafield, the store's owner. "They're a handful, Angie, I swear. Must keep you running day and night. Liveliest pair of kids I ever damn saw." Eric watched them through his store window and laughed again, shaking his head in wonder.

"The whole schoolful on Islamadora is easier to handle sometimes," Angie agreed with a smile. She put the Cokes in the picnic hamper, and, in sudden surrender, added a bag of Fritos and a box of Munchies. Some disciplinarian, she decided.

On the isolated beach, Angie sat in her foldng chair, letting the sun caress her. Her eyes were almost shut as she listened to Cay and Springy scream with delight, throwing the Frisbee while splashing through the gentle surf.

Angie felt good today. Particularly good because on Friday, just before school closed, Mr. Rudyard, the principal, had called her in and offered her the position of assistant principal, effective in the fall. It wasn't just the money, although she could certainly use that. To Angie, it was the final mark of acceptance by this wonderful community. She shifted in her chair, squirming with the pleasure that the promotion sent flowing through her whole body.

From in front of her she could hear that, as usual, Cay had quickly tired of the Frisbee contest. Maybe it was time to produce the Fritos and the Munchies. The twins' voices were distant, muffled by the sound of waves hitting the beach, and Angie was only dimly conscious of them at first, her eyes now completely shut.

"Let's swim all the way out to the barrels," she heard Cay suggest, a hint of command in his voice.

There was a pause. Springy, she supposed, was studying the line of barrels anchored off the beach to mark the limit swimmers were allowed to go. The twins would argue about it, Angie knew, but in the end would decide against it. If not, she would stop them. There was plenty of time, and the sun felt so good and the promotion was so great and she felt almost hypnotized into inaction. "I don't know, Cay," she heard Springy answer finally. "It's an awful long way out there."

"Sissy."

"No, but I get scared when I go out too far."

"Sissy," she heard Cay repeat. Then, his voice changed, suddenly trying to strike a bargain. "Look, I'll stay right with you. Promise."

"Point your finger at the sky?"

"Point my finger at the sky."

Angie's eyes flew open. She was already half on her feet, filled with a sudden dread that defied logic. She could see Cay had dived into the ocean and was waiting, treading water, yelling at his brother. Uncertain, basically unwilling, Springy dove in too, his mouth promptly filling with the warm seawater of an unexpected wave. Desperately, Angie called out to them, but knew they couldn't hear her from where she was. Quickly she raced toward the shoreline. It couldn't be happening . . .

Slowly, his breath labored, she could see Springy painfully making his way to where Cay waited, not really wanting to go, but unable to refuse his twin.

At the ege of the water, Angie began yelling to them frantically. "Cay! Springy! Come back. Right now, I said. Turn around and come back, both of you. This instant!"

Neither of the twins paid any attention. They did not hear her, they did not obey her.

Another voice was speaking to them, and it was the only voice they could hear.

Helpless, Angie began screaming.

When the Wind Blows

A chilling novel of occult terror! **John Saul**

author of *Suffer the Children*
and *Punish the Sinners*

To the Indians, the ancient mine was a sacred place. To the local residents, it was their source of livelihood.

But the mine contains a deadly secret—and the souls of the town's lost children. Their cries can be heard at night, when the wind blows—and the terror begins.

A DELL BOOK $3.50   (19857-7)

AN OCCULT NOVEL OF UNSURPASSED TERROR

EFFIGIES

BY William K. Wells

Holland County was an oasis of peace and beauty . . .

    until beautiful Nicole Bannister got a horrible package that triggered a nightmare,

    until little Leslie Bannister's invisible playmate vanished and Elvida took her place,

    until Estelle Dixon's Ouija board spelled out the message: I AM COMING—SOON.

A menacing pall settled over the gracious houses and rank decay took hold of the lush woodlands. Hell had come to Holland County —to stay.

A Dell Book $2.95 (12245-7)